Reawakening Memory
Book Five of Tales of Tasimu

By
Celu Amberstone

REAWAKENING MEMORY

First edition. March 23, 2025.

Copyright © 2025 Celu Amberstone.

ISBN: 978-1990581250

Written by Celu Amberstone.

Note to the Reader

Reawakening Memory is a work of fiction. I hope you'll read and enjoy it as such. Though I've drawn material in the abstract from places I've lived and from my own mixed race background, any resemblance to people, places, cultures Indigenous or other, and languages in our world is purely coincidental.

ONE FURTHER NOTE TO the Reader about Pronoun Usage

The characters from another dimension who can shift to be either male or female when assuming a physical form in Tas's world, I have chosen to adopt the pronouns ze and zer instead of the, they/them usage more commonly used to determine a person's non-binary gender. The ze/zer as well as the word "per" have been adopted by other SF writers in the past, and I personally have chosen to use these terms because I find, they them, confusing and I suspect others might as well.

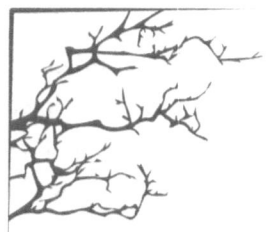

Dedication

This book is dedicated to all the refugees and displaced Indigenous peoples around the world. It is also dedicated to my children and grandchildren. Not being a woman of material wealth, my writing is my legacy to both them, and all the children who are our cherished future.

Also in dedication, I offer my eternal gratitude for the traditional teachings of my grandparents, aunties, and the other Elders I've met over the years who have taken the time to teach me. The wisdom and strength of my Elders has always been, and will continue to be, an inspiration in my life.

Acknowledgements

I would like to thank for their support, my four sons, my daughter, and my friends when I needed them. Paula, and Lila your friendship and help with proof reading cover design, and other editing was greatly appreciated.

Daniel, your edits and suggestions were beyond price for the first edition of the first book in this series. I would also like to thank the folks at Kegedonce Press for their dedication, hard work, their vision, and their fearless determination to encourage Indigenous writers of all types.

A Brief Summary of the Earlier Books

In book One, *Taste of Memory,* Tasimu is a youth with special gifts he has inherited from his mysterious father dwelling in another dimension having a portal at the bottom of Big Ice Lake. Tasimu is forced with his family to move away from their ancestral home when the invaders discover gold in their northern mountains. Tribal members who converted to the invaders' religion signed a treaty in which all the northern peoples were forced to relocate to a newly created Tribal Preserve in a southern desert.

During their traumatic journey to this new Tribal Preserve, Tasimu finds a man who knows of his unique heritage, and can teach him how to use his magical gifts, if Tasimu will agree to help with his own quest for revenge against the converts whom he blames for giving away tribal lands.

Book one ends with Tasimu morning the loss of family members and fearing what will await them in this new southern land.

IN BOOK TWO, *When Memory Dies,* Tasimu and his people finally arrive on the barren, water-starved land they have been allotted only to discover that the treaty goods they were promised are slow to arrive or never show up at all. Conflicts between different factions grow and fester, ending in violence. In retaliation for their agent's thievery, a faction of warriors leaves the Preserve to raid enemy settlements nearby to feed their starving relatives.

Caught in the middle between two warring factions, Tasimu endures beatings and scorn by both sides. When he is contacted by the outlaws who need a person with power to help them, he agrees. The desert war leader, who starts to see Tasimu like a son, is badly wounded and he and Tasimu barely escape with their lives during a raid on the agency to rescue his mother and grandfather.

IN BOOK THREE, *Abandoning Memory,* The war leader is told to seek out the Prophet. In the Prophet's camp the war leader does receive healing and he and Tasimu's mother marry. Tas will have a baby sister before spring. While living with his new family, the Kukiya war chief Golannah is summoned to a peace negotiation. Tas is included in the delegation. Once at the fort they discover the soldiers and government men plan to jail the delegates and force them to sign a new treaty, giving up more land.

By invoking his Gift Tas and the Kukiya delegation are able to escape the soldiers trap, and another ambush in the desert, but by his use of power another man, a malicer and old enemy of the war chief is alerted and seeks revenge that will set into motion events that will end in a massacre of innocent women and children and the hanging of Tasimu's beloved adopted father and Tasimu's capture.

Book Four, *Bitter Echoes of Memory*, is the story of what happens to Tasimu and the other youths captured and sentenced to the live-away school, where the students endure hunger and beatings. Tasimu is forced to use his Gift many times to save his warband of friends and relatives from cruel, sadistic priests and bullying boys.

When a high official comes to investigate accusations of witchcraft, Tasimu is jailed in an underground cell at the school where he is beaten and tortured. But this priest is far more than a temple official. He, like Tasimu, is not completely human. He is a creature in alliance with the enemies of Tasimu's Benefactor. He wants Tasimu to turn traitor and join him. Fortunately the otherworldly being who is Tasimu's true father arrives, and together father and son escape into another dimension, leaving the burning school behind.

BOOK 5: *Reawakening Memory,* begins the story of Tasimu, now a man grown, his magical lessons learned, who wants to go home.

A Tribal History of Long Ago, Rushton Archives: Fifth interview with Indigenous Zacatik subject 297

There is a rootlessness to life now that I find very discouraging. No one seems to stay in one place for very long. They go where the work or their fancy takes them with no thought to the cycles of the seasons or the land on which they dwell. I know from bitter experience that this is a lonely life, a life in which black demons of hopelessness prowl and the snares of addiction and madness are waiting for the unwary to take a single misstep. A man or woman alone, rootless and empty inside, is easy prey for these demons and their traps.

It is only with the Qwakaiva of the ancestors as a guide, and roots sunk deep into the consciousness of the land, can a person survive and live anywhere in this dangerous world our Chamuqwani conquerors have bequeathed us. The past may be gone forever but we must remain a tribal people or we will not survive our present to gain a future for our children.

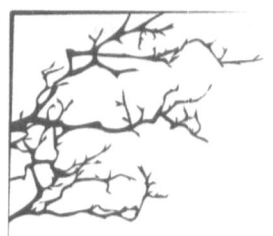

Chapter One

There are few words in a human tongue that could describe the realm to which my father brought me after we escaped from the burning live-away school. Nor can my language describe how anxious and lonely I felt when I was hidden away there. True, finally getting to know my Qwa'Nayhi Seal father was a blessing, something I had longed for most of my life, but the reality of living with him in the Beyond was very different than my childish imaginings.

Cut off from my human family and friends to live among his unpredictable relatives was *difficult,* and not without its dangers. Not being human, those I had to count on for love and friendship during that time were often fickle and disappointing when compared to the Qwani'Ya people I had always known. But perhaps it was unfair of me to expect such compassion and affection from them. They weren't human after all. They didn't understand me, or I them.

It became worse as I grew older when my fascination of being in the magical realm wore off and my father abandoned me for long periods to resume his wanderings. Without him by my side to calm my fears and yes, protect me, his alien realm made me long for even the harsh conditions of the preserve and the cruelties of the live-away school from which he had rescued me.

Though I had the Great Kunai's favor and patronage I was still only a "Siyatli," a half-breed, of sorts, and there were those in the Beyond who never let me forget that. I lacked many of the natural magical gifts born to the creatures of that realm.

Whenever my father was away and I was left without another protector, some of my "cousins" teased and tormented me mercilessly, and if my vigilance faltered, I became a victim of their petty cruelties.

But in spite of everything I grew to manhood in the shifting currents of that world and just like when I lived among Djoven's converts I learned how to survive. Though I lacked the powerful Qwakaiva of my tormentors I gained patience, cunning and the strengthening of my natural Gifts that helped to off-set my limitations.

All their tricks forced and helped me prepare for my future back among the humans of my own world I now believe. But at the time I hated them and resented my father for leaving me alone and vulnerable to their malice. I longed to be among my Qwani'Ya and Kukiya kindred again. I worried about the friends and relatives that I had left so abruptly when my father opened a portal between the worlds so we could escape into the Beyond before the enemy arrived to take their revenge on us.

Where were Kutima, Matoqwa Kuweya and Collin after I left them that terrible night when the school burned? And, what about my outlaw relatives I'd left running free and raiding the chamuqwani settlements near the Preserve? What had happened to my baby sister Kitahtla, my uncle Tli, and my cousins Samiqwas and Xyilaha? So many questions roiling around in my mind needing to be answered, and I was never going to find those answers as long as I was shielded in the Beyond.

I knew time had passed; I could see it in my own maturing body. I wanted to go back. I wanted to help if they needed me, but in spite of all I had learned as I grew older I couldn't open a portal and transport myself back to the world of my birth. My elders who took the time to instruct me, and sympathized with me at my failures blamed it on my human blood. They said there was nothing I could do about that, but I wasn't sure I believed them.

As I matured I grew more and more restless. I longed to feel the warm sun of my world on my face, smell the resinous scent of the pines upon the wind and savor the sweet taste of blueberries upon my tongue. So many little things I had taken for granted and now missed terribly.

When Star Swimmer returned at last to the rocky beach we called our home I happened to be nearby. Often left alone by those he asked to guard me I had learned that it was safer for me by the water where I could shift into my seal shape and swim away if danger threatened,

There was no sun or moon in the beyond only the shifting currents of many colored rivers of power and light. One of my first lessons in my new home had been to learn to read them for signs of danger. All was quiet, no threat lurking in their changing patterns, so I dozed. My belly was full of fish I had caught while in my seal form.

I'm not sure how long I had been lying there when I saw the phosphorescent bubbles rising from out in the jade-green liquid near the center of the lake. Someone had created a portal and would soon be approaching. I sat up, summoned my Qwakaiva and stared into the lake's blue depths. If it was Zeiva and Dathna and I caught them unguarded...

But it wasn't them; it was Star Swimmer, an exhausted Qwa'Nayhi Seal Man who appeared as tired and grim as I was myself. Brindle hair twisted into a long braid, he swam to the shore with powerful strokes of his muscular brown arms, his seal flippers whipping the water to glowing foam in his wake. With a blue-green phosphorescence still clinging to his torso he waded out of the water in his human form. He saw me sitting on the beach and came over to me. He frowned, noticing that Zeiva and Dathna were nowhere in sight.

Crouching he laid aside his spear and handed me a lumpy woven bag, motioning for me to open it. As soon as I did, a sweet fruity odor caressed my nose. I breathed in the rich smell and plunged my free hand into the bag and pulled out a deep purple oval about the size of my palm. I smiled, my frustrations forgotten for the moment.

"Teysaka, where did you get them?" I took a bite of the rich fruit, savoring the sweet taste upon my tongue. Teysaka were one of my favorite treats. I had learned to enjoy them while living in the Beyond. They came from another world similar to my own where the clans often visited. Star Swimmer had taken me there with him once. The teysaka's flavor reminded me of a honey-pear and blueberry mixture.

Star Swimmer smiled as he watched me devour the sweet treat in a few quick bites, and then reach for another. "I remembered that I have a son who likes them, so I stopped in the Yahties market to buy some for you on my way home."

I nodded my thanks and handed him the bag. I would gorge myself to bursting if I didn't return it to him soon. He took one, bit into it and swallowed. "Where is Zeiva?"

I shrugged. "Gone," I said and took another bite of teysaka fruit. He scowled, and before he could say more I added, "Zeiva said it was too boring staying here to guard me."

"Oh did ze now," he growled. I saw the red spears of anger appear in his spirit fire before he controlled his temper. "They could have taken you with them instead of leaving you alone and unprotected," he grumbled to himself but loud enough for me to hear.

They could have taken me with them? That idea had never occurred to me—or Zeiva most likely. My mood brightened as a new thought floated into my mind. Could they bring me home? Even if it was just for a little while... But my cousins were capricious beings. What would Zeiva make me do to pay for such a favor? I shuddered as several answers took form in my mind.

Reaching into the bag for another teysaka fruit he studied me carefully while he ate it. At last he spat the pit into the sand and said, "I can sense your disharmony, my son, what is troubling you?"

Taking a deep breath I struggled to sort out my chaotic thoughts. "I-I want to feel like my life has a purpose again. Father, surely it is time for me to begin the tasks among my human relatives for which I have spent much of my life being trained to do."

I sighed and looked into his eyes, deep violet eyes, so like my own. He was shielding his thoughts from me so I had no indication of his opinion on the matter. I dropped my gaze and began drawing patterns in the sand with my finger, trying to put my longing and my misery into words he could understand. At last I raised my eyes to his and blurted, "I want to go home; I want to go back to the world that gave me life.

"I am a Qwani'Ya Tsa'adi man as well as a siyatli of your lineage, father, I want to live with my mother's people again—at least for a while. I miss them. The Beyond isn't my home—and never can be. I am grateful that you brought me to this refuge, but I'm no longer that wounded child."

Taking another fruit from the bag he ate slowly while he thought about my request. When he finished, he said, "I shouldn't be surprised by this. I am aware how difficult it has been for the human side of your nature to live and be content in the ever-shifting currents of my home.

"But you are still young, Tas, though a man grown by human standards. There is still so much we have to teach you. I had hoped…"

When he fell silent the rest of his thought unspoken, I took his hand, and pleaded, "Father, please, I know I have still many lessons to learn if I am to fulfil the pledge I made to the Great One, but my Qwakaiva is telling me that it is time for me to go back."

I touched my chest to show him where I felt the power twisting and writhing within me. A picture of my baby sister formed in my mind, goading me on, though I dared not speak it out loud. Entangling myself in the affairs of my human kin had always been a weakness to my nonhuman relative's way of thinking. Though I didn't agree, I did have to admit that using my gift on their behalf had cost me dearly in the past.

"Please, just for a while."

"You know that the Crokno have your scent now and they have long memories. It would be dangerous for you if you left this sanctuary—especially if you went unguarded."

That was a sobering thought. I hadn't forgotten Grand Intercessor Hoyt, the malicer who had captured me, tortured me and nearly killed me while pretending to do the will of the chamuqwani god Djoven, The Thunderer. And yet, I knew it was time; I was needed in the human world of my birth—or soon would be.

"I fear you are right about the Crokno; I know I will have to be on my guard for their human agents like Hoyt, but I feel I must go back nonetheless."

He snorted a laugh. "You will probably not find many powerful Crokno half-breeds like Hoyt in your world, but there will be many humans who have listened to their malicious words and are there to create chaos and misery, so you would have to be vigilant always. And even so, you will need an ally and protector to guard you. It would be too dangerous for you to go without a guardian and protector like you had before and Kunai hasn't thought it was time for you to have a new ally yet."

"Then will you bring me home and stay a while among my people to guard me and continue my lessons?"

Star Swimmer shook his head. "No, I'm sorry, my son, I am needed elsewhere on another world under the Great Kunai's protection at the moment. I only came back to check on you and see if Zeiva was caring for you well. There are rumors of a traitor amongst us—and I was worried about you."

A traitor? I shuddered, recalling the unbearable pain and torture I had endured at the hands of our enemy. I had barely survived my own imprisonment; I could understand how difficult it might be for anyone of us to withstand the pain inflicted by the Crokno if captured.

"Do you know who the enemy among us is?"

"No."

"Does Kunai?"

"If the Great Dragon knows he isn't saying."

Star Swimmer yawned and stood. It was only then that I noticed the long cut on his side oozing a little blood. He saw my worried expression and waved away my concern before I could voice it.

"It's nothing." He yawned again then said, "When I return I will speak to Kunai on your behalf. If he agrees I will take you home and remain with you for a time. Then you can decide if you want to stay or return with me. But right now I need to sleep and heal myself."

"Rest and I will fish for you and make you a meal for when you wake.'

He smiled and put a hand on my shoulder as he passed. "Thank you; that would be good. I will talk to Zeiva before I go. Ze won't leave you here alone again or ze will answer to me—and Kunai."

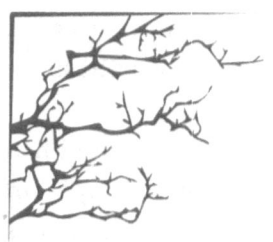

Chapter Two

Though while living in the Beyond I had little conception of how to measure time as my human family might, Star Swimmer did stay with me until his wound had fully healed. Still he left too soon to my way of thinking, leaving me once again under the protection of my unpredictable cousin Zeiva and zer *warband.*

The clans in our lineage to which Star Swimmer and I belonged were all shape-shifters as I had learned to call them in a human tongue. This meant that depending upon what gave us the most Qwakaiva we molded ourselves into a form most compatible to the element we favored.

My father and I chose seal forms for ourselves because of our affinity to Water. Star Swimmer could change into other life patterns if needed, but for me, as a siyatli, it wasn't that easy. I could physically change into a seal, and mask my tattoos and change my human form for a time, but it was only within the Beyond or within the Dream while sleeping that my spirit-body could shift more freely into a variety of different forms.

After he left, as I expected, Zeiva and her closest sibling Dathna were commanded to stay with me. Not only as my protectors but also they had been instructed to continue my lessons—a task they weren't taking seriously. I could sense they were getting bored and would be plotting to leave me behind while they went adventuring soon enough.

Showing me a new way to hide myself while slipping through unfriendly portions of the Beyond forests they snickered and sent me on a useless errand to gather plants for tea while they waited by the fire for my return. I had already fished for them, and suspecting the lesson was only a trick to get me out of the way while they escaped through a portal to elsewhere I didn't go far.

In the short time I had been gone the cousins had been joined by Utreal and another relative I didn't know. Dropping a bundle of herbs by the hearth

I knew were good for tea, though not the ones ze had asked for, I said, "I know what you are planning, you know."

In their green-skinned, mostly human forms, they stared up at me with wide-eyed innocence. "Oh, dear siyatli cousin," Zeiva cooed. "Whatever are you talking about?"

My lips curled into a mirthless smile. "Why your plans to take off and leave me here alone, of course."

Zeiva molded zer face into an expression of shock. "Why, cousin, we would never risk Star Swimmer's wrath by doing that. Whatever gave you such a crazy idea?"

Crouching I removed the pot from the flames and placed the herbs into the steaming water to steep. Setting it back beside the hearth I shrugged. "Oh maybe because I am skilled with the Qwakaiva of foretelling the future, remember? And Utreal and Dathna over there are bored." I poured zer a cup of tea and handed it to zer. Motioning for Dathna to hand me zer cup I filled everyone's cup.

When they tasted the bitter herbal brew I had made for them they coughed and scowled. I gave them my toothy smile in answer.

Setting down zer cup Zeiva grumped, "This isn't the tea I sent you to gather."

"No? Oh dear, I'm sorry. Being a poor, stupid siyatli I must have misunderstood you."

Zeiva rumbled a growl deep in zer throat, zer eyes sparking with zer annoyance. Before ze could become too annoyed and leave anyway, I said, "You know I get bored always staying around the lake, too, so instead of leaving me here, why don't you take me with you?"

The cousins stared at me with mouths agape. As I suspected, they had never considered the notion. I gave them another toothy smile. "Before he left this last time Star Swimmer said you could take me with you."

The four exchanged meaningful looks, but expertly shielded their thoughts from my probing. At last Dathna said, "That is an interesting proposal, little siyatli cousin. If we agree to take you with us this time where would you want to go?"

They hadn't wasted any time getting to the heart of the matter, so I suddenly realized they might have another reason behind their willingness to teach me the concealing art.

I wanted to go home, but if they suspected how much I wanted it, they would probably make me pay dearly for the favor. But if I didn't give them an answer, they might suggest a world that didn't have breathable air for one such as me. And then, of course, they would have their excuse to leave me behind.

I sighed; I would have to risk it, and hope their payment wouldn't be out of reach for me. "I want to go back to the world that gave me life. I want to find my Qwani'Ya and Kukiya relatives so I can guide and protect them. My gift tells me that I am needed, and will be in the future as well."

They pretended to think about my request. Though their thoughts were shielded I knew they were plotting to get the most out of me for the favor.

"My, my, that is a difficult request to fulfill, but maybe we can combine a lesson on concealment with your payment to us for such a big favor, hmm?" Utreal said zer glowing eyes alive with excitement.

I folded my arms across my chest and glared. "A big favor, eh? What do you want in return? You know Star Swimmer has promised to take me home when he returns, so maybe I should wait."

"Oh, no, no the favor isn't too difficult for a clever siyatli like you. Truly it is not," ze assured me.

I sighed; I didn't want them to leave me, so what choice did I have. "All right, what do you want in exchange for bringing me home?"

Zeiva smiled showing lots of sharp white teeth. "Well, dear cousin, you see there is a relative of Qwa'osi the Otter warrior living in a cave in the mountain across the lake that likes to collect lots of pretty, little, shiny things. And since we will need some things to trade or sell when we take you back to your world, so—"

"So you want me to steal some of his jewels and maybe a crystal of power for you, too," I suggested.

"The Otter's kinsman took some of his horde from us first," Utreal grumped. "It is only right that we take back some of our own things."

"If some of the plunder belongs to you Utreal then why haven't you gone on a raid to retrieve the stolen items yourself, hmm?"

"We tried, but Uti knows our scent and we can't get near," Dathna said. "That's why we need you to go in our place. He doesn't know you."

"He doesn't know me yet," I clarified.

"You won't have to do it alone," Zeiva offered hastily when ze thought I was wavering. "We will come with you and distract Uti while you sneak in and grab as much of his horde as you can."

"This will be a good test of your new skill," Utreal argued.

"And you might need such a skill when you return to the human world—to uh, help your relatives," Zeiva coaxed.

What did they really want, I wondered. The clans often raided and played tricks on one another that wasn't anything new, but there must be something far more valuable in the Otter's kinsman's horde that they weren't telling me about. Hmm...

"All right, I will do it on one condition."

"What?"

"I get to keep one thing from the horde—something of my own choosing. Something I might need while living in my home world."

They talked among themselves for a time then agreed.

"If I agree to go into Uti's cave and bring you out a bag of his plunder, do you give me your sacred word that you will return me to my human world and leave me near my Qwani'Ya and Kukiya relatives?"

"We swear," Zeiva said and the others agreed.

They really must have wanted to best Uti and steal back something he had taken, because I was able to coax Zeiva into teaching me the art of transporting myself physically from one place to another without any bargaining. I ended up in the lake a couple of times as I practiced on our way to this Otter warrior's cave, but eventually I mastered it.

The forest around the otter warrior's den was dark and dense with thorn and other unfriendly bushes, so I might need my new tricks before I was through. Fortunately for me a clear fast-running stream ran from a spring inside his cave and out into the lake, so I wouldn't alert the Otter by using my Gift to enter.

Utreal pointed to the stream and murmured, "When I was here before I crept through the water and into the cave. Uti keeps his stolen treasure in a large chest at the very back of the cavern where he lives."

"Hmm, and what exactly am I looking for in this chest?"

Zeiva shrugged. "Oh, just anything you can find quickly," and handed me a large woven bag.

"Anything, hmm. Alright, and while I am doing this what are you planning to do to insure I don't get caught? I have no wish to be enslaved or eaten if Uti discovers me stealing his plunder."

The four exchanged meaningful glances, and then Zeiva assumed a horrified expression on zer pretty human-looking face. "What a suspicious nature you have. Of course we won't let anything happen to you, dear siyatli cousin."

"How comforting to know."

"Yes it is. Star Swimmer would never forgive us if we let you be harmed by one of his rivals."

I snorted a mirthless chuckle. "Nor would our Benefactor Kunai, I suspect," I reminded them.

Zeiva sobered. I hoped by invoking the Great One's name ze would forgo any tricks the four of them had in mind to torment me.

"Of course we aren't going to let Uti hurt or enslave you," Dathna assured me. "We will transport ourselves to the front of the cave and distract the Otter Warrior while you swim into his den from the stream. We discussed the plan a little more until I was satisfied that they weren't going to abandon me or let me get captured.

"Just remember your new lesson and you will be fine," Dathna promised. Ze motioned to the stream. "When you hear us challenge the Otter Warrior, swim fast and enter."

When I heard their challenge I entered the water and hastily swam up the stream as we planned, until I reached the cave itself. I might have died right there in the darkness if my seal whiskers hadn't detected the net trap just before I swam blindly into it. After the cousins' earlier visit, the clever Otter had taken further precautions to keep safe his horde.

I thought about just transporting myself over the net, but decided against that plan. Uti might detect my use of Qwakaiva and come to investigate, ignoring the distraction my cousins were making at the cave's entrance. He probably would see through their tricks soon enough so I didn't have much time.

As I cautiously explored the barrier I realized the Otter had created for himself a smooth stone and slippery mud slide from his cave into the stream. To prevent taking the net trap down each time he wanted to play with his relatives he had left a thin open space between the net and the lip of the slide, which he could use to enter the lake.

Back home I had seen several slides like this where a family of the little otters my village honored created for their play. Evidently Uti thought that anyone trying to sneak into his home would fall into his trap before they reached his slide. He hadn't counted on a clever siyatli getting this far.

The slide was slippery and I had to change my front flippers back into hands with long claws to pull myself undetected under the edge of the trap and into the cave. Once inside I could still hear the roared challenges being thrown back and forth so hopefully I was safe for the moment.

Uti's cave was dark, only a faint light coming from the entrance. I wondered if Zeiva knew I was now inside because I heard a large rock crash against the stone entrance which seemed to enrage the Otter Warrior even more. I figured I was safe to explore for the time being.

I groped my way through the detritus of the main cavern feeling my way along the walls until I figured I was far back into the cave's darkness. Dropping to hands and knees I shifted into a half seal half man creature. Elongating my seal whiskers I felt my way forward and eventually brushed them against the sides of a wood-like chest.

Switching back to human form I studied the chest with my Qwakaiva searching for more traps. I found none but the chest was locked. Placing my hand on the lock and just like when I rescued my relatives from the chamuqwani jail I used my Qwakaiva to unlock it.

Opening Zeiva's bag I blindly reached inside and stuffed whatever I touched into it. I hoped whatever they really wanted was in the chest and I found it for them. They might go back on their word otherwise.

The bag was half full when I felt something nip my arm. Stifling a cry I jerked my arm from the chest. In the dim light I saw something covered in metallic scales twining itself around my arm. Fearing the being was an enemy guard Uti had placed in the chest to capture a thief my first response was to try and shake it off before it finished molding itself to my wrist. Then

I stopped and just stared when it raised its head and looked at me with sparkling jeweled eyes.

<<I am no enemy. Bond with me and take me with you, young siyatli. I have no wish to become Utreal's slave again.>>

So there was far more to my cousins' request than gathering up some pretty crystals to sell or trade, as I'd suspected. Forgetting about my task I pondered the little being's words. Though I wasn't sure exactly what it was, I could already sense that it was a being of great power.

Confused, I said, <<I can understand you not wanting to become Utreal's slave again—ze wouldn't be my first choice of a master, but aren't you worried that I might be a crueler master and enslave you, too?>>

<<Your cousin is under the shadow of a great evil; you are not. You are also favored by Kunai, as am I. I can help and protect you from your enemies in the world of your birth if you bond with me and take me with you,>> it explained.

Hearing footsteps suddenly heading my way, I agreed. <<I will bond and take you with me, but we have to do this bonding thing later. I have to go now; Uti is coming, I think.>>

<<So be it; the bonding is done. I am yours now, siyatli savior.>>

Then as I stared the little creature lowered its head, bit its own tail and shape shifted into a flat metallic scaled bracelet encompassing my wrist. I snatched up one last large handful of the contents of the chest and then dropped to the stone, crawling for Uti's slide and the way out.

Unfortunately for me Uti spotted me as I neared the slide. With a mighty roar that chilled my blood he shape-shifted into a fearsome creature that seemed to be all teeth and claws and charged after me. I wasn't going to make it; I could feel his hot breath on my neck and his sharp claws grabbing onto my shirt.

<<Transport yourself,>> the little creature on my wrist said. <<I will help you with my power.>>

I did, and then we were out of the cave and back across the lake. I landed in a heap by my father's hearth, Zeiva's bag spilling its contents on the ground beside me.

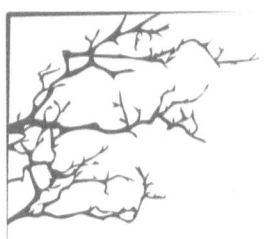

Chapter Three

I sat up, gasping for breath. I hadn't expected to have traveled that far, or so fast. I doubted the Otter warrior would follow me back into Seal territory, so I was probably safe for the moment. But where were Zeiva and her followers?

I had changed out of my ripped clothes and made tea—sweet tasting tea, and was frying meat and flat breads when they at last showed up.

"There you are, cousin," Zeiva cried. "We thought Uti had eaten you for sure when we couldn't find you."

"Then it is a good thing for you that I learn my lessons quickly and well. I would hate to know that you suffered the Great One's anger, because of me."

Ze shuddered. "Yes quite."

I gave them a toothy smile and pointed to the teapot and the platters of meat and bread by the hearth. "Come sit with me and eat. You must be starving after your long search. And you will need to renew your strength before you keep your part of our bargain and take me home." I motioned to the teapot. "Shall I pour you some tea, dear cousins?"

Zeiva hesitated. My smile a challenge I took a sip of my own brew and motioned to the pot again. Zeiva scowled then reached for the teapot, poured a cup, snatched some meat and warm bread and then sat by the fire. When ze sipped from zer cup and then ate some of my food with no ill effect, the others decided there was no tricks to the meal and served themselves.

When the meal was finished they focused their attention on the bulging bag lying beside me. Taking a deep breath I held it up to show them. "This was all I was able to gather in the time I had before Uti discovered my meddling and came to investigate."

"So little," Dathna complained. "How much of the bag's plunder did you hide away before we arrived?"

"I hid nothing; I have been preparing your meal that's all." When Utreal snorted his disbelief, I snapped, "Uti had set a trap since your visit that nearly caught and drowned me. Once in his den I found the chest, but it was locked, so I had to spend more time and Qwakaiva opening it before I could gather what was inside. You should have done a better job of distracting him if you wanted more," I said.

"Cousins, cousins let's not quarrel," Dathna cooed. "Let us open the bag and see what our brave siyatli cousin obtained for us."

"Yes I want to see," Zeiva said, so I tipped the bag and spilled its contents on the ground as they came around the fire to examine my plunder. I was amazed at the pile of glittering crystals and gold and silver ornaments that I had blindly stuffed into zer sack.

Without waiting for the others Utreal crouched and began frantically searching through the pile. When ze didn't find what ze was looking for ze snarled a curse and glared murderously up at me.

"What's wrong, cousin?" Zeiva asked.

"It's not here." Turning on me Utreal growled "You lied to us, siyatli worm. You have hidden some of the plunder you escaped with. Give it back or I will—"

"If you wanted me to get something in particular, Utreal you should have said so. I'm not stupid enough to try and steal from you or anyone of my relatives. Your Gifts are far stronger than a mere siyatli. You would have discovered my trick right away if I tried to hide plunder from you."

"I believe you, cousin. You aren't stupid; you wouldn't steal from us," Zeiva said, "but did you take something from the horde that we had agreed you could keep for your effort? If it belongs to Utreal perhaps you could give it to zer and choose something else—two something elses maybe."

Ze pointed to a red and a green stone, both radiating a glow of power. "Those two would make a fine payment for a brave siyatli such as you, cousin. Shall we trade?"

"No. And I didn't *take* anything from the bag before you came." *No, the creature took me*, I thought to myself. "What were you looking for?"

Understanding my evasion, Utreal snarled an oath and grabbed my arm pulling up the sleeve of my shirt. When he saw my new bracelet he cursed again. "Give it back you liar and thief. It's mine!"

Before I could jerk my hand away the little being on my wrist raised its head and bit into my cousin's hand. With a cry Utreal snatched zer hand away blood dripping from zer fingers.

"I am no liar and I would never steal from my relatives," I argued. "You never told me you wanted something specific from Uti's horde—and you all promised that I could choose one thing for my trouble." I held up my wrist. "This one chose me actually, but I will keep it nonetheless."

"I never promised to let you steal my property. I want it back—now!"

"Oh, Utreal, stop complaining. It's only a little qwissa dragon lizard. There are plenty more on the toskay world. We can go back there and hunt for another if you value the creatures so highly," Zeiva said.

But Utreal and I both knew the little one now resettled on my arm was far more than a dragon lizard pet, but I doubted ze would say so. "I didn't intend to take something belonging to you, cousin. The little one twined itself around my wrist before I even knew what was happening and it wouldn't let go," I explained, trying to appease zer anger. "I didn't even know what it was until Zeiva just told me. I'm sorry."

Utreal snorted zer disbelief and called me a liar and thief again.

"Oh don't be such a grump, cousin," Dathna said. "The creature has obviously chosen and bonded with him. It would kill you if you tried to take it away from him now."

"Unless I killed him first," Utreal grumbled just loud enough for me to hear." Zeiva stared open mouthed; ze also must have heard zer. "Have a care, cousin," ze warned, all teasing forgotten. "We have been charged with our siyatli cousin's care. If you hurt or kill him you would face my vengeance as well as Star Swimmer's. Are you bold enough—or foolish enough to challenge most of the clan for a little pet?" Utreal glared but remained silent, at last dropping zer eyes in submission.

Breaking up the silent battle Dathna stood and stretched. "I'm getting bored with all this jabbering. I want to go and have fun. The siyatli did as we asked and now it's time we keep our part of the bargain." Ze bent and scooped up the two power crystals Zeiva had wanted me to take and a couple rings from the pile and without looking back headed for the lake.

Zeiva agreed and picked zer own jewels from the pile as did the other relative I didn't know by name. Putting an arm over my shoulder Zeiva headed for the lake. "Come on, siyatli cousin. You did well and now we will bring you back to the human world and have some fun, too."

When Zeiva saw that Utreal was still angrily sitting by the dying fire ze turned back. "You had better come with us, cousin. Uti will suspect that you had a part in the theft of his plunder. He might venture into our territory with so many of us gone." Still muttering under zer breath ze grabbed up the remaining jewels and trailed after us.

When we emerged from the portal Zeiva and Dathna created we were in dark shadows between two tall buildings. Feeling like I might puke from the rapid transfer I staggered, nearly falling. I leaned against one of the brick walls catching my breath, my senses overwhelmed by the smells of rotting garbage, pungent urine and deafening noise.

Trying to cover my ears and my nose at the same time I frantically glanced around for help. They had tricked me—I should have known better than to trust them. Damn them this wasn't my world—it couldn't be.

While I had been adjusting to these terrible new surroundings the cousins had been molding their shapes into ones that would pass unnoticed among the beings living there. Zeiva had become a pretty pale-skinned woman with yellow hair, blue eyes, creamy breasts and rounded hips. Dathna had become a woman as well, but zer color was dark haired with honey-gold skin. Utreal and the other cousin had chosen male forms, Utreal a tall muscular yellow-haired man and the other had flaming red hair and pale skin.

Dressed in a short black dress that displayed zer figure nicely, ze came over to me and touched my face, clicking zer tongue in disapproval. I felt a tingling on my jaw and reached up to touch my face. My temper sparking, I demanded, "What did you do to me?"

"Calm yourself, cousin. I merely concealed your dragon glyph for you. We don't want to alert an enemy to who you really are, do we?"

My emotions in turmoil I stared openmouthed, trying not to reveal my vulnerability by crying. Masking my feelings with anger I waved my hand around the stinking alley. "You have tricked me and broken your promise to take me home. This isn't my world."

Zeiva stared at me zer brow wrinkled in confusion. "But we didn't break our word, cousin. This is your world, truly it is." Ze pointed to a pair of chamuqwani drunks holding each other up as they staggered past the mouth of the alley. "See, those two are definitely human. Study them with your spirit sight if you don't believe me."

I did as ze instructed. Yes, the men were human, as were the other people I could see walking down the street, but wheeled carts not needing horses to make them move? I had never seen anything like that in my world before. Nor had I ever heard the loud music coming from the open doors of the buildings further out of sight down the street.

At first I thought they might have chosen to bring me to a distant part of the Empire so they could amuse themselves by watching me exhaust myself trying to transfer back to the Preserve. But when I saw several brown-skinned people also walking by I knew that wasn't the real problem. "You tricked me," I repeated. "You agreed to take me to where my Qwani'Ya and Kukiya relatives are living."

"And we did," Dathna said. "You have many relatives—and some friends living here in Seatown."

Utreal snickered. "Even the one you love above all is here—if you are clever enough to find her—before it's too late."

My blood ran cold at that malicious pronouncement. Was my sister Kitahtla in this terrible place? I demanded ze tell me where to find her, but ze only gave me a mocking smile and walked out of the alley the unnamed cousin following."

Zeiva and Dathna started to follow but I stopped them. They must have heard the desperation in my voice because they had pity on me and stopped. "Please," I begged. "This terrible place isn't where I meant. This isn't the Preserve where my family could ever live. I sense too much evil here. I want you to take me to the Tribal Preserve, so I can help my people survive, as Kunai wants me to do."

"But that's not what you told us when we struck our bargain, cousin," Zeiva said. "We brought you back to your home world, and you have kin living in this big city. Truly you do; we aren't lying to you about that—and they do need you."

As I tried to discover the true meaning behind zer words, ze continued, "You negotiated for the 'where' you wanted to go. You never said anything about the 'when' you wanted. So if you want to be taken to another place and time we will have to make a new arrangement."

With a sinking feeling I knew ze was right. I had made a poor bargain with my oh so tricky relatives.

Zeiva put an arm around my shoulder and drew me out of the alley and onto the busy street. "Cheer up, grumpy cousin. Tonight it is time to have some fun. We often come here and there are many amusing things to see and do, so relax and enjoy your time away from Star Swimmer's boring beach."

"Will you take me home after you finish having 'fun'?"

"Which home do you want us to take you back to?" Dathna asked as ze joined us.

That was an interesting question. Did I want to go to the Preserve or did I want to go back to Star Swimmer's home in the Beyond?

Before I could decide on my answer Zeiva added, "Of course to take you anywhere would mean we would need to make another deal. Taking you back to your beach in the Beyond was never part of our original bargain, you know."

No, it wasn't. I sighed. "When are you going back to the Beyond?"

"When we get bored, of course."

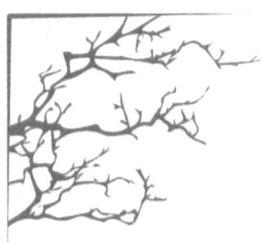

Chapter Four

With nowhere else to go, or do in this strange world I had no choice but to follow them into the noisy drinking house they entered after a short walk. Utreal and the other cousin were already there and had secured a table in the back of the large smoky room.

Hoping my relatives would tire of this place soon so I could negotiate my way elsewhere I flopped onto a wooden chair by the wall and glared at everyone around me.

The drinking place was crowded with men and women with a variety of skin tones and different colored hair, with some wearing shiny clothes and face paint that accented their lips and eyes. And, it was noisy—very noisy to my way of thinking. People were talking and laughing, trying to make themselves heard over the music blasting out of a box flashing colored lights on a side wall.

As we joined our relatives a woman balancing a tray piled high with a tall pitcher of golden liquid and several glasses unloaded the tray's contents onto our table. The handsome man who was Utreal smiled at her and thanked her. She gave him a flirty wink and returned to a long table to refill her tray with food and drinks for another group of people.

Zeiva reached for the pitcher and poured zerself and me tall glasses of the foaming liquid. "Drink up, cousin, we are here to have fun."

I glared at zer in disgust which only made zer smile. Muttering something uncomplimentary under my breath I took a sip and then nearly spit it out. I forced myself to swallow then choked out, "What is this stuff?"

Ze and Dathna had been watching me through half closed eyes trying to hide their amusement. "The people in this time call this drink beer. It's very good, don't you agree?"

Deciding to play their little game I took another bigger swallow and agreed. The brew was bitter and foul tasting to my way of thinking but I wasn't going to tell them that, because everyone else seem to like it so I went along and drank more when they refilled my glass for me.

I drank and allowed the talk and laughter to flow about me without paying much attention. It wasn't long before my cousins were joined by several pretty, young human women and men. I was vaguely aware that they were using their Qwakaiva to attract them but I was too lost in my own misery to care. I just wanted them to finish their games so we could go.

A big muscular Kukiya man caught Zeiva's eye and came over to our table. Looking down at zer creamy breast nearly falling out of zer black dress he smiled. Zeiva smiled back. Pushing me aside and nearly knocking me over in his eagerness to join zer he snagged a chair from another table and wedged himself between us.

When I protested he glared at me and said a few chamuqwani bad words that I remembered the soldiers using. Feeling grumpy and a bit daring I told him where he could go in the Kukiya language if he wanted to behave so rudely.

His eyes widened at my insult. He might have hauled back his fist and hit me if Zeiva hadn't distracted him by asking him to dance with zer. He stood up and ze flowed into his arms grinding her woman's mound against his crotch. He kissed zer and then ze guided him onto the dance floor.

As they moved away Dathna laughed. "I think, little cousin, that you need to slow down your drinking the beer. Maybe you are getting drunk and acting a little stupid, eh?"

"I am not," I said and took a big swallow of my new beer to prove it.

As the evening progressed the couples at our table came and went from the dance floor. I was asked to dance a few times myself when pretty young women stopped by our table, but I didn't know how to dance to these loud crazy songs, so I declined their offer politely and after a while they left me alone to drink and sulk.

Someone ordered food at one point and both Dathna and Zeiva urged me to eat, telling me it would be good for me to stop drinking and eat. And after some coaxing I did eat some fried meat between two slices of bread and some potatoes that had been sliced and fried.

The Kukiya that was interested in my cousin Zeiva had probably been drinking as much as I was and he definitely wasn't happy about zer paying me so much attention. When my bladder told me I had better find the indoor privy or I might wet myself he followed me.

When I relieved myself, and before returning to the noise outside, I happened to glance at a long mirror by the hallway door. In my dazed condition I thought at first another Qwani'Ya man had come in while I was peeing. I started to greet him, but then realized it was my own reflection, staring back at me.

I hadn't seen myself since leaving the live-away school, so it was a bit of a shock to see how much I had changed from the half-starved youth I had once been. I was now, like most men of my People a squarely built man with fully developed muscles on my arms, legs and chest.

I was still short—though not unreasonably so. The man looking at me wore his hair in a long braid down his back in the way I wore it in my youth—a fashion that I had noticed wasn't worn any longer by the tribal peoples I'd seen in this city so far.

Before leaving Star Swimmer's beach I had created for myself simple clothes like I'd seen the workmen of my own time wearing, but the baggy trousers and long sleeve jacket and shirt I now wore also set me apart. I would have to find a way to get new clothes if Zeiva and the others planned to be here for a while.

My dragon glyph concealed for the moment, my face still had Nachoga's tattoos that proclaimed my Kukiya adoption as his son painted across my cheekbones. But the deep violet, almost black, otherworldly eyes I had inherited from my Qwa'Nayhi Seal father declared my true lineage for those who knew enough to recognize their meaning.

All that inner contemplation reminded me that I still had to convince Zeiva to bring me home. Opening the hall door, I staggered back into the hall where the big Kukiya was waiting for me. Without any warning he slammed me hard up against the wall. His breath a sour beery cloud in my face he snarled, "I'm not going to warn you again, piss-drinkin' zaunk. Stay away from my girl."

"What girl? I don't know what you're talking about."

He swore and aimed a punch at my face. Fortunately I was able to dodge his blow and slither out of his grasp, using a touch of my Gift. "Leave me alone, dog turd. I don't know what you are talking about, really. I'm not interested in any girl."

His lips curled into a sneer. "You telling me you like boys. You a fancy boy then?"

Fancy boy? The world my cousins brought me to was so confusing. "I still don't know what you are talking about. What girl?"

"The pretty blonde with the big tits, you stupid shit! Stay away from her. She's mine."

When my slow-thinking brain figured out what he was talking about I began to laugh. "What's so damned funny?" he demanded. "If you are making fun of me I'll—"

He aimed another punch at me, but I moved out of reach still chuckling. "You are talking about Zeiva, right?"

"Yeah, what of it?"

Still trying to control my mirth I said, "Zeiva is my cousin—all those people are my relatives. I don't want to hump any of them"

He snorted his disbelief. "Sure they are. Maybe you are related to the brown-skinned one but not the blonde."

"Zeiva is related to me through my father, truly. And I don't care what you and Zeiva do together." As two other men appeared down the hall heading for the privy I brushed past the fuming Kukiya.

Me and Zeiva—humping? What a scary thought. I didn't think the big man was aware of what he was getting himself into, but he was welcome to have zer—though he might regret his rash choice by morning.

Back at the table I poured myself more beer from the new pitcher and took another drink from my glass. The loud music was giving me a headache. I so wished we could go. I hated this.

"What's wrong, siyatli cousin?" Dathna asked.

Everything was wrong, but there was no point in complaining. Ze would only laugh at me. So instead I told zer about the Kukiya man's warning for me to stay away from Zeiva.

"Oh that is too funny, cousin," ze agreed.

I drank some more and Dathna's new chamuqwani friend came back and ze went with him onto the dance floor. As the evening dragged on into the night I became aware of fewer and fewer people sitting around our table.

When Dathna came back to rest from dancing, I asked, "Where are Utreal and the other cousin?" I chuckled and took another gulp of my beer. "Did they fall in the indoor privy?"

Dathna narrowed zer eyes and studied me. Suddenly amused, ze said, "You are drunk, little cousin."

"No I'm not. Answer my kvestion, little coushin. Where'z Utre'yall?"

"They left to go to another party a while ago. This drinking house will be closing soon, so you had better find a pretty friend to stay the night with." Zer friend was back and ze stood up to go.

"Clozzing? What doesh that mean? W-where you going?"

Dathna motioned to the man waiting for zer. I'm going with him—to his house."

"C-can I come, too?"

"Definitely not!"

"But we still have to bargain; I want to go home," I pleaded.

"We will bargain later." Zer friend put an arm around her shoulder and without a backward glance they were gone, too.

I slumped back onto my chair and drank the last of the beer in my glass. I looked around for more, but the beer pitcher was empty, and so were all the glasses left on the table.

When I looked up hoping Zeiva would come back soon and buy me more I happen to see zer and the big Kukiya nearly at the front door. Fearing ze would leave me too I stumbled around the empty tables trying to catch up with them, before I lost zer, too.

The cold night air hit me like a slap in the face when I hurried outside. It sobered me up a little. Ze and zer man friend were walking down the street arm in arm, stopping to kiss now and again.

"Zeiva, don't leave me, wait for me, please!" Ze laughed at me and kissed zer friend deeply. "Zeiva!" I cried and even the drunken me could hear the desperation in my voice. "Zeiva, take me with you."

"Go away, cousin, I'm busy. We will talk later."

Stumbling as I tried to catch up to them I called, "I don't know this place – I don't know where to go—or how to find you. Zeiva wait!"

"Go away, siyatli cousin we will find *you*—later."

When I continued to follow calling out to them the big Kukiya had finally had enough of me. Whirling around as I reached them, he caught me off guard and slammed his hard fist into my jaw. Already unsteady on my feet I sank to the ground, landing in a crumpled heap.

"I told you before, you stupid shit, to leave my girl alone." He aimed a kick at my side and I grunted, nearly puking up the beer I had drunk. He might have done me more damage but Zeiva called him away before he could do me more harm.

"Oh, leave him be, my handsome sweetie," ze cooed. "His father will be mad at me if you hurt him too badly. He really is my cousin though he is one of my stupider relatives. Come on; let's go."

After they were gone I crawled to the nearby brick wall and leaned my back against its cool surface. My jaw hurt, my ribs hurt and I wanted to puke. I was dizzy the world spinning around me. I closed my eyes maybe the dizziness would go away if I just stayed still and had a little rest...

I might have stayed curled up against the closed store's wall for the rest of the night, but sometime later I was awakened by somebody kicking my feet. "Hey bud, you can't sleep here. Get up and go home." A gruff male voice said above me.

"Home?" I mumbled, still only half awake. "Yesh, I wan' go home. I wan', but don' know how get there, and my mean coushinz leff me."

Opening my eyes to slits, just wide enough to see, I saw a tall young chamuqwani dressed in a gold shirt and dark blue trousers. Atop his short yellow hair was a blue hat with a brim and a glyph of some kind on its front. He was wearing a small thunder weapon on his hip and carried a slim black club in one hand.

"Who have you got there?" The new speaker was an older and rounder man with cruel blue eyes, who wore a similar uniform.

"Just another homeless zaunk I think," the first one said.

The older one snorted. "Another one, eh? Looks like he's been in a fight, too. Look at his face."

I mumbled a protest as the older man pulled me roughly to my feet. "No fight. He hit me firsht. My cousins leave me—all alone." I choked on a sob. "All-lone." I got no sympathy from them. They weren't listening.

"What do you want to do with him? He's so drunk he can barely stand," the first man said.

"Dirty zaunk. The government should have never let them off the Preserve. All they do is get drunk and cause trouble when they come over the mountains to Seatown," the older one complained.

"So, I repeat, what shall we do with him?" the first man said. He studied me thoughtfully for a moment then suggested, "I suppose we could drop him at the temple mission. He doesn't look like he is going to cause any trouble tonight."

"The mission? Fuck that. All the old celibress in charge will do is let him sleep it off, feed him some mush in the morning and he will be right back out here getting drunk and fighting tomorrow night. Toss him in the back of the mecho-wagon with the other two. The judge can sort them out in the morning."

Putting a pair of silver handcuffs on my wrists and pulling my arms behind my back they half walked, half carried me to a large horseless vehicle one of them had called a mecho-wagon. Opening a door in the back the older one managed to bang my head against the metal doorframe as he shoved me inside. Biting my lip so I wouldn't cry out I stumbled in and sank down onto a metal bench where a third man chained me to a bar running along the side wall.

Two other tribal men were in this van thing along with me. One was about my own age, with several silver earrings hanging from one ear. He also wore black paint around his eyes and had his hair in long curls like I'd seen many of the women at the drinking house wear.

But he was very, very thin. I smelled no beer or waskyja on him, but something was wrong with him, besides the bruising on his face and arms. He was having a hard time sitting still; his muscles twitching uncontrollably.

The other tribal man was nearly bald with a bushy graying beard that spoke of his mixed race heritage. His clothes were stained and covered in dirt. A long scar ran down one cheek. He had a big belly, and stank of waskyja, pee and smoke. When he saw me his eyes grew wide in surprise.

"Hello, young buckiyo. You just come in from the Zerve to have a good time?" He chuckled. "Too bad the goldys caught you, eh?"

Goldys, Zerve? Once again I cursed my tricky cousins for bringing me to this crazy place and time. I figured out that Zerve must be one of the ways the people here referred to the Tribal Preserve. But what was a goldy? "Yes, Uncle, I am new here. There is so much I don't understand in this big city. What is a goldy?"

He stared at me wide eyed then burst out laughing. "Did you hear that, sweet cheeks? This bushy boy doesn't know what a goldy is." The thin man paid us no attention just sitting there shaking and twitching. Still chuckling the old man turned back to me.

"Your family must come from somewhere way back in those desert hills if you don't know what a goldy is. What do they call our imperial peace defenders out there, eh? Peacers, fendos, or just stupid whore sons?"

I could feel my face heating, so I dropped my eyes in embarrassment and shook my head. "I'm sorry; I don't know. I haven't lived on the Tribal Preserve in a while."

He snorted. "Well you'll learn what to call the mean pinker dog turds soon enough if you stay around Seatown. The pale-skinned people here hate anybody darker than they are, and they ain't shy 'bout lettin' you know how they feel, either."

"Yes I already noticed that many people still call us insulting names like 'zaunk'. But in the drinking house there were young chamuqwani drinking and dancing with us—and that is a good sign for the future."

"Chamuqwani... my, I haven't heard anybody call the imperial settlers that since I was a boy. Where did you say you come from, bushy boy?"

I grinned showing my canines. "As you said, uncle, I'm from deep in those wild desert hills."

He chuckled again. "Well, my young buckiyo, you just stick with old Tommo when we get out tomorrow and I'll set you right."

"Where are the goldys taking us?" I murmured. "Do you know?"

"Why to the famous Seatown House of Correction, of course. You ever been to jail when you lived in those desert hills of yours?"

Jail... I sighed. And so I was ending my first day back on Earth Mother as I had left her. "Yes I been to chamuqwani jail—long time ago."

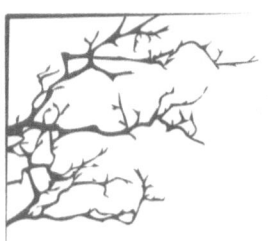

Chapter Five

Se Ho Co, as my People called the jail in Seatown, was a big gray stone building with no windows except right in front. The mecho-wagon drove through a heavy wire gate and pulled inside a large barn-like room that glowed with the flameless lights I had noticed both on the city streets and in the drinking house.

When the big doors were closed from the outside two men wearing brown uniforms opened the back doors on the mecho-wagon to get us out. One man came inside to unchain our handcuffs from the wall while the other stood outside with his thunder weapon out and pointed at us.

The man who unlocked my handcuffs refastened them behind my back and then gave me a hard shove. Get moving zaunk."

Losing my balance, and with my hands still bound behind my back, I tumbled out the door and crashed onto the stone floor. With the little one on my wrist's help I was able to cushion my fall somewhat, so that my face didn't smash into the hard surface—but now my shoulder hurt to add to my misery. Climbing to my feet I shook with rage but kept my eyes down so they wouldn't have an excuse to beat on me. I was wise to their tricks and I was completely sober by that time.

Joking with the brown-shirted guards who seemed to know him and called him sergeant, Tommo managed to climb down on his own, but not the thin man. They swore at him and called him a nasty whore of a fancy boy. He had more cuts and bruises by the time we were marched inside.

The new guards led us down a gray hall and then we were commanded to sit on a metal bench in front of a long wooden counter. There were already several chained men sitting on the bench and we took our places at the end of the row.

Just like when I lived on the Preserve and it was ration day, here also there was a fat man wearing a brown uniform sitting with a big open book in front of him. I watched as each man on the bench was brought up to the counter, asked a few questions and then ordered to take off any jewelry and put it along with other personal items into a brown bag which the fat man collected to store on shelves behind him.

To my surprise the guards also demanded the prisoner remove his belt and shoe strings, too. Murmuring so I hoped only Tommo could hear, I whispered, "Why are the guards taking away his belt and shoe strings?"

"So we won't try and kill ourselves," he said just as quietly. "It's so much fun staying here that many of our zaunk brothers try—or the guards help them try."

Fearing they would want me to remove my qwissa dragon lizard I conveyed my worry to her using the mind speech.

<<The enemy cannot see me now—nor can you unless you call on your Gift. But have no fear, I am still with you always. We should go soon. There is great evil here and one of the enemy is searching for me.>>

<<Yes, we will go and soon,>> I promised. The little one had no need to remind me about leaving. I had no wish to see judge and end up in another prison, some place where Zeiva couldn't get to me to bring me home. I doubted if ze would wait for me if I was locked up.

Hmm, searching for my qwissa, why? I shivered, feeling dread twist a knot in my gut. Had the Crokno already found me, or had Utreal bribed one of the guards to get zer revenge? Both were chilling thoughts.

When it was my turn to stand before the fat man, his first question to me was to ask me my name.

I hesitated, thinking, my name? What name should I give him? I didn't want to share with him my true name. I had no wish to give the chamuqwani, who might be a Crokno supporter more power over me....

His face turning a bright red the fat man shouted, "Speak up you stupid zaunk. What is your damned name?"

"Martin Fishspear," I blurted without thinking. That was the name given me when I lived with my uncle Royston Fishspear at the converts' settlement. It would do.

"Where do you live, Martin?"

I shrugged.

"You homeless?"

Was I? With a sinking feeling in my gut I feared I was. I looked at the man and shrugged.

"You got family here in Seatown?"

"Think so, but no find yet."

To the rest of the questions he asked me like, did I have any money, or did I have a job? I just answered with a shrug. At last he grew tired of me and ordered me to take off my belt and shoes.

I did what he wanted, but as I started to go back to the bench one of the other guards held up a hand to stop me. Reading from a paper he was holding he looked at me again, then said to the other guard, "I gotta search this one more thoroughly."

"What? Why?" the fat man demanded.

"Because he's a thief, that's why. Says here he stole a valuable piece of jewelry from some rich lord's son and the asshole wants it back."

To me he said, "Take off your clothes and bend over."

"Not right here, damn ya," the fat man protested. "I don't want any lice or other vermin he might have on him falling off in here." He pointed a finger to a door a little further down the gray hall. "Use the interrogation room if you think it's necessary."

Muttering curses under his breath the guard with the paper jerked on my chain. I was angry and a little afraid, too, but put up no resistance as he pulled me down the hall. Once we were alone I planned to find out what this was really about.

I hoped to also transport myself out of there once I discovered what I needed to know, but had to change my plans, because another guard appeared and followed us into the little room.

When I took off all my clothes the other man pawed through them thoroughly searching for my little qwissa, I guessed. But as she promised me she was invisible to their touch or sight. When they concluded that I hadn't hidden any stolen jewelry in my trousers and shirt they next ordered me to unbraid my hair. Pulling hard enough to yank some out as they searched through it they left my long hair tangled and knotted by the time they were done.

Making a sour face the guard who had brought me here took out a pair of blue gloves from his pocket, slipped them on his hands and then motioned for me to bend over and spread my bum cheeks.

Pretending that I didn't understand his order I just stood until he came over to push me down. As he drew near I stared him in the eyes and captured his spirit with my Qwakaiva. His body now unable to move and its shadow blocking me from the view of the other guard by the door, I demanded him to speak. <<Who told you about my qwissa bracelet?>>

<<Don't know. My captain said—>>

<<Who told your captain then?>>

<<Don't know. Captain just say to search—maybe beat up or even kill if prisoner resists. Rich lord give money if get his jewels back. Captain said he will share if we do this for him.>>

Strengthening my compulsion, I asked, <<Who is this rich lord?>>

<<Don't know his name.>>

The guard didn't know his name, true, but he *had* seen their benefactor. I recognized the picture the man formed in his mind when I pressed him. As I suspected; it was Utreal in zer handsome blond form.

But even if ze was angry with me for the loss of the qwissa, having me killed and risking my father and Kunai's retaliation was crazy. Did ze really think they wouldn't discover what had happened to me if these guards succeeded?

Barely able to contain my fury I became aware of the guard by the door getting restless. Time was passing and my hold over my unwilling informant was also slipping. <<We are done here. You found nothing inside me. I can get dressed now.>>

I released him and straightened. My guard stepped back shaking his head and gruffly ordered me to get dressed.

The man by the door frowned. "Did you find it?"

"No."

"The captain will be furious if we don't find it. He already took the whoreson's money. Want me to search him again?"

"Not necessary, he doesn't have it."

"Let me slap him around a bit and he will tell us where he hid it then."

"Maybe later, Ordan at the desk will get suspicious if we take much longer in here."

The other one smirked. "And want his share; too, if he finds out the real reason we wanted to question the zaunk."

The first guard agreed and together they muscled me back to the waiting bench.

"Did you find whatever you were looking for?" the fat man asked.

"Nah, must have been another zaunk."

After two other drunken men, both chamuqwani, were brought in and questioned we were all marched down another hall that ended in a row of cells with bars on their open side. One of the chamuqwani protested and started to fight when he realized he was going to be tossed in the big cell with, "a bunch of dirty zaunks." Our guards ignored his complaints and after hitting him several times with their black sticks they shoved him bleeding and dazed into our cell anyway.

When it was my turn and they took off my handcuffs I walked in with no urging and took a seat on a cold stone bench against the wall. Tommo sat beside me after guiding the twitching and bleeding man to a seat near us. The others sat on the bench or just lay on the dirty floor where the guards had left them.

When the guards had disappeared behind the now closed outer door, and the other men had either fallen asleep or were drunkenly mumbling to themselves, I studied the thin man and asked Tommo, "Tell me what is wrong with our brother there." I pointed with my lips to the twitching thin man near us.

Almost asleep himself he jerked when I spoke to him. Glancing at the thin man he shrugged. "The fancy boy? Aside from the beating the goldys just gave him, he has the red hunger that's all."

His answer wasn't very enlightening, so before he drifted off to sleep again, I asked, "I'm sorry to bother you once more, uncle, but there are so many confusing things in this big city please help me understand. What is the red hunger? I think I already know what a fancy boy is. There have always been some two spirited people among us and fancy boy is what the chamuqwani now call them, right? What I don't understand, though, is why the goldys and these brown uniforms don't like them."

He chuckled at my ignorance, but then decided to answer. "They don't like Sweet Cheeks there, because the Thunderer says it's unnatural for a man to like another man, and most people have heard that message, loud and clear, all their lives.

"As for this poor lad he gets his money from whoring—you know what whoring is, bushy boy?"

"Yes, uncle I do. Some women I knew growing up had to sell their bodies to the soldiers to feed their children. There is no shame in that. No matter what the priests say." Tommo swore and nodded. I wondered to myself if I had been speaking of his own mother, but decided not to ask.

"And the red hunger you spoke of?" I reminded him.

Nearly asleep he grunted. "Oh yeah, over the western ocean the people grow and sell a drug—a medicine, of sorts that takes away pain when used correctly, but it also makes you high—like beer or liquor and lotta guys sell it on the street for that reason.

"It's called o'piyo, or the red hunger because if you get addicted and use it all the time it turns your eyes red. Me, I'll stick with my booze, but lotta our people use it to dull the pain of just living. Sweet Cheeks there is addicted to the stuff and sells his body to anybody who can pay him so he can buy more.
"

Studying the poor two-spirited person I blurted, "But this hunger stuff is killing him."

"Yes it is, and maybe he wants it to. Maybe he would rather be dead than go on living the life the imperial dog humpers have forced upon us."

Leaning his head back he refused to answer more questions and soon enough was snoring again. For me it wasn't so easy. Our guards never turned off the lights in the ceiling above us, and someone was either puking or peeing into the indoor privy on the back wall every time I managed to fall asleep.

Trying to ignore my own bodily pain I leaned my head back, too. My thoughts were twisting and spinning like a whirlwind inside my head. All about me I tasted only grief and suffering. Sheltered in the Beyond for so long I had forgotten the pain that came with living on my wounded world. And, not feeling exactly right myself, I was finding it hard to shield from so much torment.

After listening to the two spirited one whimper and moan for a while the chamuqwani that had objected to sharing a cell with us yelled for zer to shut up or he was going to come over and shut zer up—permanently. The one called sweet cheeks heard the threat and tried to quiet down, but zer torment was too much and ze began soon enough to cry again.

Before the big chamuqwani could start yelling again I moved over beside the tormented one and took his hand. Startled he looked at me eyes growing wide with fear he tried to pull his hand away. "I won't hurt you, cousin, but I can give you some peace for a while, if you let me," I offered.

Like a small child he sounded so hopeful when he asked, "You got some stuff on you?"

"No, I have no o'piyo but I can do this for you." Placing my other hand on his middle where the pain seemed to be the worst. I used my Gift to ease his tremors and put him to sleep. When he sagged into my arms I laid him flat on the bench and made zer as comfortable as I could before easing myself to the cold, dirty floor, to doze until our guards came to fetch us. As I was drifting into my dreams I happened to glance at Tommo and saw his eyes were open and watching me.

In the morning a rumbling cart was pushed down the walkway outside our cell. Cheese inside a bread bun and cups of bitter, cold tea were pushed through a narrow slot in the door to anyone who wanted them. Not sure when I would eat next I took my share, but it was hard to choke it down. My head hurt and my stomach roiled from all the beer I'd drunk the night before.

Sometime later several guards came back and ordered us to get in line. As I rose to obey I glanced at the one I had helped. He seemed better for a little sleep, but I knew my aid was only temporary. He would need more of the o'piyo he craved soon enough. He got in line when ordered to do so, but didn't talk or look at me as he passed.

Next we were handcuffed and chained again and then we were marched out of the jail where another longer, enclosed mecho-wagon was waiting to take us to see the judge. Inside were tiny little walled off cells not much bigger than closets.

One at a time we were ushered inside, made to sit and our handcuffs were refastened to a metal bar inside each little cell. When everyone was secured the vehicle began to move.

Alone in my cramped cell I finally got the opportunity I needed to transport myself "away." I had few reference points on which to focus and project my form, so I had no choice but to choose the dirty alley where the cousins had made the portal. I hoped Zeiva or Dathna might be nearby. I needed to renegotiate our bargain, but I also needed to warn them about Utreal's strange behavior.

When the vehicle arrived at the court house and found I was no longer sitting in my cell they would be hunting for me, so I couldn't hang around the drinking houses in that area waiting for them to return. It would be too dangerous. Both the goldys and my treacherous cousin would be looking for me.

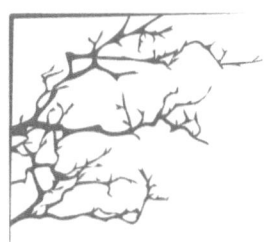

Chapter Six

As I suspected, I couldn't sense any of my tricky cousins nearby when I emerged from the alley. I walked to the drinking house where we had been the night before but its door was locked. It was early and most of the stores and dining houses I passed were still closed.

I couldn't stay here until they opened. I needed a place to clean up, change clothes and maybe change my appearance for a time until the goldys forgot about me and I became just another stupid zaunk again to them. But where could I go? I didn't know this city at all and last night I was too drunk to pay much attention to my surroundings.

The day was gray a cool breeze that tasted of rain and salt was blowing away the last traces of a thick cottony fog. The little one had reappeared as a bracelet on my left wrist after I made the transfer. Her glowing jeweled eyes blinked up at me when I pulled back my sleeve.

<<Greetings, Honored One, I am glad you are still with me.>>

<<Your respect is appreciated, siyatli rescuer. I am Aqwissa. You may call me that if you wish, because I am now your guide and protector.>>

<<Protector, eh? What about last night?>> I grumped.

The creature hissed a laugh. <<I won't risk revealing myself when you are being stupid and not truly in danger.>>

I laughed, too. <<Good point, I have no wish to get drunk again; it hurts too much. Do you know where my cousins Zeiva or Dathna are?>>

<<No, all your father's relatives are shielding from us.>>

<<Hmm, I suspected that. Got any idea where we should go so the goldys won't find us?>>

<<We must go to where the rest of the seal people live. If you join them for a time the goldys or your treacherous cousin won't find us.>>

She was speaking of seal animal people, not my Qwa'Nayhi Seal relatives, of course, but nonetheless. <<A good idea; let's find them.>>

Over the next several moons I lived among the seal people in the stinky ocean of Seatown's harbor. I kept hoping to detect my cousins, but as time passed I realized they had truly abandoned me.

Late summer passed into a stormy winter and I grew tired of hiding and eating just fish. The animal seal people and their predators left me alone, but I longed for the companionship of humankind. It was time to emerge from this saltwater refuge and explore this strange city.

Seatown was a large chamuqwani town near the edge of the ocean a ridge of snowcapped mountains to the east crowding its sprawl in that direction. To the south were flat farmlands growing foods like potatoes and berries. When I swam close enough to see, I noticed many brown-skinned people harvesting the mature crops.

There was also a large muddy river that emptied itself into the salty ocean. I considered swimming up this river, but the salmon people sang to me of mighty rapids and mating frenzy, so I decided to find another way to return to the Preserve. But the eating was good by the river, so I lingered there. I found salmon's sweet red flesh a welcome change from the bitter tasting fish of the harbor.

But at last it was becoming too hard to avoid being ensnared in the fishermen's nets, so reluctantly I abandoned my gorging and swam back to the harbor, my Gift still urging me to return to land. Earlier in the summer when I'd hunted the waters to the north I had noticed that there were long gravel and sand beaches where the city people swam and played on warm sunny days.

Behind the beaches was a forested land I heard some of the people call a park. Though Park was nearly in the downtown part of the city across the inlet it was a wild place with tall trees that seemed to climb into the nearby mountains. It promised to be a good place with many animal relatives like deer and bear living there. When I stepped over the big logs cluttering the beach and walked into the forest I marveled at the giant trees reaching high into the rainy sky. Some were so big I couldn't close my arms around them.

In the north where I was born, and in the dry deserts of the Preserve I had never seen such trees. It was such a joy to hug them and lean my forehead against their shaggy bark and listen to the wisdom they had gained after a long life.

I knew this season of the year was called winter, but though this land was cold and wet, unlike my home in the north the land wasn't asleep and it rarely snowed. Everything was so alive, beautiful and green. The giants kept their leaves, like the pine and juniper I already knew. Along the trails clustered several kinds of green shiny leaved shrubs dotted with many colored berries that the animals and I ate. Here also the fallen logs and living tree barks were coated in soft green mosses, and gray-green plants hung down from the bare branches of the smaller bushes and trees that did drop their summer foliage.

This land was a joy to me; it renewed my spirit and made me glad that I had returned to this world of my birth. I sang to it of my wonder and my gratitude, sucking in its Qwakaiva like a sponge.

Stuffing dry grasses into my jacket for extra warmth I wandered deeper into the peace of this magical world. As night approached I built a small shelter out of fallen branches with forest debris piled up along its triangular sides, just large enough for me to crawl inside. I was safe and warm, when my body heated up the tiny space. I slept well that night in spite of the rain that began near morning. Not since I had been forced to leave our family home in the north had I felt so at peace.

Next day Raven woke me when the rain stopped. I wandered deeper into the forest away from the dirt trails where I saw dogs and people walking as they enjoyed this sacred place, too. Near a stream tumbling down from the mountain above I decided to build a more permanent shelter and surround my new home with a conjure of invisibility.

There was plenty of food for me in this forest and from there I could either walk, or transfer into the city, using my Gift. I still needed to understand why I had been called to this place and time where my cousins had abandoned me.

One evening after I had caught a couple rabbits in my snares and had fished for some late arriving salmon from the nearby stream I walked down to the beach to clean my catch and offer my left overs to Raven in gratitude for showing me where to hunt.

As I was finishing my task I happened to hear the sound of a drum and the deep-voice of a man chanting in time to its cadence. His song was unfamiliar, but nonetheless it brought up strong emotions in me. I heard the music of the land in his voice. The singer was someone born to this coast, his ancestor's bones buried deep in its rich soil.

Even though they might learn the song, no person transplanted here from elsewhere could put such a wealth of meaning into his music unless he and his ancestors had deep roots here. Curious I wanted to learn more about these brown-skinned people, so I walked back into the trees to conceal my approach.

At the mouth of my stream were three men, and one of them I recognized as my companion from the jail, Tommo. An Elder with cropped gray hair had just finished singing as I crouched behind some green shrubs just inside the trees to watch.

They'd made a smoky fire a short way down the beach, and then Tommo was told to undress. One of the men clustered around the fire tossed his ragged and filthy clothes into the flames. After the Elder brushed him all over with green branches Tommo was guided into the water by another younger man.

When the water came up to his shoulders Tommo lay flat and submerged his head allowing the cool green waves to wash both his body and spirit clean. I gathered from their talk that he had been released from jail not long before. After a time, he was guided out of the water red and shivering, but smiling. He was handed a towel to dry himself and then he was given new clean clothes.

Once he finished dressing the Elder began singing a new song as the younger man painted a glyph in red paint on Tommo's forehead. To my surprise, it was a song I knew. It was one of the Prophet's healing songs I had learned so long ago when my family and I had stayed at his encampment by Saluuli Lake.

The song brought back so many joyful and painful memories of my baby sister and my dead parents that I found myself singing along with the Elder. Tears streaming down my own face, and lost for the moment in my memories I closed my eyes and just sang to ease my heart.

When I had completed the five rounds of the song I stopped and opened my eyes, finally becoming aware of the men staring at me. I took a deep breath, trying to choke down my feelings. "I'm sorry Elder. I didn't mean to interrupt the ceremony. I heard the singing from up the stream and I know some of Iyantsha's songs and…" I paused, feeling my face heat, not sure what else to say.

At last the Elder said, "If you know of the Prophet and his healing teachings then come over here by the fire and join us, young brother."

Unused to being among humans I hesitated, suddenly shy. Now a metallic scaled choker necklace, rather than a bracelet, my companion Aqwissa rubbed her head against my neck, urging me to go. I thanked him and came over to join them.

Sitting round the fire quietly talking everyone looked up as we approached. Someone built up the fire and set a sooty pot to boil for tea. I handed my willow basket of fish and rabbits to the Elder as an offering. His eyes opened wide when he saw what it contained.

"What an unexpected treat, young brother. Where did you come by all this traditional food for us?"

I felt my face redden again. "I—uh—went fishing earlier and then I checked my snares this evening."

From his space across the fire Tommo looked up and in the brighter light he saw me, and then recognized me. "Well, well, if it isn't my old friend the bushy boy. I thought the dog turds at the jail had killed you when you disappeared."

Turning to the Elder, Tommo said, "Samul, this is the one I was telling you 'bout." Then addressing me he asked, "Hey, buckiyo, however did you escape, eh? The guards were sure mad when they couldn't find you. Where you been, anyway?"

I shrugged. "I've been, around, staying here and there till the goldys forget about me—haven't been back in the city since the day we left for court. Right now I'm living up this stream a ways."

One of the young men with a golden-eyed wolf cub peering at me from his spirit fire saw my food rose and went into the brush to collect sticks on which to roast my catch. I learned when he returned that his name was Stakaya. He had heard some of what I said, and then asked, "If you are living out here in the park aren't you worried about the park patrol finding and arresting you?

"They don't like the homeless camping out here. We are only allowed here to conduct some of our ceremonies, because park access is written into our treaty rights."

"But this is your people's land, right?"

"Yes it is, but the government doesn't see it that way," another man sitting by the fire said.

Does anything ever change with the chamuqwani? I thought privately. "You shouldn't have to ask permission to be on your own land."

He snorted a laugh and agreed with me then Stakaya repeated his question. "No I'm not worried about the patrols," I answered. "I have seen them gathering up campers further down the beach near town, but my camp is well hidden and I'm careful. They never see me."

As we ate Tommo kept watching me and I sensed he was mulling over the mystery of me. At last he got up the courage to ask, "Your name is Martin isn't it? I still can't understand how you unlocked your handcuffs and left without anybody seeing you. How did you manage to do it?"

I shrugged and met his eye. "I have my ways. But my name isn't Martin—not really. One of my uncles gave me that name when he wanted to adopt me and convert me to the Thunderer's worship, but since running away from his camp I've never used it." I shrugged again. "I don't know why I gave the guard that name."

"Perhaps because you didn't want to share your true self with them," the elder suggested.

I laughed nervously. "I think you have the right of it, Honored Elder."

"And now do you feel comfortable enough with us to share your real name—or at least one we can call you by when needed?"

I took a drink of my tea and smiled. "You can call me Tas. That is my true name—at least a part of it. Officially when I was sent to a live-away school the name I used was Tassele Cougarson, though."

"Hmm, which school did you go to, and for how long? Maybe my sister or one of my cousins know you from your school days," Stakaya wanted to know, his face alight with curiosity.

Not thinking about the consequences of my words I swallowed down the mouthful of rabbit I was chewing and said, "The school I attended was Saint

Yon's much farther to the east. I don't recall any west coast people there at the time. Maybe some people came there after I left, though."

Stakaya frowned then shook his head. "I never heard of it, so I guess none of my friends or family would know you then."

"It's very far east from here, I think, so probably they were sent elsewhere."

"Yeah, we all went to Saint Royston's up the Jaspar River."

Stakaya might have asked me more questions, but to my relief another man interrupted, "Cougarson, that's a Kukiya name, I think. Are your people from one of the desert tribes?" he asked.

"No, but I have lived among them. I was born to the clans who lived on the shore of Big Ice Lake up north. When we were forced south to live with the Kukiya on the Tribal Preserve my mother married a Kukiya man, who adopted me after their marriage." I pointed to the black dots in a pattern across my cheeks.

"Hmm, and do you speak your tribal language, or did you lose it like so many of us who were made to go to those schools," the Elder asked.

"I didn't forget, Elder. I can speak my Qwani'Ya language and the Kukiya tongue—or at least the basics in that language."

"You hunt and fish, know your tribal language and know something of the Prophet's teachings that is a great achievement now days—especially for one so young," the Elder mused.

I found it impossible to hide my smile so to disguise my amusement I took another drink of my tea, before answering. "It's difficult to say how old I truly am, but I may be older than you think, Elder."

The elder named Samul gave me a knowing smile and I suddenly realized he was viewing me with his Spirit Sight. "Maybe so, tribal man. My People have a ceremonial house further down the beach. When you hear the big drums some night come down and join us. I am usually there; you will be welcome."

"Thank you, honored Elder. I would like that."

Glancing at the little time-tell strapped to his wrist Stakaya got to his feet. He yawned and stretched. Addressing Tommo, he said, "Uncle, I have to get back to the city. Gahji will be furious if we come in too late and wake her up again. She has school in the morning—a test or something. So if you want to stay at our house we need to go soon."

Tommo glanced at the Elder who nodded. "We are done here for tonight and will be leaving soon ourselves."

Getting stiffly to his feet with a little help from Stakaya he said his good byes to the others then stopped and turned back to me.

"Cougarson, Cougarson," he said, as if trying to puzzle out a mystery, "I've heard that name before, but I can't place where or when. When you get tired of the bush life, buckiyo, come find me in the city. Maybe I'll remember by then."

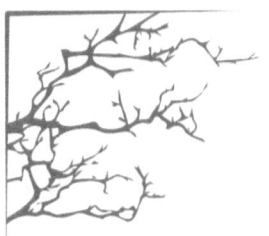

Chapter Seven

For the rest of the winter I divided my time between my secret camp in the depths of Park, and trips into Seatown. I wanted to lose myself in the peace of the forest forever, but Aqwissa and my own Gift of foretelling kept reminding me that that peace was but an illusion. The big trees whispered to me of change coming, and I needed to be ready to fulfil my part in it.

The images and feelings they shared with me when I rested my forehead against them or sank my hands deep into the fallen leaves and soil at their bases spoke to me of death and destruction. Some of the younger trees were afraid while other giants welcomed their death so that their wise spirits would be at last freed to grow again elsewhere in another place and time.

I took Elder Samul up on his offer to visit the ceremonial house a few times when I heard the singing, but I usually sat in the shadows and allowed the music and the activity to flow on around me, often without making my presence known to him. The ancestors and the spirits summoned as well to these events were aware of me, of course, but didn't seem to mind my attendance.

They spoke to me of the power and wealth of the land, and the ancestors mourned with me over the destruction brought among them after the settlers from the empire came to their stormy coast. I sang to them in the mind speech of my own people and told them how we had been driven from our ancestor's graves and the land given to us from the Earth Mother, and they commiserated with me over my loss. I thanked them for letting me live on their land.

But along with the good, I saw other things that both worried and disturbed me. As I became wiser in the ways of this time and place I saw how even at the sacred ceremonies where I knew there should be no drinking, using o'piyo, or other things that changed the mind's perceptions, many people, especially the young ones, were buying, selling, and using these unnatural substances in defiance of their Elders' wishes.

When I forced myself to ignore the noise and bad smell of Seatown I ventured into the city, and there I saw much the same thing. Shielding from the cloud of human misery that hung like a fog over everything as best I could, I watched like a patient hunter its citizens going about their daily routines—and learned. I had no wish to be taken to their jail again. I was always alert to the goldys' presence and hid when they came too near.

As I walked through the city and learned its ways, I discovered a yellow stone building called Library. It contained more books inside than I could have imagined existed in the whole world. I wasn't a good reader; the religious books at the school never caught my interest, but the patient teaching of my Qwani'Ya brother Kutima and Celibress Dinana had taught me the basics and I was now grateful for that.

When an older woman working there saw that I wasn't like many homeless people, who came in Library only to sleep, or shelter out of the weather for a time, she would answer my many questions and suggested new books for me to read. With her explanations I learned to understand paper maps which helped me to place the Tribal Preserve in relation to my northern home and this west coast city.

I read books on the empire's history and understood a little better why they came to invade our lands. I also was curious about what the books had to say concerning my own tribal history and the events I lived through on the Preserve. I didn't agree with most of what I read. Though only a child during that terrible time, I knew much of those books were lies and that saddened me.

One day when I was complaining to my friendly librarian about how tribal people recounted those events differently she handed me another book. "Here is one you might like better. This author traveled to the Tribal Preserve in his youth and fought to reform our laws concerning our Zacatik peoples."

To my surprise the book she gave me was written by my old friend Collin Golbraith, which also contained some of Willum's pictures near the end. What a shock to see a younger me, staring out at me from its pages.

When I read more about the author I discovered that he had become a famous writer and champion of the rights of the tribal peoples of his time. He and his friend Lord Bronworthy worked tirelessly after I left with my father, for the emperor's laws to be changed to protect our rights and insure better conditions for people living on the Preserve.

I stared for a long time at that picture its Qwakaiva bringing up so many memories. When my friend came around and saw the tears rolling down my cheeks she paused by my chair and asked, "What's wrong, young man; are you ill?"

Wiping my eyes I shook my head and pointed to the picture in front of me. I didn't dare tell her the truth, so I said, "He is ancestor. I remember his stories. They were very sad."

"How fascinating." She studied me more closely then nodded. "Yes I can see the resemblance. Did your ancestor know the famous war chief Golannah, too. All the stories say that he was a most fearsome man before the army finally killed him when he was trying to steal horses."

Not true, I thought. Golannah was betrayed and then tortured by greedy men looking for gold, but dare I argue the point? No, why bother.

Changing the subject I pointed to Collin's name below the books title. "I would like to talk to this Collin Golbraith about the old days. Do you know where I can find him?"

She shook her head, giving me a pitying look. "Unless you can talk to the dead I'm afraid that wouldn't be possible. Collin Golbraith died more than twenty years ago."

Talk to the dead? Well, for someone with my Gift it might be possible, but I wasn't going to explain that to her, either.

"But I'm sure some of the history professors at the Seatown Lectorium would enjoy talking to you about the events on the Preserve from that time," she added. "Why don't you go there and see them?"

"Maybe I go. Thank you." I handed her back the book. I had had enough reading for the day.

Once back on the street I decided to look for Tommo. Collin's book brought back memories of Kitahtla, and that made me wonder if she was lost to me as well. Tommo had said at his cleansing ceremony that the Cougarson name meant something to him. I hoped he had had time enough to remember what that was.

Unfortunately for me I couldn't find him. Over the next several days I searched for him in the two city parks where the children played and the elders and homeless sat on the wooden benches and drank or played card games with one another.

Early on I had discovered the mission the goldy who found me drunk that first day mentioned. They served hot meals and handed out clean used clothes to poor and homeless people who needed them. I had replaced my own ragged clothes there and eaten hot soups and bread when my hunting was poor or I was tired of fish. I knew Tommo was often there, but the celibress said he hadn't been around lately when I asked.

One evening when I was about to return to my camp in the forest I saw the one called Stakaya from Tommo's ceremony. The wolf cub was talking and joking with some other young men in one of the little parks. The men had been drinking among themselves and selling other substances to people who stopped by their little group. Usually I didn't stay to talk to men who were drunk or were using o'piyo or other things that I knew Stakaya and his friends sold. But this time I decided to make an exception.

I was worried about the old man, and if I could find him, I hoped by this time he had remembered what he knew about the Cougarson lineage. I had already asked my librarian friend, but she couldn't find any trace of someone by that name in nearly eighty years.

My cousins had assured me Kitahtla was still alive in this time, but neither I—nor did my qwissa—have any idea how to find her. I needed more information and so far he was my best source.

I sat on one of the children's swings in the shadows and watched. Like so many who came and then went again, I kept hoping that Stakaya would leave so I could follow him and ask my questions but he still had things to sell and so remained on his bench with a couple others who were getting steadily drunker.

At one point Stakaya got into an argument with a big chamuqwani with a knife scar on his face who demanded Stakaya give him money, but the big man left grumbling when two of Stakaya's friends intervened.

The little park was nearly empty and it had started to rain when he finally stood and said good bye to the homeless men who had left the benches and were seeking shelter beneath dirty tarps under the trees. Still keeping to the shadows I followed him. Walking unsteadily he crossed the nearly empty street, heading through a maze of narrow walkways that led into a district of houses and small apartment buildings near the tracks Train used.

I was about to call out to him when Aqwissa spoke into my mind. <Beware, my Siyatli, enemies are near.>>

I paused, drifting back into the shadows by an old storage warehouse coated with crumbling gray paint. Two slim men in dark clothes with hoods pulled up to cover their faces stepped out of the shadows and passed me on the other side of the street, taking the same path we followed. <<Who are they, little one?>>

<<Humans hunting like you.>>

At her words I felt a shiver slide down my spine. <<Are they Crokno emissaries hunting me?>>

<<No just humans, with empty eyes and dark currents swirling in their spirit fires, they seek the one you hunt, too.>>

<<Will you help me protect the man I follow? He may have information I need to find my sister.>>

<<Yes. We'll protect him from his enemies, this time,>> she agreed.

Unwrapping from around my neck she coiled herself about my arm just above my wrist. <<Change yourself, my Siyatli, so the enemy will not recognize you.>>

<<Good idea.>> Wiping my hand down my face I lightened my skin a bit, grew a mustache and concealed my tattoos. I then hid my long hair inside my own jacket and hood, before I followed the other hunters.

Intent on getting out of the rain, which was falling more steadily now, Stakaya quickened his pace, and turned onto a dirt trail that led into the brush by Train's tracks, and from there continued onto the other side near more houses. Too drunk himself to notice perhaps, he seemed unaware of the two enemies stalking him.

About halfway down the path he was following a third man stepped out of the brush to confront him. It was the big man from the park, still wanting his money. Stakaya stopped, swirling currents of fear appeared in his spirit fire as the other two came up on him from behind, blocking any escape.

As I crept closer unnoticed by everyone, I heard Stakaya say, "I told you, Petros, I'd settle up with you next week. You'll get your money, but right now I have to help my sister pay this month's rent or she and the children will be kicked out onto the street. I'm good for it, you know that. I always pay Benton in the end. I just need a little more time."

"Not good enough, zaunk slime eater. The goldy wants his money, and he will take it out of my hide if you don't pay up."

"I can't pay you right now," Stakaya whined. "But I will pay—and soon—I promise."

Petros refused to listen and motioned for his hunters to grab him from behind. "If you won't give me what I need then we will just have to take it, you stupid zaunk," the big chamuqwani snarled.

Petros nodded to his men and the next thing I knew Stakaya lay bleeding in the mud of the trail. I ran forward shouting for them to stop. Two of them glanced up while Petros continued to search through the groggy Stakaya's clothes for his money and whatever he had left to sell.

Brandishing a long knife the nearest of them growled, "Get lost, zaunk, if you know what's good for you. This is none of your business."

Keeping my hands down at my sides I smiled, but there was no mirth in my expression. "Ah, but this *is* my business. He is a relative and I can't let you hurt him."

Petros snorted and rose, stuffing Stakaya's money into his inner jacket pocket. His two men at his back he looked at me as if I was stupid. "Suit yourself then, zaunk." All with knives in their hands now, they rushed me, coming from different sides at the same time.

I broke the first man's wrist with a flick of my hand, causing him to drop his knife. With another flick the knife tumbled down the rest of the slope, floating away in a stream of rainwater that was cascading down the hillside.

The second man I left to Aqwissa. She leapt from my other wrist, growing in size as she landed on the ground in her dragon form. Both of Petros's men screamed and backed away, slipping in the mud and falling to their knees on the slippery trail. Regaining their feet and howling in fright they stumbled back up the trail as fast as they could. Spitting out her power in a burst of flame, she scorched their backs with a reminder to keep going and not come back.

Petros himself was a more difficult problem to handle. I took more care with him from the first moment of the fight. Freezing him in place to prevent him attacking from behind while I dealt with his minions, I crossed to him after the others were out of sight.

Radiating a white-hot fury there was no fear of me in his spirit fire, in spite of what he had just witnessed. Why was that? Did he belong to the Crokno and feared their punishments more? Perhaps. I studied him with my Gift, but detected no otherworldly taint upon him.

<<He has been using the drug his kind call bravan to give himself courage. And he fears the one who owns his allegiance far more than our Qwakaiva,>> Aqwissa supplied. <<He too needs the money collected from selling the misused plant medicines.>>

<<Maybe so, but he is a grown man who has made many bad choices and now must accept their consequences,>> I said. <<I have no pity in my heart for him—and little for Stakaya, either. It is for the sake of his sister and her children that I do this.>>

Still ensnared in my conjure, I walked in close and looked him in the eye in the rude chamuqwani fashion. "I have no wish to interfere with you collecting money owing, but I have need of this man. If he says he will pay you later then I'm sure he will do it—as he said, but right now," I retrieved Stakaya's money from his clothing, "the needs of a mother and her children are more important than you."

Petros smirked. "I doubt our boss will agree with you when I tell him. Whoever you are, you and your relative are dead men," he warned.

I shrugged. Eyes wide the man watched in fascination as I held out my hand for Qwissa to shrink and rewind herself about my arm. "Death is a hunter who will find all of us. What we do with the life gifted us in the meantime is what is important. Your hunger for power and money mean nothing to the one who hunts all of us."

Still staring at the metallic bracelet my qwissa had once more become, he breathed, "Who are you?"

I laughed softly as I released him from my conjure and created another. "Who I am doesn't matter. You have been sampling your own product. All you have experienced tonight is but an illusion." I said, urging him up the slope with my Gift. "Go now before I change my mind and invite Death to find you here and now."

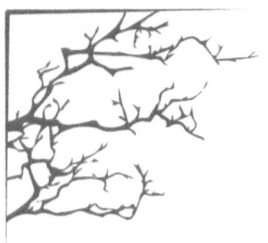

Chapter Eight

When I was sure they were all gone and weren't coming back I shifted back into my own likeness. Crouched beside Stakaya and laying a hand on his shoulder, I asked, "How badly are you hurt, brother?" Stakaya looked up, trying to bring me into focus. He blinked the rain out of his eyes and finally recognized me.

"T-Tas? W-where did you come from? How did you find me?"

I reached out a hand to help him up. "I was following you when you left the park. I wanted to ask you about Tommo. I'm worried about him. Can you walk?" With my help he had staggered to his feet then nearly fell back into the mud.

He let out a mirthless laugh. "Guess not."

"Then I'll help you." Putting his arm over my shoulder I had him lean on me as we started down the slippery trail. "Where are we going?"

Tripping over a hidden tree root half buried in the mud he groaned and then pointed with his free hand to the cluster of houses across the tracks. "Our house is the forth one on the left; we can go in the back way, so we won't disturb Gahji and the kids. My room is off the kitchen."

It was slow going and we were both soaked by the time we made it up the back stairs and into the warm kitchen. Leaving our muddy shoes by the door I helped Stakaya into his room, turned on the indoor light and shut the door. "Take off your clothes and let me see how badly they hurt you," I said and folded my arms across my chest, glaring at him.

Shivering he started to remove his soaked jacket and shirt. "I'll be all right in the morning; they just knocked me around a bit—for the fun of it, the shits. I'm really one of their best guys for moving product—"

Then remembering the reason for the attack Stakaya began fumbling at his clothes, frantically searching for his lost money and mumbling curses to himself when he didn't find it.

I watched him for a while, my anger simmering. If I hadn't needed his possible information about the old man I would have let the pack of carrion eaters have him. Finally I took pity on him, reached in my own damp jacket and tossed the wad of paper script onto the bed beside him.

"Here is the money you told Petros you needed to give your sister for the rent—I trust that was true. Petros may still have the o'piyo you had left, but I didn't bother to collect it. That will be up to you to sort out with him as well as paying him what you owe him. "

Pulling a dry shirt over his head he sat down on the bed, picked up the script and counted it and then recounted it again. Satisfied it was all there he tucked it away in a drawer in the stand by his bed and stared open-mouthed at me. "Thanks for getting me out of a jam, my sister really does need this. How did you get the money back from him?"

I waved a hand in a dismissive gesture. "How I came by the script isn't important. I helped you this time—but only this time, because of what I heard you say about your sister. If you continue to trade in substances that hurt or kill our People I will not help you again. Understand that, too. You need to pay off these men and find a better way to help her."

Stakaya sighed unable to meet my eyes. He finished getting dressed and finally said, "I know I need to stop selling. I might have gone back to our tribal preserve up the coast and kept my job fishing with a cousin, but Gahji needs help with the children and extra money while she finishes her nursing training."

"That you want to help is good, family members should always help one another, but do it in a good way, not like you have been doing."

He sighed again. "Yeah I know; she tells me the same thing. But it's hard to find work when you don't have a trade."

"Then get one."

"Yeah she says that, too." Then, changing the subject, he asked, "Why were you following me anyway?"

I let go my annoyance with him; there was no point in pursuing this topic further. He was young and didn't want to listen. "I was following you, as I said, to ask you about Tommo. I hadn't seen him around lately and I was worried about him."

"He's back in jail again. He got drunk and started a fight with another vet from the war, a guy he knew when he was an imperial soldier. The goldys came and broke it up and put them both in jail for a while."

Now it was my turn to sigh. Well that would explain why I hadn't been able to find him. "There's a cut over your ear that is still bleeding. I need water to clean it and bandages. Where are they?"

Stakaya put a hand to his face and when it came away red, he swore. "No, I can do it. I'm sure sis has bandages and some kind of pain meds around here. I'll take a couple and I'll be fine in the morning."

"All right, I'll be going then."

"No, wait." Wiping his hand on his wet shirt he got to his feet and started rummaging in a box of clothes on the floor. 'You can stay here tonight and sleep on our couch. You're soaking wet, and Petros and his gang of toughs might be looking for us—uh—you. I'll lend you some of my things for tonight and we'll hang our damp clothes in the laundry area, so they can dry while we sleep."

Curious about this little family—especially the mysterious sister I agreed. Since returning to my world in this time I had stayed away from making friendships I might have to break off when my unpredictable cousins came at last to collect me.

But even living among my father's relatives I had missed the security, warmth and connection that I had known and grown up with when living among my mother's human kin. I yearned for the feeling of brothers at my back and the loving embrace of family again.

Here in Seatown, among these west coast people I knew I was an outsider, but even if it meant watching from the shadows, I resolved to keep my eyes on this little family just to make sure that no harm came to the woman and her children, because of her brother's foolishness.

After we hung up our clothes Stakaya handed me a blanket and pillow from one of the boxes stored in the laundry area and showed me to the sagging living room couch. Thanking me again he stumbled off to the indoor privy and then to his bed. Setting Aqwissa the task of guarding the house I curled up in the blanket and fell into an exhausted sleep.

In the dim light next morning I was roughly awakened when three tiny humans plopped down on the couch beside or on top of me. Sitting up with a groan I put the little girl that had been crawling onto my hip into my lap, where she snuggled contentedly. Her long dark hair was coming out of her braids and tangled from sleep. Her mischievous eyes smiled up at me as she sucked on her thumb.

A slightly older boy, all bony arms and legs, and with the cropped hair most males of whatever age, wore in this time, took his place beside me. The older girl of about nine or ten after some hesitation sat warily down on the arm of the couch on my other side. "Good morning," I said to them.

"Are you one of Uncle Ky's drunken friends?" the older girl asked, staring me in the eye. She was a pretty little girl with short black hair that hung just below her ears and at the moment her mouth was turned down in a very adult frown of disapproval.

I laughed. "I'm not a drunk, I never drink beer, but maybe your uncle might call me a friend." She gave me a searching glare not sure she believed me. "Do you smell beer or liquor on me?" I teased.

"No, but you're wearing uncle's clean shirt so that doesn't mean you're not a drunk." She said.

I chuckled and studied her with my Gift. In her spirit fire a northern jay cocked its head and stared right back. "True enough, but I assure you I never drink beer or liquor."

"Never?"

"Well," I hedged, "I did get drunk when my cousins first brought me to Seatown and I got into lots of trouble, so I promised myself I would never do that again."

"Uncle Ky got drunk once and the goldys put him in jail. Amima was real mad at him," the young boy said.

Amima? That was a Qwani'Ya word; was this family from one of the northern clans of my own people?

His sister made a disgusted sound deep in her throat. "Tuunac, you aren't supposed to tell people about that—especially someone we don't know and isn't family. And that's not why he went to Se Ho Co, either."

"Is, too Angika doggy breath."

"Is not, little mud worm," the older girl I now knew was called Angika corrected. "He went to jail for the possession of drugs that can hurt people."

"Did not."

Before their argument could go further, I said, "It's all right. I still like your uncle even if he did go to jail—for whatever reason. The goldys have put me in their jails, too. But only once in Seatown that time I got drunk drinking too much beer. I won't tell your uncle's secret," I assured her—though she didn't look convinced. Changing the subject myself, I said, "I'm called Tas, or you may call me Uncle Tas, if you like."

Turning to the little boy, I said, "You are Tuunac, right? When you spoke of your mother just now you called her amima. That's a Qwani'Ya word. I'm Qwani'Ya, and I used to call my own mother that when I was your age. She used to call me her little rock squirrel. She called me that even when I was nearly a man," I chuckled, remembering. "And I hated that, too."

"What's a rock squirrel?" he asked.

"Oh it's a little brown animal that lives in the rocks of my northern home."

Taking her thumb from her mouth, the little girl said, "We have squirrels in the park. They have big fluffy tails and are grey. Uncle buys us peanuts to feed to them, sometimes."

"Yes, I have seen them."

"Do rock squirrels have big fluffy tails, too?" the boy asked.

"No, only tiny little ones."

"Then how do you know they are really squirrels?" Tuunac said.

I laughed again. "That's a very good question, and one I can't answer. We just used to call them that in my village."

Turning back to the older girl, I asked, "Angika is your mother from one of the northern clans sent to the Tribal Preserve? I thought Stakaya told me he was from one of the west coast families."

"He is," she clarified. "Amima's father was different from his. Ami Ethalia married more than once."

"Ah that would help explain it," I thought. But there was still a mystery here that my Qwakaiva was urging me to explore.

We talked quietly for a bit longer, and more relaxed now Angika slipped off the couch arm to also sit beside me. Then Tuunac suddenly announced that it was time for "Mighty Martiin."

"Who—or what is Mighty Martiin?"

I got my answer soon enough when Angika grabbed up a tiny box off the low table in front of the couch and pressed some buttons on its face. Over in the corner a box with a glass window on part of its front suddenly came to life the window glowing with light and then tiny images appeared inside the window and began to talk.

I stared open-mouthed and after watching for a moment I asked, "What is that thing?" I pointed with my lips to the box.

Angika looked at me in puzzlement. "What thing?" I pointed again. "The picta-view?"

"Yes. That's what it's called, a picta-view? What does it do?"

"It shows us stories about our favorite characters like Mighty Martiin and Gati the super cat."

"And tells amima the Empire's news, when she has time to sit down and watch it." Tuunac said. "What do you watch, uncle, when you are at your house?

"I don't watch anything, young nephew, because I don't have a picta-view," I said.

"You should ask Uncle Ky to buy you one. He always has lots of money for treats," he added.

"Oh, does he now. But I don't think that will work for me, so when I want to watch the picta-view can I come watch yours with you?" he smiled up at me, snuggled closer, and nodded.

I will admit that I was fascinated by the glowing, talking box. To be honest, I hadn't paid much attention to all the new machines humans had invented in my absence. So as we watched I peppered the children with lots of questions and finally Angika had had enough of my interruptions. "Oh, Uncle Tas, don't you know anything?"

I chuckled and tousled her short black hair. "I guess not, so you will have to teach me. Are you a good teacher?"

She giggled and I smiled. "You see, I grew up far back in the dessert on the Preserve and I don't know much about Seatown. I've only been here a few moons. Can you be a teacher for me? I promise I will be a good student." She giggled again and agreed.

We watched the figures moving inside the box for a while in silence, before I asked another question. The meaning of the tale the children watched I found disturbing. "And who is that one?" I pointed to a pale-skinned character with muscular arms and wearing a long flowing cape.

"That's Mighty Martiin," Tuunac answered. "He came to earth from a distant star and has a magic ray gun and can kill all the bad guys."

Angika giggled her dark eyes smiling. "He is so wonderful. Oh look, here come the bandits!" Turning to me she explained. "Mighty Martiin also has super-powers. Those bad guys won't get away with stealing from the prince—you watch."

And I did...

"Mighty Martiin is my favorite character," the boy announced, his excitement growing as the figure in the little box shot bolts of lightning from his ray gun at a series of evil-looking dark-skinned bad men who attacked another pale-skinned character riding in a fancy cart.

After Martiin suddenly appeared thebandits were frightened and then before they could run away, they were killed dramatically, to the joy of his young audience.

When the story ended the boy picked up one of the tiny toy figures lying on the low table and made swooping motions like a flying bird imitating the noises he had just heard the characters in the box making as Martiin attacked his darker enemies.

"When I grow up I'm gonna have super-powers just like Mighty Martiin," he predicted. "I'm going to kill all the bad guys just like Uncle Tommo and the Elder did when they went to war."

"No you won't," his little sister said. "You're just a stupid boy."

"Am not, Bijahgwi cow-face."

"Are so, Tuunac doggy breath."

"Stop fighting you two or you'll wake mom and she'll give you a licking for waking her early on her day off," Angika warned.

Ignoring me and their older sister's cautions the two younger ones continued to trade insults back and forth.

"I got mighty super-powers just like Martiin, even now," Tuunac announced. Hopping down off the couch he circled around behind us, continuing to make his toy swoop up and down. Then making a loud whining sound he let his toy skim across both his sisters' and my heads.

"Stop that," Angika cried as she waved him off. "Stop it or I'll give you a licking myself."

He didn't listen, continuing to fly and dive on the imagined enemies he thought were hiding in the forest of his sisters' hair.

Unfortunately on another flight he somehow got the figure tangled in one of Bijahgwi's braids. Then when he tried to release it the toy became more entangled. He pulled harder and she began to cry.

Making it worse the more he tried to free the toy I pulled the little girl closer and soothed her with both my voice and the barest touch of my Qwakaiva, to quiet her screaming. "Here now, little one, let me see."

"It's stuck and amima will have to cut it out," she whined and cried louder. "I don' wan' my hair cut."

"No, no your amima won't have to cut your hair," I promised. "Hush now and hold still and let me see."

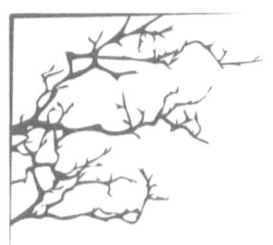

Chapter Nine

Suddenly there was a loud thump from a room down the hall, some cursing and then an angry woman with snapping dark eyes and tangled hair came charging into the living room. Her full lips pulled back into a snarl when she saw a strange man holding her crying daughter. "What are you doing to my girl? And who the fuck are you?"

At her shout everyone froze, staring wide-eyed at the thick-bodied woman wrapped in a ragged robe glaring at us from the doorway.

Answering her most important question first, I stammered, "I'm not hurting her. The toy got stuck in the little one's hair when the children were playing... I was trying to get it untangled, so you wouldn't have to cut—"

I broke off my babbling, no longer able to meet her eyes, the bear in her spirit fire continuing to snarl. Like my own grandmother, she was a formidable woman, I thought.

"Amima, don't cut my hair, please," the little one sobbed. "Tuunac was being mean again, and uncle Tas said he could—"

"Get over here and let me see," she snapped.

As she slipped off my lap I used my Qwakaiva again and managed to pull the toy free. I held it up to show them. "See it's free now and no harm done," I said as I handed the figure back to Tuunac. "And no one will have to cut it out and spoil your pretty hair."

Not at all pleased by my last comment about her daughter's prettiness the woman continued to glare. Finally Angika said into the silence, "Amima, this is Uncle Tas," she explained coming to my rescue. "He's Uncle Ky's friend. He was watching Mighty Martin with us when Tuunac and Bijah started fighting."

The woman's scowl only deepened when she heard her older daughter's explanation. Addressing her, she growled, "My girl, what have I told you about Uncle Stakaya's 'friends'?"

Her eyes suddenly wide with fear Angika jumped off the couch and backed away from me as if a bee had stung her. Confused I stared up at her mother in surprise. When I finally understood I met her glare with one of my own. Unable to prevent my own lips from curling into a snarl, I said, "I would never hurt any child in that way, honored clan mother."

"So you say, but I don't know you, do I?" she replied in an icy tone, unwilling to back down.

Just then we heard another door open and a figure stumbled out of the kitchen and down the hall to the indoor privy. The light came on and then we heard the sound of a man peeing into the bowl. The woman glanced down the hall at the open door, rolled her eyes and sighed.

In the next moment a sleepy-faced Stakaya appeared once more. "Anybody make kaf-tea yet?" He paused when he saw everyone staring at him. "What?"

His sister scowled and folded her arms across her chest. She glared at him another moment then marched into the kitchen and began opening cupboards with a bang and slamming down a pot onto the cooker. "Ky, come in here. I want to talk to you—privately."

Folding her arms across her chest in an imitation of her mother Angika glared at her uncle until he started for the kitchen. Stakaya shrugged, smiled at me and the younger children then followed his sister.

Their attention diverted to the box, the children went back to watching another picta-view program. This time the story was about a little pony named frisky, but I was no longer paying the box any attention. I rose quietly and folded the blanket I'd been using and laid it across the back of the couch.

Through the half opened kitchen door I heard Stakaya whine, "What? What did I do now, big sis?"

"What did I tell you before about bringing home with you some of your drunken friends? I don't want strangers in my house, and especially around my children. You know this, so why—"

"But he's not a drunk, sis. I've never even seen him take a drink—or smoke tishwa or use any drugs either, I swear."

She snorted and slammed another pan hard onto the cooker. "That's a laugh. I don't believe you. All you have these days for friends are drunken drug-using people. And I don't want those kind of zaunks around my family," she repeated.

"Sis, I promise you Tas isn't like that. And the guys you're talking about aren't my friends, either. They are customers, and—business associates," he clarified.

She snorted her disgust and turned away from the cooker to face him. "Whatever you want to call them, they are all dirty zaunks—a disgrace. And what happened to you last night? How badly are you hurt—this time?"

Stakaya touched the bandage he had plastered near his ear. He winced, then waved his hand in a dismissive gesture. "It's nothing. Just a small disagreement with a business associate, that's all."

She folded her muscular arms across her rounded breasts and snorted. "A business associate, hmm, Ky when are you going to smarten up? I can't understand why you keep going to the parks to spend your time around such people."

"Because they give me money," he shot back his own temper sparking. "Money we need to survive here, eh?"

"Yes we need money, but do you have to get your share on the street? And this guy, Tas, is it, what do you actually know about him?"

Pointing to his wounded head, he snapped, "I know he helped me out of a jam, so I offered him a bed for the night. It's no big deal and the kids are fine."

"That's not the point, damn it. He's probably homeless and a criminal, too. Look at him, Stakaya he's a bum, dressed in ragged clothes he probably got from one of the mission free stores—if he didn't steal them off another drunk instead."

"That's harsh sis, really harsh." Stakaya protested. He chuckled. "And, at the moment he happens to be wearing some of my things. We both were soaked to the skin by the time we got here last night."

"So he *is* homeless, eh?"

"No, I didn't say that. He has a home; it's just out in the bush somewhere."

"Out in the bush," she made a disgusted noise. "In other words he's homeless. So I repeat, what do you really know about this guy?"

"I know Elder Samul knows him—and likes him, for one thing." As her mouth fell open, he grinned and then reached for a hand full of cups out of the cupboard. From its place atop the counter the kaf-teapot was burbling happily, filling the room with its rich scent.

Setting the cups on the counter he answered her question. "To be honest, I don't know much about him. He hangs around the park a lot, sitting with the old ones, but never drinking with them."

"If he's not sharing a bottle with them then what is he doing in the park instead of working—is he a dealer then?"

"No! Not everybody who hangs in the park is a drunk or a dealer."

"Well, he's young and fit enough. Is he a soldier that has just returned from one of the Empire's peace keeping missions—with problems?"

"I don't think so, though I often see him watching and talking with the crazy vets, and they seem calmer afterwards."

"What is he doing there then?"

Stakaya shook his head and sighed. "I don't know. But what I do know is that nobody in the park or in the shelters down by the railroad tracks messes with him, not gangers, the goldys—not anybody. He comes and goes whenever and wherever he pleases, and shows up at the ceremonies on the shore sometimes. The elders like him and that's amazing for a young guy that isn't related to them."

She gave him a noncommittal grunt and reached for the quiet pot and poured herself a cup of the dark brew. "What? What else is so amazing about this ragged bum?"

"He can speak both the Qwani'Ya language and the Kukiya tongue Uncle Samul says. And not like he learned it in some government sponsored, 'reclaim your roots' language program. Old Billy says he speaks the Qwani'Ya language like the old people used to do.

"And Tas knows a lot of the old songs, too. One night last month everybody was down at the park having a good time and then some of the old ones started drumming by the fire and Tas came over and began singing with them.

"And, damn sis, I was amazed. He has such a beautiful voice; the guy can really sing. When he sings the old songs it's like you were really there in those old times. I could see and feel—"

He broke off his story as I cleared my throat in the doorway. I had found my dry clothes and changed. I was just putting on my jacket and holding my shoes in my hand. When they turned to stare at me, I cleared my throat again and said in the Qwani'Ya language, "I'm sorry if I caused disharmony in your house this morning, honored clan mother. I meant no disrespect. I will go now. Thank you for the lodging."

Gahji blinked, her mouth dropping open in surprise. She glanced at her brother and then as I turned away to leave she stopped me. "No wait. I didn't understand all of that, but don't go yet. You are a guest in my house and it is me who is forgetting my manners." She motioned to me to sit at the kitchen table and handed me another cup filled with kaf-tea. "Stay and eat with us before you go. The free kitchens will be closed by now."

Peaking around the doorway a brown face with pleading eyes whined, "Amima, I am so, so hungry. Can I have some cereal? Please, please, please? I'm sta-arving," Tuunac said.

She snorted, but reached up to pull down a box with more picta-view figures painted on it. I had learned at the mission shelter that those boxes contained the dry cereal flakes that everyone in this time liked so much.

"Why don't I make bacon and panny-cakes instead," Stakaya offered. He smiled at his little nephew and niece. "And uncle Tas can help me. Wouldn't you like that instead?"

The children all clapped their hands in excitement and jumped around shouting, "Yei panny-cakes! Uncle Ky and Uncle Tas are making panny-cakes, Yei!"

Gahji pointed to the other room and roared over the growing clamor, "Go sit down in the living room and watch the picta-view or you won't get anything!" Giggling they raced off to watch the little box again.

When it was quiet save for the people talking inside the box Gahji sighed. "I'm going to take my shower and get dressed. You two make breakfast. And try not to make a mess like last time, Ky, all right?"

Stakaya gave her a mocked salute then smirked. "We will make breakfast—and no mess. Duly noted, Mama Bear."

She growled something under her breath that sounded like a good-natured curse and stalked into her bedroom.

When he heard the water turn on and knew she couldn't hear us, he said without looking directly at me, "I'm sorry about my sister's cruel words. Her mistrust wasn't directed at you personally."

He reached for another box from the cupboard before continuing, "When she was younger she was attacked and—uh—raped by some assholes at school and, and I don't think she's ever gotten over the experience completely. She, uh, doesn't like men much. I'm always amazed she got married at all, and put up with those dog humpers as long as she did, to be honest."

Looking inward at my own experience, I said, "Abuse is a hard thing to overcome. It is a wound that can fester for years if not lanced. I didn't take her words personally, as you put it. I think she is a very brave woman."

"Yes, she is. She went back to school and never let the whispers behind her back stop her. She's getting her degree in nursing and will have a good job at the Seatown Infirmarium or on the Preserve when she's done. But it's tough being on her own with three kids to raise. That's why I stay here most of the time and help her out with the rent and food as much as I can."

"What about her children's father—or fathers; do they help her at all?" I asked.

Stakaya shook his head. "They're long gone, either in jail or dead." He shrugged and went back to stirring the mixture in the bowl.

"As I said, she is a very strong and brave woman." Then I put down my kaf-tea and asked, "What can I do to help?"

He motioned to the big white box humming to itself along the wall. The bacon is inside the ice box. Bring out the pack and set the slices on a tray to go in the oven."

Some of what he was saying was new to me, but I went to the big white box and opened it. I rooted around a while and finally found the bacon on the bottom shelf. While I was placing the neatly cut strips on the tray he handed me I asked without looking at him, "Your sister Gahji, you can see her Bear, eh?"

Pouring some of the mixture onto the heated iron griddle atop the cooker he turned to look at me with a puzzled expression. "What bear?"

Still without looking directly at him I said, "The one who lives within her Spirit Fire that is her protector and teacher. You can see her, eh? That's why you called your sister, 'mama bear.'"

Stakaya laughed. "Oh, Gahji is going to explode if she hears you talking like that. She thinks that a lot of our old ways are superstitions that are holding us back."

"That's what I was taught at the live-away school I attended, too, but I never believed those priests."

"I'm not sure she believes that garbage, either—not really—but she does believe that the prejudice the pinkers hold against our people who keep our traditions alive is real, and she wants a better life for her kids than the one we had on the Preserve."

"Pinkers?"

Stakaya gave me a puzzled look. I repeated my question. He shook his head and laughed. "You really are a bushy boy like old Tommo says. I am speaking of the paler citizens of 'our glorious Empire.'"

"Oh, thank you for telling me. I've heard the word before since coming to Seatown but I wasn't sure of its meaning."

Stakaya shook his head again and returned to his earlier topic. "So my sister pretends to be a 'modern woman' and goes to school to make everybody—including her Djoven-praising and dog-humping in-laws happy."

"In-laws? I thought you told me the fathers of her children were long gone."

"They are, and they aren't," Stakaya said as he placed more cakes on the growing stack to cool. "Angika's father died in a mecho-cart crash returning to Seatown from the Zerve. The cousin he was stupid enough to hitch a ride with was drunk and missed a turn in the twisty mountain roads.

"No, it's Tuunac and Bijahgwi's father's family that is the problem for her sometimes. Win is in prison—and will be for a long while, but his parents want Tuunac—bad. He's the first born son and that means a lot to those people. They are newcomers to the coast—sort of.

"They immigrated from across the western ocean to work on the railroad a couple generations back, found gold and got rich. Their customs are different from ours and they don't respect women much.

"Gahji wants a better life for all her kids so she thought win was a good catch and married him, but he turned out to be an asshole with a gambling problem that landed him in prison.

"When Win was arrested and sentenced Gahji refused to give his parents her children. So now they have the social workers and the supervising staff at her nursing school always checking on her and the kids. That's another reason why she gets so angry when I bring people home with me."

"Thank you for telling me all this; it helps me to understand her better. I'm not sure I agree with her reasoning about abandoning our traditions, but I can understand her wish to make a good life for her children." I smiled. "And I will be careful about mentioning bears."

He laughed. "Good idea. And to answer your first question, no, I can't see any bear in her aura. I was just teasing her. I've called her that ever since we were kids, it's just a joke."

"I didn't know about your pet name for her, but when I look at her I do see her Bear."

He thought about it for a moment while he flipped more of the cakes. "Though I can't see the bear you are talking about, to me she has always been the bear in our family—in so many ways, her fierce warrior spirit, her willingness to fight anyone to protect her cubs, so many things." He nodded to himself and placed the done panny-cakes on plates for the children.

"Yes, a mama bear," I agreed. "When she first came into the living room and saw me, a stranger, with her cubs, and one on my lap crying, her Bear snarled at me, before the human woman questioned me with her words. She was ready to fight me if my answers weren't to her liking."

Stakaya laughed. "You got that right, zaunk-brotha, she probably would have." Sobering he added, "But that's my fault. In the past I have brought friends home that did cause trouble around here. Mostly small shit like stealing money out of her purse or leaving a mess she had to clean up later when she came home tired from work.

"And she's always worried that some guy is gonna mess with Angika. She's such a pretty little girl, if anybody did that I would kill'em—if Gahji didn't get to him first."

I shuddered as a wisp of a foretelling brushed tendrils of ice across my spine and Petros's scarred face appeared in my mind.

<<Avert, avert!>> I resolved to create a protection charm for Angika—her sister, and Tuunac, too.

Then the smell of something burning brought Angika herself running into the kitchen. When she saw the smoking griddle she stomped her foot and folded her arms across her chest. "Oh, Uncle, you are doing it again."

"Doing what, my girl?" Stakaya joked as he dumped that batch of panny-cakes into the garbage.

"You know, she accused. "You are burning breakfast again."

"Well, come help me, my girl, you know your uncks is a terrible cook."

Angika let out a long sigh. "I guess I will, then."

"Is breakfast ready yet? I'm sta-arving," one of the two sorrowful faced children said as they crept into the kitchen.

Taking the tray of bacon out of the oven I set it on the top of the cooker and then got the little ones settled at the table. Angika got everyone forks and I served up the panny-cakes and bacon to them.

Hair still wet from her bath Gahji came in and took her place at the head of the table. She was surprised when I sat a full plate down in front of her and then handed her a fresh cup of kaf-tea. Confused by me serving her, she looked up at me with narrowed eyes.

Her eyes met mine and I felt her untrained power searching for the hidden motive in my kindness. I let her look. She was too inexperienced to see much, but I had no bad intent to shield from her.

Looking down at her plate she said, "Thank you. You must have had lots of practice caring for children and women growing up."

I laughed and took a place at the table. Still cooking the last of the cakes Stakaya drank some of his kaf-tea and watched us thoughtfully from his place by the cooker.

"When I was growing up I had lots of practice taking care of my little cousins and helping the women and the elders. I wasn't allowed to get out of work just because I was a boy."

She snorted a laugh and gave her brother a triumphant grin. "Too bad these west coast people haven't learned that yet."

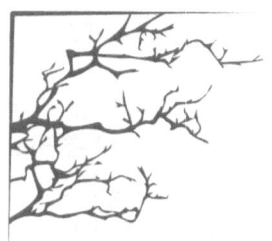

Chapter Ten

For the rest of that winter and spring I visited Gahji and her little family as often as I could without making a nuisance of myself. I justified my attentions by saying to myself and her female relatives who teased us that I was only waiting for Tommo to get out of jail—and to make sure Petros and his men didn't try to get back at Stakaya by hurting one of them.

All that was true, but I would be lying if I said that was the only reason. From the first I had admired Gahji, and as I spent more time with the family I became very fond of her indeed. Maybe we might have explored our attraction to each other faster, but because of our experiences with sexual molestation, we held back from sleeping together.

She was cautious after two failed marriages, and I could understand that and didn't press my interest. Just being a part of her family – even in a limited way – helped ground me into this place and time, and for that alone, I was very grateful.

During that period in spite of the easy-going face I presented to the family, I also managed to keep a vigilant eye on that lovable but annoying young wolf cub Stakaya and his dealings, as well as searching for Utreal and my tricky otherworldly cousins, who were all still avoiding me.

Goldys, drug dealers and irate rich grandparents I felt capable of handling. They were all just threats made by humans, though any one of them might be guided by an otherworldly hand, but a vengeful Utreal, or Crokno emissary was a whole other matter, and that possibility sent chills down my spine as my affection for the family grew.

As the days progressed into moons and Gahji saw how helpful I could be around the house and that I actually enjoyed spending time with her and her children, she softened her attitude, and I think, grew to trust me—a bit.

Which is why, perhaps, when school stopped for the summer vacation I convinced her to let me take over caring for the children much of the time, so she could study and work without worrying. Stakaya had proven to be unreliable in the past and her younger cousins wanted money, and so would a day camp program if she wanted to use that service.

With only a part-time job at the infirmarium to support her family through the summer while she completed her own classes, I knew Gahji was struggling financially and neither Stakaya nor I had jobs to help pay expenses. Hunting and gathering traditional foods as well as babysitting were ways I could contribute. It would also allow me to try and teach the young ones some of the skills I'd grown up with. Skills they might need if they ever chose to live once more upon the land.

It was my secret wish that someday I could convince Gahji—and maybe Stakaya, too, to move away from this noisy, smelly city to a more natural place either back on the Preserve or somewhere further up the west coast where the giant trees still guarded the land.

Then to my surprise help came from an unexpected source to further my plan to teach the children the basic skills I felt all young people should know. One of Stakaya's many paternal cousins gave me a small battered canoe he wasn't using any longer. It needed work to make it seaworthy, but after coaxing Stakaya away from his druggy friends to help with the project we managed—with the children's help, of course, to get it fixed up pretty good over the next moon of summer.

On the long summer days when it never rained on the coast, I often took the young ones over to the quiet beaches on tribal land where, away from prying eyes we picked berries, swam and fished together, coming back to the city sun-browned and happy to welcome Gahji home after a tiring day at the infirmarium or school.

I discovered early on that little Bijah had a Gift. She could see my Seal and I could often speak to her mind to mind. Feeling daring I sometimes changed into my seal form to swim with them—which delighted all of them. "This is our little secret," I warned them, and they solemnly agreed to keep it—even from Uncle Ky and Amima.

I knew they were young and might not be able to keep such an important promise, but so few people in this modern time believed in such things as shape-shifting seal men and otherworldly beings I thought that most would dismiss their ramblings as the imaginings of the young and pay them little attention if they happened to let it slip out.

Anchoring the canoe out from shore I would slip into the water and shift into my seal-skin. I would catch a few fish and bring them back to the canoe where giggling with delight Tuunac or Bijahgwi would take them from my mouth and then Angika would put them inside the wooden box used for keeping them cool until we got back on shore to clean them.

It was after one of those lazy, delightful days that things changed for me—for all of us. Elder Samul had gone to bring Gahji home from the infirmarium at Ky's urging. The Elder now owned an older model mecho-cart and Stakaya was always pestering his older relative to let him drive it, and going to collect his sister was a good excuse. Elder Samul knew his reasoning, but didn't trust the cub to borrow the cart without him going along for the ride, so Ky had to be content with that until he could afford a vehicle of his own.

When they arrived the house was filled with the smells of frying fish and baking scau-bread. "Mm, smells good in here," Stakaya called.

"Yay, uncle and Amima are home," came the answering call from the kitchen. "Come in; come see."

What they saw coming into the kitchen was a busy scene of me and the smiling children preparing a meal. Angika was standing on a stool flipping the frying fish while Tuunac and I were cutting and dipping the boned fish fillets into flour, making them ready for frying. Little Bijah was farther down the kitchen table sorting through the day's picked berries for our dessert.

I turned and smiled at them and motioned to the empty chairs at the table. "Please sit. The food will be ready very soon."

Gahji's eyes narrowed when she saw her young son using one of her sharp filleting knives. She might have said something to me about allowing young children to use such a tool, but the elder put a hand on her arm, shook his head and guided her to a seat at the table.

The fillets nearly done I took over at the cooker for the last batch and Angika hopped down to set the table. Inwardly I smiled. The Elder and I both knew the boy needed to learn to use a man's tools, in spite of his mother's protective nature. I had been younger than Tuunac when I started helping Uncle Tli and Ko clean our catch for the drying racks.

"We made red suma'ki tea. It's in the ice box chilling. Would anybody like some?" I said as I turned to the ice box.

"I'll have some, Tas. It's too hot for kaf-tea." Gahji said.

I poured her and the children glasses of the lemony-tasting red berry tea. She looked tired. I ventured a kiss on her forehead as I passed to set the pitcher on the table, which made her brother smile.

"I can make some kaf-tea if you prefer, Elder," I offered as I sat the platter of fish in the center of the table.

Samul chuckled as he reached to place a golden fillet on his plate before passing it to Gahji. "You keep calling me elder, and though I appreciate the respect implied, shouldn't it be me calling you that?"

I froze, nearly dropping the warm scau-bread I was just taking out of the oven. Suddenly all was quiet in the kitchen. The children paused eating and Gahji and her brother stared open-mouthed at each other and then in puzzlement at the older man. Expressionless he sipped at his suma'ki tea, waiting on my answer.

Placing the tray on the table I returned to the ice box to hunt for butter, trying to figure out how to answer. Should I deny it, laugh it off or tell them the truth?

<<Tell them if you want, my Siyatli,>> Aqwissa said into my mind. <<Them knowing will make no difference to your future, or that of the world you have sworn to protect.>>

With my back to them I was still trying to decide, taking over long to find the butter, when Stakaya, always impatient asked, "What are you talking about, great uncle? Why should Tas call you Elder? He's a bit older than me but he's still a young guy—like me."

"Are you sure 'bout that, nephew?"

Flustered Ky glanced at the elder and then at me. "Y-yeah, I guess so," he said, but we all heard the uncertainty in his voice.

Gahji put down her fork and glared at me and then her brother, her Bear snarling her suspicion. At last focusing on the elder, she took a deep breath and said, "Great Uncle, what are you trying to tell us about Tas?"

Ignoring her for the moment, the Elder turned to Bijahgwi, and asked, "What do you see, my girl, when you look at Uncle Tas with your Gift?"

Before the little girl could answer Gahji protested, "Oh, Uncle Samul don't encourage her. She will only get into trouble at school when she forgets and tells some teacher about her visions, and then I'll have a snooty social worker knocking at my door again. Those days are gone and we all have to live in this place and time. It's best she forgets about her Gift."

Ignoring Gahji's protests for the moment he repeated his question to the little girl. After glancing fearfully at her mother and then getting more encouragement from the elder, she giggled and said, "Uncle Tas is a seal man."

Samul smiled. "Is he now, and how do you know this; do you see a seal in his Spirit Fire like I do?" She nodded.

Gahji rolled her eyes and sighed. "A seal."

"He really is a seal, Amima," Tuunac chimed in. "When we go to the quiet beaches by the big ceremonial house to fish, uncle jumps in the water and becomes his Seal and then he catches the fish for us to bring home to cook for you."

"And sometimes when we are swimming he lets one of us hold on to his neck and gives us rides—and we swim real fast," Bijah added.

As the older and more responsible child at the table the adults turned to Angika to explain. After a little hesitation she dropped her eyes and then reluctantly nodded. I couldn't prevent a smile from curving my lips at that revelation. The Elder had only guessed at half of my story, and now he was surprised, too. He hadn't expected my Seal to be real in this world, and not just the spirit helper most humans were either born with or acquired during their life time.

Unable to hold back my amusement any longer I found the elusive butter and sat down at the table. "You could call me elder, though I doubt if I am wise enough yet to deserve the title." I chuckled, "And, people might think you were getting a bit senile if you did."

He laughed, too. "Well there is that to consider, old one. So how about I call you brother—or younger brother instead."

I nodded. "I would be honored. That is what Iyantsha always called me when my family and I lived in his camp and I assisted him."

Ignoring the shocked look on Stakaya's face and Gahji's scowl, he nodded as if I had just confirmed his earlier assumption. "I thought you might have known the great Prophet personally."

"I did—for a short time, before my life's path took me elsewhere. But I'm curious, what gave me away?"

"That first day when I met you, you said you had attended Saint Yon's Live-away school." Noticing my puzzled expression he continued. "Saint Yon's burnt down about ninety some-odd years ago."

"I would have thought they would have rebuilt it after the fire."

Samul shook his head. "The way I heard it from older relatives it was never rebuilt. With the director and a grand intercessor dead along with several staff and students, the Temple felt the site was cursed before the witch who started the fire died in the blaze as well."

He gave me a long searching look. "Is that how it was, brother?"

A witch, eh? So the Temple claimed that either I, or my father started the fire instead of the director and the intercessor who killed him. I made a sour face, but decided to answer. "Like other things I've read at the library concerning our peoples the chamuqwani twist the truth to their advantage."

He nodded. I knew he had many more questions he would like to ask me, but after glancing at the wide-eyed faces listening he chose not to pursue the topic further.

Choking down the last of his fish, Stakaya made a disgusted noise in his throat and then blurted, "What are you crazy people talking about? I don't understand any of this."

Samul chuckled then took a last sip of his tea and rose from the table. "Maybe if you let me put you in the ceremonial house for the winter you might understand better, eh, nephew?"

Stakaya let out a big sigh. "Yeah, maybe, but like I told you before, I'm not ready."

The Elder chuckled. "Well, don't wait too long to decide or somebody might sponsor a drubbing for you and then you will have no choice in the matter."

"Yeah, all right, all right, I told you I will make the commitment. I just need more time." He glanced at his sister, his eyes pleading for her help. Gahji refused to comment, but he prattled on anyway, as if she had agreed with him. "Right now my sister needs me to help her pay the rent and—"

Samul chuckled and shook his head. "Nice try, nephew, but I don't think Gahji needs you as much as you would like to believe." He glanced at Gahji and then met my eye. I returned his gaze and gave him a slight nod, answering his unspoken question.

When he next spoke, however, it was still to the cub. "You are forgetting about 'uncle Tas there?" he pointed with his lips at me. "I think he is more than willing to take upon himself many of the family responsibilities you have been shouldering—if your sister will let him, eh?"

Gahji scowled then grumped, "Uncle. Stop. Don't talk about me as if I wasn't sitting right here. Leave Stakaya alone—and my love-life is not your concern—as I've told you before."

"Oh, I'm sorry, my girl am I butting into your business again. As your elder I'm just expressing my concern for my favorite niece and nephew's welfare. Will you forgive me? Us old people have memory problems sometimes, you know."

She laughed her annoyance forgotten. "Oh go home, Uncle, before Aunty Megara is calling me on the far-speak wondering where you are."

As he put on his jacket to go he thought of something else and turned back to me. "Tommo will be getting out of jail again soon. I know you are anxious to see him for your own reasons, but I would also like to consult with you about doing another ceremony to try and help him. Me and a couple more of the old vets would like to talk to you about that."

"I'm not sure how helpful I might be, I'm not a trained healer like Iyantsha was, I mostly lent him my Qwakaiva for his own healings on occasion. But I will be happy to talk with you about it whenever you wish."

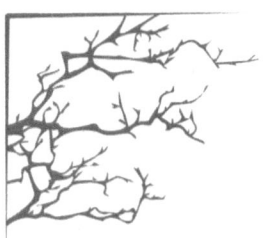

Chapter Eleven

When Stakaya had wandered off to the park, pursuing his own concerns, we cleaned up the kitchen and put the children to bed. Then we sat companionably together on the sagging couch, listening to the music coming from another machine she owned. More scau-bread and tea sat on the low table in front of us in case we needed refreshment. Content, I tucked her next to my side and put an arm around her. Resting her head on my shoulder she sighed and snuggled a little closer.

The house was quiet and it was growing late. I should leave, but I was reluctant to move. Her warm female body, smelling of sage and pine after her shower, was making it hard for me to hold back my natural desire to finish what we so often came close to and then shied away from. I desperately wanted to make love to her.

But when I slipped my hand under her plaid shirt to caress her honey-gold and oh so tempting breast, I felt her stiffen under my hand. Pulling back I looked her in the eye. "What's wrong, my heart, am I hurting you? I admit I am inexperienced, but I am willing to learn. Will you teach me what you like?"

Removing my hand she sat up, but didn't pull away. Still studying my face, she finally said, "Tas, I know the children love you, and I totally appreciate all the help you have been giving me. You are a very nice person, and I don't want to hurt you, but I can't have sex with you—or anybody—not anymore."

"Why?"

Dropping her eyes before answering she played with a loose button on her shirt while she decided what to tell me. "Because I haven't had much luck in choosing partners in the past and I've learned not to trust myself where men are concerned. Everything seems wonderful at first—and then it all goes to shit."

"It could be wonderful with me, I promise. I would never hurt you or 'let it go to shit', as you put it. I'm not just looking for a sexual partner; I think I love you and want to be your partner for all our lives."

She shook her head, but turned away when I tried to kiss her. "That's very sweet, and tempting, but I'm better off just raising my kids on my own."

To prevent me from kissing her again, she patted my hand and moved further away on the couch. Hoping to soften the blow of her next words she smiled, but there was only fear and regret in her eyes. "I'm not such a great catch, you know. I can be mean and grumpy—ask my mud worm of a brother, if you don't believe me. I'm telling you this now, because you might regret your rash choice once you get to know me better."

I laughed. "I seriously doubt that." When she scowled I moved over and kissed her anyway, then said, "Gahji, my dear one, in keeping with our Qwani'Ya tradition whether we live together as husband and wife or not, is *your* choice, and I will respect your decision and not pester you to change it. But I have also grown quite fond of the children and I would hate not to see them any longer. Please don't send me away entirely whatever you decide about us."

"All right I will promise that. They do need a good man in their lives—and I think you are a good man."

"Thank you; I want to be. And, I will promise you this. I will care for and protect your children as best I can. No matter what you decide about our relationship after tonight,"

And then I reached forward and kissed her again—deeply. "Gahji, I don't care if you are a grumpy old mama bear at times, because you are also courageous and beautiful, and-and I need you."

She snorted. "Need me? Why would a handsome guy like you need a woman burdened with three kids not his own to raise. You are a fool to want that when you could have any number of cute young things. Why would you want me?"

"Because you give me purpose and you and your family help me to put down roots and ground myself so I can feel a part of this oh so confusing world I find myself in. I've grown to love your children and I don't care if I made them. According to our old traditions babies always belong to their mothers anyway. And as a traditional man I accept that. I promise you I will always love and cherish them as if we had made them together."

Pulling away at last, and with tears coming into her eyes she protested, "How could you promise so much? You know so little about me."

I laughed softly and pulled her onto my lap, so I could hug her and kiss away her tears. "Then if it's important to you then tell me. I will listen. Stakaya told me a bit about the children's fathers—and the rich grandparents who torment you from time to time. But he hasn't said anything about your own family or where you grew up. Why don't you start by telling me who was your grandmother and your mother?"

"My Ami." She smiled, recalling a beloved Elder. "My Ami Thonna was a famous show woman who traveled all over the empire preforming tricks on horseback and with her rifle.

"A man named Barklyo came to the Preserve after the Zacatik wars ended looking for people who could do trick riding and shooting for his entertainments. After seeing her ride and shoot he hired her and that dog humping bastard she married. They called Ami a Zacatik princess and she traveled all over the Empire, and was payed lots of money—which Ati spent, leaving her broke."

Her mouth hardened into a hard line as she continued, Ati Matoqwa never beat on her, probably because she carried a gun and knew how to use it, nonetheless he was a mean bastard, always getting drunk and fighting. Amima and I hated him and I was glad when Ami left him...."

My heart gave a lurch at the mention of my war brother's name. Could this woman be a descendant of my old friend? My thoughts tumbling like a whirlwind, I finally broke in on her ramblings to ask, "Did your Ami Thonna have another name?"

Gahji paused and stared. "Y-yes."

"Was it Xyilaha?"

Narrowing her eyes at me in suspicion she said, "That's the name friends and family used, but her name on the agency books was Thonna Fishspear and that was the name the pinkers wanted to use for the performances. So even though she hated that name and what it represented to her, she was forced to use it. How did you know? Have you let me babble on when you already know the history of my family?"

Before she could work herself up into a temper I held up a hand to stop her. "I didn't know about her preforming for the chamuqwani, nor that she had married your grandfather Matoqwa, but I did know your grandparents when they were younger and we were all still living on the Preserve."

She narrowed her eyes scowling. The Bear in her Spirit Fire curling her lip as she studied me as well. "All that stuff you and the Elder were talking about over dinner tonight you really want me to believe you are some ancient creature come to this city to—do what?"

Serious now and my sexual interest forgotten for the moment, I said, "I do want you to believe me, because it is all true, as hard as that may be for you to accept.

"But actually I'm not sure why I am here at this time and place—not yet, anyway. Until coming here with some paternal cousins, who then abandoned me I had been living with my father's relatives since he rescued me from the fire at Saint Yon's.

"I bargained for my tricky cousins to bring me home—to the world of my birth. They did bring me back, but not to the Preserve in the time when your grandparents and everyone I knew were still alive."

"All that is hard to believe, Tas. It's so, so unreal. I don't know what to think. Did you really know the Prophet, and my grandparents?"

I kissed away her frown. "I did. My mother and I lived with Xyilaha's family for a time, but I probably knew Matoqwa better, because we grew up together in the far north before the soldiers marched us south to the Preserve. He must have been a tormented man; he lost so much during those troubled times."

I chuckled. "My poor body carried many a bruise from him growing up, but he was also loyal, brave and in the end he saved my life—more than once, so don't judge him too harshly. Let go your anger and be grateful for the strength, power and determination you have also inherited from him."

She snorted her disgust. "That won't be easy for me; I've hated him all my life."

"And yet even if you hated him, you have inherited his bear. I can see her glaring at me from your spirit fire every time I look at you, my dear one."

"Oh, please don't start about that again."

"All right, if you insist."

She gave me a long-suffering groan then fell silent considering my words. At last she said, "All right, it won't be easy to let go, but I will think about what you've said."

"That's all I ask. My entire story I will save for another time, a time when I have earned more of your trust, and you know me well enough to understand the truth in my words."

Then changing the subject, I said, "Tell me about your mother and your father, before it grows too late."

She sighed and then decided to humor me. "My mother was Ethalia Tall Tree. She was Qwani'Ya as you know, but after graduating from Saint Royston's Live-away school she married a man from the Preserve named Benji Tall Tree. We lived on the Preserve, but there was no work and it was hard living on doled out commodities. When he got a job here we moved.

"After he died Amima married again—the cub's father—a man from one of the west coast tribes. So we stayed here in Seatown and I finished my schooling here. Amima Ethalia died of cancer not long after I married Angika's father. Since then Aunty Megara, Elder Samul's wife, has been like a mother to me."

Her expression souring again she reluctantly continued, "After I had Angika, and lost my first husband. I went back to school to become a nurse—didn't finish—had some problems. Got married instead—had two more children. That marriage didn't work out, either. Went back to school and then had more unpleasant relationships with men for my trouble."

"Not all those relationships with men were bad," I teased. "You have three beautiful children to show for it."

"That's true I guess, the past has left its scars nonetheless."

"Well, who cares much about the past, we all make bad decisions; that's how we learn, I guess. The now and the future is what is important."

Suddenly thinking she understood what I might be referring to she pushed me away and glared. "Did my brother or the Elder tell you about what happened at the school? Did he tell you that everybody blames me for the failed relationships and even my rape—did he?" Her voice quivering with pent up anger and frustration, she leapt from the couch and began to pace around the living room.

Horrified I watched her open-mouthed. "Gahji, what's wrong? I don't understand. What did I say?"

'You don't understand, eh? Well, damn you, too! How can I let go the 'past' if everybody keeps reminding me of it, eh?"

"...Whatever happened at the school isn't important—not to me. I still love you—"

"Well it matters to me. Ky told you, didn't he? Damn the little shit, damn him!" turning her back on me she began pacing again, tears of frustration and rage streaming down her cheeks. Glancing over at me she said, "This is just another reason why I don't trust men—any men—even the ones in my own damned family." Then when I remained silent just watching her, she snapped, "I think you better leave."

Leave? Right now—or forever? My heart in turmoil I watched her stomp back and forth for a while longer, uncertain what to do. Did she really want me to go as she said?

<<No she does not,>> Qwissa murmured. <<Go to her, comfort her, Siyatli bungler.>>

Taking the advice of my qwissa dragon—also a female—I rose when her back was to me and enfolded her in my arms. Snarling, she whirled round faster than I expected and punched me. "I said I wanted you to leave."

Jerking my head back when she tried to punch me again, I tightened my embrace instead. She resisted, but couldn't free herself and finally stopped. Breathing heavily she growled, her Bear showing its fangs, "Leave, it's a simple five letter word. What part of it don't you understand? I don't want to be around a man—any man right now!"

"Good, then we don't have a problem, because I'm not a man—well not completely anyway."

Staring as if I had just grown moose antlers, she said, "What are you talking about—of course you are a man."

Trying to hide my grin I shook my head. "No I'm not."

Pushing me back and folding her arms across her chest she growled, "All right, smart ass, what are you then—a seal like my children say?"

I nodded. "Yes, like the children said, I'm a seal man, a siyatli, half man, half Qwa'Nayhi Seal."

As I'd been speaking I'd been guiding her back to the couch. Still holding on to her I settled us back onto its cushions. "Do you know what the word Siyatli means in our language?" When her only answer was to frown, I hastily babbled on. "A Siyatli is a half breed—of a sort. You see my mother, a good Qwani'Ya woman happened to take a fancy to one of the Qwa'Nayhi Seal men living at the bottom of Big Ice Lake. And then, after a suitable amount of time there came me." I smiled and thumped my chest. "A Siyatli—neither man, nor seal—but always stuck in the middle."

She snorted a laugh, but took the cup of tea I offered her and drank. "You are such a stupid ass. I'm not sure I believe you and the children's claim to be only half human, but you make me laugh."

My smile widened and I challenged her. "Come swimming with me and the children tomorrow and I will prove it."

Thinking I was making a joke she glared, then answering my unspoken challenge she nodded. "Maybe I will."

I hugged her and kissed her again. When we paused, I said, "To be honest the cub did mention the rape—without going into any details. He saw that I liked you from the first and was trying to warn me that you might not be receptive to my interest. I told him, as I did you, that it doesn't matter to me—and I mean it."

"Most men would run far and fast if they knew. Why are you so different?"

Taking a deep breath before opening the door on my own painful memories, I said, "Why? Because I have scars, too—lots of them, on my body and in my heart. While I was a prisoner at the live-away school I was accused of witchcraft and one of the grand intercessors from Djoven's temple tortured me. Part of the pain and torment he inflicted was sexual in nature."

My vision looking inward I shuddered, my voice barely above a whisper as I said, "I would have died the night of the fire if my Seal father hadn't come to rescue me. I need you, my lovely bear woman, can't you see that? I could never hurt any woman or child after what those priests did to me..." Lost in my memories I stopped, letting silence come between us.

With a nip from Aqwissa I let go the past and gave Gahji a tentative smile. Yawning I rose. "There is much more to that story, which I can share with you, if you would like some other time. But it grows late and I should leave like you want."

As I reached to grab my jacket and shoes she stopped me. "Don't go. It is late and the goldys will be prowling the streets looking for people to beat up and throw in jail. You can stay here tonight."

I glanced at the couch, but she shook her head and took my hand, heading towards her bedroom. "It's my day off tomorrow. I was going to study while you babysat, but I think I'd like to go on a picnic instead. You invited me to go swimming with you and the children, remember?"

Banishing my ghosts, I grinned. "I do remember."

Reaching her bedroom door she put her arms around my neck and kissed me. "You are a very complicated man, Tassele Cougarson, and I'm going to trust that I'm not making another mistake, but I think I might enjoy discovering more about you." Then pulling me inside she closed the bedroom door.

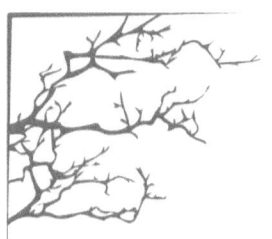

Chapter Twelve

The cub's mouth dropped open when he saw me coming out of Gahji's bed room the next morning. He grinned and started to say something, but I gave him a stern look and he closed his mouth before uttering a sound.

"Is the kaf-tea ready yet?" Still staring he finally nodded. "Good." I brushed past him and pulled down two cups from the cupboard and filled them with the rich dark liquid. Then passing him again I headed back to his sister's bed room.

As I reached the door he called after me, "Hey, you two—uh—want some breakfast—in bed?"

"We'll come out to eat—when it's done."

"What do you want me to fix?"

"Anything but mush." I didn't hear more because I closed the door.

Much to the children's delight we went on a picnic that day up the coast and I was happy to see my lovely bear woman's mouth soften and the tension around her eyes disappear as she lazed around enjoying herself, school and work forgotten for the moment.

I showed her my Seal as I'd promised. At first I think she was a bit frightened, because as of yet we couldn't speak mind-to-mind, but noticing how accepting the children were of my Seal she soon relaxed and even played water games with me when I was still in my Seal form. And as summer continued she joined us more and more whenever her work and school schedule permitted.

One day nearing the end of summer, we hurried to our beach, knowing our lazy time together would end soon. It was a cooler day than we'd grown used to, though it was still warm enough to swim by our sheltered beach, but we could still taste autumn in the air. A fire dozed within its rocky nest if anyone grew chilled, the grub box nearby filled with our morning's catch, when we got hungry. Knowing this might be our last day to enjoy here with school about to start, no one was ready to get out of the water and end our fun.

Engrossed in some noisy water play none of us heard Samul's mecho-canoe and the other small park patrol vessel approaching until it was too late. Gahji saw the canoe first, recognized her great uncle and waved. I was in my seal form under the water at the time, diving deep and swimming fast hoping to come up under her and, giving her woman's mound a good nuzzle as I passed between her legs.

My plan was to let her fall back onto my shoulders, so I could give her one last ride before we got out and built up the fire to cook our catch. I had already committed myself to the dive, ignoring any possible danger when I heard her talking to someone. Thinking that we were safe on tribal land I'd grown careless, and failed to catch the warning that was now in her voice.

When I bumped her she let out a startled cry and toppled backwards on top of me and then fell off spluttering as she got back to her feet in the shallow water. No children's delighted laughter greeted my antics as she stood. "Tas, you mud worm, stop! We have company."

Detecting the urgency in her voice I hastily dove deeper, and in the concealment of the blue-green water I shifted back into my human form before surfacing. Shaking the water out of my eyes I stood and waded over to her, putting a comforting arm around her shoulder. Though only a grim anger could be seen on her face I could feel her trembling. I gave her a slight hug to reassure her, and murmured, "What's wrong, love?"

Without looking at me she pointed with her lips to Samul's canoe and then to the two chamuqwani men in green uniforms sitting in the park vessel not far away. "Park patrollers? What do they want?" she shook her head slightly, but remained silent.

Before I could ask that question to the strangers, Elder Samul and another man I'd seen before but didn't know his name guided their canoe closer and asked, "Is there a problem, patrollers?"

The older of the two, a red-faced man with a wide-brimmed brown hat and a bushy gray mustache glanced from the grim-faced men in the canoe to me, holding Gahji protectively at my side and then to the wide eyed and frightened children on the shore.

He cleared his throat, and then said, "We got word from a couple tourists driving by that there were people up the beach that were feeding and bothering a seal. You folks know that it's against the law to mess with or come near any of the wild animals living along the coast and in the park."

Gahji glared at me, but I saw the fear in her eyes as well. I knew without using my Gift that she was thinking that a report from the patrollers could be used against her by Tuunac's grandparents should they hear of it. Her Bear lifted her lip to show her fangs, agreeing with her that I was an idiot. "I'm sorry; I will be more careful in future," I murmured.

<<Want me to kill and eat them,>> Aqwissa said.

<<No! They would be missed and that would cause more trouble. Just help me be more careful in future. I have no wish to make more trouble for Gahji.>>

The men were watching us intensely. They must have seen my mouth move but were too far away to hear us. Glancing about the beach with eyes wide, I said, "I'm new to Seatown so thank you for telling me about the law, but I don't see any seals around here. I think those tourists were mistaken."

The younger of the two scowled and said to his partner loud enough for me to hear, "Sergeant, he's lying. My eye sight is better than most. I'm sure I heard and saw a seal when we were coming here." The sergeant grunted, only studying us thoughtfully.

<<I think I should eat them; I'm getting hungry.>>

<<No.>> Quickly conjuring a piece of dark gray cloth out of nearby seaweed under the water I held it up for the men to see. "I often wear this gray hood when I'm diving to keep my hair out of my eyes. Maybe this is what the tourists and your companion saw."

Still scowling the younger man glanced at his partner. Before he could speak, the man in the canoe whose name I didn't know said, "Patrollers, as our brother says, there are no seals near this beach. You are no longer in the park. You are on Smotahlik land. If there is a problem then it is a Smotahlik problem—and 'we' will handle it."

"I am aware that we are in Smotahlik territory, Chief Rickson, but the Emperor's law is the law no matter where we are." The sergeant gave me another suspicious glance. "If these people have been feeding, or bothering seals then the law says—"

"I am aware of the law, patroller, but I see no seals here, so you have nothing to write up a report about—except for some tourists who need new glasses, eh?"

After a long hesitation the sergeant nodded and pulled the cord to start up their vessel. "But, Sergeant," the younger man protested.

Cutting him off with an imperious gesture, the sergeant steered his craft back into the channel.

When they were out of sight I breathed a sigh of relief and apologized again for being so careless. "He probably did see me."

"He probably did see—something, mud worm," Gahji agreed and jabbed me hard in the ribs. "But they weren't going to argue the point. Not with the chief and the Elder right there. Chief Rickson has some powerful friends in the current government who make all the trouble they can for the park patrol, and the goldys, for that matter."

We followed him and the chief as they paddled the canoe closer into shore. "Come eat with us," Gahji offered as she stepped out of the water. "Tas went fishing earlier and I'll make some scau-bread to go with the fish. I'm assuming, Uncle, you wanted to talk to Tas, which is why you and the chief followed us out here."

"I did come to speak with your man, my girl, and a meal would be nice," Samul said.

As I helped the men beach the canoe I shouted to the children in our Qwani'Ya language to build up the fire and fetch more wood and water from the creek, because we had guests for the meal. They answered me in the same language and hurried off.

Samul saw and nodded his approval. "You are teaching them both your language and your bush skills, I see. That's good."

"The children are in part Qwani'Ya it is proper they know how to speak to their ancestors and living relatives. As for the bush skills I am teaching them, how to live on the land is always good to know. Even if when they are grown they choose to take a job in the city—any city, those teachings can be useful."

Chief Rickson agreed. "We never know what the future may throw at us, so it is good to be prepared for anything."

Canoe secured, I held out my hand to the newcomer. "I've seen you a few times when I've visited the ceremonial house, but until just now I didn't know your name. I'm Tas Cougarson."

The chief took my hand and shook it. He wore his hair in the cropped fashion like most men, a habit learned at the live-away schools, no doubt. He was younger than Samul by maybe ten years and carried some extra flesh on his frame that was turning from muscle to fat as he aged. He had sharp dark eyes that saw much, a flattened nose and full lips.

"As Elder Samul told me and I think I saw, you are a very interesting, uh, man. And, I want to welcome you to our territory, elder brother."

I nodded and then made a face and laughed. "I gather Samul has told you a bit about me, though right now I'm feeling like someone's idiot younger brother rather than an old one. Did you and those park patrollers see my Seal?"

"Y-yes, maybe. Not sure 'bout the greenies—they were farther away than we were. I wouldn't worry 'bout it though. Who would believe 'em back at headquarters, anyway."

"I'm not worried, it's Gahji who is worried. She fears that Tuunac's paternal grandparents will give her more trouble if the park patrol makes a report on her."

The chief scowled, suddenly serious. "I'll tell her not to worry about that. Our attorneys will handle it if those people try to make trouble again."

Before meal preparations were completed two other canoes of tribal members noticed us around the fire and came over to join us. We spent a delightful evening eating and telling stories.

As it grew late, and knowing that the Elder and the chief wanted to talk to me without all the listeners, my sensible Gahji took the tired and now grumpy children back to Seatown with her aunty and a couple older cousins to help paddle.

When they were gone the three of us sat around the little fire sipping cups of tea and staring out over the quiet ocean gathering our thoughts. In no hurry we watched a crescent moon climb above the giant trees to spill a silver thread across the dark water.

Finally elder Samul threw sacred boughs onto the dozing fire, allowing the fragrant smoke to flow over us. I bathed my hands and face in its essence, saying a silent prayer of gratitude to the unseen Ones for the Unexpected blessings I had been gifted, after my return to my beautiful wounded world.

"Old Tommo will be getting out of jail in a few days," Samul said, getting to the point at last. "His lawyer tells me that faction in the government wanting to crack down on zaunk offenders is growing in strength in spite of the reformer party's efforts.

"Many of the veterans, like Tommo, who can't seem to adjust to civilian life are going to be in trouble. The courts are getting tired of their constant relapses. If Tommo gets picked up for getting drunk and fighting again they will put him in prison—maybe for the rest of his life this next time. Which won't be long, I'm thinking. He isn't a healthy man. I'd like your help with a ceremony to see if we can prevent that."

"I see. I'd like to prevent that, too," I agreed. "But unlike Iyantsha—or my own grandfather I have little skill with the healing art, beyond the simple herbal lore that most people of my youth would have known. So I'm not sure what use I could be to you—or him."

"That may be true, but perhaps that isn't the whole story," Elder Samul said. "You have admitted that when you stayed with the Prophet he called upon you for help with his healings from time to time. What did you do for him—and others during that period of your life?"

"Hmm.... Mostly I lent Iyantsha my Qwakaiva which he could use and skillfully direct for a healing. Elder Samul, you have to understand that for most of my early years I was unaware of my unique parentage. My Qwakaiva, my power was raw and untrained. Once I pledged my life and my service to the Great Kunai for the survival and the service of this world I was given allies and teachers along my journey, but it was only after my Seal father took me to live with him in the Beyond that I truly began to learn how to use my natural Gifts."

"So what are those gifts, old one?" Chief Rickson asked. "If you are willing to tell us."

I studied the chief with my spirit sight for a long moment before answering. His spirit fire pulsed with indecision. He was a modern man who had been taught at school to disbelieve heathen superstitions, but deep down in his soul he desperately wanted to believe in something that validated his ancestors' traditions. He hoped Samul's claims about me were true for that reason.

<<As chief of his people, he also wants to know how he might use you and your Qwakaiva for his own advancement,>> Aqwissa warned, expressing the darker aspect of his interest. <<So have a care, my Siyatli.>>

<<Yes, I see that, too. Thank you for reminding me, honored one.>>

"The Gifts I have most commonly used in service to my people concern my gift of foretelling future events—though that power comes when it chooses. I can rarely summon it when I want.

"I also can speak to the dead and help them to find their way into the world where our ancestors wait to greet us. I can create simple illusions and summon other forces for the protection of my loved ones or myself on occasion, but I prefer not to speak of that at this time."

Samul nodded, looking thoughtful. At last he tossed more sacred boughs onto the flames and as the smoke rose skyward he said, "I think your ability to speak to the dead might be what is needed here. He doesn't speak of it when sober, but I believe, like many vets, he is tormented by the ghosts that have followed him back from the Empire's wars abroad."

Recalling the ghosts of vengeful chamuqwani miners I had once encountered I frowned. "Though I certainly have seen chamuqwani ghosts who were killed during the old wars I have never tried to sing a ghost home that wasn't one of our people. I don't know if I can do it."

Samul placed a brightly-colored new blanket on the ground between us. "If Tommo is prepared to work with us again, would you be willing to try a healing with me and a couple elders, nonetheless?"

So it is beginning, I thought to myself, feeling a shiver of apprehension slide down my spine. I suspected my sweet bear woman was pregnant with my child and I had been blissfully content these past few months to enjoy my new loves and becoming just a family man with no other responsibilities to trouble my heart. Ah but I had made other, earlier commitments that I was obliged to honor as well.

I hope I was ready for the coming storms. "I might be," I said hesitantly. I reached for the offering and stood. "I will need some time to think about this and pray, before I will know if I can be of help to the tormented old man and others you might wish me to help."

"That's fair," Samul agreed. "We will speak to him when he is released and make our plans from there."

Samul and the chief rose as well, pouring the last of the tea and the bucket of water onto the fire. As I headed away from them the chief called, "Are you coming with us, old one?"

Blanket thrown over my shoulder for warmth in the evening chill I paused and turned to face them. "No. But so she won't worry about me please tell my Gahji that I will spend the night at my campsite. I want to pray and speak to the spirits of the land and my own guardians about the work you wish me to do for you. I will come home before she has to leave for work in the morning—tell her that, too."

Just before I made the transfer in the shadows under the trees I heard Rickson say, "Without a canoe how is he going to get back to the city by morning?"

Samul laughed. "Don't worry about him; he has his ways."

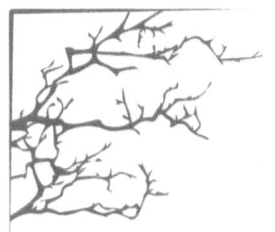

Chapter Thirteen

To my surprise the ritual the Elders envisioned for Tommo and other vets wouldn't take place in the large tribal ceremonial house a short ways up the coast from Seatown. No, it was to be held in a small chapel dedicated to the Mother of Mercy and her son located down by the ocean just outside tribal land. And also to my surprise some of the congregation would be present.

Samul saw my dismay when I showed up with Stakaya and a couple of his cousins in tow for the ceremony. "It's all right, really," he assured me. "Most of the people who will be attending are tribal people, including the reverend himself."

"Why aren't we using your larger ceremonial house for this?" I asked.

"Because they are in the midst of preparing for the traditional winter ceremonies and the Elders didn't want anything to interfere with that."

Interfere? I knew they did healings weddings and even funerals in there on occasion as well as the initiations for new ceremonial dancers.

<<Though Elder Samul may trust you, the others in their ceremonial society don't know you,>> Aqwissa said.

<<I can understand that—but in a temple?>> An amused hiss of a laugh in my mind was my only answer.

Reading the sour expression on my face correctly Samul hastily continued, "It's not like what you remember. Here the harsh rules and the threat of prison and the witch trials that were a part of Djoven's worship on the Preserve were never so brutally enforced out here.

"Another branch of the temple had more of a say in our 'civilizing' than did the tribes living farther east. The rev there won't call you a witch if you use your power. He's attended rituals in our ceremonial house before."

Not sure I believed him about the reverend, but I nodded and agreed to go ahead as planned. This was his territory after all so he and the local

Elders had the right to make the rules. One thing I did insist on was that there would be no children or other vulnerable people here when I went into the Dream and confronted the enemy dead.

He saw the wisdom in that and after speaking with the reverend and some other elders a few women and children sitting in the pews were escorted out and Stakaya and a few of his younger cousins were posted by the temple door to see that no one entered once the rite began.

I was directed to sit on a chair by Tommo just in front of the altar. He had been given an herbal brew that would help him relax and I could see it was already having its effect. He yawned and then nodded when he saw me take a place beside him, Samul on his other side. "Hey there, buckiyo," he said his voice slightly slurred. "You think you can handle my demons, eh?"

I snorted a laugh. "Well, it's me or nothing, so you take what you get."

He made a face but chuckled and agreed. "Let's give it a try then."

Serious again, I said, "I have never tried to sing on their journey ghosts who were not of the People, uncle, but I will do the best I can for you. I promise you that."

"That's all any man can ask, but I also will warn you, that you might not like what you see."

"I probably won't, uncle, but don't forget I have already lived through the old wars and I have a powerful ally who will also be traveling with us, which you will see once we enter the Dream."

There was no more time for talk, because at that moment the indoor lights were turned off and then the hall was illuminated only by candles, a multitude of them, on the altar table in the front of the pews, and along the walls in hanging metal holders. A man stood and began to ring a small bell in a slow cadence. As the congregation began to sing an unfamiliar hymn in time to his ringing, the old green-robed reverend rose and lit a wad of resinous incense and walked down the aisle swinging the smoky holder over and around the gathered people.

I breathed in the fragrant cloud and tried to set aside unpleasant memories which also came to mind when I inhaled Djoven's smoke. Was I ready for this? Too late to back out now, I scolded myself, and I did want to help the old soldier, no matter if it clawed open old wounds for me personally.

I allowed the songs and the prayers to flow about me without becoming immersed in their substance. I felt the spirits hovering, curious about me, none were hostile and some were even sympathetic when they recognized one of their own needing a healing.

Scooting my chair behind Tommo's I directed him to lean his head back into my cupped hands. With a little nudge of my Qwakaiva I felt him relax and enter the Dream. Aqwissa and I were right behind him.

Tommo's dream-world was a grim rocky desert plain, pock-marked with large craters wisps of blue smoke curling around some of their edges. No sun or moon illuminated the dark sky, but now and then a fiery red light lit up the horizon followed by a thundering boom. I shuddered in spite of myself. The soldier attacks I had lived through were terrible, but nothing like what the warriors of this modern time were forced to endure.

Suddenly nearby came the rattle of a smaller chamuqwani weapon. I saw the sparks from its barrel pepper the dark and heard a whistling sound as a missile from the enemy weapon passed by my head.

<<Get down, damn ya,>> Tommo shouted and pulled me with him behind a burnt out building. Taking his own weapon off his shoulder he aimed out into the dark and let loose a burst of answering fire.

When all was quiet again he turned to me and snarled, <<Stupid fucking recruit, don't they teach you new boyos anything? You are supposed to aim and fire that rifle on your back at the enemy not just stare gawking like an ignorant civilian when we are under attack.>>

Becoming more aware of myself I realized that I was now dressed in a dusty and stained soldier's uniform just like the younger Tommo beside me. I took the chamuqwani gun off my back and examined it. I had never owned let alone shot one of the enemies' guns—though Nachoga and many of my relatives had, and prized them dearly.

<<I guess I wasn't paying enough attention, Sergeant; will you show me now?>>

Muttering a long stream of curses under his breath he showed me how to aim, fire, and reload the alien weapon. So next time we saw the shadows of enemy soldiers approaching we both fired on the enemy until they were all dead.

Walking over to view the bodies with him, I saw that they were all of a deep brown skin with tightly curled black hair, not the blue-eyed pale skinned men I thought we would be fighting.

<<Who are these people?>> I asked, looking down into the vacant dead eyes of a youth about Stakaya's age.

<<They are the enemy, that's all. Don't know more—don't want to know more,>> he growled. <<Captain says we have to kill them and take the village. I got my orders and so do you, soldier, so let's finish it.>>

Hovering over his body was an angry enemy ghost. Mouthing curses at us he trailed along behind us as we moved further into the village.

Inside the village of mud shelters we saw more mutilated bodies; some wearing the empire's uniform, while others wore the enemy's ragged long robes. We also saw many women and children among the dead and I could hear the echoes of their death screams, so like what I remembered from the Gold Creek Massacre I lived through as a youth when I lost my mother and grandfather.

On my arm Aqwissa nipped me, urging me to keep strong. We were here to help Tommo; this was no time to be sucked down into a whirlpool of my own memories of loss and grief.

Shadowy empire soldiers surrounded us as we moved deeper into the enemy stronghold. At times I would hear gunfire and one or more of the shadows accompanying us would let out a cry of pain and fall away into the gloom at our backs. Muttering to himself Tommo kept moving forward, me keeping pace at his side.

Finally he stopped and pointed to a dark house ahead that was larger than the other dwellings we had passed. <<Our informant says that house belongs to the leader of this bunch of rebellious scum. Our orders recruit are to take that house and capture or kill their leader. Got that, recruit?>>

<<I understand those are your orders, Sergeant Tommo, but the fear and uncertainty I see in your spirit fire tells me you don't want to carry out those orders and kill those people. People that look so much like our own relatives, people who are living in huts not much different than you might find on the Preserve. Is that not also true, uncle?>>

<<No, no, they are enemy; we have to kill them or they will come across the ocean to our coast and enslave us.>>

<<Look at them, Sergeant, how can they do that, eh?>>

<<No, don't want to see... Me and my men will be thrown in jail or killed if we don't obey our orders.>>

Ignoring any further argument I might raise, he rushed forward and entered the looming house, his shadowy escort right behind him.

The house was richly furnished with colored blankets hanging on the walls and layers of rugs covering the floor of each room. Several of the ghostly soldiers brushed past me and ran up the stairs to the second floor. From the dimness above I heard more shouting and gunfire and women and children screaming.

When I caught up to Tommo he was standing just inside the doorway to what appeared to be a kitchen area. He had just fired his gun, smoke still wafting from its barrel. On the floor nearby lay a woman and two young children, an old grandfather with a long knife still clutched in his hand lay sprawled on the floor in front of them.

His aura radiating his grief and anger, Tommo stood there just staring at the mutilated bodies and the ghosts with blood pouring down their faces staring back at him. <<All this killing was for nothing,>> he finally said. <<We got bad information. There was no rebel leader in this village. All this—this whole damned war was for nothing, we fought and died just so a few rich lords could keep control of the mines they operate in these people's country.>>

He pointed a shaky finger at the old man. <<They come to me in my dreams—like now—accusing me... He was just trying to defend his women-folk. Probably thought I was going to rape his daughter, maybe, I don't know. I'm so, so sorry. I wish—I wish I was dead instead of them,>> he admitted with a sob.

<<Then instead of running away and hiding in a bottle you need to speak to your dead and tell them how you feel,>> I said. <<Tommo, what you haven't let yourself understand is that you are a victim here, too.>>

<<What are you talking about, recruit? I killed these people. They are the victims, not me. I am their murderer.>>

<<Yes, you are a murderer, I won't deny that, but you are also a victim of the chamuqwani lords' senseless war. You are a victim of other men's greed and hunger for power.>>

When he just stared, missing my point, I said, <<Why did you join the emperor's army in the first place, eh?>> when he still didn't answer, I rushed on, <<If I were to guess I would say that you joined to escape the poverty and misery you grew up with on the Preserve. There were few choices available for a young man who wanted a better life for himself and his family but joining the army back then—and it isn't much better now, if I believe what Stakaya keeps telling me.

<<There is no shame in wanting a better life and taking the opportunity given you. The blame falls on the greedy men who lied to you and tricked you into fighting and dying for them in their stupid wars.>>

Addressing the ghosts I said, <<Come away with me into the front room I noticed with all the beautiful rugs and wall hangings. This man wishes to talk to you, and if I can I will ease your journey into the Beyond where your ancestors are waiting to welcome you.>>

Taking Tommo's hand I led him back into the front room of the house where there was no blood or signs of violence. I sat him down on the carpets and we were joined by many other ghosts, both enemy and Tommo's own men. When all were assembled I began, <<This man has things he wishes to say, but before I ask him to speak I would like to share some of my own story, so that you may better understand us and the soldiers sent to invade your land.>>

Gathering my courage I opened the door on my own memories of terror and pain. I lived again the hard times we faced after being driven to the Preserve and then the nightmare of the massacre that killed my mother and grandfather. I showed them how in his way Tommo was a victim as much as they were and how the guilt and shame he felt for causing their deaths had tormented him throughout the years.>>

When I finished Tommo spoke. He told them about his life on the Preserve and how in desperation he had joined the Emperor's army to help support his mother in her old age. With deep emotion radiating from his spirit fire he said how sorry he was for coming to their country and killing them. And at my urging he asked for their forgiveness.

At last the grandfather, speaking for the enemy dead addressed me and spoke, <<Thank you, honored teacher, for explaining more about your people to us. I can see how all of us are victims of other men's lies and greed.

In order to pass on into paradise I know we must set aside the anger and bitterness that is keeping us tethered to this place and time.>> Addressing Tommo he said, <<For this reason I will offer you my forgiveness.>>

He chuckled, but there was little mirth in the sound. <<Now it is up to you to forgive yourself if you wish to avoid your own destruction. It will be up to you to make what you will of your life in the living world from now on. We will not be there for you to blame for your failures. This is my challenge to you, my enemy.>>

<<Fair enough,>> Tommo said. <<I accept your challenge, my enemy. From now on my life is my own to make right—or fuck up—as I choose.>> The old ghost laughed and agreed.

That completed I asked the enemy elder, <<Is there more I can do for you and your people that are still lingering here, honored elder, to help you pass? I have been taught by my own elders how to open a passage into the Beyond that might help you.>>

<<That would be good. Pray with us, brother, and open the way.>>

And so I did. As we prayed I opened a portal and the enemy dead passed through. Still keeping the portal open after they were gone I addressed the imperial ghosts still hovering in the room. <<Brothers, my strength is waning. It would be best if you follow into the place where your own ancestors' dwell while this door remains open. There is nothing remaining here for you. Go home. If you have final words for a loved one, tell me now and I will try and get a message to them.>>

At last it was over and my Qwakaiva nearly spent. Intent only on returning us to our physical bodies Tommo and I rose and stepped outside the enemy dwelling—where I nearly died.

A dark specter controlling two metallic creatures, like the ones I had seen hunting my father when I spied on my mother's dream were waiting for us. With an unspoken command the two metallic hunters focused their gleaming eyes on me and then a bolt of blinding white light shot from the red eye of the nearest, hitting me right in the chest. Startled, I cried out falling to the ground spirit ichor spilling from the gaping wound just below my right shoulder.

I might have died both in the Dream and back in the physical world if not for the quick reactions of the soldier-trained Tommo beside me. Before the other hunter could focus on me Tommo pulled his weapon and fired several bursts of flame at this new enemy.

At almost the same moment, Aqwissa sprang from my arm and leapt for the shadowy figure directing them. With a startled screech of pain the specter burst into flame as it tried to get away from her ferocious onslaught.

Ignoring the pain like a hot knife cutting through my shoulder I grabbed for my own weapon and fired at the second metallic being before it could focus on me or Tommo again. Putting much of the last of my strength into the weapon's fire, I had the satisfaction of seeing the hunter explode into blinding white light.

When it was over and our enemies smoldering nearby, I offered him my thanks. <<Uncle, I think your quick reactions might have just saved both our lives.>>

Tommo grunted and helped me to my feet muttering curses about treacherous, lying enemy scum.

<<The old one didn't lie to us, uncle. Your enemies are gone.>> I waved to the smoldering bodies nearby with my uninjured arm. <<These, are *my* enemies. My guardian and I were so focused on releasing the trapped ghosts that we spared no thought to our own peril.>>

<<Your enemies, eh?>> He walked over to inspect the charred wreckage. <<This one appears to be a man, but the other two,>> he pointed to the larger metallic coated figures, <<They look like the robots I saw in an old Mighty Martiin comica book. I've never seen their like. What—or who are they? And what, for that matter is that dragon-like creature by your side?>>

I reached down and patted her silvery scaled head. <<This is Aqwissa, she is one of the guardians and teachers that I spoke of.>>

Pointing to the scorched metallic creatures now devoid of life and movement, I said, <<I don't know exactly what they are, but I have seen their like once before.

<<What I *do* know is that they are not from our world. From what I have overheard from my paternal relatives they might be compared to a kind of otherworldly bloodhound, maybe. They can be given someone's ethereal scent and then they and their master are hired to seek out the enemy for the one offering the bounty.>>

Tommo snorted a laugh. <<What did you do to piss somebody off bad enough to send these fuckers after you?>>

I let out a mirthless laugh. <<Well, my father and I killed one of the enemy's favored sons, for a start. Then I rescued this one from another of their treacherous enemy spies,>> I stroked Aqwissa again, who purred under my hand, <<which also probably pissed them off.>>

Tommo grunted, giving me another speculative look. <<Seems like I've been wallowing in my own misery for far too long. Sounds like there is more going on around me than I realized.>>

<<Yes, there is. What is happening in our world is mirrored both in the realms of the Beyond and in other physical worlds within the Starry River. My father's clan—and I are pledged to use our Gifts to protect the world we live in—and others from an enemy who wants to destroy all human life.>>

Coming over to the humanoid figure I reached out a hand to touch its essence, but Aqwissa held me back. <<Don't touch it, Siyatli,>> she warned. <<When the Crokno come they will taste your essence upon the corpse and know where to hunt for you sooner.>>

Tommo's eyes widened when he heard her speak. I laughed. <<Aqwissa is far more than a dragon-lizard attack dog—which is probably why their agent is so mad that she chose to bond with me when I rescued her.>> He nodded his understanding. Returning my attention to the corpse I asked her, <<Can you detect who sent this bounty hunter after me? Was it Hoyt's angry mother, other Crokno relatives, or Utreal?>>

<<Your treacherous cousin, but the Crokno may also know of your return if he has dared to tell them that he has lost their gift to him—me.>> she nuzzled my side with concern. <<We have stayed over long in the Dream. You and the human are weakening we must go—now.>>

Suddenly feeling the strength almost completely drained out of me I swayed and agreed. <<Yes. We need to go. Can you help me—us, my beautiful qwissa dragon?>> She purred and nuzzled my hand then transformed herself back into the silver bracelet upon my arm.

Taking Tommo's hand we made the transfer back into our bodies in the Physical World.

I awoke to the disconcerting experience of being bathed in Djoven's smoke and the reverend waving a candle over me and praying, while a worried Elder Samul dabbed at a bleeding scorched wound on my chest.

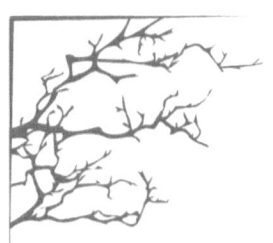

Chapter Fourteen

Gahji was mad at everybody when they finally brought a wounded me home for her to tend. Promising to talk more in the morning, the Elder and a discomforted Stakaya and his cousins beat a hasty retreat, fearing to become the focus of her ire, no doubt—the cowards.

That left me to face the furious mama bear alone. I knew she was angry—and had every right to be—I'd been stupidly careless, but I also saw the fear and worry pulsing in her spirit fire as well.

"Gahji, please don't be angry or yell at me," I gasped out as she bandaged my shoulder—none too gently. "You might wake the children and they will be frightened if they see me like this. I will tell you all of it, and more of my own story that explains what happened tonight, but I need to lie down—rest a bit—please."

Finished with wrapping my shoulder she saw the wisdom in my request, nodded and helped me to our bed. I lay down gratefully and closed my eyes to begin my healing process.

When next I awoke the gray light of dawn was showing behind the pulled drapes of our bedroom. When I turned my head she was lying on her side watching me. "Good morning. Did you sleep at all?"

"A little," she admitted, "but I was worried about you. I kept waking to check on you."

I picked up her hand and kissed it. "I will be all right. I heal quickly." Glancing at the growing light illuminating the drapes I struggled with one arm to rise. "I need to get up and wash before the children wake, so you can get to work."

Gently she pushed me back down "I'm not going to work today. I called in sick. I'll make breakfast and get the kids off to school. You can stay here and rest."

"You don't have to do that, my dear one; I can get Angika and Tuunac ready and walk Bijah to her school in the afternoon. I'm not that injured," well maybe I was—but I wasn't going to admit it, "see..." I reached over and pulled her to me and kissed her with tenderness and passion.

Laughing she pushed me gently away. "Oh, no you don't. You aren't going to distract me so easily—and you *are injured*, and bad enough to need your rest, without being pestered by a five-year-old all morning. I'm staying home—and that's that."

"And besides," she added, "you promised to tell me what happened—and more about your own story if I let you rest last night. I'm gonna hold you to that promise this morning, if I can find a way to distract Bijah while you tell me, that is."

I smiled and sat up again. "I think I might have just the distraction in mind. Bijah will be entertained and kept safe, as well,"

"What are you talking about; what kind of distraction?"

"You'll see." I laughed at her frown and rose a bit shakily to my feet.

"Hey, where are you going? Come back here."

My grin widened. "I have to pee, but I will be back—be sure of that."

She laughed and patted the bed beside her, unbuttoning her nightgown. "Hurry back, seal man."

Stakaya hadn't returned by the time the older children were fed and ready to go to their school. I offered to take them, but Gahji said she would do it and refused to argue about it. I knew she feared for Angika's safety and worried that Tuunac's grandparents might try to kidnap him if she wasn't always on her guard, so I nodded and let her go.

When she returned I was propped up against several pillows on our old couch a fresh pot of kaf-tea and last night's scau-bread and berry jam on the low table in front of me. In the bedroom she shared with her sister Bijah was happily playing with Aqwissa.

Not fooled by my relaxed appearance Gahji noticed the absence of her other daughter right away. Then she heard her talking to someone in the bedroom and asked, "Your distraction? Who is she talking to?"

I pointed to my bare wrist. "Aqwissa offered to amuse her for a while."

Thinking I was teasing her she scowled. "She is talking to your bracelet—and how long is that going to last, eh?"

I laughed softly. "Her distraction will last as long as we want it to." I motioned towards the bedroom. "Go see for yourself. Aqwissa is one of the things we need to discuss." Still scowling at me she did as I suggested.

Without following her I knew what she would find. When I checked on her a while ago Bijah was sitting atop her bed with a snaky silver-scaled dragon lizard, about the size of a cat, curled in her lap. Aqwissa could only speak to her with the mind speech, but Bijah hadn't mastered that yet, so she would be answering her friend with her voice.

I heard Bijah greet her mother then went back to playing with the dragon lizard. When Gahji returned her frown was still in place, but her Bear wasn't snarling at me, so she was more curious than angry.

"What is that thing?" she asked as she sat down beside me and took the fresh cup of kaf-tea I handed her.

"My bracelet—like you said."

She growled and punched me playfully on my uninjured side.

"Ow! To be honest with you, my heart, I don't know everything about her and her race. She came to me when I rescued her during a raid into a rival clan's territory while I was living with my father's relatives. She bonded with me, offering her protection to me and now my family when it seems necessary."

"But if she is yours, why is she in my daughter's lap at the moment?"

"Bijah can see her and Aqwissa seems to have a special affinity to her as well. She tells me that your younger daughter has the blood of dragons in her lineage, so that makes them kin of a sort."

"Must be from her father's side of the family, I never heard of a dragon in my lineage."

"Nor would you. Most northern peoples, including my own Qwani'Ya family feared Kunai and the Aseutl dragons living in the earth or at the bottom of Big Ice Lake."

"Our protection, hmm... And you are sure the creature isn't going to hurt Bijah or the others in my family?"

"No, no she won't hurt them, I am sure. In fact that first night when I helped the cub home it was Aqwissa that warned me about the men following your brother and helped me defend him."

She sipped her kaf-tea, thinking. Finally she sat her cup down and said, "This is weird and maybe a bit creepy, too. I guess like your Seal-self, your bracelet dragon is just another one of the strange new things I am going to have to get used to since I accepted you as my husband."

I smiled. "Along with my Seal to play with you, and my fishing and hunting skills to feed you, think of her and her unusual Gifts as a part of my groom-price."

She snorted a teasing glint in her eyes. "Unfortunately for me that groom-price comes with no money or job."

Suddenly serious I swallowed another joking remark and asked, "Gahji, I'm sorry I haven't been able to help you in that way. I'd hoped by babysitting and helping provide most of our food it would be enough. But if it's important to you that I get a job and help with earning money I will ask your uncle Samul to help me find—"

She leaned over and kissed me to shut me up. "I am teasing you—mostly. Without proper papers it would be hard for you to find work—that isn't paid poorly at slave-labor wages."

"For you I would work for slave-labor wages."

She shook her head and drank more kaf-tea. "No I don't want you to do that. I get worried about the bills from time to time—especially right now, but I shouldn't take it out on you. You are doing more than your share to help out around here. Ignore me."

"You said right now, what has changed to trouble your mind?" I thought I knew but I suspected it would be better to let her tell me.

She sighed. "I guess I should tell you—if you haven't guessed with all your otherworldly powers. We are going to have a baby in the spring. I will be finished with school before then, but I will have to quit work sometime over the winter and I guess I'm a little worried about how we are going to get by with only a small maternity leave pension to pay the bills."

I put my hand on her slightly rounded belly and smiled. "This makes me so happy. And I understand. You have every right to be worried. I'm forgetting that I now live in this 'modern' world and my hunting and fishing skills aren't going to be enough to support us." I smiled and teased, "Unless you want to come stay in my bush camp when you quit work."

She punched me again and I caught her hand and kissed it. "You are such a mean, mean nursy. Please, please don't hurt me I'm already wounded—and in pain," I whined.

She laughed and then kissed me. "You are such a mud worm—and you aren't that injured. You told me so a while ago when you begged me to climb on top of you and we were—" she kissed me again. "Doing this..."

We got distracted for a while, but time was moving along and one of us would have to get Bijah fed, and off to her afternoon classes, so when we decided to stop and eat some scau-bread—just to keep up our strength—she reminded me of my promised explanation and so I began.

Holding her hands to strengthen our connection I asked her to close her eyes and then projected images into her mind as I told her the story of my life. I was doing pretty well until I got to the part of my life where I was accused of witchcraft and imprisoned by Grand Intercessor Hoyt.

Losing control of my tale at that point, I became ensnared in the terrible memories of that time, sharing far more with my sweet Gahji than I'd planned. Tears streaming unnoticed down my cheeks I relived my torture and my rescue by my Seal father and her brave ancestor who killed the grand intercessor, who wanted to kill me or make me his slave.

Pulling her hands out of mine she broke the connection and threw her arms around me and kissed me. "Tas, stop! That's enough. All that happened a long time ago. You are here with me now and I love you—we all love you. Just like you said my grandfather did, I'm gonna take care of you—and our family."

When I got my emotions back under control I sniffed and said, "Thank you for listening and putting up with me," I said to Gahji. "I thought I had healed from that old wound while living in the Beyond.I guess I still have some healing work to do."

"I'm your wife. Don't apologize for sharing with me." She rose and kissed me on the top of my head like one of the children as she moved into the kitchen. "Talk to Uncle about that stuff. I'm sure he will be around to check on you sometime in the next day or so. But right now it's time for our daughter to get ready for school and all of us to have our lunch."

Calling Aqwissa to my arm Bijah and I followed her into the kitchen to help with the preparations.

When Bijah was ready for her young scholars class, which only ran for half the time that the older ones spent at the neighborhood school I dressed with Gahji's help and came with them, my wounded arm nested in a triangular cloth sling.

As we walked slowly home holding hands, my mind was still mulling over the events of last night and how they were connected to my past.

"It's kind of crazy but I have to thank Hoyt for some of the things he taught me."

At her horrified stare I hastily added, "Oh, not the abuse, but when he was trying to win me over to his way of thinking he showed me how to perceive the world—and my enemies, in a way that was totally different than what I'd been taught by my own Elders.

"When I was confronted by Tommo's enemy dead during the ceremony Hoyt's teachings, gained through so much pain, helped me to understand them and the Empire's soldiers sent to kill them. I was able to create a portal and send them home. I'd only guided our people before and as I told Tommo before we started I wasn't sure I could do it."

Guiding her to the weathered chairs on the porch when we reached home I pulled her down beside me.

Voicing more of my thoughts I said, "You know Hoyt was a sort of half-breed like me. His Crokno mother made a child with a chamuqwani man, and then when he was weaned she abandoned him to his drunken father's abuse and molestation.Later when he survived his early years she returned to claim him."

"That's terrible. How could a mother do that to her own child?"

I gave her a sad smile and patted her hand. "Unlike you, my beautiful mama bear, the beings that dwell in the beyond have different priorities to ours sometimes. His otherworldly relatives, the Crokno work for the destruction of all humankind."

"Why?"

Because many among them can see into the future, they see us as a cancer that might spread our corruption to other worlds if allowed to achieve our destructive, imperialistic potential. Unloved and abused, Hoyt became a perfect weapon to aid them after he was trained."

"And what about your own otherworldly relatives?"

"Oh, they aren't without their faults, but they don't wish us gone. They are aware of our potential for harm, but because of their connection to the Traditional tribal peoples of our world they think we are 'salvageable,' if those teachings can be preserved and nurtured to grow anew along with all the lethal machines humans are making along the way.

"To teach and preserve our heritage and our teachings is what I have pledged my life in service to do, and why I wanted to return here myself."

She was quiet for a long moment toying with a loose thread on her sleeve while she thought about my words. At last she looked up and I saw the gleam of moisture in her eyes. "That is such a noble calling. All you have suffered, all you are striving to achieve with your Gifts, why would you want to burden yourself with me—with my children?"

Feeling a lump come into my own throat I leaned over to kiss away her tears. "Oh, my lovely bear woman, you and the young ones mean everything to me. Besides being beautiful, smart and gifted with your grandmother's healing touch, you help ground me in this place and time. As I told you before you give me purpose and make me want to put down roots and grow.

"Without you and the children I probably would end up just like my father Star Swimmer, just drifting throughout time, swimming from world to world, battling our enemies, but with no real sense of belonging anywhere. I have neither the magical talent, nor the desire to take on that task.

"Oh I'm sure, like many fathers he would like me to follow in his footsteps. But as my dear paternal cousins are in the habit of reminding me, I am too human for all that.

"My place is here, my purpose is here. I'm too rooted in the soil of the world that gave me birth. And I will use what gifts I have to make this wounded world a better place for all who want to dwell upon her."

Elder Samul came by with his wife Aunty Megara and Chief Rickson, the next evening after the children were in bed. Aunty had made a carrot cake with creamy frosting for us to share. Sitting at the kitchen table eating cake and tea we told our visitors our happy news about the baby. They were delighted and wished us well.

After I finished giving them an account of my part in Tommo's healing, it was growing late, so after asking me a few more questions our guests rose to go. Ushering them to the door I followed them out into the night. Following the chief to his mecho-cart I stopped him before he could climb in and drive away.

"Chief Rickson, I have a problem and I wonder if you might be able to help me solve it."

He turned to face me. "If I can, certainly. What is it?"

I took a deep breath. "With the baby coming, my Gahji is worried about money once she has to stop working. My hunting and bush skills have been feeding us much of the time, and my babysitting means she doesn't have to worry about paying for childcare, but that won't be enough once she has to stop working.

"I want to help her more; I want to get a 'real' job and make money to help pay rent and buy baby clothes and things. The problem is twofold. One, I don't know how to go about finding a job. And two, I have no proper papers. Any written identification I might have had once would be too old—and unbelievable—even if it could be found."

I gave him a nervous laugh. "You see, according to the Empire's officials I don't really exist in this place and time. I'm hoping you or someone you know can help with this difficulty. I don't want her to worry."

"Hmm, I can see your problem." Patting my shoulder he opened his mecho-cart's door and climbed inside. As he started the mecho device he turned back to me, and said, "Let me think on it for a while and talk to some people. Sometimes the homeless or tribal members coming to town from the Preserve lose their documents and they have to be replaced. We can probably work something out before Gahji has to quit work, so leave it with me and don't you worry."

He chuckled. "If it comes to the worst I have a somewhat shady cousin who has a fishing boat, who fishes from time to time—when he isn't smuggling, that is. He can always use an extra hand—no questions asked."

I laughed. "I will do it, if I have to. I'm used to hard work, but I'd rather be legalized and get some work a little closer to home, with the baby coming and all."

"I can understand that, too," he said. "We will talk again soon."

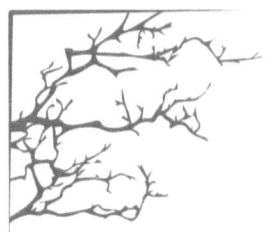

Chapter Fifteen

Gahji was at work and I had just walked the older ones to school and I was returning home to clean up the breakfast dishes when Bijah riding on my shoulder pointed out the chief's mecho-cart pulling up in front of our house. Hanging on to my braid with one hand she waved and called to him, kicking her feet in her excitement.

When we were close enough to talk without shouting he opened his window and asked, "What plans do you have this morning, Tas?"

Setting Bijah down so she would stop kicking my still tender shoulder I shrugged. "Not much, just cleaning up the breakfast mess, why?"

"Come take a ride with me there's someone I want you to meet."

When I glanced at Bijah, he smiled. "She can come, too. Get in."

Curious, I settled Bijah in the back seat and climbed in beside Rickson. Riding in one of these machines never ceased to amaze me. "Where are we going?"

"To the Zacatik Friendship House, have you been there yet?"

"No but I've heard of it—sort of. Why are we going there?"

"Because the imperial government is giving them more money for their language programs. When I mentioned to Director Rabbitson that I might know someone they could hire to help out the old man who is currently teaching the Qwani'Yan portion, he was very interested.

"The Elder is quite ancient nearly a hundred years, so some say. But he is very dedicated to passing on his language. Unfortunately at his age, well, his health isn't the best. The program if it is to continue after he is unable to carry on will need another teacher.

"Right now they are just looking for someone to ease the burden from the old fellow who tends to take on too much, but who knows what might come of the opportunity in the future.

"If you are interested the director has promised me that he will hire you for the winter," he snorted his disgust, "or until our fickle government cuts off the funding again.

"But in the spring and summer I have already applied for a grant to offer camps to teach our children the bush skills they so desperately need to learn if they want to be proud of who they are and withstand the troubles haunting earlier generations of our people. You would be first on my list to hire for that program as well. Are you interested?"

"Possibly."

We had arrived at a large house with a big shaded porch and a wide open door inviting us in. several people were sitting inside and on the porch laughing and talking. From the back seat Bijah let out a shriek of delight next to my ear.

"Yey! I wan' go see Aunty Terry." Without waiting for me to open the door to let her out she climbed over the back seat and landed in my lap, the chief ducking just in time to miss a flying foot.

Holding her still with my Qwakaiva I looked into her eyes, making her focus on me. "Calm down, little one. You are being rude and disrespectful. You almost kicked me and the chief. We will go find Aunty Terry in a moment."

Chastened, Bijah apologized to the elder and me, but almost immediately she was excited and wanting to get out and find this unknown aunty again.

As we got out of the cart Rickson smiled and answering my unspoken question said, "You may not have been here before, but she obviously has. Terry Red Bird is one of the childcare teachers. Gahji has probably left her children here, before you came to help out. You can let her go. She will be all right and she knows the way to find the classrooms on the lower level where the children enrolled in the childcare program play."

As we climbed the stairs to the front door in a more dignified manner, Rickson stopped to greet several people as we went. I was not unknown here myself, much to my surprise, and I was welcomed as well. By the time we reached the entrance I was feeling a bit overwhelmed, not sure if I was ready for all the life-changes that were suddenly being tossed my way.

Inside the front door was a large open area, furnished with several comfortable, but well used, couches and chairs, where people could sit and talk while they waited for an appointment or a program to start. By one wall was a long table with a couple large kaf-tea pots, and several plates of cookies for anyone to take who might be hungry.

At the far end of this central area was a large room with a wooden floor. Men and women were busy setting up tables and chairs for an upcoming meal. On either side of the center were hallways containing several smaller rooms which I learned later contained the offices of the people hired to work there.

On the lower floor and the upper were classrooms and a large room called a gym where people played ball games when it was too cold and wet to play them outside. Bijah had disappeared down the stairs to the lower level where I could hear the excited laughter of young children at play.

Following Rickson over to the large wooden desk by the entrance I heard him ask for the director. We were told to have a seat, he wouldn't be long, the woman at the desk said.

We grabbed cups of kaf-tea and a couple cookies and sat down in a quiet corner. Using my Gift to discourage meaningless interruptions I set down my cup and asked, "This is all very interesting, brother, but what about my papers? Does this man know who I really am? Is he willing to give me a job without government identification?"

"No, I haven't told him who you really are, old one." Rickson said. "And if you agree, our lawyers and I are officially enrolling you as a Smotahlik tribal member. By her mother's marriage to Stakaya's father Gahji is already part of our band, along with her kids. Samul has decided to adopt you as a long-lost nephew after the rest of your family back on the Zerve died. We figured that was the best way to get your Zacatik identity cards and other documents—if you agree, of course."

I thought about his explanation for a long moment then agreed. Neither Aqwissa nor I could detect anything in the ethereal currents that would cause harm by this. "Thank you for working so hard on my behalf. Having a job and proper identification does ease my mind."

"You are very welcome. I think you will become a treasured member of our community who has valuable knowledge to contribute to our band."

He might have said more—especially what he expected from me in payment for his generosity, but the director came out of his office to greet us at that moment, and we followed him back to a large, quiet office decorated with wood carvings and other art down the hall away from the open area.

Director Rabbitson was a tall thin man with wide green eyes and a thin black moustache that spoke of his mixed race heritage. Taking his seat behind his cluttered desk, he studied me critically and wasn't sure he liked what he saw.

Turning to Chief Rickson he ignored me for the moment and said, "When you told me you knew of a fluent Qwani'Yan speaker I was expecting a much older man."

Rickson caught my eye and we shared an amused smile. "Don't be put off by his boyish good looks, Director," the chief joked. "He is older than you might think. And though I personally don't speak that language, old Billy Blueshirt says he speaks it quite fluently. Tas here also tells me he can speak the Kukiya language as well, which makes him of a double value to your program."

"Hmm, well at the moment we don't have the Kukiya portion going just Smotahlikan and the northern tongue." Turning to me for the first time he asked, "How did you come to learn both those languages?"

"Qwani'Yan is my first language. For many years that was the only language I knew. I learned to speak the Kukiya language when my mother married a Kukiya man and he adopted me." I brushed a finger over the tattoos on my cheek.

"Hmm, I didn't know some people still did the old tribal tattooing on the Preserve."

Rickson laughed, but there was a hint of nervousness in the sound. "Rabbitson, aren't you one of the first to tell the Empire's funding representatives that we are keeping our ancient cultures alive in these modern times? Tas is living proof that our traditions are still with us, eh?"

Rabbitson made a face but nodded his agreement. I didn't like this man. I sensed no enemy taint on him, but our personalities were so different that I found dealing with him irritating. I hoped he was a better administrator than he was an interviewer.

"I don't know if other families practice the old arts," I said, trying to swallow my annoyance. "But my family did, and I am proud of my tattoos. They tell the world who I am. And that I am honored by my mixed heritage."

He scowled, and without meaning to I realized that I had irritated him in return—though I wasn't sure what I had said or done.

Confused as well and realizing the interview wasn't going quite as he'd planned, Rickson chuckled, trying to smooth over the problem, whatever it was. "Oh come now, director this man is a treasure, you would be foolish not to snap him up, before he gets netted by some other Zacatik organization in town. Why, I plan to steal him away from you next summer for a youth summer camp program I have cooking up."

Rabbitson nodded, still not totally convinced of my worth, but not willing to dismiss me completely. Including the chief in his next comment, he turned to me and said, "As to whether we hire you, or not, the final decision will be up to our head instructor, who is a fluent speaker. He will be the one to decide if your 'skills' meet his standards. After I hear from him we can discuss your job prospects."

"Fair enough," I said. "Is the head instructor here today? I will have to bring my daughter to her young scholar's class in a while. I'd like to meet and speak to him before I go—if he's available."

"That is an excellent idea. He usually comes early enough to have lunch with us in the dining hall, so he can visit before his class starts."

Rabbitson looked at the time-tell on his wrist. "His great-grandson should be bringing him over soon—if he isn't here already. You are welcome to stay and have lunch with us, too. I think scau-bread and deer stew is on the menu today." He rose and motioned for us to do the same. "Let's go see if he's here and I will introduce you."

When we arrived back in the central area a large muscular brown-skinned man with gray eyes was just carrying a bony old man up the last of the front steps. Behind him came another man carrying a wooden chair with wheels instead of legs under the seat.

Misinterpreting my stare the director said defensively, "A grant to create a ramp that will bypass the front stairs is on our list to build." He sighed. "Unfortunately, to construct an indoor lift is beyond our budget at this time.

For that reason Elder Keveneth teaches his students in the dining hall or in an empty office, depending on the day's activity schedule."

Keveneth... The director had no need to give me the elder's name. Looking with my Gift I had recognized the ancient already. It was my old war brother and friend Kutima—or to use his chamuqwani name, Keveneth.

Placing the Elder in his wheeled chair, the young man put a blanket around his stick-thin legs and then went to get him a cup of tea. Taking advantage of the quiet Rabbitson walked over to the old man the chief and I trailing along in his wake.

"Good afternoon, Elder Keveneth, Chief Rickson I think you already know, but I'd like to introduce you to this young man, who is looking for a job and the chief assures me, can speak your language."

Smiling I stepped forward so he could see me better. "Greetings, old friend and war brother."

Kutima glanced up saw me for the first time and gasped. Clutching his chest he slumped forward in his chair, breathing in ragged gulps of air.

As I hurried forward and crouched beside him taking his limp pale hand I heard an onlooker say, "What's wrong with him; is the old one having a heart attack?"

Blotting out other distractions, I opened a channel of Qwakaiva between us and sent my power into his ancient heart to ease its rhythm. Holding his stare, I said in our Qwani'Ya language, "Don't you dare go and die on me now that I've found you again."

His breathing steadier he blinked at me and stammered in the same language, "T-Tas, is it really you I'm seeing?"

I chuckled and released my hand to pat his shoulder. "Didn't I tell you before my father took me away that I would come back and you would see me again before you passed into the realm of our ancestors?"

He nodded. "You did, but I'd just about given up hope."

I dropped my eyes and took his hand again to strengthen our connection. "I hadn't planned to be gone so long, but my relatives had other ideas. And, as they keep telling me, I'm only a Siyatli and lack the Qwakaiva to transport myself from one reality to another without their help."

"I understand. How *is* your father?"

"He is well, as far as I know—off on another mission for the Great Kunai, I suppose. I haven't seen him since a couple of my tricky paternal cousins brought me to Seatown and then abandoned me here about a year or so ago."

"You've been here so long? I wish I had known sooner."

"I wish I had known about you as well, lost and abandoned as I was, and not sure if a Crokno agent was hunting me it's taken me a while to figure things out in your modern world."

Looking worried, he said, "A Crokno agent? Tas, should you have come back at all?"

"Yes," I assured him. "My Gift tells me it is time; I am needed here—or will be soon."

He might have asked me more, but breaking in on our private conversation the muscular young man who had carried him in, asked in the common tongue, "Ati, are you all right?" and then giving me a menacing glare he said in our language, "Who is this person? Did he hurt you?"

"No, no, grandson. I am all right now. It was just a shock to see him again after so long. Martin, he is the one Collin and I have been waiting to see, for all these long years. He came back just as we said he would."

Glancing up at that point I suddenly realized we had drawn quite a crowd. Even my little Bijah was standing beside me staring at the elder wide-eyed with her thumb in her mouth.

Pulling her close I murmured next to her ear, "Did you sense my use of my Gift?" not taking her thumb from her mouth she nodded. "Well, everything is fine now. This Elder is an old friend I knew when I was a child like you. He was just surprised to see me, and I had to help him get over the shock, that's all."

Kutima had noticed Bijah and asked, "Is the little one yours?"

Still speaking our language, I said, "This is Bijahgwi. She is my wife's child—and mine in the way of our old traditions." When I coaxed her she greeted him in the same language, and then shyly hid herself behind my shoulder.

Hoping our mind connection was still strong, I said, <<I don't know what you have told your grandson and the rest of your family, but it would probably be best if you tell everyone that I am the grandson of your friend Tas from the old days, who looks very much like his ancestor.>>

His eyes widened at my use of our old link, but I think he understood enough of what I was trying to communicate, because that was how he introduced me to the worried onlookers gathered around us. His grandson Martin wasn't fooled, however. He continued to watch me over the meal with a mixture of awe and suspicion.

"Well, listening to you two, I guess the question of whether he can speak Qwani'Yan has been answered." The director said. Turning to Chief Rickson he said, "I guess we can discuss his job prospects over lunch." He waved a hand towards the dining hall. "I think they are ready for us now."

Not wishing to be parted from Keveneth so soon, I took the handles on the back of his chair and wheeled him into the table set aside for elders at the front of the room.

As I brought over a couple extra chairs for me and Bijah, I took a moment to speak privately with Rickson. "I don't know how these things are done in your time. And since Gahji isn't here to speak for me, will you be my advocate and make all the arrangements in this job hiring matter?"

He nodded. "I would be honored, old one. If I am understanding what just happened correctly, Elder Keveneth knew you in the 'old days'?"

"Yes, we grew up in the same northern village, but his father was our trader, so he didn't go on the long march to the Preserve with us. Later when I was sentenced to a prison term at Saint Yon's I ran into him again."

Over the meal we chatted companionably, Kutima telling me a bit about the language program and what he'd been doing with the variety of students—and their skill levels—he'd been trying to teach. "Some of the older ones learned the basics from relatives back on the Preserve growing up. For them it is more a task of listening to a fluent speaker and regaining a lost skill," he explained.

"For the younger ones," he shook his head discouraged. "I don't know growing up in this city, watching the picta-view and attending chamuqwani school, I don't know if they will ever know more than a few words in our beautiful language," he confided.

I laughed softly. "You were always a good teacher—you taught me how to read and write didn't you? If you can achieve that task you can accomplish anything."

He snorted, sharing my mirth. "Well, there is that. I can't say you were the worst student I've had in my teaching career, but you weren't an easy one, either."

I smiled. "We will do the best we can, and even if they never become fluent speakers they will learn enough to be proud of who they are."

Soon enough it was time for me to leave and take Bijah to her young scholar's class. Before I left him I invited him and his family members to our house for dinner four days from then. "I know my wife will want to meet you, old friend. And, that will give me time to hunt and fish for the occasion."

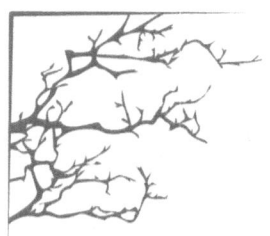

Chapter Sixteen

When I told her that night that I had met an old friend and I had a new job she was excited. "You mean I get to meet someone at last from the old days—someone who can tell all your childhood secrets?"

I laughed and cuddled her close. "Well, maybe not all of them, but he did grow up with me when we lived at Big Ice Lake. And he knew Matoqwa, too." Before she could ask I shook my head. "No, he didn't know your grandmother as a child. Her village was farther down river from ours, though he may have known her later in her life."

"Hmm, I will have to ask him."

Making a small fire in the back yard on the big day, I decided to cook the fish and some of the small game I'd caught in my snares in the old way. I thought Kutima would appreciate it—and I knew I would.

Inside Gahji, Angika and Bijah were making rabbit stew, chocolate cake, scau-bread and a large salad with fresh wild greens I'd also gathered to mix with the vegetables like tomatoes we grew in pots on our porch.

When our company arrived I was surprised to see two vehicles rather than one pull up in front. Calling Stakaya to watch the meat I hurried down the front steps to help Martin carry the elder and his chair into our home. Along with his elder, Martin had also brought his wife Esusi, a pretty young girl with long dark hair and a shy smile.

A balding middle-aged chamuqwani with dark eyes that seemed somehow familiar got out of the second vehicle and walked over to us, holding out his hand to me, his eyes a light with his excitement. Studying me for a long moment as I took his hand, he at last turned and said to Kutima, "I think you are right, Elder. He looks just like the pictures in great uncle's book."

Enjoying my confusion my old friend chuckled. "Preceptor Ruston is Collin's great nephew, Tas."

The stranger laughed nervously. "I'm sorry. In my excitement I'm forgetting my manners. I'm Rushton Golbraith. Keveneth told me on the far speak that you had returned and it is so amazing to meet you at last. My great uncle Collin always said you would come back. I just wish he could have lived long enough to welcome you back himself."

"I regret that, too." Seeing Gahji and the children standing in the doorway I picked up Kutima's chair and motioned for the others to precede me into the house.

Preceptor Ruston hesitated suddenly shy. "I hope you don't mind that I invited myself to this party. But I think I may have something that belongs to you."

"All people of good heart are welcome in our home, brother, do come in and join us." I said.

We spent a very enjoyable evening laughing and talking about the old days as we devoured all the good food prepared for the event. Gahji did ask my old friend embarrassing questions about me as she promised, and I took their teasing with what I hoped was good natured tolerance. She also got another perspective of her grandfather and his childhood.

"I did meet your grandmother Xyilaha when she was touring with Barklyo's show, though I didn't know her well," Kutima admitted. "It was Matoqwa who always came by with tickets for Collin and I when the show was in town."

Including me and the preceptor in his next comment, he said, "You know, both Matoqwa and Kuweya testified at the Emperor's inquiry into the mismanagement of the live-away schools run by Djoven's temple. Their evidence helped us change the laws concerning how the schools were administered and also enabled later reformers to pass laws giving citizenship to all Zacatik peoples throughout the Empire. You should be very proud of him, granddaughter."

Gahji blushed and nodded. "Thank you for telling me that, grandfather. You and Tas have shown me a different side of him that I didn't know as a child."

Kutima chuckled. "I'm not surprised. He wasn't an easy person to know and love. But be proud of him nonetheless."

We talked a bit longer, but all too soon I could see Kutima was tiring and the children, who were also fighting sleep, needed their rest. "We will do this again soon," I promised my old friend, "and then you can tell me more about what you and Collin and the others in our little warband got up to while I was 'away.'"

Placing his folded up chair in the back seat of Martin's mecho-cart I leaned in the vehicle's window and took his hand. "And you will see me two days from now when I show up at the Zacatik Friendship House to be your assistant instructor, eh?"

He brightened. "Yes, that's true. I'd forgotten about that."

"You can tell me all about our warband and Collin in our language and see how much of our conversation your students understand."

He chuckled. "Probably not much, but truly it is good to see you again, Tas. I've missed you."

After Martin and his family drove away Rushton was still standing by his vehicle. When I joined him he reached inside his coat and drew out a small carved wooden box and handed it to me. "My great-uncle, whom I admired very much, made me promise to give this to you should you return to our world in my lifetime. If you didn't return I was to pass it down to a trusted descendant until you came to claim it."

Puzzled, I took the box and opened it. Inside was a small gray stone with a natural hole in its middle. It was threaded on a braided cord made from my mother and father's hair. I had forgotten about the token I gave Collin at my trial, afraid Djoven's demons would take it from me and destroy it. Feeling the tears come to my eyes, I held it up to show him.

He smiled and I saw the tears come into his own eyes. "I think it is safe for you to reclaim it now. And so I return it to you at last."

"Thank You," I said and placed it around my neck. "This means a lot to me. My mother wove this cord from hers and my father's hair. For a long time it was all we had left of my father, and now it is all I have left of her. You are welcome at our house anytime you wish to visit."

"Thank you, Tas, I would like that. My great-uncle spoke of you with fondness many times over the years. I hope we can become friends, too." Swallowing hard, he patted my shoulder and climbed into his cart. "Please come see me at the Lectorium. I work in the history department and I would like to talk to you about your memories."

I laughed. "I can talk to you, but if you write down what I tell you and show it to anyone they will think either you are, or I am, crazy."

He shrugged and smiled. "Maybe both of us, but even if your account is just for family and friends it should be written and collected for the future." I studied him with my Gift for a long moment, trying to decide what prompted his offer.

<<He would like to use your story to enhance his academic career, but it is also true that he is a vehicle to record our story for all Traditional Peoples in this world's future,>> Aqwissa said into my mind.

Returning my attention to the waiting man, I said, "I will think about it. Maybe—someday. But do come again for a visit in the meantime."

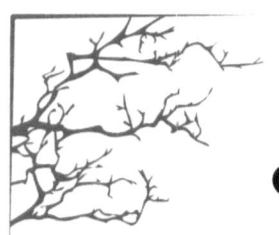

Chapter Seventeen

The coming days were full of new experiences as I learned more about how to live and function in this "Modern" world. I learned how to pay and ride the mecho-transit that ran about the city carrying people from one place to another. I also learned to use Gahji's far-speak, and she helped me open a bank account when I got my new identification papers so I could exchange my earnings for script we could use to pay our rent and buy other things we needed.

We fell into a daily routine in which I walked the older ones to their school and then three days out of the seven, Bijah and I went on to the Zacatik Friendship House where she spent the rest of the morning in child care while I worked on language materials or helped out in other ways when I was needed.

After lunch I took her to school and then went back to ZFH to help Kutima teach the Qwani'Yan language classes. In the afternoons either Gahji or I picked the children up and brought them home to begin meal preparations and supervise homework.

And somehow I managed with the help of Aqwissa and my Gift to hunt and fish for us as well. Until Gahji quit work near the end of her pregnancy it was an exhausting schedule for all of us, but for me it was also stimulating with all the new things to learn and do.

About a moon after I started work at ZFH, Tommo ran into me when he showed up for the midday meal the Friendship House offered on a regular basis. I was glad to see him, though I felt a little guilty for not going to visit him at the mission as often as maybe I should have. Busy with family, a new job and gathering our traditional foods whenever I had a spare moment, I had more than enough to occupy my days.

I was sitting with Kutima at the Elders' table engrossed in that afternoon's lesson planning when Tommo and my new Uncle Samul joined us.

Chattering away in our language I was startled when his familiar raspy smoker's voice hailed me.

"There you are, Buckiyo, I heard you were working at ZFH and here you are."

Clean and sober the old soldier was looking much better each time I saw him. I smiled. "Greetings, Sargeant Tommo. I'm glad you are feeling well enough to come to Friendship House, since I don't seem to find the time to visit you these days."

He waved my apology away and chuckled. "Does me good to get out of my room and away from the holy celibress always preachin' at me to convert and dedicate what life I have left to the temple." He snorted his opinion of that idea. "No way that's going to happen. Though if I have to listen to her sermons much longer the bottle might start looking mighty tempting again."

When he saw my horrified expression he laughed, letting me know he wasn't serious. Taking a bite of his buttered bread he studied me thoughtfully while he chewed. "Samul tells me you were looking for me when I was locked up. What did you want to talk to me about—if it isn't too private to discuss right now."

I smiled and shook my head. "No, it isn't too private to talk about here." I took a deep breath before continuing. As Gahji's belly grew with our child I couldn't help thinking about my baby sister Kitahtla, and wondering what had happened to her.

To taunt me, Utreal had told me that I would find her alive in this time—and maybe living in this city, but as of yet I hadn't been able to locate her, or anyone who knew of her, or her descendants.

"That day when I came across you and Elder Samul on the beach and I told you my name, you said you had heard of the name Cougarson, but you couldn't remember what it was that made it stick in your mind. I was hoping you might have remembered by now. If I have Cougarson relatives living here I'd like to find them."

"Cougarson." Tommo took a few more mouthfuls of his soup while he thought about it. Finally he put down his spoon and said, "When I was growing up on the Preserve there was an old Kukiya-breed woman and some children by that name."

I felt my heart skip a beat. Could old Tommo tell me how to find Kitahtla at last? "Not sure if the old woman is still around, though, but I think her children changed their names once they were grown."

"Do you know what the children changed their names to?"

"No. I don't know—if I ever heard. The girls took their husband's names, of course, and I'm not sure about the son. Being a breed he may have just left the Zerve as soon as he was able. The family wasn't well liked by the agent and the temple converts and they had a rough time of it, as I recall.

"There was some story about them also being related to the famous outlaw Jimmy Shoeless, and since the convert faction in those days was in control all over the Zerve a lot of people would have been afraid to associate with them. Once he was shot and killed I'm not sure how they fared—if any better."

Jimmy Shoeless? I had to think a long moment before I remembered that he was talking about my uncle Tli using his chamuqwani name. I sighed, another branch in the trail becoming a dead end.

Seeing my disappointed expression he apologized, "Sorry I can't be of more help."

"I'm sorry, too. It certainly sounds like it might be my baby sister and her descendants. I knew this Jimmy Shoeless you mentioned. We were all branded as outlaws and chased by the soldiers for trying to take back our stolen treaty goods and feed our starving relatives back then."

I pointed to the tattoos of adoption on my cheeks and gave them an ironic laugh, before continuing, "And though still a youth I used my Gift to help them on their raids. I was proud to say I was an outlaw, too."

Tommo snorted and gave me an approving smile. "Damned right. Good for you, Buckiyo."

We ate in silence for a while, and then Kutima surprised me by saying, "Tas, I didn't know you were looking for Kitahtla. Never living on the Preserve I didn't pay much attention to life there. As you wanted I stayed with Collin and became his scribe for a while after I completed my education. But have you mentioned this to Rushton? His field is history, you know. If she is still alive he would be able to help you, if anyone can. Call him on the far-speak and go see him at the Lectorium."

Kutima had also advised me to make an appointment with him, instead of just showing up at the Lectorium as I'd planned. When I at last got through to him on our far-speak he was delighted to hear from me and we agreed to meet the following day at his office after I took the older children to school. Bijah would stay home with her mother because I had no idea how long my talk with Rushton might take.

The Lectorium campus was green with flowering shrubs, ivy climbing the walls of older buildings and tall trees shading its pathways. It was also confusing, like so many things in this modern city I now lived in. Forming an image in my mind of Rushton I sent Aqwissa on a hunt to find him while I sat on a bench to watch the activity around me and wait for her return.

Shrinking down to the size of a small insect so she could travel unnoticed, it wasn't long before she molded herself once more onto my arm and formed an image of our friend in my mind. With her help I found the building where he was working easily enough after that, though once I arrived I had trouble convincing the plump blue-eyed chamuqwani woman behind the big desk in the history department that I did indeed have an appointment to see the distinguished preceptor.

She took one look at the long-haired tattooed savage dressed in faded trousers and shirt facing her and her mouth curled with her contempt. I heard the words "filthy zaunk" as clearly as if she had dared speak them out loud. She refused to believe that Preceptor Rushton really did want to see me, and no, I wasn't on her appointment calendar.

Threatening to call security if I didn't leave, I walked back into the hallway frustrated. I sat down on a wooden bench down the hall and tried to contact him by using the mind speech, but I had no real connection with him as of yet and he was too focused on the student papers he was grading for him to hear my call.

Finally in frustration I released Aqwissa again to fetch him. A moment later I heard a startled yelp and I stepped back into the history department's reception room again. The chamuqwani woman opened her mouth to order me out again when Rushton opened his office door, saw me and smiled.

"Ah, Tas, there you are. Sorry if I kept you waiting. I got caught up in grading papers and forgot about our meeting." With a bemused expression he glanced down at the silver snaky-dragon bracelet now adorning his wrist. "Uh, I think I might have found something that belongs to you."

I laughed. "Yes, I think you have."

Rushton glanced at the chamuqwani woman who was scowling at me murderously and sighed. Lifting his other hand he studied the time-tell on his other wrist. "Come with me. I'll buy you a meal at the instructors' club."

Returning his attention to the secretary, he said, "Madeline, take any messages for me. I won't be back until after my class at two." Her scowl deepened, but she nodded and returned her attention to her own work.

Out in the hall once more Aqwissa slipped from his wrist and came back to me. As I fell into step beside him, I said, "It's kind of you to offer to buy me a meal, but will you have trouble if you take me to this instructors' club you spoke of. We could just sit in the shade and talk if you like."

Staring down at his now empty wrist, his mouth dropped open. When he saw her back on my own arm he laughed nervously and said, "No, it's all right. I want to. I already have the reputation of being an eccentric preceptor anyway; bringing you will just enhance my reputation a little more, which is fine with me."

Glancing back at the building we had just left, he added, "I'm sorry, you must have had a bit of trouble with Madeline. I apologize. She is the dean of the department's hire and I had no say in the matter. I will speak to her; you won't have that problem again. When you called me at home I forgot to tell her you were coming this morning."

I snorted a laugh. 'She is very protective of her charges—and doesn't like zaunks. She threatened to call security if I didn't leave—which is why I had to send my companion to fetch you. It's me who should apologize if Aqwissa startled you."

He laughed again. "Your—uh—companion did that, but great uncle and Keveneth warned me that if you showed up again in our lifetime I should expect the unexpected." Opening the door for me we stepped inside the club and he led me into a wood paneled room with a thick carpet, and flowers in glass vases on top of each starched white tablecloth.

We found a quiet corner overlooking a shady garden dotted here and there with benches and colorful flowers, sat and ordered. Over a good meal of grilled steak, baked potatoes and green salad, I told him of my search for my sister Kitahtla Cougarson.

After he thought about it while we finished our dessert of fresh berries over a small cake topped with whipped cream, he finally said, "The name is vaguely familiar, but I would have to check Uncle Collin's records of his informants to be sure."

Still frowning he added, "But there was a student I had last term named Mathrom, I can't recall his enrolled, official last name, but about midway through the term he said he was reclaiming an ancestral name and wanted everyone to start calling him Cougarson."

When he saw my hopeful expression, he glanced down at my brown arm resting on the table, and added a cautionary word. "This particular student may not be your relative. He had fair coloring, dark blond hair and green eyes."

I glanced down at my arm as well and chuckled. "He may still be related, in spite of his chamuqwani looks. His grandfather—or great grandfather Nachoga was a chamuqwani. He was taken as a young child on a raid and grew up to become a feared Kukiya war leader and brother to the famous war chief Golannah."

"Hmm, now that you refresh my memory I seem to recall something about that in Uncle Collin's notes."

Feeling my excitement rise, I asked, "Do you know how to find this Mathrom Cougarson? Is he still attending the Lectorium?"

"That, I don't know. As I recall he was very interested in our unit depicting the Gold Creek Massacre, but he wasn't one of my better students, so he may have been forced to leave. He was always getting into trouble with administration because of poor grades and his politics."

"Politics?"

Rushton chuckled. "Yes, politics. I'm surprised you haven't run into him at Friendship House. I've heard that a group of young radical Zacatik Rights advocates meet there to plan their protests."

"No, I haven't come across them, but I'm rarely there of an evening so I'm not familiar with everything going on at ZFH. Could you see if you can find him for me?"

"I would be happy to. I also recall that he has a sister who was enrolled at the Lectorium. She was a much better student, so there is a good chance she is still attending classes here if her brother isn't. Unfortunately I might have to ask Madeline's help, because the new family name isn't coming to mind at the moment. But I will keep looking—I promise you that. I will find them for you."

As I was walking Rushton back to his office Aqwissa raised her head from my wrist, stuck out her long tongue to taste the etheric currents swirling around us, and then hissed a warning in my mind. <<What is it? >>

<<I taste an enemy and maybe the relative you seek.>>

<<Are they one and the same person?>>

<<No, but they are linked.>>

Feeling a sliver of ice slide down my back I paused to gather my defenses, before asking, <<Is there a Crokno agent at this Lectorium I need to worry about?>>

I sensed Aqwissa testing the currents again as she pondered my question. At last she said, <<There may be an agent, but if so, the Crokno isn't near. The enemy taint is from your past and carried through the bloodline of a powerful human malicer to his descendants.>>

Her words had me puzzled for a long moment, then an image of an etheric hairy creature all teeth and claws formed in my inner vision and I knew. Azogi. <<Where? Can you show me this enemy and the one who might be a possible relative?>>

<<They are among the humans clustered by the fountain.>>

Already on my guard I saw the malicer first. He was a thin mixed-race youth with wavy dark hair, a black moustache and sly eyes. On his shoulder perched a shadowy creature with red eyes and gleaming teeth.

<<I see the malicer, honored one, but where is the other?>>

<<He is bending over talking to the dark-haired woman, sitting on the bench,>> she said. <<I will make him turn to face you.>>

When I looked in the direction she indicated my heart skipped a beat. There, by the fountain, laughing and joking with a group of scruffy-looking young people, and suddenly straightening to slap at a nonexistent insect, was Nachoga.

Oh not my adopted father—I *had* watched him hang, after all—but a young man who could have been his twin, in truth. Dressed in ragged modern clothes he had my father's paler skin, green-gold eyes and dark yellow hair. Only instead of the two neat braids Nachoga favored this man had a straggly beard and tied his long hair back in a tangled ponytail. The young man himself hadn't become aware of me yet, but his cougar certainly had. The big cat in his spirit fire watched our approach with feline intensity.

Rushton had been prattling on as we walked, but I hadn't been paying attention. Finally putting a hand on his arm to stop him I pointed with my lips towards the group by the fountain. "No need now for you to check your files. I think I have found him," I said quietly. "If there is still time before your class will you introduce me to him?"

Startled out of his monologue he stopped, glancing around, confused. "What? Who?"

Remembering that most chamuqwani didn't point with their lips but only with their hands I motioned to the group standing by the fountain. ""The one with the ponytail that's Mathrom Cougarson, isn't it?"

Rushton looked then turned back to me, an amazed expression on his face. "Y-yes, but how did you know? Did you—"

I chuckled. "No it was no use of any magical power that drew me to him. He could be Nachoga's twin. And," I admitted, "His ancestor's Cougar is staring at us from his spirit fire."

"Oh." Still flustered, he glanced down at his wrist. "I will make time. Come on, I will introduce you. And then I really do have to go to my class."

As we wandered over I touched his arm again and asked, "Do you also know the breed in the red shirt among that group?"

Rushton frowned then said, "I think his name is Rody—something. He was never in my classes, but my colleague who did have him, had trouble with him, as I recall. Why do you want to know?"

I laughed, but there was no mirth in the sound. "Because he is a malicer and a witch. So avoid him if you can in future." When he frowned, wondering whether to believe me I laughed again. "Oh come now, after meeting me and my living bracelet, as well as growing up listening to your great-uncle's stories, surely you should know by now that I speak true."

He laughed along with me this time. "Yes, I should—even if it goes against all my academic training."

As we drew near the malicer's demon ally became aware of me first, then the young man himself looked round and saw me. I gave him a toothy smile, showing my elongated canines. <<Greetings, enemy fish slime. I see you, so have a care.>> My smile widened. <<If you are planning to renew the old blood feud and harm me or mine think again—if you want to survive, that is.>>

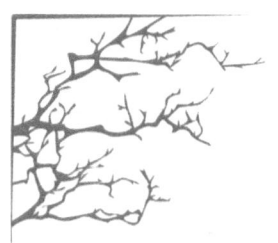

Chapter Eighteen

Rushton hailed the group as we approached. With grim satisfaction I noticed the one called Rody slipped away without a word to his friends. The preceptor smiled and spoke to several of the students by name as we came closer, and asked about their current classes.

They smiled and welcomed him in return, happy that he had remembered them. Judging by the easy way they behaved in our company I was pleased to realize that my new friend was respected and well-liked by these young people.

Turning to the one called Mathrom at last, he said, "Mathrom, I need to leave for my next class now, but before I go I'd like to introduce you to my friend, Tas Cougarson. He thinks you two might be related."

At first the young man's mouth opened in surprise, then suspecting a trick of some kind his eyes narrowed with suspicion. "Really? I never heard of anyone with that name but members of my family."

"I never have either—just family." I held out my hand and eventually he took it. I smiled and firmed up my grip so Aqwissa could taste him. "You look just like him, you know." *—or at least you would, if you cleaned up and braided your hair properly,* I thought privately.

His scowl deepened and at last he pulled his hand from mine. "Who do I look like? Who are you talking about?"

"Why the famous war leader of the Kukiya, Nachoga—of course—or to use his chamuqwani name, Mathrom Cougarson, I noticed the resemblance right away when I saw you. You could be his twin brother."

Turning to Rushton I asked, "I know Nachoga wasn't at Black Rock Fort for the negotiations where Willum took a lot of his pictures, but didn't any pictures of Golannah's brother survive?"

Rushton thought about it for a moment then shook his head. "I'm not sure; I would have to check the old records." Glancing to an ivy-covered building across from the fountain, he said. "I have to go; will you be all right if I leave you now?"

I chuckled and waved him on. "Go teach your class. I will have to get the children from their school soon myself, so I won't be staying long."

"Call me later and let me know how you fare."

"I will do that." Then turning back to the young man, I said, "Before I go I would like to speak to you for a while—if you don't have to leave for a class." I waved to a bench under some nearby trees. "Can we sit over there and talk?"

Mathrom glanced around, but didn't see whoever he was looking for. The group was breaking up, grabbing book bags and heading off in different directions.

"Hey Rina, where did Rody go?" A pretty brown haired woman with pale skin turned at the sound of her name. Walking backwards, she called, "I don't know. He left just before Preceptor Rushton came by to say hi." Then turning she hurried after her friends. Mathrom cursed and muttered something about their meeting being fucked now.

"Since your plans have changed," I said, "Come sit with me so we can talk a while, eh?"

He seemed surprised that I was still standing beside him. When I repeated my offer he shrugged and followed me to the shady bench I had pointed to. When we were seated I created a shield around us so we wouldn't be interrupted.

Taking the offensive he demanded, "Who are you really?"

"I'm Tas Cougarson, as I told you."

"Right, sure you are. You seem to know a lot about my family, I admit, but for what reason? Are you a history instructor too, like the preceptor?"

"The only history I know is what I have lived, or read from books in the library." I chuckled. "As to me being a teacher like Rushton, well, recently Zacatik Friendship House has hired me to teach in their language program, but that's the only teaching I've ever done."

"Hmm," Suddenly curious, he asked, "What language do you teach?"

"At the moment I am helping the Elder who is teaching Qwani'Yan, but I speak good enough Kukiyatan to teach the basics, if they had such a program running."

"Yeah well don't hold your breath. It will be a long time before they begin that program," he snarled.

"I wondered about that. I've noticed since coming to Seatown that many Kukiya people live here. Why isn't there a program for them?"

"Zacatik politics." Noticing my puzzled expression, he laughed and looked at me as if I was stupid. When I continued to just stare without saying a word, he snapped, "Think about it. This is Smotahlik territory, and who did the Kukiya raid for fish and slaves, eh? The Smotahlik.

"Old feuds live on and on down the generations, and now that they have the imperial government's money safely in their hands they aren't going to share—unless we make them."

Down the generations... Thinking of Azogi and his curse I doubted if this angry young man knew how prophetic his words truly were. "Hmm, I wondered about that, thank you for telling me."

He snorted again and gave me a disgusted look. "You're brown enough in color, but so are some of the immigrants that come here from other parts of the Empire. Since you don't seem to know even the basics about Zacatik life these days, who are you really if not an academic?"

"Do I look like an academic?"

He laughed. "Fuck no."

I smiled. "No academic. I am exactly what I said I was, family." I touched the tattoos on my cheek. "Do you know what these mean?"

He studied my face continuing to frown. At last he admitted. "No, what do they mean?"

"I was raised in a very traditional way, deep in the Desert Mountains, both off, and on the Preserve. My mother was Qwani'Ya, so I spoke that language from my childhood. But when I was older and my father had left us my mother remarried a Kukiya man." I pointed to the tattoos again. "When he adopted me he gave me these. So I am both a Kukiya and a Qwani'ya person."

And much more, but I wasn't going to reveal that to him—not yet, anyway. My smile widened as I decided to tease him a bit. "You may call me Uncle Tas, if you like."

He snorted again. "I don't have to call you anything. Just because some old Kukiya fart adopted you somewhere, sometime, doesn't mean we are related."

"But we are, truly. Somewhere in your lineage you have an ancestor named Kitahtla, don't you? I am related to her older brother."

Mathrom looked shocked that I knew his relative's name, then growing suspicious again, he said, "Yeah, I do have such an Elder, but Granny Kitah never said anything about an older brother."

"Maybe she never mentioned him, because her brother was captured and imprisoned by soldiers when she was still a baby."

Hedging a bit on the truth for now, I said, "Her father was Nachoga, the man you were named for when your parents gave you his imperial name of Mathrom, right? But what she probably didn't tell you was that Nachoga had two wives. We *are* related, truly."

He shook his head stubbornly clinging to his earlier opinion. "I don't understand why you want to keep lying about that. Neither I, nor my sister Saskina ever heard that the old warrior had another family. We were always close to Granny Kitah—she would have told us."

"Is Kitahtla still alive? If so, you can ask her about me."

"If you're so smart and know so much about my family then why are you asking me that? You should already know if she's alive or dead."

Yes, and I could find it out right now if I stripped it from your mind like your malicer friend would do.

"I think you're just making things up, because I look like some chief's picture that you found in an old book? Are you thinking that you can use me for your own research paper about the 'good old days'?"

I sighed. So we were back to that again?

"Well, that's not going to happen, so you can fuck off," he added.

I reared back as if he had slapped me. This young cat and his belligerent attitude was trying my patience. Detecting my emotions, Aqwissa stirred and raised her head to hiss her own threat. I put my other hand over my wrist to quiet her, before either of us did something stupid—something I would regret later. He might look like my beloved father, I reminded both of us, but with every word out of his mouth he proved to me that he wasn't.

After taking several deep breaths I calmed down enough to say, "As I told you before I am no academic; I'm not writing a paper on our family."

Though Rushton would certainly like me to let him use what I could tell him to write his own paper about my people.

"True, there is the physical resemblance you share with your ancestor, but more importantly you have inherited his Cougar," I said, in what I hoped was a calm voice.

"When I look at you with my Gift, my spirit sight, I see the old war leader's Cougar watching me. That is how I know we are related. Hasn't Cougar come to you in your dreams to try and teach you and guard you?"

At the mention of spirit beings his eyes widened in surprise, all his earlier suspicion had been set aside for the moment when I mentioned his cougar spirit guide. Toying with the strap on his bag, he dropped his eyes before he next spoke. "I have dreams sometimes about cougars," he shyly admitted, "but I don't know what to make of them. My friend Rody says that there is a big cat trying to capture my spirit because it is evil. I have to fight it to protect myself and my sister."

Stupid, stupid tom kitten! I could feel my temper bubbling up again. Thanks to the teachings of Djoven's damned priests the ignorance of these modern people was unbelievable.

"And do you listen to this bad advice and fight Cougar when he comes to teach you?"

"Sometimes, but mostly I just try to run away or hide from it."

Barely able to control my rage, I demanded, "Why aren't you listening to what your gut—your intuition—to use a modern term, is telling you about the cougar? Stupid dog turd, who is this man you call Rody? What right does he have to tell you such lies and deny you your birthright?"

Unaware of my mounting fury Mathrom shrugged. "He's just a guy I know. He used to date my sister, but she dumped him and she gets mad at me when she knows I've been hanging out with him. But the guy's a breed Kukiya, like me, and claims to be a Puhani."

"A Puhani?" I made a disgusted sound deep in my throat that sounded more like a growl than human speech. "A Puhani is someone with puwa/power who is a healer and a teacher. And that, this Rody is not. Your sister is right not to like him—and neither should you."

"But—"

"Yes, I would agree he has puwa,' I said, cutting him off. "But the puwa he has he uses for selfish purposes. He is a malicer and he means your family no good." Barely able to contain my fury I stood. I was done with talking to this gullible, ignorant young relative. It was time for me to get my children anyway.

Mathrom rose as well, the flush of anger coloring his pale cheeks. "Rody is my friend, someone I've known since our childhood. He's had my back several times when the goldys have tried to beat us down when we're fighting for Zacatik rights. Why should I believe you, a stranger, a man I don't even know?"

My own temper flaring again I called him a bad name in the Kukiya language and smiled as his color deepened. He'd understood me. At least he knew enough of the old language to know when I was insulting him.

"Believe what you want, nephew. I don't really care. Ask someone older in your family—or Golannah's to tell you about the blood feud with Rody's ancestor Azogi. I don't know your mother, but if you trust your sister, ask her why she doesn't like this man.

"And then listen to the one in your dreams trying very hard to protect you. Nachoga's power came from Cougar, Kitahtla's power came from Cougar, the spirit and puwa of the big cat is one of the beings linked to your lineage.

"And that knowledge and power that uniting with Cougar would give you is what truly frightens this man and his demon ally. He says he is your friend—but is not, and I hope you are smart enough to figure that out one day. Until then, it is you who can, 'fuck off.'"

As I started to walk away he called to me, "Wait, are you saying that you yourself are a Puhani?"

I turned. "Some have called me that, but I am definitely not like this man Rody."

Hurrying to catch up to me, he called out, "Please, I need to ask you things. Rody says he's a Puhani, but I think he doesn't know as much as he claims. Could you teach me about Cougar Puwa?"

"Maybe. I could teach you, if you ever smarten up. Cougar's puwa could be yours one day—if you survive your stupidity that long. Come find me when you are willing to change your ways, and make the necessary sacrifices to be worthy of that Gift."

"Wait, I don't understand."

I laughed, but there was no mirth in the sound. "No, I'm sure you don't, disrespectful kitten. To become a true warrior of the Kukiya you must pledge your life, and your Gift in service to the People like the man whose name you want to claim."

"I will do whatever you want if you will teach me. When can I start?"

"Not yet, you aren't ready. Right now you are like your malicer friend; you want Cougar's Gift for your own selfish reasons. As I said, come find me when you smarten up."

"But how will I find you? Give me your address and far-speak number, at least."

I snorted my disbelief. "The teachings to gain the power of a Puwa Gift isn't like taking a class at the Lectorium. You will have to prove yourself worthy. Finding me will be your first lesson—after you rid the malicer from your life. No more talk now; I have to go."

It was growing late, the children would be out of class soon and I had neither the time nor the patience to argue with him or wait on mecho-transit right then.

Feeling daring, and maybe hoping to shock and frighten him a bit I made the transfer when he could still see me.

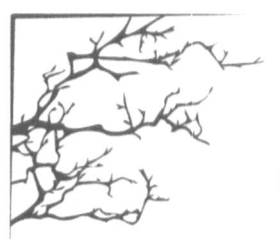

Chapter Nineteen

The children could tell when I retrieved them from their school that I was upset about something, so I tried to mask my feelings. Collecting Bijah, I took them to their favorite park to run off some of their energy before we all went home for the evening meal. Bijah wasn't fooled, however. She could read the disruptive currents in a person's spirit fire nearly as well as I could, thanks to Aqwissa's tutelage.

Knowing that, I made sure that the little dragon-lizard assured her that yes, earlier I had been angered by someone—not her—or anyone living at our house, but now I was calming down, and would be myself again soon.

Later when Gahji and I were cuddled close in our bed I told her about my frustrating day. She too had sensed my inner turmoil, but knew she didn't need to press me about it. I would tell her—eventually.

When I finished my tale she was suitably comforting and enraged by Mathrom's disrespectful behavior.

"If Rushton or any of the other instructors at the Lectorium had to put up with a fraction of what he said to you, I can understand why the little mud worm is labeled trouble. I would have expelled the little shit before now."

She thought about it a moment longer then said, "They probably haven't, because if he's registered as a tribal member, in spite of his looks, he comes with Zacatik money and the greedy shits in administration wouldn't want to give that up—unless he did something to piss them off really bad."

I chuckled and kissed her. "I love you, my protective mama bear." She punched me playfully and then returned my kiss.

For the rest of that winter I avoided Mathrom's efforts to contact me. He was smart enough to remember that I worked at the Friendship house, but not smart enough to realize that I could tell without speaking to him that he hadn't done what I told him to do. The stink of Azogi's curse was all over him. He was playing games with me, and so I ignored him.

One time when he came in with a pretty young woman, fair of skin, with a reddish tent to her long brown hair, and family features that reminded me of my mother's, I used my Gift to ensure he didn't see me.

I was sitting at the Elder's table with Kutima when I heard him asking someone by the door for me. When the person told him where I was, he and the woman with him came into the dining room. With some amusement I watched him scan the room, his glance passing right over me without seeing me.

After he and his companion walked around a few times, talking to people they knew and asked about me, Mathrom gave up in disgust and left. They young woman, however, decided to stay for the meal and sat down at a far table with some other young people she knew.

I watched her closely for the rest of the meal, wondering if this was a trick the two siblings had cooked up between them to try and flush me out into the open. When time passed and Aqwissa confirmed that Mathrom wasn't hiding and waiting to pounce on me, like the big cat he truly was, I decided to go speak to her. She had remained reading a text book and taking notes after her friends ate and left.

Turning to Kutima, I said in our language, "I need to talk to that young woman sitting over there." I pointed to Saskina. "I might be a little late for our class."

With a puzzled expression Kutima glanced in her direction then returned his attention to me. "I saw her come in with a young man a while ago and I thought they were asking for you, but you didn't invite them to join us. What's going on? That isn't like you."

"I know, but I have my reasons, which I can explain later. Those two are my sister Kitahtla's grandchildren. My niece I have no problem talking to at the moment, but the young man is another matter."

"Kitahtla, have you found her at last?"

"I've found her descendants anyway—I'm not sure about her. I hope to find out more by talking to my niece."

"Go ahead then; I know this is important to you."

I excused myself from the Elders, and with the explanation of bringing mine and Kutima's empty bowls and plates to the kitchen I sat down uninvited next to Saskina when I finished my task.

Startled she looked up from the book she was reading. The little desert fox in her spirit fire cocked its head to stare at me. "Greetings, niece, did you like the meal we had today? Most Kukiya I know don't care for fish much, but I caught some of the ones used to make the soup, so I hope you enjoyed it."

She stared at me for a long moment, her mouth falling open. At last she gathered her wits enough to say, "Yes I did, thank you—uh, uncle?"

I smiled. "That's good. It makes me happy to know people appreciate my efforts."

She studied me then asked, "You must be Tas Cougarson? Did you just come in and somebody tell you we were looking for you?"

My smile widened. "No, I've been sitting at the Elders' table over there beside the elder in the wheeled chair this entire time."

Surprised, she glanced at Kutima and then returned her attention to me. "How?" When I only continued to smile she swallowed hard, and said, "My brother has been looking for you."

"I know, but I'm not going to let him find me until he does what I told him to do. If he wants me to teach him about his inherited Cougar power he will need to learn the disciplines of a warrior and a Puhani."

Curious now, she thought about my words then said, "I always wondered about the Cougar in his aura that Granny Kitah saw. She also wouldn't teach him—said he wasn't ready."

Then she frowned. "If you can see the Cougar what do you see when you look at me?"

"I see a little desert fox. But you already know who is your guide and teacher. Now no more little tests, you either accept who I say I am, or not. I won't play childish games with another Cougarson relative."

Startled that I had seen through her ploy her eyes widened. At last she cleared her throat and looked down at her notes. "If what Mathrom told me is true about Granny Kitah having an older brother, it is so unbelievable. I didn't mean to offend you."

Looking me in the eye, she asked, "Why did you let me find you?"

"Because you seem like a more sensible person than your brother and I wanted to find out. Women usually are, according to my wife, anyway. To her all men are idiots—accept for me, I hope. I am the exception—at least most of the time."

She laughed. "She sounds like my kind of woman. I would like to meet her someday."

"You will I'm sure. I'm not hiding from you—as long as you keep my secret. It's only your brother I am avoiding for the moment."

"And why is that, if I may ask?"

"You may ask. When I first saw him at the Lectorium I recognized him right away, because of his physical resemblance to his ancestor Nachoga. I told Mathrom that he was in danger from his association with a man called Rody. That one is a malicer and he wishes your brother and your whole family ill.

"Whether Rody is strong enough in his puwa at this stage in his life to know and use the forces that drive him I haven't taken the time to find out. He may be just an unknowing vessel for the old curse, but I told Mathrom if he wanted me to teach him he was going to have to abandon his friendship with that man."

"But he has, uncle, and that's why I agreed to come here with him today. He confessed to me what you told him about Rody—and I agree with you. I didn't know he was a malicer, but I always knew there was something about him I didn't like. Mathrom assured me he wasn't seeing him anymore."

Saskina dropped her eyes and admitted with some embarrassment, "He was hoping if you saw me with him you might come over to talk to us."

I laughed. "Then the more fool he— and you can tell him that for me, too. I smelled the stink of Azogi's blood feud curse all over him before he even stepped inside the dining room. He lied to you and is playing games with me—and I won't have it."

All joking aside I rudely stared her in the eye so she would understand how serious I was. "If he thinks to trick me and play games with me, then as a great uncle in your lineage I will gladly see to his discipline. He will learn—in most unpleasant ways—what it means to mess with someone who truly has power."

While we'd been talking the cleanup crew had come in and started putting away tables and chairs. I stood, Saskina rising, too. "I have to go help teach the Qwani'Yan language class in a room down the hall. You are welcome to join us if you like."

Glancing at the time-tell on her wrist she shook her head. "No, another day maybe, but I have a test to study for, so I better go. But I would like to talk to you again—if you permit."

"I would like that, too. When I was taken away from the desert I hadn't planned on being gone so long. There is so much I would like to know about the family. And, if you permit I will come visit you in the Dream and then we can get to know each other better and talk more freely."

She turned back to stare at me. "You can actually do that?"

"I can, but I am no malicer to force my way into your dreams. I will only come to you, if you give me your permission."

Unsure if she believed me she considered for a moment then nodded. As she started to leave once more, I stopped her again. "One last question, is your granny Kitah still alive? Your brother wouldn't tell me."

She muttered something uncomplimentary about him under her breath before nodding. "Granny is, but she doesn't live here in Seatown anymore. She's quite old—in her mid-nineties, I think. She said the damp air on the coast bothered her bones, so she went back to the family rancha near the Preserve where my mother is still living."

Alive, she was alive. Excitement rising like smoke offered in a prayer, I smiled. "Niece, we will definitely have to talk more then."

I waited about four days, before contacting Saskina directly in her dreams. I checked on her a bit before that, I will admit, without letting her know. Ethically I knew I was balanced on the knife's edge by doing so, but I was also worried about her. If Rody found out about our connection...

As I suspected when I spied, she *had* told Mathrom of our conversation and he was furious about it. They had a big argument and I was pleased to see that she stood up to him and told him he had lied to her about Rody and it was his own fault if I was ignoring him.

The night I did come into her dream to speak to her for the first time she was sitting in an empty classroom, her books open on the table before her while she pondered the results of the test she had taken that day.

With the silver dragon-lizard curled around my chest and her head on my shoulder, I took a seat at the desk facing her. <<I'm sure you did just fine on the test.>>

Startled she looked up and then smiled, delighted. <<Are you really here and I'm not just imagining you?>>

I laughed. <<No, you aren't imagining me. I am truly here in your dream and I can prove it.>> I stroked Aqwissa who rumbled her dragon purr, enjoying my touch. <<You never saw my companion Aqwissa when we met before, so you couldn't be imagining her with me, eh?>>

She laughed, <<No I guess not.>>

We talked for a long while that night and before I left her I pressed a stone amulet that I had carved with my dragon glyph into her hand and folded her fingers tight around it. <<As more proof of my presence, when you wake you will find my token in your hand.>>

She examined the stone then looked up at my face, puzzled. I touched the similar dragon glyph on my face, which was visible while we were in the spirit world of the Dream. <<Keep my token with you to strengthen our connection. It will also protect you from the old curse. If you hold it and think of me, I will know.>>

I laughed at her expression. <<Have a little faith, niece, eh? >>

Over that rainy winter we were both busy with classes so I didn't see her in the flesh as often as I might have liked, so I had to be content with our dream visits. On one occasion, after another frustrating attempt on Mathrom's part to confront and corner me at Friendship House when he knew I was scheduled to teach, I asked her, <<What is your brother's obsessive attraction to this man who means him no good?

<<Rody is using his power to strengthen his connection to your brother, but Mathrom himself is using his untrained Gift to enhance the bond, too. Even though a part of him knows this man is dangerous for him. Why is he doing that?>>

She thought about it for a long moment before speaking. <<We didn't go to a live-away school like most of the kids on the Preserve we knew growing up, so that set us apart. We went to a day school in the closest imperial settlement, like a lot of mixed race people, and some tribal kids, like us, too.

<<Caught in the middle it wasn't easy for us—Mathrom especially. Looking like an imperial we got the racism in reverse, you could say. Mathrom became a fighter even as a young one. He is fierce and very loyal to his friends, and giving his all to whatever cause he believes in.

<<Mathrom was fair enough to pass and hang out with the imperial settler kids, but he chose to proclaim his Kukiya heritage and champion our People's rights. Unfortunately the browner members of our tribe and family often turned on him and didn't accept him as one of the People no matter what he did. Rody was one of the few darker tribal members who welcomed his friendship. That's probably why it's so hard for him to do what you want.>>

Her words saddened me. Such prejudice was another wall the imperials had created to divide us.<<Though a true chamuqwani by birth your ancestor Nachoga was raised Kukiya, and somehow he inherited the family's cougar puwa, too. But because of his fair skin, he, like you and your brother, always faced that racial problem, as well. Even though he was Golannah's brother and a fierce war leader, there were families like Rody's, who hated him and worked against him whenever they could.>>

<<I don't understand how you know all this?>>

I smiled. <<Because, niece, I am much older than I look. Kitahtla is my younger sister, our mothers are the same. Amima died at the gold creek massacre,and your Granny Kitah was raised by my uncle and his wife after I was captured and Nachoga was tortured and hanged.>>

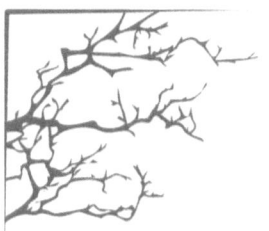

Chapter Twenty

Our baby boy was born just as the frogs began to sing in the reedy ponds in the forest, and the cold weather ceremonies were ending for the year. I had just arrived home with the older children when Gahji unexpectedly splashed the baby's life water onto the kitchen floor.

Soon after that her pains started, and she had me call Aunty Megara on the far-speak. As the women arrived for the birth, all the males in the household were ordered to leave.

Aqwissa, also being a female, I argued should stay. To ease my mind, if for no other reason, my sweet bear woman finally agreed. Slipping her as a silver bracelet onto Gahji's arm I kissed her on the forehead and hastily left before Aunty could yell at me or find the willow switch she joked she might have to get if I didn't go on my own.

Elder Samul collected me, Tuunac and Stakaya and our bags of clothes and bedding in his mecho-cart and we made the short trip over to his house to stay for the seven day confinement.

During this time it was customary for all male relatives to stay away. But with Aqwissa and Bijah there, with whom I was linked, I would be present in spirit at least. I was there, I told myself, to ease my bear woman's pain and shield her and my son from any evil intent that might be aimed at my loved ones during that vulnerable time.

My beautiful bear woman gave birth to a healthy baby boy after a short but intense labor. Through my link with Aqwissa I was able to be at his birth and together we eased her discomfort as much as we could. I also was able to assure Bijah when she started to cry that her mother wasn't going to die when she saw all the blood that arrived with the birth of her new brother.

At Uncle Samul's I announced the birth of our son moments before the far-speak rang officially giving us the news. I knew by observing his spirit fire that Tuunac, too had been worried about his mother, so I hugged him close, and told him that as a nearly grown man he was going to have to help me take care of the little one in the future.

During our exile I kept him out of school and took him with me to my secret bush camp sometimes, teaching him how to set snares and other things a boy of his age would have known, if he had lived in my northern village. "Someday you will have to help me teach the little one how to do these things," I told him and he seemed proud to be treated in such an adult way.

Soon enough we were allowed back into the women's sanctuary and I was so excited to really see him. Through my mind link with both Aqwissa and Bijah I had witnessed the little one's birth, but to hold him in my arms for the first time, and feel his soft cheek next to mine filled my heart with both joy and wonder. He had a cap of wavy dark hair, a red bow of a mouth and enigmatic dark eyes that hinted of the otherworldly blood in his lineage.

To my amusement, the guardian that watched me from my son's spirit fire wasn't a seal like my father's or mine, but my grandfather's lake otter, who, in turn, gazed back at me with his own ironic mirth.

<<Oh, little otter, I think you are going to keep your seal father always swimming fast to keep ahead of your playful tricks,>> I told him.

When I told Gahji that night about his otter guardian as I held her in my arms, she smiled at the little pup, sucking greedily at her rounded breast and said, "I wonder if he will also inherit the Elder's healing Qwakaiva as well."

"Possibly, he could even be a great Qwakaihi if so, inheriting the healing Gift from his mother as well as his grandfather. And that may mean trouble for a poor seal father like me."

"Trouble? What are you talking about?"

I explained a bit about the traditional rivalry between Qwa'osi the Otter and Co'yeh the Seal that I had heard stories of as a child. She chuckled.

"I guess, like always it's going to be up to me, as the mama bear in this family to keep the peace and smarten everybody up."

When all the trees were green and bright colored flowers bloomed everywhere, our little otter, O'siyan, was about three moons old. Unable to contain our joy any longer, we decided to have a party to celebrate his birth in the modern fashion. Soon enough Gahji would have to go back to her job at the Seatown infirmarium—part time—and we would be too tired and busy to host an event if we waited till the summer feasts.

While Aunty Megara took charge of the aunties and cousins cleaning the house and cooking, I was kept busy fishing and gathering traditional foods with Tuunac, Stakaya, and a couple of his older cousins, one of whom owned guns and an old mecho-cart.

It amused me when Stakaya and his cousin Denny both managed to kill a deer on tribal land up in the mountains, but then didn't know what to do with it. It was a good thing that they brought me and Tuunac along, because neither of the young hunters knew the proper way to make an offering, or skin and prepare the meat. So, I ended up giving the young hunters a lesson on how to care for the animals properly, before we were finished that day.

I had decided, with Gahji's approval, to invite Saskina to the party. Contacting her through our dreams I told her about the new baby and the celebration. She was delighted, excited and agreed to come. She had been wanting to meet my family, I knew, but before then I hadn't felt comfortable with inviting her to my sanctuary.

On the special day I sent Stakaya off to collect the mysterious relative from a kaf-tea room near the downtown library, because, as I told her, we lived in a dangerous part of town and she should have an escort.

Gahji and I exchanged an amused look when the grumpy young man who had been awakened early and then sent to fetch her was all smiles, laughing and joking when he returned with this pretty new cousin in tow.

We had also wanted to let Star Swimmer know about his new grandson, so I had tried contacting my father within the Dream, but was unable to reach him.

At the time, I recall that I wasn't too worried about that. As I explained to my sweet bear, "Time swirls and twists in unpredictable patterns from one realm of reality to another. What seems like years here on Earth Mother might be no more than a blink of an eye in the realm where he is swimming at the moment. I will keep trying to make contact, but in the meantime we will just have to wait to share our news."

By the afternoon our house was brimming over with people and noise. The scent of roasting fish and deer meat competed with the fragrance of baking cakes and scau-bread.

To avoid chaos in the kitchen I borrowed a couple long tables from work to set up outside in the back yard. Most of the food and drink we made, or relatives brought, was set on them and neighbors and a few of the homeless who always gathered by the railroad tracks were also welcome to share in the feast if they left their drugs and bottles behind.

I had made our bedroom off limits, and using my Gift I created a quiet space within it, for the baby and Gahji to retreat into, whenever she felt overwhelmed and needed a rest. This quiet place was available for Kutima as well, should he need it, but with a little help from me and Aqwissa he had remained alert and happy, chatting with younger friends and relatives.

The afternoon shadows were lengthening into the soft shades of evening when someone turned off Gahji's music player. And a few Elders and their students brought out hand drums to begin the more traditional singing and dancing.

I was thinking about joining them when suddenly Aqwissa hissed a warning. <<Siyatli brother, the enemy malicer is near.>>

Muttering a chamuqwani curse under my breath I followed as she guided me away from the backyard activity. Using my Gift as I stepped out onto the front porch I saw him right away.

His red-eyed demon perched on his shoulder Rody had ineptly concealed himself within the foliage of a clump of overgrown bushes by the vacant house across the street. And, just behind him among the leaves was a nervous Mathrom.

As I stepped quietly out and closed the front door behind me Rody saw me and smirked. Then he said loud enough for both Mathrom and me to hear, "Didn't I tell you that I could find him for you? I have more puwa than that fake Puhani who claims he is your uncle. He can't hide from me."

Glancing around Mathrom also saw me then, and murmured in an urgent whisper, "All right you did it—you found his house, but there's too many people here let's go we can come back another day and talk to him about this curse stuff you never heard of."

Talk to me? Not going to happen, dog humper!

My rage suddenly turning to ice in my veins I returned the malicer's smirk with a toothy smile, showing my canines. I stepped down off the porch and walked slowly towards them. In the middle of the empty street

I stopped,. Still smiling I said to my companion, <<I will take care of the humans, my qwissa. You deal with the demon.>>

<<Can I kill and eat it?>>

<<If it won't make you sick, yes, but have a care, others of its kind may ambush you if you have to give chase into the Beyond.>>

<<It will not last long enough to run.>> she promised.

Without giving the malicer time to shield from an attack I lifted him up and slammed him hard against the brick wall of the vacant house next to their hiding place. At the same moment the little dragon-lizard sprang from my wrist to leap upon Rody's shoulder. She grabbed the hairy demon between her fierce jaws and shook it like a dog killing a rabbit. The creature screeched and clawed frantically at her and its human host, hoping to escape.

Slumping to the ground Rody let out a terrified scream as blood appeared in long claw marks on his face and down his arm.

As far as anyone without spirit-sight could tell I hadn't moved; I was still just standing in the middle of the street, staring at the crazy man, bloody and writhing trying to defend himself from an invisible adversary.

"I warned you, malicer, what would happen if you came near me and mine," I hissed through clenched teeth. He would have like to run away, but I held him frozen in place. I curled my hand into a fist as I tightened my hold around his throat. "Stupid dust eater," I snarled in Kukiyatan. "Maybe I should just kill you here and now like your demon, eh?"

"My what?" Realizing at last that his demon was now gone, Rody let out a scream of anguish and began to cry uncontrollably. "It's gone—it's gone," he wailed. "What did you do to it—to me."

"What did I do? I stripped you of your power to do more evil in this world, malicer," I snarled. "But if you find another someday to enslave yourself to and come at me again, I will kill you—and that is a promise."

"Not if I can get to you and your family first," he growled back.

"Tas, look out!" I heard Stakaya shout a moment before I saw a dark shadow swing a thick branch at my head as he charged me.

"Damn you, we just wanted to talk! It's you that's the malicer! Leave him alone!" Mathrom shouted.

I barely had time to duck his blow, before the branch clipped me and I staggered, losing control of my hold on Rody. Taking advantage of my distraction the malicer lurched away in a stumbling run. Ignoring my command for her to go after Rody, Aqwissa decided that Mathrom was the more immediate danger.

She materialized, enlarged and pounced, bearing him to the ground under her, claws digging into his shoulder, her fangs at his throat.

Racing over to us, a trembling and tearful Saskina grabbed my arm and pleaded, "Uncle, don't kill him. He's my brother—even if he *is* misguided and stupid."

Focused totally on the threat I hadn't noticed Stakaya and Saskina sitting in the shadows cuddled together in the basket swing, when I came out of the house. Though neither had more Qwakaiva than what normal humans have, they had witnessed my attack and were shaken up by the experience.

I sighed, and shook off her hand, but my temper had calmed by then. Still visible to them Aqwissa crouched atop my nephew snarling every time he tried to move. I walked over to them and looked down at my terrified nephew. Cougar watched me approach, but didn't snarl or make an aggressive move towards me. He knew this lesson was well-earned.

<<Oh, Father Nachoga, It would seem that the reverberations from the old curse are still echoing through the generations. If you are still linked to the Cougar guardian that is trying to protect this stupid descendant of yours, please advise me what to do with this poor deceived relative.>>

"I'm not going to kill him, niece. Unless he pushes me too far, I love my sister Kitahtla too much for that."

Standing over him I called Aqwissa to me. She leapt off her pray and reformed herself back into the silver bracelet upon my arm. Before Mathrom could get to his feet and run away, too, I used my power to jerk him to his feet, then froze him in place. From the neck down he couldn't move. "Stupid, stubborn, tom kitten, do you know how close you came to dying just now?" I hissed.

I touched my arm to make my point perfectly clear. "This one would have killed you if you had been more of a threat to me. Remember that, before you try to hit me again."

"I-I will remember. But we just wanted to talk. Rody said he'd never heard of any stupid family curse," Mathrom stammered. He glanced at his sister, his eyes pleading for her help.

"Really? And does that denial include the Aka demon sitting on his shoulder and directing him?" Mathrom stared at me as if I had just grown moose antlers.

Suddenly I realized that this modern child had no idea of the unseen forces massing about him. Unable to bond with Cougar he couldn't see with his spirit sight—he didn't know.

"What do you plan to do with him, old one?" Elder Samul said from behind my left shoulder.

When I glanced around I saw a shocked and frightened audience of Saskina, Stakaya, and little Bijah with her thumb in mouth, staring wide-eyed at me, and the bloody and disheveled young man I held up with my Qwakaiva. Expressionless, Elder Samul held Bijah's hand to comfort her and repeated his question.

Then he added, "Bijah came and got me, she knew something was wrong and was worried."

I brushed a hand across my face and scowled when it came away red. I swore a soldier's oath and glared murderously at Mathrom. "I'll be fine. But I'd better get cleaned up before Gahji sees me."

"She's in your bedroom with the baby taking a nap, I think."

"Good, maybe she won't see me before I wash the blood off."

The singing and noise from the backyard had drowned out any cries made by my battle with the enemy and no one had come to investigate my absence. I'd been lucky about that and also because no one had called the goldys yet. Only these few had witnessed.

Glaring at Mathrom, the Elder asked as if reading my mind, "We should get out of the street before the goldys come by. What do you want to do with this piece of shit?"

"A piece of shit he may be, but he is also a relative. I don't know yet what I will do with him. But you are right, we need to get out of the street."

"Please, uncle Tas, just let me go. I won't come back—I promise," Mathrom begged.

I laughed, but there was no mirth in the sound. "Want to call me uncle now, eh?" I snorted. "Well, your leaving isn't one of your options at the moment, nephew. Bringing that dog-humping malicer to my home to threaten the safety of my wife and my children has changed the rules. You aren't going anywhere for a while, till I decide what to do with you."

Motioning for Stakaya and elder Samul to help me carry Mathrom's immobile body into the house we plunked him down in a chair in the corner of the living room, where I glued his feet to the chair's legs and one arm to the chair as well. While I did that, I sent the two young people off to the indoor privy to quietly gather up supplies to clean and bandage our injuries.

"I'll go back outside, and keep anyone from coming in to disturb you, younger brother," Elder Samul offered. "Call me if you need me."

"Thank you; I will."

As we were cleaning up I happened to notice that Kutima had been sitting in the living room for the entire time. He'd been watching the proceedings without comment, an amused smile curving his thin lips.

"Ah, old friend, did we interrupt your rest? Are you getting tired at last? Do I need to get Rushton or Martin or someone else to bring you home?" I stammered.

He wheezed a laugh and shook his head. "Not just yet. You can teach tomorrow while I stay home and sleep if need be. There's too much excitement going on here for me to think about being tired."

He chuckled again. "Watching you and young Stakaya hauling your frozen prey into the house just now does my old heart good. It reminded me about the time you and the warband took Ronalton out of the dorm in a snow storm to teach him manners and the error of his ways."

I laughed with him. "Yes, I remember. Do you know whatever happened to that bully of a head boy? Did he die in the fire?"

"No, he was badly burned but survived. But after I left with Collin I never heard much about what happened to the rest of the survivors."

"Who is Ronalton?" the ever curious Stakaya wanted to know.

"A dog turd that liked to beat up on other children when the Elder and I were at Saint Yon's Live-away School. And, since Kutima was often the victim of his malice, as our little warband's Puhani, I helped take care of the problem he posed for all of us."

"What happened?" Intrigued, Saskina wanted to know.

I shook my head and started for the kitchen. "Ask the Elder to tell you, if you want. He was there and a part of our warband. But for right now I should go check on the people outside."

Kutima's eyes were alight with mischief, "Do you really want me to tell them about your exploits at the school and running wild with the Kukiya outlaws, Tas? Though I wasn't there for that part of your early life, Kuweya told me quite a bit while he was waiting to testify for the Imperial Commission, you know."

Anxious to leave before I forgot about my intention not to strangle my nephew, I just shrugged and kept heading for the kitchen. "No, I didn't know. Tell them whatever you like."

Kutima chuckled and glanced at Mathrom. "Well, Tas, you know how I love to tell stories and here you have given me a 'captive' audience, how can I resist? Is he the one you were telling me about?"

I laughed and turned back to face him. "Yes he is. Both Mathrom and Saskina are Kitahtla's grandchildren."

"I see. What do you plan to do with him, if I may ask?"

"You may ask, but I haven't decided yet. Tell the dog turd whatever you want, and Saskina can bring him something to eat and drink, but he stays in that chair until I say otherwise."

"But what if I have to pee," Mathrom whined.

I gave him a disgusted glare. "Hold it or wet yourself—I don't care. You are staying put till I say so."

Suddenly needing a way to express the tangle of my pent up emotions, I headed for the kitchen again. "I think I hear the drum starting up and I want to sing." I called over my shoulder to them.

As I went out the back door I heard Saskina say, "Did you know our Granny Kitah back then?"

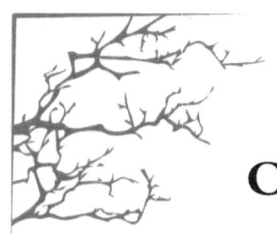

Chapter Twenty-One

O nce more in the back yard I saw that most of the families with younger children were packing up to go home. Some of the adults might return later, if the goldys didn't arrive to break things up. The Elders and their students were standing near a fire someone had built warming the drums for the next song.

I think Samul could see that I was still unsettled. He raised his drumstick to call me over. "There you are, younger brother, someone was just asking about you." He began quietly tapping the hand drum he held, the line of other drummers joining in. "Give us a song, eh?"

Walking over to them I could feel the tears forming in the corners of my eyes. After all I had gone through during my turbulent childhood I rejoiced in the family and the life I now had. But after what had happened earlier I knew how fragile my happiness truly was—and I was afraid. I took Rody's threat seriously. If not him there would be another enemy waiting in the shadows to snatch my prized contentment away from me.

Picking up the skin bag of smudging mixture lying on a rock by the fire, I tossed some of its contents into the flames. Gathering the smoke between my hands, I bathed my face and body in its healing breath.

As I did that I prayed for my ancestors and the Unseen Ones to guard my family and to give me the strength to guide and protect them, and this wounded world I had sworn to Kunai I would love and defend.

Crossing to stand by Samul I opened my mouth and began to sing. I sang and I sang, enhancing my music and the images I formed in my listeners' minds with my Qwakaiva. My hopes, my fears, my memories of the past, I let my feelings unravel and reform in the Kadence of my songs until my throat was dry and hoarse.

When I fell silent at last no one spoke, still enthralled within my conjure. Only the crackling of the flames could be heard in our yard. Suddenly exhausted and overwhelmed I sank to the ground, bowed my head and tossed more of the sacred herbs into Fire. I whispered a silent prayer of gratitude and placed my hands flat on the earth to draw up her strength.

When I finished Elder Samul placed a hand on my shoulder and thanked me, murmuring his own prayer of blessing in the Smotahlik language, as he drew me to my feet. When I rose I turned and happened to glance up at our back porch. Gahji was sitting in the rocker I had bought her, our baby resting in her arms. Our eyes met and she smiled at me, telling me with her eyes how much she loved me.

Farther down the porch I noticed that Kutima had coaxed some of the onlookers to carry Mathrom, still glued to his chair out to the porch so he could be a part of the festivities. There was an expression of both confusion and wonder on his face when I met his eye. I tried very hard not to smirk.

I guessed that with the malicer's hold over him broken for the moment, Cougar had enabled him to experience the images I had been projecting. He had learned tonight a small taste of what it meant to be a Puhani of the People. I hoped he would change; I hoped he would prove receptive to my teachings.

I was encouraged, but I wasn't prepared to release him and risk him slipping back into old habits. So with that in mind, I kept him bound to his chair in our home for the next four days.

Smiling in a wide grin that displayed my canines, I told him when everyone was getting ready for bed that night and he begged me to let him go home, "Don't think of your confinement as a punishment—though it is that too—but more as a modern-day spirit-vigil."

When he opened his mouth to angrily protest, I warned him, "I can always close your mouth with my puwa, if you make noise and awake our baby, so don't push me. You may be family, but until you prove to me that you can be trusted, I intend to treat you as enemy.

"Stakaya has agreed to stay with his cousin Denny, so we will put you and your chair in his bedroom for your vigil. That way you won't disturb my wife and the children. She can't release you, when I am away hunting or at work, so don't bother asking. Use your time to pray and welcome Cougar into your life."

"But I have things to do—people counting on me—"

"You have no classes at the Lectorium at the moment, so your sister tells me," I interrupted, "and as for your 'other' concerns, you will have to make choices.

"If you want to pursue your political protests and other things of that nature after this confinement I won't stop you. But I won't teach you, either."

"But that's not fair," he complained. "Protesting how the government treats our People is important. And if I could use my puwa to help us gain our goals, that's a noble use of a Puhani's gift, right?"

"If you are sure you know what the best path is, yes. But in order to do that, your emotions must be unclouded with anger, fear, or even love. You have to fly high like Eagle and see the whole situation before you ask for the power to change it. If you don't have that Gift, the unforeseen consequences of your conjure may not be to your liking."

He thought about it for a moment and then grumped, "But the Elder told me that you used to go on raids and use your power to help the warriors, so why is it different when I want to do something to help our people now, eh?"

"It isn't, if your intent is true and honorable, but did Kutima also tell you that I made mistakes back then and suffered for it?"

"N-no."

I snorted my disgust. "There is a price for using your Gift, so a Puhani also has to be willing to pay it before he invokes help from those living in the Beyond. I paid for my uses—especially my mistakes—with abuse and torture. Are you willing to endure such consequences for the use of your power, if you are wrong?"

He frowned, suddenly confused. "I don't understand."

"When you become a Puhani – a true Puhani – much of your life is no longer your own. You are committed to a life of sacrifice and service to the people, not to your own selfish desires, like a malicer."

"But I'm not a malicer, and my friend Rody wasn't using his power for selfish reasons. He and I really do want to help the People. Our activities were carried out to force the imperial government into making things change."

Remembering Dotsuwa and his quarrel with Nachoga over a woman, I said, "Jealousy is a terrible sickness affecting some people. Are you sure about Rody's motives?"

"Yeah, I'm sure."

"Then why did he tell you that the Cougar you kept seeing in your dreams was evil, hmm? You knew in your heart what he said wasn't true, so why did you keep listening? Saskina told me that your Granny Kitah told you that Cougar was your guide, and then she refused to teach you when you ignored her warnings and continued on your destructive path.

"On the surface Rody's actions may have appeared noble, but dive a little deeper, nephew. Why did that man—who claims to be your friend, use his puwa to blind you from your true source of power? Could it be so that you would remain dependent on him to direct and advise you?" And more importantly, why did you let him? Think on that while you sit in your chair for the next few days."

When I came home next day after collecting Tuunac and Bijah I found Angika and Gahji in the kitchen cooking with a cleaned up Mathrom drinking kaf-tea at the kitchen table. His clothes were the same dirt and blood-crusted mess, but Mathrom's hair was washed and neatly braided, and his scruffy beard had been removed—and unfortunately for my peace of mind, he resembled his ancestor even more.

Gahji burst out laughing when she saw my face. Folding her arms across her breast she gave me her "give me no nonsense" mama bear look. "He stank and his hair was a tangled mess. I wasn't going to have any stupid zaunk in my house looking like that, so Angika and I did the best we could. Now if you want him back in Stakaya's room you can put him there yourself, but take off his nasty clothes and give him some of my brother's things to wear while I decide if I want to wash his—or burn them."

"All right," I said meekly, "I will do that, but how did you get him out here to the kitchen?"

"I called Aunty Megara and she sent my brother and cousin Denny over to help us."

Trying to hide my amusement I kissed her, so she wouldn't see my smile. "Well, my sweet mama bear, I will do that for you."

I released Mathrom from his chair. He stood up gratefully and stretched, but made no move to run. I would only send Aqwissa to fetch him if he did, and he was smart enough to realize that by now. Motioning him to the indoor privy down the hall, I said, "Go take a shower, so your aunty won't have to smell you. I'll bring you some of Stakaya's or my old clothes to put on, before I put you back on your chair."

"Do you have to do that? I promise I won't run away."

"Yes, if you want to become a warrior for the people you will need to endure pain and discomfort—make sacrifices. Sitting in a chair, in a warm dry room, under the protection of caring family is nothing compared to what me and your Kukiya relations lived through during the wars."

"Were you confined like you are making me do?"

I snorted and shook my head. "You have no idea..." I motioned down the hall. "Go before I change my mind and put you back dirty."

When I heard the water running I went back into the kitchen. The meal was almost done. I poured myself a cup of kaf-tea and leaned against the hall doorway, staying out of the way of my women.

Using our Qwani'Ya word for father, Angika, who was setting the table asked, "Appi, should I set out a plate for the new cousin?"

I sighed. "Do you want him to eat with us?"

She thought about it for a moment then giggled and nodded. "Yes."

I glanced at her mother for her permission. Gahji rolled her eyes and went back to her cooking. Deciding to tease her I said to Angika, "And you want Mathrom to eat with us because you think he's cute, eh? Want to sit by him, too?" When she giggled again and blushed I laughed. "My sweet eldest girl is growing up. What's a poor seal man to do, eh?"

My bear woman groaned. "Don't encourage her. You will be sending your little pet to chase away unwanted male admirers soon enough."

I laughed and went into the laundry area to search for clean clothes.

When Mathrom's time of confinement was nearing its end his sister called me on the far-speak all excited. "I was able to speak to granny when my mother was in town to get groceries. I told her about you coming back, and I explained about Mathrom's troubles.

"She is so excited. She wants my brother to come stay with her for a while. She has things to pass onto him if he's finally ready. I told her about your family and the new baby. She hopes you will come see her, too, when you are able."

"I will have to work on that, but I do want to see her as soon as possible. Can your mother or another relative bring her out to Seatown instead? We can have her stay with the girls or put her in Stakaya's room."

She hesitated and I sensed there was a problem. At last she took a deep breath and admitted. "I don't think that would be possible. My mother Qwadalah is a hard woman to deal with. Granny is almost a prisoner under her care. She never takes her anywhere except to the doctor."

I knew she couldn't see my horrified face, but Gahji could, and came over to hug me to offer her support. "I don't understand, why would she do that?" I said into the far-speak.

"I'm sure you've heard our family had it tough, being the children of renegades and outlaws. Mama always wants to be in control—maybe because of what happened to her back then—I'm just guessing. As a child I tried to stay on her good side, but Mathrom has always been a rebel. She was very mean to him growing up and they fought constantly. Both of us left home as early as we could."

"This is terrible," I said, "but what about other relatives? Rushton told me that my sister had three children, where were that aunt and uncle when you and your brother needed them? And what about Golannah's descendants, for that matter, didn't they want to help you?"

"My aunt Janata I haven't seen in years—not sure where she is living now. Uncle Rigby died as a soldier years ago. As for Golannah's family, no they didn't help us. I don't know what started the talk, but Golannah's relatives blamed his chamuqwani brother for the chief's capture and death. Mathrom got in terrible fights at school defending his reputation from the hateful things they said."

Far-speak in hand I groped for a kitchen chair behind me and sank blindly into it. "Whatever those lying dog turds said about your ancestor isn't true. I'm so sorry you and your family had to go through all that.

"As pale of skin as you and your brother are, it's a wonder to me that you didn't just forget about your heritage and disappear into the Empire."

"Granny's love and teachings made it impossible for us to forget. She tried to protect us when she was younger and her health was better. She brought us to the rancha to stay with her when mama moved to the nearest town to live with her succession of boyfriends. But that didn't last.

"Mama lied about the imperial money and after a while she feared they would find out we were living elsewhere and cut her off. By that time her last stupid boyfriend had had enough and left, so we were made to go back and live with her.

"Later when granny took a bad fall off her horse and her health suffered mama quit her job in town and went back to the rancha. Now she gets money from the imperials to take care of granny instead of us."

I was silent for a long time before I spoke again. "Thank you for telling me. I wish I had discovered all this sooner. When you come to take Mathrom away I will give you a talisman similar to the one I gave you. Give it to my sister when you see her. Then I will at least be able to come to her in her dreams so we can talk, until I can figure out how to visit in person."

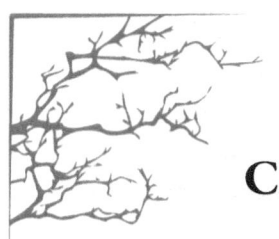

Chapter Twenty-Two

By the third morning of his confinement, when I checked on Mathrom before heading to Friendship House I could tell he was well into a spirit communion. He had asked the day before for me to close the drapes in his room and had refused the midday and evening meals. When I saw this I backed out and closed his door. I told Gahji and the children to leave him alone so he could continue his journey.

On the fourth day when Saskina arrived with a friend's borrowed vehicle to collect him, a cleaned up and subdued Mathrom was waiting for her. With my sight I sensed that something had changed for him, but I didn't ask. I would wait for him to share with me what he chose. I wasn't Kukiya, and I had no Cougar puwa of my own. I could only guide him so far; I was glad he was going to stay with my sister for a time.

I had decided to make a talisman for him as well as Kitahtla. I wanted to keep in contact at least in the Dream to see how he was faring. When I gave it to him he surprised me by thanking me—for everything. I smiled and patted his shoulder before he got in the vehicle.

"You are welcome to come back to visit at my home when you return, if you like. Until then, a safe journey to the both of you."

I heard no more from the siblings for about a moon. Immersed in my work and hunting and fishing for the family I sank into sleep each night exhausted. Gahji had started back to work part time when the children finished school for the summer, so at least I had Angika to help me with little O'siyan and the other two.

I did, however hear from my sister. One night when I swam into my dreams a Cougar with soft golden eyes came to *me*. She rubbed her head against me and purred. I through my arms around her and buried my face in her soft tawny fur.

<<Oh, my sweet baby girl, I am so glad I found you at last. I hoped we could communicate with each other by using my talisman and here you are. I'm so sorry I haven't been able to come in person yet.>>

She rumbled a laugh and licked me with a scratchy feline tongue. <<It is of no importance. We are coming to see you instead. The children told me of your new family. I know it would be difficult for you to leave to visit me right now.>>

<<Is your daughter bringing you? Saskina told me a little about your problems with her. I am more than willing to look after you and have you live here with us. Your big brother is here now to help take care of you.>>

<<No, the grandchildren are bringing me. Qwadalah is going into town to get her hair done and get groceries tomorrow and we are sneaking away with only a note left on the kitchen table to let her know I am fine.

"I am supposed to go into the local imperial infirmary for some medical tests next month; I'm just going a little early and doing them in Seatown at your wife's infirmarium instead, that's what we wrote in the note.>>

She purred a laugh and rubbed against me again. <<As to your offer, I will have to think about that. I've grown to love my hot thirsty desert, so we shall see once I get there.>>

That night I told my Gahji and she seemed as excited as I was by the news. She was quiet for a while mulling over the problem at last she said, "We can put her in the girls room. The beds are newer in there and it's quieter on that side of the house. Bijah can either bunk with Tuunac, or sleep on auntie's camp cot in here."

I pulled her into my arms and kissed her. "Sounds like you have it all planned out, my sweet, mama bear."

After talking to Samul I figured out that by mecho-cart the journey could be done in a day, but because of my sister's age her grandchildren were taking it slow and doing it in two. That, of course gave me time for Angika and I to clean the house and for me to do some hunting in the mountains. I did some fishing in my seal form with Tuunac, too, but I was also happy when Denny offered to drive me into the mountains so we could hunt for deer.

Being part Kukiya and raised Kukiya I figured my sister would enjoy the deer meat. Our deer relatives were kind when I called them, asking for their life gift and we managed to bring home two fine young bucks. Leaving a special portion for her Cougar spirit with the rest of our offerings we butchered our catch and headed home late on the night before her arrival.

Gahji didn't have to work that day and neither did I. We spent the day cooking, cleaning and waiting excitedly for them. Late in the afternoon a mecho-cart I recognized pulled up in front of our house with Mathrom driving. Inside I could see the silhouettes of two others.

As he parked Saskina opened the window and waved smiling. "We are here at last," she called.

Bounding down the front steps I went to meet them. Gahji and the children were watching from the porch, but let me have this special moment alone with her. In the back seat of the cart was an old woman with long gray braids and warm golden eyes nestled in a nest of blankets and pillows. She smiled when she saw me and I opened the door to help her out. Kitahtla when she emerged was a plump woman, nearly as tall as I was myself. As she studied me in the physical world for the first time since her babyhood the golden skin around her eyes and mouth wrinkled into familiar laugh lines as she smiled.

"Big brother Tas, at last."

Unable to speak and with tears streaming down my cheeks I enfolded her in my arms my whole body trembling. She rested her head on my chest her own tears dampening my shirt. "Oh my sweet baby girl," I choked out at last. "I've missed you so much, but I couldn't come back and let my enemies find you. I'm so, so sorry I wasn't able to come sooner, to be there to protect you and your family throughout the hard times."

She looked up, smiled and caressed my cheek. "My dear one, I kept the talisman you made me so long ago, so you were never far away in my thoughts. Mama Sagila and papa jimmy told me the stories about you about my parents. I always knew I was loved by all of you. Papa always said he had a feeling you would come back."

I hugged her tight again once again unable to speak. "I just wish I could have come sooner—to help you—protect you."

She chuckled and touched my cheek again wiping away my tears with her finger. "Now, now don't grieve over what can't be changed. And if you had come earlier, who knows how the future might have turned out."

She was right about that, I reminded myself. And if I had come back into an earlier place and time I might not have met my beautiful Gahji and had the family I now had. I hugged her again and then guided her to the porch to meet my wife and the rest of the people waiting so patiently to greet her.

Kitahtla hugged Gahji when I introduced her and was delighted to see baby O'siyan and the other children. The older ones heard Mathrom and his sister calling her Granny Kitah and decided, with her approval, to call her that, too, instead of great aunty. Over dinner we traded stories and caught up on some of the family news. But in spite of the excitement I sensed that Kitahtla was tiring.

Over whining protests from Bijah and Tuunac I got the little ones ready for bed while Gahji and the two Kukiya siblings helped clean the kitchen and put away the left overs. Angika was delighted to have my sister bedding with her and after Bijah put up such a fuss I let her stay in her bedroom, too.

"Let her be, Tas. She can sleep with me in the bigger bed. It will be like old times for me having a little one to snuggle with," Kitahtla said.

I snorted a laugh. "You might regret that decision before morning. She can kick like a soldier's mule at times."

She laughed. "We will manage. Now close the door and turn off the light, so we can sleep."

I paused at the door and in what I hoped was a stern voice I said to the girls, "I'll let you stay, but your new granny needs her rest. So if I hear a lot of talking and giggling in here—I will be back and somebody will be sleeping on the couch or in Tuunac's room," I warned.

Saskina was just leaving when I came back down the hall. "I have to bring my friend's vehicle back," she explained, "but I will come by soon to visit."

"You are welcome anytime, my girl." When I turn to also say good bye to her brother I found him still sitting on the couch.

Clearing his throat, he said, "Uh, can I stay here for a few days, Uncle Tas? Aunty said it was all right with her if you agreed."

I studied him with my gift, wondering if there was another motive behind the request. "You can stay, but you will have to sleep on the couch. Stakaya's room is too small for the both of you. And I can tell you from personal experience that it's not a comfortable bed."

He made a face but nodded. "It's all right, I'll manage. Can I stay?"

I came fully into the living room and sat down in a nearby chair facing him. "You can stay, of course, nephew, but what's really going on, eh?"

He sighed. "My—uh—roommates, when I didn't come back for so long, packed up my things and moved in another guy to help pay the rent. If I plan to go back to the Lectorium in the fall I will have to find another place to live before then."

I laughed and went to the storage shelves in the laundry room for a blanket and pillow. When I came back I tossed him the bedding and joked, "Well there's always my bush camp if you get tired of the lumpy couch."

To my surprise he took my joke seriously. "I may take you up on that offer. Granny has given me some 'work' to do and your bush camp sounds like it might be a good place to start."

"Hmm, let's talk about that more in the next few days."

The house had grown quiet by then baby O'siyan babbling with his mother in our bed room behind the closed door the only sound. As I moved down the hallway to join them, Mathrom called me back for one more revelation.

"Uncle, I know sis told you a bit about our mom. Well we might have a bit of trouble coming this way from her."

"How so? Please explain."

"When we were coming back we passed several peace defender vehicles that were searching for something—or somebody. I'm not sure if it was us they were looking for, but I wouldn't put it past our mama to have sent them. She might be claiming we kidnapped granny in spite of our note.

"I had to do some very creative driving a couple times to avoid them. That's one of the reasons we were so late getting here today."

"Thank you for telling me. I will be on my guard for any trouble coming from that direction. Saskina told me about the medical tests, so your grandmother has a good reason to be here staying with relatives.

"And if the goldys come to investigate we will tell them that I am the grandson of her older brother. I agreed to let her stay with my family until it's time for the medical tests. If Qwadalah wants to press the issue then it will be me, who has to come up with a 'creative' way to deal with her."

Kitahtla enjoyed the children and blended in well into our daily routines, for which I was grateful. My eyes couldn't get enough of seeing her, or listening to her soft voice as she talked with the children. I hated to leave her for work, but I couldn't abandon Kutima to our classes and soon enough the program would be ending for the summer, hopefully to be renewed in the fall.

One afternoon a few days after her arrival I came home from work to find her sitting alone in the basket swing on our front porch. I smiled when I saw her, but the house behind her seemed unnaturally quiet. "Where is everybody?"

"Mathrom and Stakaya took the older ones to the park to play and Gahji and the baby are asleep in your bedroom, I believe."

I nodded, went in the house to grab a cold drink from the ice box and came back outside with two in hand. Kitahtla smiled and took one then patted the cushion beside her. "Come sit, brother dear, and talk to me. Tell me about what has happened to you since you left us."

I should have known she would ask and have been more prepared, but I told her as best I could my story, beginning with the family's stay with the Prophet where Nachoga and my mother Qwadalah married. Reluctantly, I went on to summarize the Gold Creek Massacre that killed our mother and got me captured and sent to the imperial prison for children. And then I ended with the tale of how my seal father came to rescue me from the Crokno agent who captured me, and accused me of witchcraft, and how my seal father took me with him into the Beyond to teach me while I grew to my manhood.

When I was done we both had tears in our eyes and we just sat cuddled together silently rocking for a long time, content to share our grief and our love for each other, and the ones who were gone, in silence.

Finally I got up the courage to ask her some of my own questions.

"Tell me a bit about what happened to you and the rest of the family. Last I saw, you were crying, strapped to your cradleboard while Sagila raced away with Xyilaha covering your retreat."

Kitahtla chuckled. "That girl was a wild one, no doubt about it. Did you know she joined Barklyo's show and did trick riding and shooting all over the Empire?"

"Yes, I did know. Gahji is her granddaughter. She told me first but I also heard some of the tale from Kutima and Rushton, Collin's great nephew."

"Ah Collin, such a sweet man, he and his friend Lord Bronworthy worked so hard for our people back then."

"When I came back I spent quite a bit of time in the downtown library studying history. What a shock to see myself in the pictures in one of Collin's early books."

She laughed. "I bet it was."

"I know a lot of what I read in those histories wasn't true. I know Uncle Tli was killed but what of his son and my cousin Samiqwas? Are they still alive and living on the Preserve?"

Kitahtla shook her head and chuckled as she brought forth the memories. "Samiqwas and Binahgwinn? Ah those two were crazy wild boys, too. After Papa Jimmy was killed trying to rob a settler's bank those two ran off from the Preserve and formed their own outlaw gang. They raided and stole all over that country for years afterward and always shared their plunder with friends and relatives. Neither the soldiers nor the tribal peace defenders could catch them, because the People always hid them away when trouble was near.

"Alas, the boys were betrayed by one of our own in the end. Some said it was a man from a family that had blood feud with chief Golannah, but I can't say for sure.

"The defendos captured the boys, and Samiqwas and Binahgwinn went to prison for a long time. Samiqwas died there. When Binahgwinn got out he returned to the Preserve and stayed to help out his mother Sagila, who was quite old by then. After she died he just drifted away and I never heard what became of him after that."

I hugged her. "That is a very sad tale, but I seem to recall that you were supposed to marry Binahgwinn at one time. I guess that didn't happen, eh?"

She snorted. "That's what papa Jimmy wanted true enough, but mam was having none of it. After her first two husbands had been killed by the soldiers for making war she wanted a peaceful life for me. She found me a nice young chamuqwani who was one of Collin Golbraith's scribes sent to the Preserve to gather information for one of his books."

She chuckled. "And in the end he gathered me up, too. Lord Harrington Lander was his name. He was a younger son of his family, sent away to live on an allowance and warned to keep out of trouble. We fell in love and he purchased my rancha for me.

"While he was working with Collin he lived with me and gave me two of my three children. But our union—even though it was temple blessed wasn't to his family's liking and at last he couldn't stand their constant criticism and threats and he left me.

"I couldn't manage the rancha alone with two small children, so I tried marrying a Kukiya man who was good with horses to help me. He gave me my little Janata, but he died when she was about ten. Rigby was nearly grown by then and he took over the rancha for me.

"Through Collin I managed to get the children's father to pay for the two older ones education. Rig looked a lot like his father. When my boy finished his schooling his father bought him a commission in the Imperial army. After that, he left us and the rancha behind. I rarely saw him in the remaining years before his death."

"Saskina told me about her mother but what about your younger daughter? Do you still keep in contact with her?"

"A little, she favored her father's people and was much darker than her siblings. Qwadalah can be a mean bitch, as I'm sure you've heard from the children. Janata was shy and took her sister's teasing and ridicule to heart. I stopped it whenever I could, but even though I told her she had to stand up for herself and ignore her sister's bullying she all too often just hid away and cried."

"What happened to her?"

"She married early and has a bunch of kids and an old mother-in-law to care for down by the salty lake on the southern half of the Zerve. We talk on the far-speak sometimes but I don't see her much anymore."

"I'm not sure what I could do to help her, but thank you for telling me. Maybe someday I can take you to see her, if you want."

She patted my hand that would be nice. "I would like to see how she is getting along."

With Kitahtla around to supervise child care when Gahji was at work that freed me up for more traditional food gathering. Borrowing a larger boat from Elder Samul, I sometimes took the entire family berry picking and seaweed gathering and I let Tuunac show off to his mother and granny his newly acquired skill of setting snares and catching and cleaning the rabbits and small birds he caught in them.

Unfortunately, Chief Rickson didn't receive the money to run the summer camp sessions on tribal bush land in the mountains as he'd hoped, but he did obtain funding to hold the series of social dances that were usually held each year in the summer.

And, he managed a small endowment to hire me and a few Smotahlik elders to teach traditional bush skills to a group of young men and women who would become next year's instructors for an expanded program. The students would also be paid a small wage, to encourage them to complete the course, with the promise of a job next summer.

To keep them out of trouble, I coaxed the chief into letting Mathrom and Stakaya join the program as well. It was a sweet beginning to the summer, unfortunately it was just the lull before the storm.

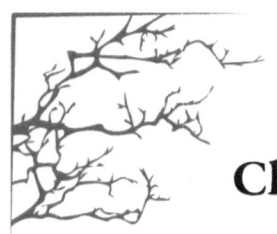

Chapter Twenty-Three

Our troubles began when my irate niece Qwadalah finally found us and showed up with a couple goldys in tow. I had been helping out at Friendship House when Aqwissa hissed a warning into my mind.

<<Trouble at home, Siyatli Brother. We must go now!>>

Excusing myself from helping set up tables for the midday meal with the explanation that I was urgently needed at home I stepped into an empty office and made the transfer to a clump of tall bushes by the railroad tracks behind our house.

Walking around the corner I saw Mathrom and a fat middle-aged woman with muscular arms and short graying hair, dressed in trousers and a short-sleeved man's shirt, yelling at each other near a dusty vehicle. Not far away two young goldys stood by their mecho-cart, looking bored. Kitahtla holding O'siyan in her arms was on the porch with three wide-eyed and frightened children just behind her.

As I approached I spoke into Mathrom's mind, hoping he would hear me before the goldys decided to arrest him. <<Enough, nephew. Calm yourself; I am here now.>>

To my relief, he did hear me, paused and turned in my direction. To the goldys I said, "What seems to be the problem, Defenders?"

The goldys turned to me as well, probably wondering where I'd come from. "And you are?" the dark haired one said to me.

"I'm Tassele Cougarson; I live here. What's the problem?"

"This woman," he motioned to Qwadalah, "says that her mother, a senile and feeble old woman, was kidnaped from her home by her grandchildren in the hopes that they can convince her to change her will."

"That's a load of shit, mama, and you know it—" Mathrom blurted. He might have said more, but I held up a hand to stop him.

I'd seen my niece's smug expression; she was baiting him, hoping the goldys would arrest him. I turned so the goldy couldn't see my face and lifted my upper lip, showing her my canines. She wouldn't find me such an easy adversary to control.

To the defenders I said, "I assume you are speaking of the Elder holding my youngest son. Does she look feeble or senile to you?"

The men weren't willing to commit to an answer instead they turned their questioning back on me. "Why is this woman here in the first place and what is your relationship to her?"

"She is my great aunt. We recently found each other through her grandchildren and another contact at the Lectorium, Preceptor Rushton of the history department by name."

"That's a lie. This man is trying to trick an old woman—maybe with my children's knowledge, or maybe he is tricking them, too. My mother never had a long-lost relative with the Cougarson name." Qwadalah screeched.

When the goldy turned to me, I said calmly as if I hadn't been interrupted, "I've recently been tracing my lineage and discovered my late grandfather's sister Kitahtla through old records and her grandson Mathrom Cougarson."

I motioned to Mathrom. "I met Mathrom through my preceptor friend, and when he and his sister were visiting the rancha they told me their granny has medical tests here at the Seatown General Infirmarium in a seven-day or so. My family and I invited her to stay with us until then."

"My mother's tests were at our local infirmary. Somebody changed them. And, you're lying about being a relative," Qwadalah interrupted. "I think you and your lazy wife just wanted a babysitter for your passel of brats while you go off somewhere to party."

I could feel my temper heating, but I also knew she was baiting me. The woman was a master at the art. "My wife is a nurse at Seatown General Infirmarium. Normally I am home from my job before she has to leave, but she must have been called in to work early today. We don't need the Elder to 'babysit.'"

"And you work where?"

"I work at the Zacatik Friendship House in one of their cultural programs. Chief Rickson and Director Rabbitson can tell you that I am not a person who drinks or goes to parties."

He looked at me as if he wasn't sure he believed me. "If that is all true why was there so much secrecy about her visit?"

I shrugged. "I can't comment on that, I haven't been back to the Preserve since I left as a child."

Kitahtla handed the baby to Angika and came down the steps to join us. "I'm the one who changed the location of my tests. They will do a better job here than at the infirmarium near the rancha. I left you a note on the kitchen table, Qwadalah, there was no secrecy or need to make such a fuss and bring in the defenders for a family matter. Nobody is kidnapping me or forcing me to change my will or anything."

"Mother is keeping granny on the rancha like a prisoner" Mathrom blurted, barely able to contain his fury. "She can't go anywhere except to the doctor's office. That's why we left a note instead of waiting to tell her in person. And she's done exactly what we feared—call the fendos to enforce her control. She just wants the rancha. She doesn't really care about our granny Kitah, mama just wants the government money she is getting to care for her—"

"That's a god-cursed lie, you ungrateful little shit," Qwadalah cried. "I love my mother and I want only the best for her!"

Mathrom snorted. "Yeah, like you did for me and my sister, eh? Collecting a government stipend for us when we were living with granny and you spent it all on your boyfriends and never gave granny Kitah a cent to help pay for our food and clothes. And now you are doing it to granny, instead of us. Is that your idea of caring?"

"Grandson, stop," Kitahtla said. "I know you mean well, but I can speak for myself."

"Mathrom, be quiet," I said just barely loud enough for him to hear, "or I will 'make' you be quiet. You aren't helping."

Turning to the goldys Kitahtla said, "I asked the grandchildren to bring me into town for my medical tests and to visit with newly found relatives because I wanted to avoid just such a deplorable scene as you are now witnessing.

"My daughter is the only one living on our rancha these days who still drives, so I am dependent on her to get our food and other supplies. She often is busy running the rancha and doesn't have the time to take me for visits. So, I must admit the grandchildren are right—in part. I rarely leave our rancha."

Turning to her daughter she added, 'But just because I am here in Seatown doesn't mean I plan to change my will or live here permanently.'

Tears of frustration pooling in the corners of her eyes, Qwadalah whined, "Mama, I only want what is best for you, truly I do."

"I know, dear," Kitahtla said in a soothing voice, "and right now that means I need a vacation, so I can visit with my refound relatives."

Qwadalah scowled and gave me a murderous glare. "I still believe this man is lying and trying to trick you—and maybe the children in some terrible way."

"Qwadalah, cousin, if you go to the library and look at some of the old historys written by a Collin Golbraith you will see a picture of my ancestor, for whom I was named, Tas Cougarson. This ancestor looks like me. I just want to get to know my relatives, that's all."

When she looked like she still wasn't convinced, I snapped, "If money is the real problem here, and you don't want to believe me, then have your attorney draw up some legal papers stating that neither myself nor my children will ever make a claim to the Lander Rancha. I will sign whatever you want. My only interest is spending time with my aunty before she passes into the realm of our ancestors."

"Don't worry; I will. You'll never own even a grain of sand on the Lander Rancha," she said through gritted teeth. Then with a snarl of disgust Qwadalah got back into her vehicle and drove away in a roar of noise from her cart. The goldys looked at one another, shrugged and returned to their vehicle to leave as well.

After the evening meal Kitahtla took Mathrom onto the front porch for a little private talk. I suspected she wanted to speak about his behavior that day. I let them be; she was capable of disciplining him as well as I could and he might take it better from her, than me.

Next morning I was planning on taking our canoe out to do a little fishing with Tuunac when Mathrom sought me out to ask, "Uncle Tas, can you take me with you and let me stay for a few days in your secret bush camp?"

"Does this have anything to do with your granny's talk with you?"

He shrugged. "A little, maybe. She told me I needed to look at how I entrap myself in behavior patterns that another wants, because they are trying to get me into trouble."

I patted him on the shoulder and smiled. "That is a lesson we all have to learn at some point in our lives. Of course I will take you to my camp. Let's pack you a few things—like some dry meat, a sleeping bag and extra clothes—so you won't get too hungry, or cold at night, eh? You modern young men aren't used to really 'toughing it,' as they now say," I teased.

"Ah but just wait till I have you and the other students under my power for your 'wilderness instructors' training course, eh?"

He made a face, laughed and followed to help me.

I wasn't joking—but he would find that out soon enough.

On the seventh night of his vigil I went to Mathrom in the Dream and asked him if he was ready to come back to Seatown. He said he was, so the next day Tuunac and I took our canoe across to fetch him and do a little fishing on the way.

When we'd caught and cleaned enough fish for our needs and Tuunac had set a couple snares for rabbits we could collect on our way back, we beached and hid the canoe and walked up the stream, tumbling down from the mountains above. My camp was concealed further up the slope near where another little creek joined the bigger flow.

Stream was full with snow melt and loud as it playfully jumped over the many rocks hidden in its bed. We were out of sight from the occasional hiker on the forest trails, so I allowed Tuunac to babble on telling me about his days with his new granny, and his grumbling complaints about his younger sister Bijah.

I doubted we could be heard over Stream's noise, so I would let him talk until we reached the smaller creek nearer the camp. Only then would he need to be quiet as we traveled the last off-path distance to my shelter.

We were nearing the little creek when raven cawed a warning. At almost the same moment Aqwissa and I sense the alien enemy. Jerking to a stop, I grabbed Tuunac and froze, all my physical and otherworldly senses straining, exploring the way ahead.

One look at my face and Tuunac stopped babbling. He opened his mouth to ask what was wrong, but I motioned for him to keep silent. Color draining from his face, he stared up at me trembling.

Half-carrying him I hustled him back down the stream till I found a hollowed out nurse log that had fallen and was now starting to be covered with small saplings and berry shrubs. I motioned for him to crawl inside the log's cavity. My voice stern I commanded, "Stay hidden here—and quiet until I come back for you."

"But I want to help if there's trouble," he protested. "You said I was growing up and Mighty Martiin says—"

"Not today! This is no game, son. I need to make sure Mathrom is all right and you can't help me with this enemy. You need to stay here, so I won't have to worry about you, too."

When he protested that he wasn't a baby like O'siyan, I snapped, suddenly out of patience with this modern child who had never known true danger. "You do what I say and stay here and keep quiet or I will glue your mouth shut and stick you to the ground inside this log. What will it be?"

He knew I was completely serious, and trembling crawled into his refuge. "Can Aqwissa stay with me?"

Softening my tone, because I knew I had frightened him, I shook my head and said, "No, I will need her. You will have to be the brave young hunter I know you are, and not give into your fears. Pray to the forest spirits and they will protect you. I will come back for you when it's safe."

Releasing Aqwissa, and using a small portion of my Gift to conceal my scent, we headed up the little stream towards my camp. The acrid burnt stink of the alien enemy grew stronger the closer we came. Unwilling to reveal myself before knowing the adversary I was facing, I asked the raven sitting in a tall fir nearby to lend me his sight while I checked out my camp.

From his perch among the branches I could see Mathrom with his back against the giant cedar whose canopy sheltered my earth-covered forest hut. He was clutching a sturdy branch like a club in one hand and his long hunting knife in the other. With teeth bared he was snarling like the big cat he claimed as spirit protector.

Facing him were two squat creatures, their shapes reminding me of a mix between a spider and a beetle. I had seen them before in my father's mind pictures. Half living flesh, half alien machine, the insects were about the size of a child's pony. Sabiyan scent-detectors, they were not of my world and I had been warned about them.

These two had a glowing collar of colored lights clasped around the thinner area between the two sections of their armored bodies. The glowing collars allowed their keeper to sense what they did and issue commands to control them. Radiating from the central mass were several jointed limbs that could smell and track the prey their keeper had been hired to find. On top of their small metallic heads were swiveling eye stalks to sight their victim and large fanged mandibles to capture, hold or kill their quarry.

<<Where is the master who controls these creatures?>> I asked Aqwissa, now hovering beside me in her snaky dragon form.

She huffed out her disgust. <<Probably hiding nearby in the Beyond, after what happened to the last set of hunters the Crokno hired to track us it is afraid to come to near. I am a hunter, too,>> she boasted. <<I will find and kill it. I am hungry.>>

<<Be careful if you want to track it. It probably knows what happened to the other pack Utreal hired. These Sabiyan hunters are cunning. Your capture is probably a part of the bounty, be clever yourself. It will want you alive after its pets kill me.>>

<<If you think you and the young cougar can kill the hunter's scent-slaves I will find the master. The Sabiyan may get away otherwise.>>

<<We will manage. Go, but be careful. I don't want to lose you, honored one.>> She rubbed her snout against my cheek and then vanished into the Beyond.

Raising their eye stalks to stare at Mathrom the aliens each lifted two front limbs, the nose-holes on their tips flaring to better taste his scent. The largest of the pair opened craggy jaws to display long yellow teeth. <<You stink of our prey, little human, where is he? Give him to us and we won't kill you.>> it promised.

Mathrom took a deep breath. He had heard their mind talk, but chose to answer with voiced words. "I have no idea what—or who you are talking about. Get away from me; go back to whatever black pit of Djoven's fiery abyss you came from," he snarled and raised his stick.

<<Stupid human. We hunt the siyatli seal man who is our patron's enemy. Tell us where to find him—or we will take what we want from your unprotected mind before we kill you.>>

I stepped into the open to reveal myself, but before I had the chance to call out, I felt the atmosphere nearby suddenly shift as Cougar's puwa entered its human companion for the first time. With Cougar's battle scream echoing through the forest the young warrior leapt into the air, and landed atop his nearest adversary's armored back, beating with his club at the unprotected eye stalks of the creature until they were smashed and useless. Then he continued to pound at its now blinded head as it swirled in circles trying to grab onto him with a clawed limb or its lethal fangs.

Before its partner could get over the shock of Mathrom's attack and come to the aid of its companion I let it see me. To distract it from attacking Mathrom, and knowing its master could hear me through the creature's collar, I said, <<Looking for me, Sabiyan fish slime? Are you a coward to hide in the Beyond while your slaves do your work? Come show yourself and collect your bounty, if you can.>>

Agile as the big beetle it had been modeled after, the creature sprang at me with only a moment for me to raise a shield, before its gnashing mandibles were scraping at the glowing fire protecting my face.

No longer a helpless child needing my father to fight for me, as a man I was able to create my own otherworldly weapon in our physical world as my father had done, when he fought Hoyt during my rescue. I leapt backwards and jabbed at the creature's carapace with a sharp spear made of otherworldly Qwakaiva.

Not quick enough, however, to strike a vital spot, or hit its glowing collar, my first blow struck its armored back in a shower of sparks. I cursed, whirled, throwing up my shield as it leapt with lightning speed for my throat.

Somewhere off to my left I heard Cougar scream again. I needed to help Mathrom; I doubted he could fend off or kill the alien even with Cougar's help. And though we were far from the well-used park trails, the noise of our battle was going to attract unwanted attention—or start a forest fire, if it continued much longer.

The alien being was incredibly fast, even with my gift to help me I could barely keep it from tearing me apart with its lethal jaws as we battled and dodged each other's attack through the nearby forest.

Then I had another idea. Not sure how quickly the controlled alien could respond to a change in my tactics I decided on a different approach. If I was wrong it would surely grab and kill me, but I had to risk it. As it charged me again I ducked and moved in closer, hurling myself under the creature's softer belly when it jumped to land where I'd just been standing.

As I rolled I managed to slice off two of its segmented legs with my next blow. The alien toppled over, the legs on its uninjured side waving helplessly in the air. I stabbed at the glowing collar again disabling one of its lights, my blade slicing along the creature's softer under parts, a smelly dark ichor spilling out of the wound as it flipped itself out of reach of my next thrust.

Before it could retreat and maybe recover, I channeled my Qwakaiva into lifting a nearby boulder about the size of the creature itself, out of its mossy nest in the soil and dropped it on top of its struggling form.

The stone hadn't landed quite in the center of the unnatural thing, but close enough. Shifting my power back into a long knife I hacked off its remaining limbs. Then pushing the boulder away I proceeded to dismember the alien and smash to tiny bits the collar that controlled it.

Breathing hard I put out a fire smoldering on a nearby bush and glanced around for Mathrom and the other attacking alien. I hadn't heard the big cat's scream for a while, and I didn't see them in the ruins of my camp under the big tree. Afraid that Mathrom had tried to run and the Sabiyan tracker had gone after him, my eyes darted around the detritus, hoping I wouldn't find his limp and bloody remains among the berry bushes.

Then raven cawed and I looked up. Perched on a thick limb within the lower branches of the big cedar crouched Mathrom. The human part of his melded being had retreated to allow Cougar to command the body they now shared. Below on the ground the blinded alien insect was using its sensitive fore limbs to snuffle around the tree's base as it tracked him.

Mathrom curled his lip and Cougar's rumbling growl began deep in his throat. As I watched, the tracker found his scent trail and began to slowly climb Mathrom's tree. The Cat's growl deepened and became louder.

Mathrom balanced like a dancer upon the tree branch and leaned slightly forward to watch the alien insect, feeling its way up the trunk.

Frozen in place with shock I could neither speak nor move to help him. With my spirit sight I saw the blue glowing image of the big cat enveloping the frailer human male totally within its Qwakaiva.

When the alien crawled onto his branch, but was still not balanced, Cougar using Mathrom's hands, with etheric claws extended, together they swatted the giant insect from the branch. It tumbled with limbs flailing to the ground, landing with a loud plop on its back, its armored shell cracking open. Cougar screamed his triumph and leapt after it to finish the kill.

Mathrom landed as lightly as a feather, though he had been perched quite high in the canopy. Picking up his discarded club he proceeded to smash the alien and its controlling collar into an unrecognizable mass of fragmented parts.

Then, he stopped and through down his branch, an expression of bewilderment on his face. Breathing raggedly the melded being that was my nephew remained crouched over the kill uncertain what to do next. The Cougar whined, its instinctual response was to feast on its fallen prey, but Mathrom's nose wrinkled in disgust, holding back. The carcass had already begun to stink, its alien flesh out of harmony here in our world.

I walked into the clearing so he could see me. The big cat put a possessive hand on its kill and snarled at me. I stopped and held myself perfectly still, but I didn't move away. The air around us tingled with danger and otherworldly power.

"Mathrom, come back. You must thank Cougar for his help, but the threat is over. You have to take control of your physical self again or the Spirit will destroy you."

<<Cougar, there is no good meat here. This kill is enemy—but it is also poison. Let your companion guide you now. You will hunt again together soon, I promise you.>>

I remained unmoving. They both had heard me. I hoped he could transition without my intervention. I wouldn't want to hurt him.

It took a bit more time, but at last his eyes closed, and when Mathrom opened them again I knew he had managed to balance the parts of himself somewhat back into harmony. Cougar had vacated his body and was once more only within his spirit fire.

Rushing forward, I caught him before he sank to the ground. Holding him up, we staggered together away from the smelly carcass and at last I eased him and myself down by the big fir where raven still perched. Taking deep breaths, he leaned into me trembling.

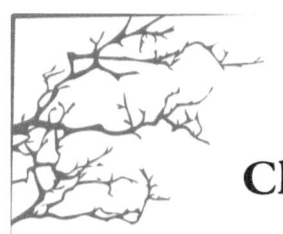

Chapter Twenty-Four

I wrapped my arms around him and just held him. "You did well today, young cougar warrior. I'm very proud of you."

Still trembling he stared into my face searching for answers to his many questions. At last he choked out, "Who—or what were those things?"

"Sabiyan scent-trackers, I'm sorry you were here when they entered our world. They were hunting me."

He made a face then winced. "I figured that out, but why?"

I sighed. "That is a long story, one which I am willing to share with you at another time, now that you have come into your true power."

Recalling Cougar and the battle he shuddered. "The transition won't be like that next time," I said. "Ask my sister for her advice in that. For most people who have strong puwa, they never have such an experience, their spirit guardians are merely there as advisors for their entire lives.

"But you, like your ancestor Nachoga have the natural Gift to embrace Cougar's Spirit entirely when needed."

"I now see the seal in your spirit fire like Bijah and Elder Samul tell me they can. Is that the way it is for you?"

"No. For me it is different." I chuckled. "I am, like you, a breed. As you already know, Kitahtla and I have the same human mother. Only my real father, a Qwa'Nayhi Seal man isn't human, and not of our world. Your ancestor Nachoga adopted me when he married my mother.

"You, and other people like you, invite the spirit of your protectors to enter your human form when needed, but for me it's different. I am as much my Seal as I am human." I stood, pulling him to his feet with me. We had no time for long explanations now.While I waited for Aqwissa's return we needed to dispose of the enemy corpses and salvage what we could of our things. I sighed as I glanced around the shambles that had once been a valued retreat for me. My hut was caved in on one side, blankets, clothing and other personal items were broken and scattered everywhere many covered in smelly alien ichor and human blood. Once we left here today I would never return. I would have to find another sanctuary in this beautiful forest.

I wiped a hand across my face and when it came away red, I sighed. I would also have to do some creative explaining when I got home. I glanced at Mathrom who had been surveying the mess. He too was bloody. The worst of his injuries seemed to be a long cut running down one arm, and a slash across his chest, but I couldn't tell if he had other wounds under his filthy clothes.

"How badly are you hurt?"

He seemed startled when I spoke. Staring down at himself he noticed the wound on his chest and his still bleeding arm. He shrugged. "Nothing hurts too much, so I guess I'm all right."

I snorted a laugh. "You will hurt later, trust me." I focused on our surroundings again, my senses alert for any danger. Where was Aqwissa?

Without looking at him, I said, "We need to clean up this mess before we leave. Do you want to come with me while I fetch Tuunac?"

"No, I can stay here and begin sorting," he mumbled, still pondering what had taken place and his part in it all. Then my words finally penetrated the fog and he spun back to face me. "What? You mean little Tuunac is out here somewhere—by himself?"

"Yes, we were coming to get you when I sense the enemy. He is safe I hid him away, but I need to go get him now."

Mathrom glanced back to the destroyed camp with eyes wide. "You mean to bring him here?" He waved an expressive hand about the clearing, "and let him see all this?"

"Yes, as my son I will protect him as best I can but I'm not going to coddle him, either. He needs to know what dangers might lie waiting for him in our world, instead of just seeing the made up stories he watches on the picta-view. Do you want to come with me or not?" I repeated, my voice hardening. These modern tribal people!

He sighed. "I'll stay and begin the job."

"Good." I left without another word and hurried to collect my son. As I came closer I knew he could see me, but I was pleased to note that Tuunac waited till I told him it was safe before he came out to me. Trembling and ashy, he stared wide-eyed at the blood and ichor covering my clothes.

So intent on collecting him to reassure myself he was safe, I'd forgotten how I must look to him. I put a hand on his shoulder and slightly squeezed, to reassure him that I was alright. "Come back with me, my brave, young hunter. The enemy is dead and you can help me and Mathrom clean up the camp site."

Before returning I took the time to strip off my shirt and wash it and myself as best I could in the icy stream water. I had managed to collect an impressive amount of scrapes and scratches while racing through the underbrush dodging my alien enemy. Fortunately none of my wounds were deep enough to cause concern. Gahji was going to be mad at me, but the care of my injuries could wait till we got home.

Holding hands with a silent Tuunac we were nearing the clearing when I heard Mathrom shout, calling out urgently for me to come. Scooping up Tuunac I bounded up the slope for the clearing.

Near the berry bushes at the base of the fir I saw my nephew staring down unmoving at something on the ground at his feet. There didn't seem to be an immediate danger, so I set Tuunac down and walked over to him.

My face must have revealed my dismay when I sensed what he had found, because he said when he saw me, "I felt something a moment ago, and then I saw her—just lying there." He hesitated and then added, "I wasn't sure if she would let me touch her after—" He broke off, uncertain how to continue.

Lying on a bed of last year's fir needles was a crumpled and bloody little dragon-lizard, her silver scales tarnished and darkened in several spots. With a strangled cry I sank to the earth, cradling her in my arms, and hugging her to my chest. She was alive, but had used much of her life force to return to my world—and me. I wasn't sure how successful her hunt had been, but she had suffered many wounds whatever had happened.

<<The enemy is dead,>> she murmured weakly into my mind, <<but I may follow it.>>

<<Not today you won't, Honored One.>>

I leaned back against the fir, and asked for its help as I prepared to share some of my Qwakaiva, and the tree's with her. I was glad there was no enemy following at the moment. I was fairly depleted of power after the battle, but the tree's sharing would help.

When I enlarged a cut on my chest enough for the wound to trickle some blood Aqwissa lifted her head to lick at the flow. I closed my eyes and sent my Qwakaiva deep into the earth to gather up more healing power from the forest around us. <<Our world has been invaded by enemies who wished to destroy all life,>> I explained to the lurking Spirits. <<I am a sworn emissary of the Great Dragon, Kunai. I have pledged my life to help protect this beautiful world. I need the Gift of your Qwakaiva now to help me continue my task.>>

It wasn't long before I felt the answering surge of the Gift flowing upward into me, like sap in the spring rising up to green the branches of the trees. With eyes closed so I could focus on my task better I said to Mathrom, "Aqwissa will need my help for a while, please continue with the cleanup. Tuunac can help you with some of it. I will take care of the disposal of the aliens as soon as I can leave her."

He gave me an answering murmur and then he spoke to Tuunac in a low voice as they moved away to continue the sorting.

When she had gained back some of her strength, Aqwissa said, <<You were right, siyatli brother, the trackers were only a distraction to separate us. Your cousin and another were waiting for me in ambush when I found the scent-detectors' keeper. I killed the keeper easily; he was focused solely on the battle you and the young cougar were fighting with its minions. The alien hadn't expected such a fierce resistance from you. When I bent to feed off its corpse the others sprung their trap for me.>>

<<Did you manage to kill Utreal or the other, before you escaped?>>

<<I wounded the traitor Utreal—badly maybe, then the uninjured Crokno, who had held back from the attack, left supporting your traitorous cousin—I hope thinking I was dead.>>

"Uncle," Mathrom said hesitantly a while later. "Tuunac and I have sorted things as best we can for now." When I opened my eyes he pointed out a couple piles, containing our things.

"There wasn't much we could save, a couple of your blankets, a cooking pot and a basket containing a few of your medicine things tucked well back in the shelter that I wasn't using." He motioned to a willow basket and a neatly made up blanket roll. "Unfortunately, most of our camp supplies were ruined."

He next pointed to a larger pile that contained his bedding, most of his clothes and many more of the camp's cooking utensils and simple furnishings that were now either broken and smashed, or coated in blood and enemy ichor.

Misinterpreting my stern look he said hesitantly, "I'm sorry, Uncle Tas, I know I made a mess, but I had planned to clean up before you came to get me. I guess it's kind of my fault that some much of our stuff was damaged."

Well, he might be right about that, I thought. If he had kept things he wasn't using tucked away in the baskets and wooden boxes I kept within the shelter, there wouldn't have been so many things ruined during the battle. Instead of getting angry I decided this was a good lesson for the future and I gave him an evil grin.

"It's not a problem, nephew. It just means you will have less to bring with you when you attend the bush training course. I had only a blanket and a knife when I began the long march to the Preserve. Guess you will be following in my footsteps, eh?" He shuddered then gave me a tentative smile, not sure if I was joking or not.

I wasn't.

But I didn't tell him that I would be sharing his lack, too.

"Uncle, the shovel isn't broken. I can dig a deep hole and burry the ruined stuff," he offered, hoping to placate me, no doubt.

"Do that, while I see to the corpses."

Intending to leave the recovering Aqwissa resting in her fir-needle nest, or on Tuunac's lap, she spoke into my mind, offering a different plan.

<<I don't wish to drain your Qwakaiva too much in case there is another enemy nearby. Take me with you, siyatli brother. I may be able to feed a bit off the dead as well.>>

Rising with her wrapped about my shoulders I walked the short way from the clearing to where I had left my kill. Kneeling I set her near enough so she could crawl to the corpse. <<The alien is decaying rapidly on my world. Can you still draw its life essence from the body?>>

<<I will try.>>

<<Don't feed on it, if it might make you sick. This world and I can provide what you need honored sister.>>

<<Go help your relatives. I will call when I am done here.>>

When Aqwissa was finished with the alien trackers there was not much more than a scattering of brittle metallic parts and blackened skin as thick as the substance used to make mecho-cart wheels left. We shoveled it into the holes dug for the rest of the garbage that we weren't going to pack out with us. Aqwissa had more healing yet to do, but with my gift and her feed she had acquired enough Qwakaiva to transform herself back into a somewhat tarnished silver bracelet like I usually wore.

As I headed out of the clearing behind the others I looked back to check our work. Except for broken branches on the nearby shrubs there was little evidence to show that the peace of this forest had been so brutally disturbed. In time it would heal; no lasting harm had been done that day. Raising my gaze to the silent trees I said a prayer of gratitude for the many blessings they had so willingly given me during my stay among them. I was going to miss them and this place. It was hard to say good bye.

It was growing late and Sun already sleeping by the time we made the beach and retrieved the canoe, grub box, and other items hidden away in the brush nearby. Tuunac slipped off to check his snares and proudly returned with two fat rabbits. He asked me if he could give one to Aqwissa to eat. He wanted to save the other to give to Granny Kitah.

On the way home Tuunac sat in the center of the canoe while Mathrom and I paddled across the inlet. Aqwissa unwound herself to sit in his lap while she feasted on the young hunter's prize.

When we had stowed away the canoe in the tribal boathouse and disposed of the camp's garbage we began the trek home, with our fish and other plunder. We agreed to take the long way round, in spite of our exhaustion. We figured it would be safer using back ways through the brush in the rough places by the railroad tracks rather than risk being spotted and then picked up and "questioned" by a cruising goldy patrol. And they surely would stop us—if they saw us, because I knew we all looked a mess.

As I trudged up our front steps, barely able to put one foot in front of the other, Tuunac and Mathrom right behind me, the door burst open and a crying Bijah launched herself in my direction, nearly knocking me off my feet. Staggering I dropped my blanket bundle and hugged her.

"There, there, my sweet baby girl, everything is alright now. Don't cry. We are safe."

Glancing over her shoulder my wife and sister and Angika stood in the doorway looking fearful and uncertain. I gave my women a lopsided smile. "Sorry, I guess we are a bit late for the evening meal." I pointed with my lips to Mathrom and Tuunac. "But we caught plenty of fish and a rabbit for tomorrow."

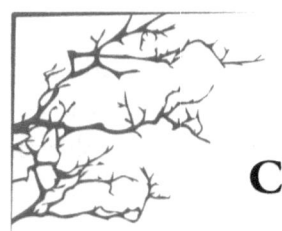

Chapter Twenty-Five

Not sure how badly Aqwissa had injured my traitorous cousin, or maybe Utreal and the Crokno thought Aqwissa hadn't survived, but for whatever reason they left us in peace to lick our wounds, for which I was grateful. To foster the illusion of her death I decided that I alone would maintain the shielding of the family and our home until she was fully recovered, hoping the truce would continue throughout the rest of the summer.

I had no illusions that it was over, however, Utreal's petty grievance against me for taking Aqwissa was minor compared to my father and I killing the Crokno-breed Hoyt, an agent in our world, in which the enemy had invested a lot of their time and power to create. A reckoning for that was a terrifying specter looming sometime in my future.

I was also grateful for my sister's presence in our home. She was able to work with Mathrom as he came into his true Cougar puwa. Her Gift coming from the same source she was able to teach and guide him better than I could, having no cougar puwa of my own.

Kitahtla proved to be a wise guide in another aspect that I hadn't considered. One night soon after our return home when I was still suffering from my wounds I went to bed early only to be awakened later by a chill at my back and the sound of someone softly crying in the living room. Noticing Gahji was no longer by my side I crept down the hall towards the sound.

Before I could reveal myself I heard someone else enter from the kitchen and then Kitahtla said, "Sit up, my girl, and drink this."

Venturing a quick peak around the corner I saw my tearful Gahji huddled in a blanket on the couch, my sister sitting down beside her and handing her a cup of steaming herbal tea. As I watched from the shadows Gahji sat up, wiped her eyes and took the offered cup.

After a few sips, she said, "I'm so afraid, Granny Kitah. All my life I dreamed of having such a man as Tas in my life. He is the answer to all my prayers. I don't know how I could survive if I lost him."

Kitahtla nodded and patted her hand. "I won't lie to you and say that isn't a possibility. I have a pretty good idea how you must feel. He has returned wounded to you, twice now, after encounters with his enemies.

"As a child I can recall that we were constantly running away from the soldiers. Always afraid, often hungry, I had to learn to live with the fear that soldiers would find, and kill, some or all of us. Mama Sagila lost two husbands to war and I wouldn't wish that pain on anyone."

"How did you do it? How did you go on knowing the ones you loved constantly risked their lives and might be taken away at any time?"

Kitahtla sighed. "It isn't easy, my girl, truly it isn't. You learn to take one day at a time. Each morning you pray and give thanks for your many blessings, and you pray for the courage and the strength to survive if Death's shadow falls over the ones you love before you sleep again."

"But why? Why are so many bad things happening to our people? What have we done for the Unseen Ones to curse us so?"

Kitahtla was silent for a long time before she said, "I don't know why, my girl, and I'm not even sure that's the right way to think about it, though blaming a god's punishment for the bad in our lives is certainly what we've learned since the live-away schools. Though our Traditional Elders viewed our situation, before the Empire conquered us differently, I've heard."

"How then?"

"Many of them blamed malicers for their troubles back then, but that isn't the whole truth either. As best I understand it, all our thoughts, our feelings, and our actions, both as individuals and as a People have consequences. Consequences we can't always predict the outcome of. Without laying blame we have to choose how we respond to the events in our lives and one choice may affect our own and many other lives in future.

"Men like Papa Jimmy, his warband of outlaws, and yes, Tas himself, made a choice to pledge their lives to the People—and in Tas's case, to our world for its protection, even to the point of sacrificing their very lives to insure others' survival."

"You, like Mama Sagila, have chosen to love a warrior. He needs you and your love, my girl, never doubt that, but like the warriors of old who often had more than one wife you too have a co-wife to contend with. So, instead of fighting her presence, it will be up to you to find a way to work in harmony with that other, for the good of us all."

Gahji chuckled and took a drink of her tea. "His other wife, you are speaking of his pledge to Kunai to help protect our world from these Crokno invaders who wish to destroy us, right?"

"Yes, them, but his pledge also includes the destructive forces among us humans. The Crokno aren't killing babies in wars, cutting down our forests, or poisoning the land with mining projects, for example."

She snorted. "Yes, that is true, humans—and men especially, can be destructive shits."

Kitahtla chuckled. "That they can, but you will have to include women in your condemnation as well. My daughter Qwadalah can be a mean vindictive bitch at times, as well."

Gahji laughed softly acknowledging the point. "I can be a bitch at times, too." She fell silent a while sipping her tea Kitahtla letting her think. At last she set down her cup and said, "I want to be strong for him—and my children, granny, but it's so hard."

"I know it is, my girl. But you have powerful Bear Puwa through your lineage to help you. Pray, my girl, and be guided by those ancestors and the Spirits bonded to your bloodline who are there to help."

I heard no more after that. With a lump in my throat I crept back to our bed to wait for her.

Over the next few days while we recovered Mathrom and I stayed home with the younger children and my sister, while Gahji went to work. My nephew was still trying to understand his inherited Cougar power and how to use it. I was grateful Kitahtla was with us to help with his training.

Stakaya had a new girlfriend and was spending a lot of time over at her house, so Mathrom was able to get a break from the lumpy couch and sleep in his room some nights.

At other times I suspected he slept with Tuunac. They had grown quite close after their shared experience at my camp. Even though he hadn't seen the actual battle with the aliens my son started having nightmares about what he had undergone and witnessed.

Having Mathrom, who had been there nearby to comfort him I think helped him set his fears aside so he could return to being the boy who used to torment his younger sister one moment and in the next trying to persuade me and his mother that he was nearly a man grown.

I was glad the language program had shut down for the summer so I didn't have to do a lot of explaining about my battered condition, but I was also worried about our money situation. O'siyan needed his mother too much for Gahji to go back to work fulltime, and my summer jobs were not going to bring in much money—though they would be challenging and interesting for me personally.

I also suspected that Stakaya was back dealing tishwa smoke and o'piyo to help out after he lost a job delivering boxes for a local warehouse. I suggested to him that he go work on one of the fishing boats owned by the tribe when I confronted him about the dealing, but he was reluctant to leave Seatown for the north, because of Jula, the new girl in his life. So, rather than spend a lot of time arguing with him, I left the matter for him to figure out on his own.

Coping with the stresses of this modern world made me feel like an inadequate failure when I couldn't support my family well. Though I was hunting and fishing nearly every day to ease our money situation, it wasn't enough. No one ever blamed me or complained about not having new toys or clothes, but I blamed myself.

To be a modern man I figured I had to provide modern items, like a desperately needed new couch, and other expected things so apart of this modern world. It was very frustrating for me, because when I called the tribal office on the far-speak everyone was vague about when the government money would arrive.

With Kitahtla and Mathrom living with us to help out I was considering asking Chief Rickson to get me a job smuggling with his shady cousin when he came to me with another proposal.

It was too hot that day to use the cooker in the kitchen, so I was out in our back yard building a small fire to cook the fish I had caught in my seal form just before dawn that morning. As if I had conjured him with my troubled thoughts, when I looked up, there was Rickson with kaf-tea cup in hand on the porch behind me.

Setting the last of my catch on a long forked stick leaning over the flames to cook, I waved him to one of the log rounds placed near the fire.

Taking a seat he sipped at his drink and smiled. "Seeing you like this brings back so many memories from my early childhood."

I sighed and nodded. "Me, too. I'm lucky that we live in a part of the city where the neighbors don't complain about my cooking or other traditional projects like," I motioned to the drying frame containing a stretched deer hide ready for tanning by the porch.

"But in spite of the extra freedom living here affords me it isn't safe for Gahji and the children when I'm not around. I still would like to move us away from all this," I waved a hand at the tangled shrubs and undergrowth that led from the back yard down to the railroad tracks and the homeless encampment on the other side. "But with both Gahji and me only working part-time that isn't going to happen for a while."

Rickson made a noncommittal grunt and took another sip of his kaf-tea. "They told me at the office that you were looking for me and asking about the summer programs I wanted to hire you for.

"We are still waiting for the instructors' training grant to come through, but I came to tell you that the first of the Wachedai social dances will be held at the end of the month. I can hire you—part time starting next week to help set up the grounds and organize security on site during the event."

"Me? Become a goldy? Why me? Surely there are other tribal members better qualified."

Rickson laughed when he saw my face and in the next moment I joined him. "Well, that's certainly a job that I've never considered before."

"There are others qualified, true," he added, "and I hope you will include them in your planning and patrols, but I figured you might be our best choice."

"Why? The only thing I know about peace defenders I learned from visiting the *inside* of their jails a few times."

He laughed again. Then leaning forward he looked me in the eye in the chamuqwani fashion. "You see in the past we have lost funding for these cultural events, because of drugs and booze being used on site and the goldys called to keep the peace and prevent further violence.

"Now that the government is giving us another chance I don't want to risk more trouble this year. And you, with your, uh, special talents might help prevent that."

It angered me that a proud man like Rickson had to grovel to the imperial officials for our basic needs like good housing, healthcare and permission and money to hold our cultural events, but I was not in a position to do much about it, so I would have to bend like the willow in a storm and learn how to survive until a better time came along.

I thought about my answer for another moment then agreed.

The chief rose and set his empty cup on the round where he had been sitting. "Good, we will talk again later, after the Wachedai dance."

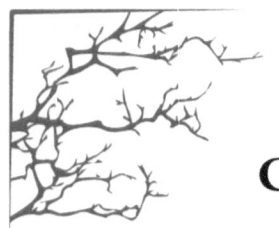

Chapter Twenty-Six

I had never heard of a wachidai dance during my childhood. When I asked Elder Samul about them he explained that they had started about fifty years before.

"There were children from many different tribes all thrown together at those damned schools. We made friends from tribes from different parts of the Preserve or elsewhere. The Wachidai Dances started I heard as a way for people to get together in the summers after they grew up and left school. We could gather, visit and have fun—and no damned priests were there to break it up.

"It was an act of defiance against the Empire, too, I guess. It showed the pinker officials and priests that they couldn't kill our spirit or our culture—no matter what they did to us."

Later Kitahtla added to the chief's explanation when she said, "The people back then created new songs, new dances to disguise a hidden way of honoring our traditions and secretly praying to the Unseen Ones as we danced and sang."

And like the dances back home at Big Ice Lake it was a way to dress in our finest regalia and display our heritage to everyone, I thought, as I watched the family get ready on the first day of the celebration.

I remembered the woolen shawls fringed with brightly colored ribbons and yarns that the women and girls wore in my youth, only now instead of tunic dresses of leather or trade-cloth to wear under them, Gahji pulled out a box from the back of the closet containing a few long skirts made with patchwork designs and sewn with rows of colored ribbons.

She had one for herself and one for Kitahtla, Saskina already having one of her own. There were also little dresses similarly made for the girls. Angika cried when her dress was too small and she had to give it to Bijah. Then her mother surprised her with a new skirt similar to her own and she was all smiles again.

The men of the family weren't neglected either. Tuunac Mathrom and Stakaya had brightly colored shirts and woven belts to wear and my sweet bear woman surprised me with a new shirt of my own and an embroidered leather vest to wear over top of it. Her gift being a total surprise she laughed when my mouth dropped open and then she kissed me.

Rushton had recently given me a broad-brimmed chamuqwani hat decorated with a leather headband strung with engraved silver disks. The women made me try everything on, and pronounced me quite handsome which made me blush.

Elder Samul and cousin Denny were picking us up in their mecho-carts, so when they arrived we loaded up all our children, blankets, food and folding chairs and off we went.

The dance ground was a large grassy field which at other times of the year teams playing ball games used. Around the central open area set aside for dancing was a circle of tents and other types of open-walled shelters. Some of these were set up by people selling food and craft items, while others closer to the dance itself were places where those wanting just to watch the dances or needing to rest could sit and visit with friends.

Unlike the hand drums I was used to from my childhood, on the dance ground itself were four large drums and chairs surrounding them for the singers who would play them.

Behind all the bustling activity, near the back fence and the scrub beyond was an area where people had been allowed to set up tents and park their mecho-wagons. Most were just relatives from the Preserve visiting family and wanting to share in the celebrations. Others, however were here for a darker purpose and it was in those shadowy places I would be focusing much of my attention.

Officially there was to be no drugs or booze on the site, but as Stakaya laughingly informed me that wasn't going to stop anybody.

"You," I told him sternly, "had better not be one of the ones I might catch dealing back there, because you won't like it if I do." He shuddered, probably remembering what happened to Mathrom when he disobeyed me.

A few days before the dance was to take place I met with the men and women the committee hired for the security patrols. Several were young and inexperienced but most were warriors who had served in combat and had been hired before for the wachidai dances.

Most were comfortable with me being the one in charge, because I listened to what they had to say and considered their suggestions valuable. The only person I suspected was going to cause trouble for me was a scarred veteran who I'd heard grumbling about Rickson during the lunches at ZFH.

He took one look at me after I was introduced and made the assumption that the only reason I got the job was because I was a favored younger relative.Contradicting me whenever he could throughout our meeting, I asked him to stay when everyone else was leaving.

Danyo was his name and he gave me a withering look and started for the door. Over his shoulder, he growled, "I'm no snot-nosed kid staying after school 'cause some puffed up young fancy ass sucking up to the chief thinks I'm a bad boy."

I let him get nearly to the door then I froze him in place, his hand out stretched for the knob. He struggled for a long moment, before I walked over and shut the door so we could be alone.

Eyes wide he opened his mouth either to cry for help or to curse me out again, but before he could decide, I looked him in the eye and said, "I can glue your mouth closed as well, so don't push me."

When he nodded, I continued, "As I said, I want to talk to you. If you think you can behave like a sensible person I will release you and we can go back to the table over there and have our talk. What will it be, eh?"

"We talk," he snarled. "Let me go."

His words said one thing, but using my spirit sight I could see radiating flames of anger in his spirit fire. He was planning to attack me as soon as I released him. I smiled showing my canines. "What you are planning would be most unwise."

Aqwissa uncoiled herself from around my neck to perch upon my shoulder, a low threatening growl deep in her throat. "If this one saw you as a real threat she might kill you and nobody wants that." I motioned to the table again. "I repeat, shall we sit and talk?"

When he nodded I released him and he walked stiffly to the table and sat. When I took a chair across from him he pointed to Aqwissa and said, "What is that thing? And who are you, for that matter?"

"The answers to those questions would take too long to explain at the moment. If you know old Tommo you can ask him about me later. Right now we have more important work to discuss. As you may have figured out by now, I'm not a young man sucking up to Rickson to take your job.

"I was hired because I have certain, 'Gifts,' that the chief felt might insure that there will be no trouble this year that might cut off future funding for the Wachidai.

"If you think you can set aside your bitterness and work with me then I would like to leave much of the organizational details up to you, because you are the better man for that, and I'm not shy about saying so."

"And if I can't work like that?"

"Then you are done here; you won't be working this year. We will get someone else to replace you."

Glancing at Aqwissa and then looking me in the eye, he knew I wasn't joking. "So if I'm gonna run the show like I've always done what will you be doing—cept collecting a paycheck?"

I stroked Aqwissa and smiled. "Whatever I need to. You've just experienced a taste of what I can do to prevent a situation from exploding into violence that will bring the goldys on the dance grounds. Rickson and the committee don't want to give the city and the Seatown Peace Defenders the excuse they want to stop the wachidai forever."

It took a little more talk, but both of us wanted to prevent the city from stopping the dances, so he grudgingly agreed to work with me and take my orders when necessary. By the time we left I was certain we could work together—though we would probably never be friends.

After we arrived on the dance grounds I helped get the family's baskets and chairs arranged in a shelter erected to shade the people watching the dances. When we were settled, my sister resting in a comfortable chair to supervise, I decided it was time to report to Danyo and tell him I was here and I would be walking around.

Earlier we agreed that officially I wouldn't start seriously patrolling till the evening, so I had the day to enjoy the dance and visit with family and friends. I would begin my vigil later, after officially everything closed, and would continue throughout the night.

Leaving O'siyan strapped into the old-time cradleboard I'd made for him next to Kitahtla's chair, Gahji took my arm and we headed off to browse the vendors' stalls and check in with Danyo in the command wagon. The three younger children had already left with Mathrom and his sister Saskina to do their own exploring.

Though the wachidai was full of strangers, who might possibly be human enemies under alien control, I wasn't too worried about the children; they were wearing my talismans, which would alert me to any trouble, and the older siblings would see no harm came to them from drunks and other normal dangers.

I had talked Mathrom—and Stakaya into signing up for some security patrols during the three-day event. Since his battle with the alien trackers Mathrom had become a trusted young warrior that I was starting to rely on.

When we arrived at the command wagon to report, Gahji laughed at my expression when an evilly smiling Danyo handed me a long golden strip of cloth. Puzzled, I asked, "Uh, what am I supposed to do with this?"

"Put it around your hat wear it on your arm or tie it around your neck—though I wouldn't advise that—I don't care, just wear it."

"All right, but why?"

Sharing her amusement with the scarred veteran Gahji laughed at my expression and then explained, "So if someone needs help they will know you are a wachidai goldy, that's why, my dear, sweet seal man."

"Oh." I wasn't sure I wanted everyone to know I was a goldy. I could almost hear my warbands' ghosts laughing at me. Muttering my dismay under my breath I tied the cloth to my upper left arm.

Before returning to our seats to watch the dancing we bought some fried scau-bread and wandered around the booths, stopping to talk with relatives and friends, and marveling at all the beautiful things that were on display. I would have liked to buy her everything that caught her fancy, but we had no extra money to spend on pretty things, which brought up my feelings of being an inadequate husband and man again.

When Gahji paid special attention to a pair of long earrings I resolved to come back later and see if I could trade for them with meat or fish. With

Mathrom content to stay at the house and Saskina dropping by nearly every day I also resolved to steal my Gahji away from time-to-time so we could be alone and do fun things together that didn't involve children and work. I was a modern man now, I reminded myself, I needed to think of such things and keep my partner loving and happy.

When we returned with drinks and snacks for my sister and the others we found Kitahtla surrounded by several women cooing over O'siyan strapped in his cradleboard. I hadn't thought about it but I suddenly realized I hadn't seen any modern babies being carried that way.

When I sat down beside my sister and handed her a cup of tea and some bread, she leaned over next to my ear and whispered, "They all want to know where they can buy a board for their own babies. You could probably go into business selling them if you wanted.'

I snorted a laugh. "I don't want. And the one Nachoga made for you was much better than my bumbling attempt for O'siyan."

She patted my hand. "You did a fine job. Don't be hard on yourself."

The regalia and the dancing were amazing to me. Beautiful and powerful I sat for a time with the women and allowed the Qwakaiva generated by the songs to envelope me. I was so proud of my People at that moment. We had lived through so much. We had survived and were still strong and powerful.

Unable to totally relax I got restless after a time, the gold cloth on my arm reminding me I had other obligations. Leaning over I kissed Gahji on the forehead and rose. "I'm going to have a look around. I will be back."

She frowned, but her eyes said she was only teasing me. "You had better or I will come looking. You promised you would dance with me when they start the couple's dances."

Actually I had forgotten that promise, but I smiled and nodded.

"You better," she warned. "I don't want to come looking and find you with another woman who has singled you out for *her* dance partner, eh?"

I laughed without turning. My mind suddenly focused elsewhere, I called over my shoulder, "No chance of that. You are the only one for me."

A moment ago I had sensed a disturbance in the otherworldly currents surrounding this place. I couldn't determine if that meant trouble, but someone—or someones had opened a portal and entered my world from the

Beyond. Aqwissa had sensed the portal opening, too, but also wasn't sure of its significance.

Trying not to alert any alien visitor to our knowing we wandered among the people and booths along the outside of the dance ground, searching for the intruder.

Responding to my role of wachidai goldy I helped a young mother locate a lost toddler, and later caught a couple of teenaged girl stuffing jewelry into an open handbag.

Quietly coming up behind them I reached over the taller one's shoulder and plucked the bag from her hand. At their startled look I smiled and opened the bag. It was crammed with earrings, bracelets and necklaces. "My, my, such a lot of pretty things. You must have worked hard all year to get the script to pay for all this."

"Yes we did—so give it back," she growled. Noticing my gold armband at last she balled up a fist and swore.

"I don't think so. I watched you stuff this in your bag," I held up a brightly colored necklace. "It's from the table behind us. You didn't pay for it."

"Yes, I did."

I wasn't going to get in an argument with them so I only smiled showing my canines. The girls were skinny and were dressed in ragged clothes, no regalia. The only decorative items they wore were pairs of long earrings, which they might or might not have already stolen.

My silent stare was unnerving them, finally the tall one blurted, "You gonna arrest us, stupid pretend goldy?"

"Should I?"

"No, cause we didn't steal that stuff."

"But if you try we'll say you are a pervert who tried to molest us. Then you'll be the one in trouble, eh?" the other one threatened.

Startled, I jerked my head back as if she had slapped me. Taking advantage of my surprise the taller one ducked out from under my hand and opened her mouth as if she was going to scream and do just that. Anticipating her shout I glued her mouth shut, and her friend's mouth, too.

Before they could think to run I grabbed both of them and hustled them out of the central walkway. Over by some of the parked mecho-vehicles I turned them to face me. Eyes wide they stared at me, now too frightened to think of running. Seeing Danyo talking to a couple dancers in the parking area not far away I hailed him.

He scowled when he saw the two girls I was holding. When he reached us I handed him the bag of stolen items. "I caught these two stealing from the vendors over there." I scowled and added, "When I confronted them, that one," I pointed at the taller girl, "threatened to tell everyone that I had molested her."

Danyo snorted. "Yeah the little bitch tried that on me last time we held a wachidai. It didn't work then, either, but she's a slow learner. Aren't you, Larissa?"

Telling him that I sensed trouble elsewhere I left him to deal with the girls and headed back into the vendors' area. Those from the Beyond were near my children, and Bijah was frightened.

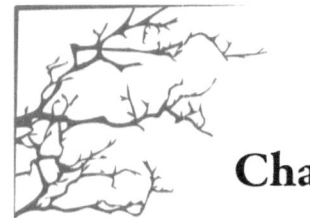

Chapter Twenty-Seven

Fearing it was Utreal or another Crokno agent I tried not to panic. Everything would be alright; I would find them, I kept telling myself. With the big drums booming like my frightened heart I frantically searched the happy crowd for a sign of them.

<<Calm down, Siyatli brother, you are blocking your power with your anxiety,>> Aqwissa said. <<The little one is fearful, but the intruder is only Zeiva. The children are in no danger—and the cougar warrior is coming. See, they are over there near the food stalls.>>

Slowing my pace, I headed in the direction she indicated and then I saw them. Bijah was standing a part from Angika and Saskina with her thumb in her mouth, a tall slim woman with golden skin and golden hair, bending over her. Zeiva was saying something to her but I couldn't hear what. There was too much noise with the drum and the singing.

The older girls looked worried, but hadn't worked up enough courage to interfere yet. Out of the corner of my eye I saw a grim faced Mathrom also heading in their direction, Tuunac and a puzzled Stakaya coming along at a slower pace in his wake.

Bijah saw, or sensed me first and raced over to me, clutching my leg. I picked her up and she buried her face against my chest, frantically sucking her thumb. In a soothing voice I said. "It's all right, little one. Zeiva didn't mean to frighten you." Then to my tricky cousin, I said, "Asiya, Zeiva, what are you doing here?"

When she straightened I noticed that Zeiva was dressed in a dance shawl and long skirt like most of the women here, but her shirt was unbuttoned enough to show lots of golden breast. I sighed. Ze was hunting—for willing male prey—as usual. And judging by the adoring hungry look Stakaya was giving her as he approached I suspected she was also enhancing the men ze encountered interest with her power.

Green eyes laughing at me ze grinned. "Ah, Siyatli Cousin, how nice to see you again at last. I was just asking the child where I might find you."

"Umm hmm. Why?"

Zer grin widened. "Why to see if you want to bargain, of course. Still want to go home?"

I snorted. "A little late for that now, as I'm sure you know."

Setting my daughter down I nudged her in her sister's direction. <<This being is my cousin; everything is fine. Go with Saskina and your sister and stay with your mother. I will come soon.>>

Using my voice I called to Stakaya, "Take the children and Saskina and go back to where granny Kitah is sitting. I'll be along in a while."

Glancing at Zeiva he hesitated, reluctant to leave. "Do what I say, Ky—now!" I snapped. He heard the warning in my voice and with one last longing glance in my cousin's direction he ushered his charges away.

Zeiva's eyes widened at my use of the mind talk with Bijah, which made me smile. By that time Mathrom had joined us. Under my breath I said, "Did you sense our visitor from the Beyond?"

"Not sure what I felt but Cougar warned me there was trouble and I knew I had to find the girls," he murmured. Mathrom's lips thinned into a hard line and his green cougar eyes glared at my otherworldly cousin. The Cougar in his spirit fire snarled.

Zeiva had heard us and chuckled. Ze looked him over and liked what ze saw. With a red cloth banned across his forehead, his long tawny hair in braids and a colorful dance shirt covering his muscular torso, my nephew was a handsome young man. Ze also could see his cougar guardian and was amused by their hostility. Enhancing zer power to ensnare him, ze gave him an enticing smile, showing lots of teeth.

Mathrom curled his lip and stepped back. He didn't exactly know what ze was trying to do to him, but he knew instinctually he wouldn't like it if ze succeeded.

"Mathrom, maybe you should go with—"

"I'm staying with you, uncle," he announced in a firm voice, his green cougar eyes fixed on the intruder.

I sighed again. "Oh, Zeiva, stop. He's family, so leave him alone. He knows in part what you are trying to do because he has already killed one of the enemies from the Beyond and can smell the Beyond on you as well."

"Really?" Ze narrowed her eyes and studied him more closely. "That is a tale I'd like to hear, handsome tom kitten man. Will you tell it to me sometime?"

The creature just couldn't help zerself. Seduction was in zer nature.

Mathrom looked uncertain how to answer zer. To help him out and change the subject I said, "Where is Dathna and Utreal, and what are you really doing here?"

"Why, looking for you, cousin, among other things, as I said, and talking to that lovely little human child. Is she yours?"

"Yes, she's mine in our traditional Qwani'Ya way."

Zeiva chuckled. "Such a sweet little thing, she has a bit of the old dragon blood in her. Did you know that?"

"I know she has been gifted from her father's heritage," I touched the choker around my neck. "Aqwissa told me and has been teaching her. But never mind my daughter; where is the rest of your hunting pack?"

Zeiva shrugged zer golden shoulders. "Dathna is around—hunting a new friend—somewhere. Utreal... I don't know where ze has taken off to. We haven't seen zer in a while. I was wondering if you had—seen zer?"

Mathrom muttered a curse under his breath and we exchanged troubled looks. "No I haven't seen the traitorous fish slime, but I definitely want to."

"Really? Why? I never thought you two were that close."

"We aren't. I want to find the dog humping piece of shit, because ze has tried to have me killed three times since you abandoned me in this place and time and I want to return the favor."

Zeiva laughed, dismissing my accusation with a wave of zer hand. "Oh, that's too funny. You are so amusing, little cousin. Why would ze do something so foolish as to risk Kunai and the clan's wrath by killing you? And over something as trivial as a little dragon lizard ze wanted? How ridiculous!"

"I know you don't think much of my half-breed skills, but I tell you ze is a malicer and a traitor.

"Impossible!"

"Why? Is it really so impossible that a breed like me might be right?"

Zeiva jerked back as if I had hit zer. I saw the flare of rage encircling zer form and braced myself for an attack. All serious now Zeiva hissed, "Yes-s-s it is. Utreal would never do something so stupid. Ze is no traitor? That's preposterous! Dathna and I have known Utreal for hundreds of your human years. It couldn't be true."

Like so often before when I lived among my paternal relatives, ze was dismissing me and my Gift. My temper flared and I snapped, "Why not, because it's me, Star Swimmer's poor little half-breed, someone with only inferior abilities, someone who can't be trusted to know and use true power? After all I'm only a stupid 'siyatli' making that claim, eh?"

Zeiva was silent for a long moment before saying, "That is a grave accusation, little cousin. If you want me to take you seriously tell me more about why you think that? What evidence can you offer to prove your claim?"

Motioning for zer and my nephew to follow me I led them to a quiet spot by the fence then I turned to face zer, and began, "Utreal would risk it, for two reasons as best I can figure." I held up one finger. "One, because ze is the Crokno traitor and spy Star Swimmer warned us about. And when my father and I killed their favored human agent the Crokno wanted revenge, and so along with his spying ze's been commanded to kill one or both of us, if ze can."

Before ze could launch a counter argument I held up another finger. "And two, because Aqwissa is far more than what she appears to be, and Utreal knows it. Ze wanted her to bond with zer, so ze would have power enough to kill Star Swimmer. But Aqwissa resisted, and managed to insert herself into Uti's stolen horde to prevent him from trying to enslave her."

"Interesting, I know ze was unusually angry over the qwissa dragon-lizard, but that doesn't prove ze wanted to kill you."

"No, on its own it doesn't, but I have other reasons. When you left me that first night the goldys arrested me. Guards at the jail were paid money to kill me and take Aqwissa. While one of them was ensnared in my conjure, I asked him who had paid them to take Aqwissa and kill me. He couldn't name the one, but he did show me an image of Utreal as ze appeared in human form earlier that night.

"The second time ze tried to kill me ze hired a Sabiyan hunter and its creatures to find me in the Dream. I killed its slaves and Aqwissa followed their back-trail, and killed the master. Once again the creature revealed before its death the image of Utreal."

Before I could account the third time Mathrom rolled up his sleeve to show zer a long half-healed scar on his arm. "I got this a few weeks ago when another pack of alien hunters discovered me at Tas's camp in the forest where I was staying. They told me they were looking for him."

"Fortunately I happened to be coming to get Mathrom and was nearby. Together the young cougar warrior and I managed to kill its scent detector slaves in my world, while Aqwissa went hunting in the Beyond for the master.

"Unfortunately Utreal and an unknown Crokno were waiting for just such a move. Though she wounded Utreal when ze tried to ensnare her my little Aqwissa was badly wounded and barely made it back to me." I stroked my living choker and heard her purr next to my ear.

Zeiva gave me a noncommittal grunt and turned away. "You have given me much to think about, I will admit. But before I can return to the Beyond I have to hunt—and have some fun while I feed."

Before ze could leave I grabbed zer arm in desperation. "Zeiva, please, you may not believe me but at least find Star Swimmer for me and tell him what I told you. If he says I'm being foolish then I will say no more."

Turning back to me ze frowned. "Find your father? Ah, you've just reminded me. That was the other matter I wanted to talk to you about. Have you seen him?"

An icy chill sliding down my back bone I shook my head. "I tried within the Dream to contact him when my son was born some moons ago, but I couldn't find him. I just assumed he was off somewhere doing something for the Great One and would contact me when he returned to our beach and found me gone."

"Hmm, Co'yeh and the elders sent me to ask you if you had seen him, because he is missing, too."

"That is most troubling news, cousin," I said, feeling a knot of fear growing in my gut.

Ze removed my hand from zer arm and stepped away. Ze was distracted by the need I saw in zer eyes. Ze wasn't going to take my warning seriously until ze replenished her Qwakaiva with some of a human lover's life essence.

"It's probably nothing to worry about," Zeiva reassured me. "He may have found a new love, or is spending time with one of his other families." Ze smiled, a mischievous gleam in zer otherworldly green eyes as ze studied me carefully. "The ones he never told you about."

Other families? Well that certainly was a stunning revelation, and would explain a lot of his long absences when he left me alone with other relatives, but I wasn't going to let her know ze had surprised me—and maybe hurt me a little, too.

Hoping my face and my spirit fire wouldn't give my inner turmoil away, I said, "I don't think so; not this time. There is something wrong and my father is in trouble."

Ze thought about it for a moment then gave me a condescending smile as a new thought came to zer. "Since no one has heard from either Utreal or Star Swimmer, perhaps they are together somewhere battling the Crokno enemy."

When ze spoke those words the foretelling hit me like a hammer blow. Gasping for air I staggered and might have fallen if Mathrom hadn't rushed to catch me. Violent images of combat exploded in my mind. Red beams of light blinded me, I heard my father and others shouting and the thunder of alien machines roared, drowning out all other sound. The stink of blood stung my nostrils and its coppery taste clogged my throat as Zeiva's prophetic words reverberated in my head. <<Perhaps they are together...>>

My body trembling with the power of the sending I was still ensnared in the horror and I couldn't answer when a frightened Mathrom called to me. "Uncle, speak to me. What's happening; what's wrong?" He shook me gently and glared at Zeiva his lips curling with a snarl. "You alien bitch! What did you do to him?"

"Don't insult me, little tom kitten." Ze snarled indignantly. "I've sworn an oath to care for, and protect him, and I keep my word." Zeiva studied me for a moment longer then waved zer hand, banishing the horror. Still gasping I leaned into Mathrom, trying to center myself and catch my breath.

When ze saw that I was calmer and grounded, ze said, "What did you see, little Siyatli cousin?"

How much to tell zer? How much was in the past and how much of my vision was a possible future? Taking another deep breath I stood straighter and said, "You are right, cousin; they are together, but not as allies. Star Swimmer is imprisoned and Utreal is his jailer—and the angry Sabisa, mother of Hoyt, is coming to have her revenge on him."

Having the gift of prophesy, like all the creatures born in the Beyond Zeiva didn't dismiss my words, but ze wasn't sure I had interpreted what I witnessed correctly, either.

Ze reached out to touch me this time. "Show me what you saw. I will consult Dathna about this and if we see truth in your interpretation we will alert the clan and the Elders," ze promised.

I shuddered, but I relived the foretelling and allowed zer to take it from my mind.When ze was finished ze released me, and then said, "That is a most troubling sending, true enough, cousin. When I return to the Beyond I will speak to our Elders right away." Zeiva grinned. "But first I need to—feed."

Catching zer arm again, I begged, "Zeiva, please I know you must feed before returning, but Star Swimmer is in great danger, truly he is. Don't stay over long in my world, playing your games."

And then, before I could argue further, my scowling wife found us.

Snatching my hand off Zeiva's arm I whirled and swallowed hard. I don't know what the children and her brother had told her, but my Gahji was not happy with me at that moment.

Distracted by the interruption and curious about the newcomer Zeiva sensed her displeasure and smirked, amused.

Coming up to us, Gahji took in the picture we three made and was not happy. First there was me with my hand on the arm of a pretty, smiling woman with her shirt half open, and then there was Mathrom looking dazed and uncertain, like a child caught stealing scau-bread from the grub box. Gahji folded her arms across her breasts and glared at everybody without speaking. Her Bear lifted her lip in a snarl.

I didn't know what to say. After an endless tense pause Mathrom plastered a smile on his face and said, "Hi, auntie," he pointed to Zeiva with his lips. "This is our relative from the Beyond, Zeiva."

"Zeiva is a paternal cousin," I babbled quickly. "Ze and another cousin came to find me to give me news about other relatives."

"Hmm, is that so."

I took a step away from my tricky cousin and nodded vigorously. "Yes, truly it is."

She kept me anxious for a long moment then dismissed Zeiva and zer games, and said, "When the children told me where I might find you, I came to remind you of your promise. They will be calling for a couples dance soon. But if you are busy..."

Flustered and uncertain what the children had told her about our alien visitor I wasn't sure what to do or say. "Uh, no I'm not too busy." I glanced at Zeiva. Enjoying my discomfort, no doubt, ze smirked. Knowing Gahji was watching, ze thrust zer breasts forward to display them more fully.

I sighed. <<Zeiva, please stop.>>

To my relief just then the couples dance was announced and Gahji took my arm with a possessive firmness. As she started to lead me away, she turned back and surprised me by saying to Zeiva, "I am forgetting my manners. Since you are a part of Tas's family you and the other cousin here with you to enjoy the wachidai are welcome to join us in our family's shelter. Tas can introduce you to everyone and you can watch the dancing with us."

Zeiva seemed as startled by the generous offer as I was. Her eyes opened wide and then ze bowed zer head and smiled. "Thank you, I just might do that. I will admit, I am curious to get to know the human kin our little siyatli cousin was so anxious to return to in this world."

As Gahji lead me away, a watchful Mathrom trailing in our wake, I murmured, "Oh my sweet generous Bear Woman, I'm not sure you know what you have gotten us into."

She snorted and quickened her pace as the big drum began pounding out its insistent rhythm. "No, it's that tricky bitch from the Beyond who doesn't know what ze has gotten zerself into." She grinned. "And if she tries to mess with my stupid brother, ze is going to have trouble with me and my Bear."

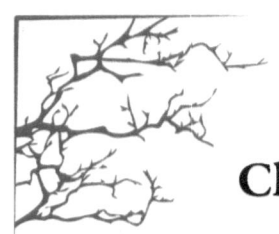

Chapter Twenty-Eight

Hands clasped we joined the circling dancers. Never having known this kind of dancing as a child, I allowed Gahji to lead us into the pattern of the swirling couples. While we danced I gave her a brief account of Zeiva's troubling news and my foretelling. After the first song ended we stayed, holding hands to dance several more while we discussed the problem.

Talked out at last with no solution coming to mind we continued just to dance, allowing the drum's rhythm and the singing to fill our hearts and spirits with their peaceful Qwakaiva. Letting our body's movement become our offering to the Unseen Ones, we each prayed for Star Swimmer's survival our children's protection, and the healing of our troubled world.

When we returned to our portion of the shelter I was startled to see sitting on the grass by Kitahtla's chair both Zeiva and a male Dathna. This time Dathna was wearing a brightly colored shirt, long dark braids, and sunglasses covering zer otherworldly green eyes.

I also noticed with some amusement that Kitahtla had managed to convince Zeiva to button up zer shirt and tone down her seductive power. Ze was talking quietly with my sister and Saskina, and both of my tricky cousins for once seemed to be behaving themselves—though for how long was anybody's guess.

Still wary of the visitors Mathrom had disappeared with the younger children I noted, and that was probably for the best.

Kutima and Rushton had arrived and were also sitting and watching the dancing nearby. Rushton looked a bit dazed and uncomfortable probably sensing Zeiva's allure and didn't know what to do about it. He seemed relieved when he saw me returning. I doubted he could detect who they really were, but I could tell he did sense the unnatural power ze radiated and was flustered.

Having already met my father, Kutima I was certain did know our visiting relatives were from the Beyond. When Gahji and I arrived hot and breathless from the dancing, he was engaged in an animated conversation with Dathna and didn't notice me till I greeted him in our language.

Far over by the edge of the next family shelter hovered Stakaya and cousin Denny, pretending to joke with the young men sitting there, but secretly watching Zeiva every chance they could.

Gahji saw their glances too and frowned, sending her brother a murderous look. Placing a hand on her arm, I shook my head. "I will talk to them for you, but don't worry about the boys. Even if they don't heed my warning and agree to go with zer for some fun, Zeiva isn't going to harm them—not really.

"If ze ensnares him Ky will wake up tomorrow feeling like he has the worst hangover he could imagine, but he will regain his strength and Qwakaiva in a day or two. And it might be a valuable lesson over all."

She snorted, understanding the point I was making, but not sure she agreed with me, all her mama bear instincts not liking the idea.

My cousins left us after sharing our evening meal. The fish, potato salad and scau-bread with berry jam wasn't going to give them the Qwakaiva necessary to create a portal and leave our world. They needed to "hunt" and I wished them a speedy capture and feed. I wanted them gone, so they could tell the clan elders of my sending and my fears.

Midway through the evening's dancing I sensed my sister's exhaustion and the baby and the older children were also getting tired and grumpy, so I kissed my Gahji and sent everybody home in Rushton and Martin's mecho-carts, when Martin collected his grandfather.

It was growing dark; time for me to begin my patrolling. Mathrom and Stakaya had stayed behind when the family left to also patrol for a shift that night. Deciding that Stakaya was the more likely of the two to stray into temptation, of one sort or another, I asked Danyo before he went home to assign him to me. Mathrom he paired up with another veteran, who had worked security at such events before.

As they headed down the row of vendors' booths I watched Mathrom call his Cougar to him. Though still only partially in our physical world its glowing form curled around his head and shoulders to enhance his human senses. They were on the prowl and ready.

Nearing dawn I felt a portal open somewhere in the trees outside the dance grounds. My cousins were at last leaving. I was relieved. I hoped they would heed my warning and tell the elders of my father's clan about my sending, since my own powers to do that were limited and often ignored, even when I was able to contact someone.

There was nothing much to report after that first night of patrolling. Mathrom and his partner broke up a drunken fight before it could get out of hand and another pair on security surprised a couple teenagers who had been smoking tishwa, and tried to break into a closed stall for some snacks.

Right after I started my patrolling I became aware of a couple mecho-wagons of goldys parked just outside the dance grounds. They were looking for any excuse to close the dance, but as of yet they had no reason to invade our gathering and I wanted to keep it that way. The following day and night were the focus of the main ceremonies and dancing. If there was going to be trouble it would probably come then.

Leaving another experienced vet in charge until the afternoon Danyo gave me and my two young warriors a ride home to catch some needed sleep. When it was time for me to return the family decided to come back with me. We had left our chairs and some other items in our assigned spot, so it was easier for everyone to pile into Samul's vehicle and head back to the dance ground for the day's festivities.

I decided to let the family go ahead with the excuse that the vehicle would be too crowded with me as well, but that wasn't my true reason. I had talked to the vendor selling the earrings Gahji had admired and I was secretly bringing her a couple red fish and a deer roast as payment.

My sweet bear woman had tears in her eyes when I gave them to her just before the first couples' dance was announced that day. She put them on right away and then threw her arms around me in front of everybody. I buried my face in her hair to hide my own emotions, and I hugged her close. Smiling she dragged me out to join the circling couples as the drum sounded and the singers began to sing. I loved her so much.

The serious trouble we were all worried about came about midnight after the dance had closed down for the night. By then most people had gone home or returned to their tents and wagons to relax and sleep. Stakaya and I were just coming up to a cluster of rusty vehicles parked in the dark near a hole in the fence when I heard a woman's angry cursing. Then it was cut off abruptly in the next moment by the sound of someone being smacked up against the metal wall of a mecho-wagon.

Stakaya cursed and would have rushed over to help, but I put a hand on his shoulder to hold him back. "Patience, wolf cub, a good hunter studies the land before running into danger."

Danyo had warned me to keep a close watch on this bunch before he left that evening. "Jakko and his cousins are a rough lot. They come in town from the Zerve every summer to sell their crop of tishwa and make trouble for anyone who gets in their way. Even you might not be able to handle them on your own, so be sure you call for back up if they start something," he warned me.

"If they cause trouble each summer why don't the goldys arrest them?" I asked.

Danyo snorted and gave me an incredulous stare. "Because they pay the goldys to ignore their dealings and anybody they beat up or rape while doing their business, why else?"

My mouth hardened and I gave him a grim nod. "Thank you for the advice." I tapped my silver choker. "We will keep a close watch on the area where they are camped. And I will call for back up if they start anything."

Reminded of Aqwissa's presence he grunted. "Yeah, well don't get too over confident," he motioned to my living jewelry, "even with that thing—whatever it is—to help you if five or six of the dog-humping shits jump you all at once you could go down."

That was true; I could be jumped and "taken down," especially if one or more of the enemy was guided by an otherworldly hand. But if that happened Aqwissa would act to protect me and would kill every enemy in sight. And that would create its own set of problems. Such a slaughter couldn't go unnoticed. It would be impossible to conceal from the goldys and the dead men's friends and relatives.

So, with Danyo's warning in mind I spoke to Mathrom with the mind talk, letting him and his partner know there was trouble brewing and to come this way if they could. Then I approached the vehicles slowly and cautiously, motioning for Stakaya to circle and close in from the other side.

Coming around the vehicle at last I saw a man with a shaved head bending over a sobbing and cursing girl on the ground. "What do you mean no, you fuckin' little whore," he snarled as he caught his breath and wiped at the bleeding scratches on his face. "I gave you my tishwa and some reddos at a bargain price. Now it's time to pay up, bitch!"

"I paid you money for the stuff, fucking you wasn't part of the deal."

"Fucking is always part of the price with me, bitch. Everybody knows that? You wan'na play with the big boys and deal product then you better learn the rules of the game." He reached down and yanked her to her feet.

Under the grime and blood I saw that the girl the man was trying to molest was the troubled girl from yesterday that I caught stealing, Larissa. Danyo was right; she did seem to be a slow learner—or just desperate.

I was about to show myself when from the other side of the farthest vehicle I heard Stakaya give a startled yelp and then he said, "Oh hi, Jakko how you been? I didn't know you and your cousins were back I thought... Uh, does Benton know you're back this year?"

"No, and we plan to keep it that way." The next thing I heard was my brother-in-law being slammed against another mecho-wagon.

Then Stakaya choked out in between gasps for air, "Leave me be, damn 'ya! The piss drinking goldy isn't going to hear it from me zaunk-brotha, truly! I'm not even working for him anymore."

What to do...? Larissa and the man were tussling again, but Stakaya was kin and his situation sounded like more of a threat. Releasing Aqwissa, as I raced around the vehicle to help Ky, I said, <<Change yourself into a big dog or another fearsome creature of this world and chase off the man who is trying to harm that foolish girl. I am going to help Stakaya.>>

"Let him go," I snarled as I stepped out of the shadows behind them. Like his relative, Jakko was a big man. His head was shaved, except on the top where the hair had been clipped short and greased into spikes. He had muscular tattooed arms, but around his middle was a roll of fat, bulging over a large metal belt buckle.

Wheeling round he let go of the cub, who staggered out of reach, choking. "Who the fuck are you?"

"I'm Tas." I pointed to Stakaya. "He's my brother-in-law. My wife would be very angry with me if I let you hurt him anymore."

I pointed to the gold cloth tied around my arm. "Before the goldys find an excuse to invade the wachidai you and the rest of your family pack up and move on. You can sell your tishwa and other things elsewhere. The rules are no drug or booze on the dance grounds."

Jakko dismissed me, my rules and my golden armband with a laugh. Then without warning he charged me. I stepped aside and with a wave of my hand I slammed him hard against the vehicle behind him. His bald head hit the metal with a loud booming sound, which unfortunately woke other people sleeping in the two other vehicles.

Then from the darkness we heard a ferocious growl and a man cried out in pain. There was the sound of teeth tearing flesh and then a man running and the girl shouting encouragement to the one giving chase.

Shaking his head to clear it Jakko roared and came for me again. From one of the mecho-wagons a door suddenly flew open and three men with clubs stormed out shouting and swearing.

Picking Jakko up with my power I hurled him at the charging men. Together they went down in a tangled chaos of kicking and punching arms and legs. By this time we had created quite a commotion and I heard men and women groggily asking each other what was going on and then someone else shouted for everybody to, "Shut the fuck up, so he could get some sleep."

Before Jakko and his cousins could untangle themselves Mathrom, his partner, and a couple more experienced veterans showed up to help sort things out. Uncertain what had happened to the girl and Aqwissa I told Mathrom and his partner Lorn about the rape attempt.

"Go ahead and look for them I already called Danyo on my rad-speak," Lorn said. "He is on his way with more guys. This bunch is going to be permanently barred from any further events the tribal committee holds in future, this time."

"Good, I'm sure that will be for the best." Motioning for Stakaya to come with me, we hurried off to find Larissa and her attacker.

They hadn't gone far.

When we found them in the trees behind the fence Aqwissa had the man pinned down and an enraged Larissa was cursing and darting in now and then to kick or punch her fallen abuser.

"Larissa, that's enough, back off and let me deal with him now," I said as we hurried over.

Startled she whirled around with fist upraised. "Don't tell me what to do, dog humper," she snarled at me, "he—"

"I know what he tried, and he will pay for the attempt, I promise you that, but right now he needs to join his cousins. They are leaving."

I called to Aqwissa to let the man up. Swearing and glowering he got to his feet, mopping at his bleeding arm with his torn shirt. "I'm gonna kill that damned dog and you, too, fucker." Focusing his malice on the girl he snarled, "And then I'm coming for you, bitch!"

I smiled, showing my canines. Where were my tricky cousins when I needed them? I would let them suck this loathsome man dry with my blessing. "Is that so? But I don't think you are going to be bothering any girl or woman for a long time—if ever again."

I called him a name in the Kukiya language that the old warriors used to call a cowardly and contemptable enemy. His eyes grew wide at my use of the old term, but he had understood me well enough.

Then without touching him I showed him my raised hand, closed my fist and squeezed. The man let out a horrified scream and fell to the ground clutching at his crotch and writhing. Realizing he might call the goldys with his noise I sighed, realizing my mistake, so I glued his mouth shut, too.

Turning to Ky in the sudden silence, I said, "Aqwissa and I will take this one to join his relatives. Bring Larissa along, so I can see how bad she is injured in the better light by the command wagon."

She stared at the man, swallowed and straightened a satisfied smirk curving her lips. "I don't need your help, pretend goldy," she said, her voice quavering in spite of her attempt to show her toughness. "I'm fine."

Jerking her now whimpering attacker to his feet with my Gift, I turned back to her and snapped, "Too bad, because you are going to get my help, like it or not. Now go with Ky."

My help and my judgment, too, because you are partially to blame for his attack on you as well.

"And don't make me sent this one," I motioned to Aqwissa now at my side, "to find you. You won't like it if I do."

Grabbing a hold of the man's shirt I pushed him back through the hole in the fence and toward the main command center where Danyo and his men were waiting for us.

Behind me I heard Stakaya talking to the girl and telling her I was a good guy and a man with special powers, so she should do what I wanted, and not to worry about Jakko and his bunch.

At the command wagon I shoved the attacker down on the ground with his relatives. Tears were streaming down his face, but he was unable to answer when they asked him what was wrong. Then, as an added precaution I froze them all in place. Grinning as I watched them struggle when they figured out what I had done I told Aqwissa to guard them.

I walked up the steps and into the mecho-wagonhouse. Danyo, in the doorway raised his eyebrows when he saw the big hairy dog with snarling white teeth I had with me. "Where did you get the dog?"

I smiled and touched my bare neck. His mouth dropped open when he figured out what I meant.

Though many of the security guards wanted to turn the whole lot of troublemakers over to the goldys, after a call to Rickson, who was still worried about funding being cut off for future events, it was decided that we would hold Jakko, Larissa's attacker, and another cousin, at the command wagon as our hostages while we sent the other two caught up in the fray back to their encampment to wake up the people and pack up everything. They would be leaving as soon as it could be quietly arranged.

The sky was now graying in the east; it would be day soon. Mathrom and Lorn went with them to make sure they did what we wanted. Breathing a sigh I decided to grab a cup of kaf-tea and relax while we waited.

It was then that Stakaya called me into the other room where he had taken Larissa to clean and bandage her wounds. There was blood all over her torn shirt, so he had given her a bed sheet to wrap around herself like a dance shawl. Her hair pulled back into a ponytail and her face and arms clean and plastered with tiny bandages where needed, she looked better than she had a while ago.

I thanked him and took the girls hand without asking. When she would have pulled it away I firmed up my hold and gave her a warning glare. I needed to see if she had internal injuries that needed a doctor's care. Her eyes widened when she felt the touch of my Gift flow through her body, but she remained silent and just looked into my otherworldly eyes.

While I examined her, I said, "The man who attacked you was partially right. No matter how much you thought you needed the money selling his poisons would give you, you were a fool to try to buy and deal without understanding all, 'the rules of his game.'"

"So?"

"So, all our actions have consequences. He is paying right now for his, but you will have consequences, too. Think about that, before you try this again. You may end up in jail next time—or dead."

She snorted, dismissing my predictions. "Yeah, and do those preachy words apply to you, too, eh?"

"Yes, they do. I will suffer in my own way for using my Gift tonight to punish a bad man and rescue you. I hope you are worthy of my sacrifice."

When I'd finished and released her Stakaya said, "Tas, we have another problem. Larissa says her friend Franzi was with her tonight. She went off with one of Jakko's guys to try some reddos they got, in a new shipment. She doesn't know where she is."

"Is that the girl I saw you with yesterday?"

"Yeah, what of it?" Larissa said, wrapping the sheet tighter around her shoulders. "You need to let me out of here so I can go find her."

"Tas, I can go with her if you are worried about somebody else attacking her," Stakaya offered. "I know the family. Franzi is her cousin and Larissa's sister went to school with Gahji."

Having a sudden bad feeling about the missing girl I motioned for them to get up and follow me. "We all will go."

"But what about Jakko and his guys?"

I snorted. "They aren't going anywhere until I say so."

He puzzled over my words for a moment then his eyes opened wide when he figured it out. "Oh, you mean like Mathrom when he—"

"Ky just go." I motioned for him to lead the way out of the room.

Chapter Twenty-Nine

Telling Danyo about the missing girl we headed towards the trees at the edge of the camping area where Larissa thought she might have gone. Sun was just clearing the horizon. Most of the people staying on the site were up, and the smells of kaf-tea and frying bacon wafted on the air making my stomach rumble with hunger.

In the center of the dance ground people were gathering by the big drums for sunrise prayers. As a man began the singing my heart longed to be over there joining them, lifting my voice with the others to thank the Unseen Ones for the new day and our many blessings.

But not today; I had work to do. Offering up my prayers silently I followed Stakaya and the girl over to Jakko's family's camp.

Mathrom and Lorn were surprised to see us until we explained about the missing girl. Both shook their heads when I asked if they had seen her.

"I have been checking each mecho-wagon," Mathrom said. He grinned. "I, uh, we smelled lots of other interesting substances inside those wagons, as well as lots of stinky dirty clothes, but nobody is hiding a girl."

Mathrom was referring to his spirit helper. I could still see Cougar's otherworldly glow encircling him and augmenting his weaker human senses. I could trust his evaluation of the vehicles and their contents.

Widening our search we at last saw Franzi lying in a crumpled heap, just off the trail leading up to the road that went into the dance grounds. It was Larissa who saw her first. Breaking away from Stakaya, she rushed forward to flop down beside her, pulling her head and upper body into her lap. Tears suddenly streaming down her cheeks she called Franzi's name over and over but got no response.

Sinking down beside them I took the girl's limp hand. "Stop crying, she isn't dead." I snapped at the blubbering Larissa.

"Are you sure? How do you know?"

"Because I can't see her ghost... and I can feel a faint pulse. Now be quiet so I can check her more thoroughly." As I closed my eyes to focus on the girl and her injuries better I said to the hovering Stakaya. "Go back to command and tell Danyo we found her but she is in a bad way. And mind where you step," I warned. "I will need to see if she was carried and dumped here by someone or she dragged herself out here looking for help when she knew she was in trouble."

"Sure, Tas, I'll do that, but what shall I tell him is wrong with her if Danyo asks."

"She's been poisoned—by taking bad drugs is my guess. I can help her by sharing some of my Qwakaiva with her for now, but she will have to go to the infirmarium where they can better care for her. With my Gift I can only do so much."

"I'll tell him. And I'll go up the trail to the road so I won't mess up any tracks from the camp that might still be there. It's shorter to go that way and will attract less attention anyhow."

When he was gone I opened my eyes and said to Larissa, "Did you give her the red pills or did she buy them herself?"

She opened her mouth to lie, then thought better of the idea, swallowed hard and tearfully admitted, "She's been having a hard time at home. Her mom has a new boyfriend, and... She just wanted to relax for a while and have a break—and some fun. She begged me to buy some of Thauny's reddos along with the tishwa with the money we stole from her drunk of an uncle last night. So we did, and then she took a couple, she said she wanted to try them out, before we sold them all today."

My heart ached for all the stupid hurting children in this troubled world. I grimaced and held out my other hand. "You had better give the rest of those bad pills to me; you aren't selling reddos today."

"And the tishwa, too?"

"I don't care about that; it's probably just dried plants, though Jakko and his bunch may have soaked the plant leaves in something before drying them to enhance its effect. Better ask Stakaya about that if you are still foolish enough to try and sell it."

With some hesitation she reached into the pocket of her trousers and handed me a small folded brown paper. "Are you going to tell the goldys what I told you?"

"No. What good would that do now? Sending you to jail or maybe prison won't help your cousin survive and heal."

She was quiet for a long time, then just as we heard a mecho-cart stop on the road nearby and Danyo calling my name she said in a trembling voice, "This is what you meant about all our actions having consequences, isn't it?"

Lifting the still unconscious girl into my arms, I started up the trail to meet them. "That will be up to you to decide."

When we arrived at the road I was surprised to see Chief Rickson's vehicle, and him at the wheel waiting for us. Danyo got out of the front seat and opened the cart door. With a medical bag already opened on his lap the man in the back motioned for me to lay Franzi on the seat beside him.

"Yonny was a medico-aidman when he served in the Imperial Army he can take care of things from here," Danyo explained as he closed the door and stepped back to wave them away.

Larissa grabbed my arm and pleaded, "Can I go with her? Please!"

I knew someone would need to ask her questions, but they could wait. I motioned her into the front seat.

As I turned down the trail to check for tracks, I handed Danyo the packet of reddos. "These are the cause of the trouble. The one called Thauny is the one Larissa said sold them the red pills. As best I can tell with my Gift they have been corrupted with another substance that may kill or injure others if used. We need to find the rest of those pills and also find out how many the dog turds have already sold."

Danyo swore angrily for a long moment. At last he calmed down enough to say, "Damn it this changes everything. Before Stakaya showed up with his news I was going to send your nephew to tell you that Jakko's bunch is all packed and ready to leave." He smirked. "Unfortunately they can't until you come to release them."

I chuckled. "I had forgotten about that. Good thing though, eh? Because we need to find and destroy those pills."

Danyo smirked, his dislike for Rickson plain upon his face. "Yeah, and Rickson isn't going to like it, but we are probably gonna have to involve the goldys now."

When I checked Franzi's back trail I could find no sign that anyone had dumped her unconscious body in the bush. She must have gotten disorientated when she felt herself growing sick and went in the wrong direction, so I hurried back to command.

Danyo was right about the goldys, however, but it happened in a way that satisfied everyone but Jakko and his family. After dropping off his passengers at the infirmarium Chief Rickson showed up at the command wagon with another committee member.

Danyo and I had just started to question Jakko about the poisoned reddos when they barged in and told us to let them go. Spluttering and purple with indignation I thought Danyo was going to explode he was so furious. I was surprised, but curious. I saw the gleam of mischief in the man's eye and the swirling colors in his spirit fire suggested the chief was up to something.

Putting a hand on Danyo's shoulder to stop him from doing something stupid, I murmured, "Wait and have a little trust. Let's see what the chief has planned."

Danyo gave me a murderous look but didn't stop Rickson when he told the men they wouldn't be welcome at future events that were tribal sponsored, but at the moment they were free to go. Maybe after working with me during the dance he had learned to trust me a little. "If I am wrong then you and I, and anyone else who wants to join us, will take our own brand of justice—like the warriors did in the old days, eh?"

He grunted and transferred his murderous glare to Jakko, and gritted his teeth when Jakko promised revenge to taunt us as he left.

When they were finally gone I poured myself some kaf-tea from the nearly empty pot and said to Rickson, "Along with their other items for sale those men are selling tainted reddos which may kill some of our people if they aren't stopped. You know that, eh?"

He chuckled. "Yes, I do. Which is why I got the far-speak number of his former employer from your brother-in-law. Benton received an anonymous tip a while ago that Jakko was leaving the dance ground and was carrying tainted reddos and other banned items for sale. He was happy to get the information and said he would act on it right away when he also learned that there was a young girl in the infirmarium who might die after ingesting some of Jakko's poisonous stock."

As we hoped, we learned later that day that Jakko and his bunch were surrounded and arrested at a road block not far from the dance ground. The tainted pills were found and the whole lot were carted off to Se Ho Co to await trial.

The family didn't return that day for the last of the festivities. Gahji had to work later that evening and my sister was exhausted. Fortunately for everyone Saskina came over to help with the baby and the other children when she heard about the trouble on the dance site.

Having been awake for nearly two days I was exhausted, but stayed with my security crew until the final ceremony and the clean up afterward. For me personally, it was like being in the traditional ceremonies in the old days where people often stayed up all night or even longer. I wasn't in prayer in the traditional way but my fatigue and my service were my gifts to the Unseen Ones as my offering for my people's healing and survival.

There was another wachidai dance held in a smaller community nearby, and to my surprise it was Danyo who recommended that they hire me along with Lorn and another veteran for security. This time he was totally in charge, which was fine with me. I just needed the extra money.

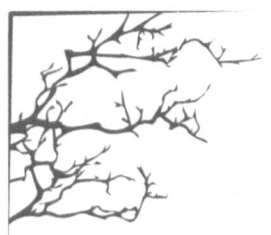

Chapter Thirty

The rest of that summer passed with no further word from my otherworldly cousins or my father. I was worried, true enough, but I could do little about it. For fear of being tracked if I stayed too long searching for him within the Dream I transformed my fretting into work. And there was plenty of that to occupy my mind and hands.

Chief Rickson did get his grant for training instructors for a more in depth program next summer, but it wasn't for as long as I would have liked. I had only a half-moon with the group of young men and women enrolled rather than the moon or more I had hoped for.

I brought Tuunac with me to keep him from pestering his sisters in my absence, and to let him know I recognized him as a growing young hunter and teacher. Between the Smotahlik Elders, him and I, we taught these modern" tribal young people what we could in such a short time, but it wasn't enough—nowhere nearly enough. I couldn't squeeze in several years of my own learning into just a few days in the forest.

Rickson was disappointed, too, by the meager allotment of money for such a vital program I suspected, but when I asked him he only shrugged and said, "That's often the way with Imperial government funding. We usually ask for more than we hope to get for that reason," he confided. "And they have a bad habit of cutting the money off just when a program is starting to show results, too."

Though he didn't say so, I took his words as a warning for the future funding of the language program that I was also counting on to help us pay our rent and other things. If ZFH lost their funding I might have to resort to making cradleboards or smuggling with his shady cousin, neither of which appealed to me.

With my sister's urging Mathrom decided to go back to school in the fall. Once our "wilderness" training class ended he picked up a part-time job delivering meals for a local dining house. Part of his pay he gave to Gahji in exchange for staying at our house and the rest he told me he was saving for books and supplies once the term began. He also was looking for a room closer to the Lectorium once his tribal funding started up anew.

And then the summer was over. School and my language classes were starting again. This would be Bijah's first year going to school full time, like her brother and sister and she was very proud. This also meant that only Gahji, the baby and I would be home for much of the day alone and we could manage child care and work schedules between us.

But unfortunately with the chill and dampness of the rainy season drawing near I also sensed my sister's restlessness. Qwadalah had been pestering her all summer to return home even though I had signed the legal papers she'd sent me, giving up any claim to the Lander Rancha.

Kitahtla had resisted her nagging, caught up in the excitement of our family life, Mathrom's teaching and the summer gatherings. But as much as I didn't want it to be so, my sister was an old woman and the strain was starting to show, in spite of my frequent sharing of my Qwakaiva with her when I saw her tiring.

So it was with a deep sadness that she came to me after I had walked the children to school to tell me that she wanted to go home.

Sitting beside me on the couch she handed me a cup of kaf-tea and began, "It has been such a blessing to be here with you and your family, but the weather is changing and my old bones are starting to feel it. I need to go home—at least for a while now. In the spring, well, we shall see…"

"It will be much quieter now that the children are back in school, so you can rest," I argued, "And with Stakaya spending so much of his time at his girlfriend's we can clear out his things and give you his room, so you can rest without the children bothering you—and I can help you with my Gift more—"

Kitahtla laughed and patted my arm. "I know you want me to stay and I will miss you, too, but we will visit each other in the Dream. This is for the best, truly it is."

She waited letting me master my feelings, before she continued, "I called Qwadalah yesterday when you were at work. She is coming to pick me up at the end of the month."

"So soon? The winter storms won't be here for at least a moon or more. Why do you want to go so soon?" She hugged me and for just a moment I let my head rest against her soft breast as I felt her old heart beating next to my ear.

"Because it's time for me to go back, big brother dear, I feel it in my heart and in my bones."

A lump of sadness suddenly choking my throat I swallowed hard a few times before I could speak. "But what about Mathrom's teaching? Cougar's power isn't mine to give him. He needs you."

I need you. "If you are in pain I can—"

Kitahtla patted my hand to stop me. "I know you will miss me—and I you, my dear one, but I'm tired and," she chuckled, "and I miss my old mare, my lovely desert and the purple mountains beyond."

"I wish, I wish I could go with you—take care of you..." Feeling the tears gathering in the corners of my eyes I choked out, "I promised Nachoga I would take care of you, but I feel like I failed both you and him I was hoping now I could make it up to you—"

She hugged me again and I heard the tears in her own voice when she said, "Oh, Tas, you haven't failed either me or our father. You have done the best you could for me and the family. I don't blame you for not being there to help out when I was younger, so don't blame yourself. Even with your Gift to aid you, you were just a child back then. I'm glad your Seal father came and took you away. You wouldn't have survived otherwise."

She leaned forward and kissed me on the cheek. "And I feel so blessed that I've gotten to know you again now, before I pass into the Beyond to be with our ancestors."

Swallowing down my own feelings I nodded. "If that is what you want then so be it. I will enjoy the little time we have together before my niece comes to take you away." I took a deep breath. "And hopefully next summer, when the weather is warm again on the coast you will come back and stay with us again. Baby O'siyan and the other children need to spend more time with their Granny Kitah."

"I would like that. And maybe if the snow isn't too deep in the passes around the winter holidays you and your family could borrow a mecho-cart and come visit me on the rancha. Do the children know how to ride? I would love to teach them. Do you remember how to ride a pony yourself, or will I have to teach you, too?"

Sniffing back my tears I laughed and hugged her. "Though I could never ride like Xyilaha, I can manage, I guess."

"Good then that's settled you will all come for the holidays. Mathrom can drive you. I will tell Qwadalah to expect you."

I snorted. "Your daughter isn't going to like us coming, you know."

"I know, but she will just have to learn to like it or she can go stay in the old trapper's cabin down in the canyon if she doesn't want to be sociable. I plan on asking Janata and her family to come for the holidays as well. They need to meet you and your family, too."

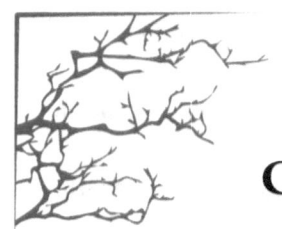

Chapter Thirty-One

Over the next few days I spent as much time as I could with my sister, but all too soon Moon had turned her silver face away and Qwadalah called to say she was coming. Cousin Denny had been teaching me how to shoot one of his deer rifles and I had persuaded him to take me hunting so I could send Kitahtla home with meat.

The children all knew she was leaving so the evening meal that night was a somber one and at last my sister had had enough. Putting down her spoon Kitahtla forced a smile and said, "Now, now there's no reason for all this sadness. I will see you soon enough when you all come to the rancha over the winter school holidays. Do you know how to ride a pony?"

They shook their heads no. "Well I think it's about time I teach you, eh? There are two or three gentle old ponies at the rancha that would love to meet all my new grandchildren. Would you like to meet them, too?"

Eyes wide everyone nodded.

"What color are they?" Bijah asked.

Kitahtla leaned her chin on her hand and pretended to think. "Hmm, one is gray with black socks and a black mane and tail. And there is a brown one with white spots on her rump and another that is golden color with black socks and a black mane and tail."

"Why are the ponies wearing black socks instead of white ones," Bijah next wanted to know. "What color are their shoes?"

I laughed, but before I could explain to her, Tuunac made a rude noise, and looking to my sister for confirmation, said, "Horses wear shoes made of iron and they are always gray."

"Are not. Nobody wears iron shoes; they would be too heavy."

Kitahtla and I exchanged smiles, trying not to laugh. Before those two could get into a heated argument Kitahtla said, "Horses don't think they are too heavy, my girl. And the shoes help protect their hooves from sharp stones and other things that might injure them in my desert mountains."

Turning to me Angika asked, "Appi, can you ride?"

"I suppose, but it has been a long time since I've ridden a horse. When I was young like you there weren't any mecho-vehicles, people either rode horses or walked, so I learned, because I had to, but I always liked the dogs that pulled the sleds in my northern village better."

The meal passed in more cheerful talk as the children peppered their granny with excited questions about horses, cai beasts, and other animals they might see when they visited. But in spite of her promise to teach them to ride, as the evening passed, and time for bed arrived, our sad mood returned. We would all miss her.

When Gahji and I were finally alone in our bedroom and the fussy baby was asleep, Gahji cuddled close, but I could tell she had something on her mind that was troubling her. When I asked her what was the matter, she distracted me with her kisses and then when we finished she turned on her side away from me and pretended to sleep. I wasn't fooled, however.

Moving closer I put my belly against her back and kissed her neck. "You are trying hard to convince me that you want to sleep, but your Bear is wide awake and watching me. You had better tell me what's bothering you, or you aren't going to get any sleep at all tonight."

She muttered something uncomplimentary about me under her breath and then turned to face me. I chuckled and wrapped my arms around her, kissing her again. "Tell me, my beautiful bear woman what is troubling your heart tonight. Is it my sister's leaving?"

Gahji sighed and admitted. "It is in part, my love. I have grown quite fond of her I will miss her, like you and the children."

When she fell silent I waited a long moment then prompted, "There is more, please tell me."

"I promised her I wouldn't tell you—she didn't want to worry you. I only found out because one of the nurses who did part of her tests knew she was family and told me. When I asked your sister she admitted the results weren't good, but she begged me not to tell you."

She shook her head then kissed me. "I can't keep such a secret from you, my heart. I think you have a right to know."

Though her face was only a dark blur in the dimness of our room I could hear the troubled grief in her voice and it sent icy chills down my spine. "There's no need for you to carry this burden alone, my heart. Please tell me."

"You have been so busy with other matters this summer that you forgot to ask her—or me about the medical tests she came here to have done at my infirmarium."

Medical test? Another icy chill slid down my spine. "Now that you mention it I do remember something about medical tests," I said slowly. "What about them? They were just something normal for old people to have in these modern times, right?"

She hesitated, then sighed and said, "No, Tas, they weren't. Your sister has a wasting illness that is slowly killing her."

...I was an idiot! I had assumed they were just an excuse made up to stay for a visit, to satisfy her daughter. Obviously they were much more. Sharing my Qwakaiva with her as I had over the summer how could I have missed the signs—how could I have not known?

It was obvious, because she was using her own Gift to mask her symptoms, and I? I had offered my Qwakaiva, but hadn't swum into the depths of her being, my worry for our safety and my wounded Aqwissa had allowed her to keep her secret unchallenged. I was an idiot!

<<It was her right to keep her secret,>> Aqwissa said, breaking in on my self-accusing thoughts. <<You aren't an idiot and the disease is one even the Prophet or your grandfather might not have been able to heal. You two were able to find each other again in this lifetime, so be grateful for the blessing you were given and stop feeling sorry for yourself.>>

Then like a knife stabbed into my heart I knew, Kitahtla was going home to die. "How long does she have; did your friend tell you?"

"Nobody knows that for sure. A few months, a year at the most the doctors say."

"Then we will definitely have to find a way to visit her rancha during the winter holidays." I gave her another kiss. "Thank you for telling me."

"What are you going to do, now that you know?" she asked a worried tone coming into her voice.

"Nothing. It's her choice. Go to sleep now; we will have a busy day tomorrow."

We decided to keep the children home from school next day, so they could say their good byes to my sister. And though Stakaya had to work that morning he did manage to wake early enough to join us for breakfast and say his own farewell. Abandoning school for the day themselves Mathrom and Saskina showed up at breakfast time to be with us.

Just as we were setting down to a meal of fried potatoes, eggs and deer meat fried in bacon grease, we heard a mecho-cart pull up out front and someone honking for our attention. Mathrom who was just coming down the hall from the indoor privy went to the front window and peered out. Coming back into the kitchen with a scowl on his face he announced, "It's mama and she wants granny to come out."

Gahji matched his scowl with one of her own. "What a rude bitch," she muttered to me as she set a plate of fried eggs on the table. My sister had just been served her plate. Ignoring the implied summons, she picked up her fork and began to eat. I put down my cup and rose. "I'll go and invite her in. Mathrom, bring in the extra chair on the back porch."

Walking over to her vehicle I leaned my head down to the window and said, "Your mother is eating her breakfast. It's going to be a long drive and a long tiring day for both of you come in and eat with us, too."

At first she gave me a murderous glare, but when I refused to snap at her bait she finally got out of the vehicle and followed me into the house. As we climbed the front steps she said, "I did look in the old history books Collin Golbraith wrote. You do look like your ancestor, so I guess you truly are one of the family."

I turned and smiled at her. "And as I told you from the beginning I have no interest in the Lander Rancha, so there is no reason for you to fear me spending time with Kitahtla, either here in Seatown, or if we should come to the Preserve for a visit."

Qwadalah had relaxed a bit by the time breakfast was over and it was time for them to leave. Everyone had tears in their eyes when they hugged their granny Kitah one last time before she entered the vehicle.

I was the last to say my farewells. As I held her Aqwissa transferred herself from my wrist to hers. Feeling the shift Kitahtla's eyes widened in surprise. I chuckled and kissed her forehead. "I am sending Aqwissa with you to keep you safe on your journey and share her life-essence with you so you won't get too tired."

She touched the silver bracelet now adorning her arm, and stared up at me with wonder. "But what about you; won't you need her for your own protection?"

I smiled. "She will leave you and come back to me when you are safely at home. I will manage in the meantime. Don't worry about me and the family. We will be fine."

I hugged her close and murmured into her hair "I'm sorry. Gahji couldn't keep your secret. I know about your illness. I wish it was otherwise, but I respect your decision to go back to the home you have always known to die. But I hope when your time draws near, you will call for me to come to sing you away on your journey."

'I would like that, brother mine, truly I would. I will send for you."

"And, another reason for sending Aqwissa with you is to help me make the transfer if I need to come quickly. I can't project myself to somewhere I've never been," I explained. "Aqwissa, by going with you wil learn the way and then she can help me make the transfer if there isn't time enough for normal travel."

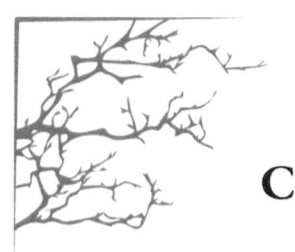

Chapter Thirty-Two

My sister arrived home safely and Aqwissa returned to me without incident. Knowing as I did that Kitahtla hadn't long for this world reminded me that my oldest and dearest friend Kutima too was an old man and soon would be leaving this realm as well. And with their passing, all the links to my old life would be severed. I needed to thank the Unseen Ones for my blessings and enjoy their company as best I could while they still lived among us.

But in spite of my brave words to myself, each day I did miss Kitahtla. The silence in our home during the day when the children were at school was a deep ache in all our hearts. Of course we still had baby O'siyan to keep us alert and busy, trying to keep him out of mischief. And as he grew older that was proving to be a full-time job.

O'siyan learned to crawl at about six moons and from then on we had to, "baby-proof" our house, as Gahji called it. Though he could be strapped into his cradleboard at times, especially when he knew we were going somewhere he was full of tricks and giggles once we arrived and he could be set free.

Tipping full laundry baskets over on top of himself when he tried to stand, or crawling into the kitchen to pull onto the floor our pots and pans to bang their lids together gave him endless pleasure but usually had his mother roaring for quiet like a grumpy old bear when she needed to sleep.

I usually strapped him in his cradleboard and took him with me to work when Gahji's schedule meant she had to work nights. I got a lot of curious looks when we hopped on the city mecho-transit but the women we met thought he was "so cute" and they entertained him for me for the ride.

At Friendship House I would prop him up against the wall in the central area where he could see everything and greet the people coming in.

After Gahji and I talked about it, we decided to help Stakaya buy a mecho-cart like he wanted. The money came with conditions, however. He would have to buy a vehicle large enough to carry the family and sturdy enough to make it over the mountains so we could visit the rancha during the winter and summer holidays.

Like most young men he had wanted something smaller and shiny to impress his girlfriend, of course, but he hadn't been able to save the money on his own, so had to settle for our terms. Elder Samul and cousin Denny helped with his selection. It wasn't what he wanted but it was better than nothing, as we kept telling him. His mood improved when Mathrom promised to buy the vehicle from him in a few moons when he got his tribal bonus allotment, so that made him a lot happier with our choice.

Time passed and we fell into our usual routine of school and work, and then the winter holiday break was approaching and everyone was excited. Stakaya decided he wanted to stay in Seatown with his girlfriend and her family, so he generously agreed to lend his vehicle to Mathrom for the trip. When the day finally arrived we loaded up the vehicle the night before so we could get an early start after breakfast next morning.

The trip over the snowy coastal mountains was a wonder to me. This was my first long ride in a mecho-vehicle and I was as excited and thrilled as the younger children. Holding Bijah or the baby on my lap they let me sit in front next to our driver, either Mathrom or Saskina, while the others squeezed together in the back seats or lay atop our bags in the very back.

I marveled at how fast the world passed by. No horse or a man running could have traveled a fraction of the distance we covered in such a short time. The views out the vehicle's windows of the dark forests and snowy peaks were breath taking, but it was cold and in places on the high passes treacherous with ice. Mathrom proved to be a good driver under those conditions, but I couldn't resist using my Qwakaiva a few times when it was snowing or particularly icy.

Except for a few rest stops to get out and stretch our legs, eat and pee, we had been traveling for most of the day. We had crossed over the mountains and were now heading down into the dry country on the other side. When we stopped to fill up the vehicle with the liquid fuel it needed to keep moving, I walked to a clump of nearby scrub pine and took deep breaths of the cool resinous air as I looked down into the wide purple and gray valley spreading out below.

Though not the desert I had grown to love while living among the Kukiya, I could feel these desert mountains welcoming me back. My spirit soared high rejoicing in the land's love and greeting. Pinyon and sage, rocks and wind there was an ancient wisdom to touch in this dry land that spoke to me in a special way. Though I had grown to love the tall trees and stormy coast of my new home, I suddenly understood why my sister had wanted to come back to this ancient land to die.

Coming over to stand by me at last, Mathrom waited for me to acknowledge him before speaking. I smiled to myself—he was learning.

"Everyone is ready to go, Uncle."

I nodded still gazing at the sage covered slope dotted here and there with pinyon. At last I said, "How much farther will we have to travel to reach the rancha, if we keep driving?"

Mathrom thought about my question for a long moment before answering. "About four hours maybe."

"Hmm... Then it will be quite dark and everyone asleep by the time we arrive."

"Yes, it will be late," he agreed.

I turned back to the vehicle. "We should find a place to camp while it is still light enough to set up the tent. Everyone is tired. We will leave early tomorrow and get there by midday, eh?" Mathrom looked troubled, but didn't question my decision. "What is it? Tell me."

He sighed. "I agree everybody is tired and that includes me. I was going to have Saskina drive for a while, but camping alongside the road... Well it isn't like the old days when people could go anywhere they liked.

"Now the land is owned by somebody, or it is park land and you have to stay in certain places and pay the patrollers for the privilege."

I snorted and swore under my breath. *Greedy chamuqwani.* I put a hand on his shoulder, urging him back to the mecho-vehicle. "Thank you for warning me, but don't worry we will find a place and I will make sure we aren't bothered tonight."

I had spoken to my sister in the Dream the night before and told her our plans. When we arrived mid-morning in the rancha yard Kitahtla, Qwadalah and several other people were waiting on the porch of the rancha long house to greet us. My heart skipped a beat when I saw how much weight she had lost and how frail my sister had become in the three moons since she left us.

Not waiting on the adults, the children bounded from the vehicle and raced to hug and greet their Granny Kitah. After taking my sister into my arms for a long hug we were introduced to the other adults on the porch. There were a couple old rancha men, who had been on the rancha so long they were like family, and the others were Kitahtla's daughter Janata, a thin dark woman with tired eyes and her big-bellied husband Rafton. There was also a frail elder that was introduced as Janata's mother-in-law Nansi.

Their eyes popped wide when I spoke to them in their Kukiya language. I pointed to the tattoos on my cheek and explained in the same language that I had been adopted by a Kukiya warrior when my mother remarried. Then they were curious about who that might be, and I had to get creative in my evasions.

Of course, the first thing the children wanted to do was go see the horses, so Janata's oldest boy was put in charge of the expedition to the barn with a stern warning not to let the city cousins get hurt.

Inside, the house was decorated with pinyon boughs and bright orange clusters of cacha berries. Wafting out from the kitchen were the good smells of baking bread and frying mushrooms, bacon and onions. We sat around the big kitchen table drinking kaf-tea and getting to know one another while we waited for the evening meal.

I could see that my Gahji and Janata liked each other right away, which pleased me. They both had little ones about the same age, so they had lots to talk about. I doubted Qwadalah would ever warm up to any of us, but it was comforting to know that I could keep at least one connection alive with Nachoga's descendants still living on the Preserve.

During the afternoon Kitahtla rose and excused herself from the table, saying she was tired and needed to take a nap. Without asking I rose too and followed her down the hall to her room. When we were alone and she lay upon the bed I pulled over a chair and sat down beside her. "You are in pain. Let me help you," I said as I took her hand.

She breathed out a long sigh and nodded. "That would be lovely, brother dear."

I'm not sure how long I stayed with her using my Gift, but it was long enough for Qwadalah to get suspicious. I had leaned back with my eyes closed the better to focus on giving her my Qwakaiva when I heard the bedroom door open. Without opening my eyes I murmured, "I will be along in a moment. Please don't wake her."

I heard the door softly close and her footsteps retreating down the hall. I waited a bit longer to be sure Kitahtla was sleeping soundly then I released her hand and closed her bedroom door.

As I came down the hall I heard Qwadalah complaining, "My mother needs her rest. I don't know what that man thinks he's doing. He shouldn't be bothering her."

"He's a Puhani, mama," Saskina said. "He probably saw she was in pain and decided to help her."

"Puhani?" Qwadalah snorted her disgust. "If she is in pain she has pills the doctor prescribed for her. She doesn't need some crazy man spouting some mumbo-jumbo and getting her upset. That stuff never works anyway."

Mathrom snorted a laugh. "Oh, you have no idea. Tas is a Puhani alright, as sis says. And whatever he does with his power definitely works."

"Oh yeah?" Qwadalah shot back. "Then if he is such a great Puhani why is my mother dying?"

"Because it is her time, and my Gift isn't one of healing," I said as I entered the kitchen and took my place next to my Gahji. "I can share my puwa with her, to use the Kukiya word for it, but I have no power to take away her illness."

"Then what can you do for her?" Qwadalah grumped.

"I can do the one thing she has asked me to do when it is her time."

"And what's that? Oh so wise and powerful 'Puhani'?"

I put a hand on Gahji's arm to stop her from making an angry remark that would only add fuel to the fire my niece was trying to start. Qwadalah didn't want us here—any of us and she was already starting her campaign to make us angry enough to leave. I wasn't going to let her do that. I would glue her mouth closed or stick her to a chair if she kept it up.

Mathrom and I exchanged knowing smiles, he knew what might happen if she pushed me too far. But I hoped it wouldn't come to that, because I could see the fear for her mother swirling in her spirit fire, so I was willing to curb my annoyance. I knew she loved her mother even though she was unable to show it.

"When it is her time she has asked me to come to sing her spirit home to the ancestors."

Qwadalah snorted her disgust. "Our priest might have something to say about that," she snapped.

"Djoven's priests will have no say in the matter. Your mother has already seen to that. She told me that she has contacted her attorney and had it written into her will that she wishes to have as close to a traditional Kukiya funeral ceremony as can be done in these modern times."

Catching her eye and holding her with my power, I said, "And I will be here to see that her wishes are carried out."

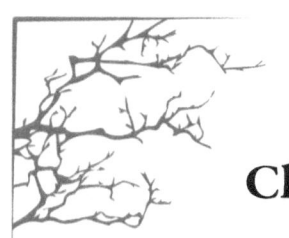

Chapter Thirty-Three

It turned out that it was a good thing we had brought our big tent with us, because there were too many people visiting to sleep in the house. There was a bed room set aside for Janata, her husband and their youngest, a toddler of about two with a drippy nose. Gahji, the baby and I were also given a room, but I told Saskina to take my place. I planned to sleep in our tent with several of the older children.

Our tent was like the ones I grew up with when we were out on the trap lines. It had a small wood stove to keep us warm and there was enough straw in the barn to stuff under our blankets so we wouldn't be sleeping on the cold ground. They were all excited about the idea and it would give me a chance to teach all of them some of my bush skills.

My sister by this time was too ill to teach them to ride the ponies as she'd promised but Mathrom, Saskina and Janata's oldest boy Neko agreed to give them lessons. Children occupied I helped out with whatever needed doing including chopping wood and cleaning stalls, which surprised the rancha men who thought, because I lived in Seatown I wouldn't know how or want to do such work. It had been a long time, but it felt good to put my hand to such hard physical tasks again.

I also tried to spend as much time as I could with Kitahtla while the women worked preparing the food for the big feast. She wanted to stay up and visit with all of us, so I gave her respite from the pain as best I could, because the doctor's pills made her too sleepy, and I knew everyone being here was important to her. This was the last time her family would all be together and she didn't want to miss anything.

The next afternoon Kitahtla and I were sitting on the porch when Mathrom came riding into the yard on a fine gray stallion a hunting rifle cradled across his saddle. I had been sharing my Gift with her, my eyes half closed, when I looked up at the sound of hooves and saw him. For just a moment the images of horse and rider blurred between the past and present and I wasn't sure who I was seeing, Nachoga or his grandson.

I must have made a noise because Kitahtla opened her eyes to stare at me. "What is it, brother mine?"

I blinked several times and turned to her. "I'm sorry if I woke you." She repeated her question. I turned back to the young warrior on horseback trotting into the yard. "Most like you wouldn't remember, but your grandson could be our father's twin. Just now for a moment I wasn't sure who I was seeing."

"Ah, my dear one, I know he touched your heart deeply, both in his life and in his death. But you need to let him go. You need to be here and live the life you have been gifted in 'this now'. Mathrom is not our father."

I laughed and patted her arm. "Truer words have never been spoken, sister mine. And you are right. I need to let go of the past; my Gahji says the same thing. And I am trying—truly I am."

"Your wife is a very wise woman, and I am glad you have someone like her to share this new life with."

By this time Mathrom was sitting atop his horse smiling down at us.

I gave him a puzzled look, but the corners of my mouth twitched, wanting to smile. "And just what are you looking at, nephew?"

His grin grew wider. "Nothing much just two old people sitting on the porch enjoying lazing around."

"Lazing around, eh? Where were you when I was chopping wood for the cook pit this morning, hmm?" I joked. "Riding around on that fine gray horse is hardly 'work'."

"Actually I was scouting for a hunt later. Mother is being difficult about butchering one of her precious beasts for the cook pit, so I thought if I went hunting..."

"And you want me to go with you."

"Rafton said he would," he hesitated, then said, "Cougar wants to hunt with me and—"

"And you don't know how well he would handle that, or if you could trust him with the horses."

He nodded, then glanced at Kitahtla, and then back to me. "If you aren't needed here, of course, and you still know how to ride a horse, 'old man.'"

Kitahtla chuckled. "I think that's a challenge, brother dear."

"Ha! Just because I have chosen to do work around the rancha rather than go riding off into the canyons with you and the children doesn't mean I have forgotten how to ride."

"Care to prove that boast?"

My sister giggled with delight. "You are truly being challenged by my kitten, Tas. So to save your reputation of being an outlaw and a warrior you had better saddle up and go with him. The brown gelding with the white blaze is probably the best one for you to ride. He is used to the guns and doesn't scare easily. And while he does that, grandson, tie Pepper to the porch rail and come sit by me. I want to give you a teaching about hunting with Cougar."

I found the horse and saddle no problem after I stopped by the kitchen to tell Gahji where I was going and grab a bit of food and some water for our hunt.

We managed to sneak out of the rancha yard without the younger ones seeing us and wanting to come along, which was a small blessing. I learned later that they had gone into the village for ice-pops with Rafton while he got some groceries the women needed.

I let Mathrom lead the way. He knew the land here and he struck out with a particular goal in mind. It felt good to be atop a horse again, though I was going to be sore tomorrow, no doubt.

I had been with Nachoga several times when he called Cougar to him during a hunt and each time it sent chills down my spine. With my spirit sight I could see when the big cat's essence entered its human companion's physical form. It was the same for Mathrom.

We followed the tracks of a small herd of black eared deer that Mathrom had seen earlier. The trail led into a steep sided gulley with a small spring and tempting green plants near the base of some big red rocks. Dismounting and using the horses as our shields we allowed them to graze along with our prey as we slowly crept closer, following the herd deeper into the gulley.

When he decided we were close enough I took the reins of both the horses, and he called Cougar to him and slipped further into the rabbit brush and tall grass. Using a touch of my Gift I kept the horses contentedly grazing, so they couldn't give an alarm.

We managed to kill two fine young bucks just as the evening shadows were stretching long across the hillsides. Taking advantage of the water in the pool by the spring we set to work gutting and cleaning our catch. Engrossed in my silent prayers and the job of gutting and skinning one of the bucks I was surprised when Mathrom spoke.

"Granny isn't going to make it till next summer to come back and stay with us in Seatown is she?"

I sighed and put down my knife to look at him. He hadn't looked up from the hind leg he was skinning when he spoke, but I could read the grief and sadness in his spirit fire plain enough. "Unfortunately no, she isn't. When we leave in a few days it would be best if you say your farewell."

He continued working without speaking. He was making a mess of the skinning but I let him continue without comment. I knew how much he was hurting—I was hurting, too.

I had just gone back to my own task when he spoke once more. "Can I come with you when you return for the sing?"

"If there is time, of course you can and Saskina, too. But I may have to make the 'transfer' if she fades very quickly. And if that happens we will hold a burning for her next year and feed her and the other ancestors hungry and waiting for us in the Beyond," I promised him."

And as I spoke those words I knew that was what I had to do to let go of the grief I too was carrying for Nachoga, my mother and all my dead. I needed to feast them and honor them in the best way I could, because even with all the Qwakaiva I had inherited from my Qwa'Nayhi Seal father I hadn't been able to save them. And by doing that, I hoped I would also free myself of my own guilt and shame for not protecting them. I would have to talk to Elder Samul about the feast when we got home.

After leaving a hind quarter for Cougar we each tied a carcus over the backs of our pony's rump and headed back to the rancha. We arrived bloody and tired that night only to find the cook pit dug and a yearling calf roasting over glowing coals.

I heard Mathrom curse under his breath as we guided the horses to the barn and fed them. I only smiled. Qwadalah was still playing her games, but it didn't matter. We would have plenty of meat for the feast and some to send home with everyone as well.

The next morning everyone got a good laugh as they watched me hobble into the kitchen from the cold tent like an old man, searching for a hot cup of kaf-tea.

"Ah, poor, poor baby seal." Gahji placed a plate of steak and eggs in front of me and kissed me lightly as she cooed something soothing next to my ear. Reaching for her to return the kiss I found her already back to stirring a big pot on the cooker.

From her seat in the rocker by the fireplace Kitahtla hid a smile behind a raised cup as she sipped her own tea.

Still grinning Rafton said, "Old Harley makes a salve for sore muscles that will set you right, city cousin. Next time you limp over to the barn ask him to give you some. Then come back and get your woman to help you put it on the sore muscles—between your legs, eh? You'll feel good as new in no time." He laughed at his own joke, but out of the corner of my eye I saw Kitahtla scowl and Janata flush with embarrassment.

"Thank you, cousin. I will definitely ask Harley about his salve," I said, hoping my expression didn't betray my true feelings concerning his crude joke. I had already smelled the waskyja on his breath more than once, so I knew he was a man with a drinking problem.

The big feast was planned for the next day and several neighboring families had been invited to join us for the festivities. So with that in mind, later that morning Gahji told me she was going into a larger town away from the Preserve with Janata, and some of the younger children with Saskina along to help supervise while the women shopped for presents and any forgotten food items.

"I'd like to try and have some alone time with her to talk about what she could do to improve her situation, if that's alright with you. She's a smart woman, really, and needs to go back to school and get out from under her husband's control."

"Sure it's fine with me, but what about her elder?"

"Rafton can take care of his own mom for once instead of going off to drink in the barn with the rancha men," she growled. "I know she is old—and frail, but so is Kitahtla and you don't see her whining and demanding attention like Nansi. The woman is too clingy, difficult to please, and it's half killing your niece. She needs to leave that dog humper, come to Seatown with her kids and go back to school."

I chuckled. "Now who is it trying to fix everyone's problems for them, eh?" she gave me a murderous look and I thought she might punch me, but then she only laughed.

I took her in my arms and kissed her. "You are right to want to help her, and I will support both you and her decision, whatever it may be. If you want to bring her to live with us, we will make do, but remember as you keep telling me, people have to figure things out for themselves if they are to learn and grow."

Later when Kitahtla and I were sitting on the porch and the house behind us was quiet, she turned to me and asked, "If your old bones can stand to get back onto a horse this morning, while Qwadalah is off seeing a new buyer about some of our yearlings, I'd like you to take me for a ride. I'm not sure if I could manage to straddle my old sweetie anymore by myself, but if you could carry me..."

I chuckled. "Well, it won't be the same as when I carried you in father's cradleboard, but I think we can manage. Where would you like me to take you?"

"There is a special place that I've always loved a little ways into the hills. It's where I used to go when I was troubled, or just wanted to give thanks and pray. I will show you."

The old rancha man Harley was startled when he saw Kitahtla on my arm enter the barn and ask him to saddle up her old mare, Sweetie, for us. His expression was troubled, but he made no comment when he lifted her up and I settled her comfortably on the blanket draped across the saddle in front of me. "I'll take good care of her, elder, she is very precious to me, so don't worry about her safety," I promised him.

He grunted a reply to me then asked my sister, "But what shall I tell your daughter, Misa Kitah, if she returns before you get back?"

Kitahtla leaned back against me, let out a contented sigh and smiled. "Tell her the truth that I went for a ride."

When I saw his expression I couldn't help but laugh. "Maybe there's some project away from the barn that desperately needs your attention this morning, eh?"

He thought about it for a moment then smiled. "Yeah, I think there is."

Still chuckling, I said, "Smart man."

Following Kitahtla's directions we headed north and east into the higher ground of the sage and pine covered hills. Over to the west the snow-capped peaks of the coastal mountains were a blue shadow on the horizon. As we climbed the slope of a hill a bit higher than the rest, the broken lands of a gray and purple desert spread out to the south and east below us.

Near the top of the slope a flat rock outcropping thrust its way like a rude tongue out from the mouth of a small cave. Cougar tracks criss-crossed the sandy ledge, but they were old and blurred and I doubted if a mother and her kittens had denned there this year. It would be a good spot for it though. We had passed a small creek flowing out of a cleft in the rocks a little ways below that would draw many animals to drink and make the hunting easier for her.

"This spot is always had a special place in my heart. I used to leave my mare down below and climb up here even when mam cougar still denned here. She never bothered me. I don't remember when I realized we had a special connection, but sometimes she would come out to lie in the sun nearby, purring. I would just sit and look over the rancha and the land beyond and pray—for you, and for all our people," she said in a dreamy voice as she recalled the past.

"What happened to mam cougar," I asked when she was silent for a long time.

She made a disgusted sound still looking out at the land below us. "She was old, like me, but I think some fool shot her, and none of her daughters came back after that to occupy her den."

"That is a very sad story."

We fell silent after that and I let her be alone with her thoughts. Moving back down the slope I collected a bit of firewood and filled our water jar at the creek then returned to make us some tea before we headed back to the rancha.

As we sipped our tea and ate the bread and meat I had also brought she said to me, "I wanted to bring you here because I remembered what you told me about needing to know a place in order to find it when you transfer, as you put it.

"If I have the strength I want to come here when it is my time. Look for me here first when you come to sing me home."

I glanced over the land spreading out below us and the cave and the slope behind us, fixing the images in my memory. "I will remember. I will sing you into the loving arms of our relatives that are waiting for you."

Suddenly letting me see her uncertainty, and the glimmer of the fear she had been so desperately trying to hide, she asked in a quivering voice, "Do you think Amima and papa Nachoga and Papa Jimmy and mama Sagila will be there to welcome me, truly?"

I reached out and took her trembling hand and gave it a squeeze. "Yes, I believe that with all my heart. Amima was so happy to at last have a daughter to carry on her lineage and Nachoga loved you so much. The last thing Nachoga said to me before the rope took his life, was how glad he was that you still lived, and he and our mother would be waiting for you."

On our way back to the rancha we ran into Mathrom and Neko who had been sent out to look for us. As he reined in his horse next to Sweetie Mathrom smiled, a mischievous gleam in his eye. "I kept telling everyone that you two were fine, but mama wouldn't listen." His grinned widened. "Everybody is mad at you and you're in a shit-load of trouble for not leaving a note, uncle."

I sighed. "I guess Harley took my advice and went somewhere safe to wait out the storm, and I should have thought of the note. I will apologize to our worried women as soon as we get back and I get your granny settled in her bed or a comfy chair."

"Now, now nobody should be mad at you, big brother for our little adventure. I'm the one who asked you to take me for a ride and I'm the one who should have remembered to leave a note."

We arrived back at the rancha house to quite a commotion, because everyone was back and no one knew where we had gone.

Qwadalah was almost hysterical and lit into me as soon as we arrived in the barnyard. Flying out of the kitchen door she charged me with fists upraised. I had just handed my sister down to Mathrom's strong arms and was climbing down myself when she came at me screaming curses and threatening to kill me if I had hurt her mama.

Before Aqwissa could react and come to my defense I whirled, threw up a shield to stop her first punch and grabbed both of her arms. Reminding myself not to use my power so openly, I exerted just enough of my Gift to prevent her from a further assault. The woman was incredibly strong in spite of her bulk. With her anger fueling her attack, she made it difficult for me to hold her without doing something more drastic that would only frighten her and cause more trouble in the end.

Mathrom laughed. "You finally found someone you can't use your fists on like you used to do with me. Lucky for you his bracelet didn't jump off his arm and bite you."

I sighed "Shut up, Mathrom, you aren't helping the situation." I turned back to my niece opening my mouth to apologize when Kitahtla surprised me and spoke sharply to her oldest daughter.

"Qwadalah, stop this right now I know you were worried and were frightened for me, but it was me who forgot to leave a note, and it was me who asked Tas to take me for one last ride into the desert. So don't blame him for anything."

"But why? I would have taken you in the wagon if you wanted to go somewhere on the rancha. Why did you ask him and not me?"

"Because I had things to show him, and talk over with him concerning my death. I didn't want to ride around in a mecho-wagon, or even a horse drawn one. I wanted to ride Sweetie and go into the hills and I knew with his Gift I would have the strength to do what I needed and that I would be completely safe with him."

I asked Mathrom to take my sister to the house and Neko to take care of Sweetie for me. When they were gone I said to Qwadalah before I released her, "I am sorry about not leaving a note. I know you love your mother, even though you aren't always able to show it. I should have remembered even if Kitahtla didn't.

"I don't like that you seem to think if Kitahtla loves others like your sister or me, or the grandchildren she won't love you. That is a stupid chamuqwani way of thinking and it isn't good for you, your mother or anyone. I am neither your rival nor your enemy, so try to remember that in the little time we have left for our visit, eh?"

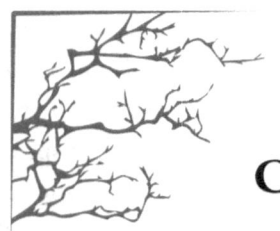

Chapter Thirty-Four

T hough it was hard to leave Kitahtla and the new cousins we had met at the rancha, the weather favored us and we arrived home without any trouble. And, wonder of wonders Stakaya hadn't had too many friends over to make a mess of the house, which delighted Gahji. Unknown to her I had taken the cub aside and told him he might be my next victim stuck to a chair if he got Gahji upset, which may have had something to do with his compliance to her rules.

We settled in and everyone went back to our usual routine of work and school, but I still felt uneasy. Throughout the rest of that stormy winter when I was hunting out upon the land, or visiting the Smotahlik ceremonial house, listening to the drums and the deep-throated singing I tried to burry my foreboding and pretend all was well while cradled within their power.

But then I would hear the storm winds crashing through the tree boughs outside and my unease would return. The spirits of the ancestors who hovered near were troubled and restless. They sang to me of changes coming and warned me of danger, urging me to be ready.

What I was dreading happened in early spring not long after my son's first birthday. Kitahtla reached out to me within the Dream and told me to come. It was her time. Mathrom who was still staying with us and putting up with our lumpy couch startled me awake with a haunting cry that also woke up the rest of the house.

Leaving Gahji soothing a frightened O'siyan, I walked into the living room and found Mathrom huddled in his blanket shivering, tears streaming unnoticed down his cheeks. I sat down beside him on the couch, suddenly glad he had chosen to stay with us instead of looking for another room closer to the Lectorium, so I could help him through this difficult time.

I took his hand allowing my Qwakaiva to flow gently into his body. "Relax and don't resist what is happening, nephew. My sister is passing on her Cougar puwa to you, her well-loved descendant. Don't fight her, it's not a malicer's conjure you are experiencing. She has called me, too."

He turned to me and swallowing hard before speaking, said, "Thank you—I wasn't sure."

I let go and stood. "Go sit in Ky's room until you are at peace with your new self. He stayed at Jula's last night, so no one will bother you. I will need to tell Gahji what has happened—and Kutima—and get ready to make the transfer soon. I'm sorry I will have to leave you, but she needs me now."

"I know you can't take me with you, but I am coming in the mecho-cart as soon as I can. I want to be there with the family."

The trees were starting to bud on the coast but I knew the snows were still deep in the mountains, making travel difficult, but he had a right to come and I couldn't refuse him. "Drive safely then and bring your sister. I will send Aqwissa to aid you if I can."

The light of a new day was a gray band on the eastern horizon when I stepped out of the pinyons by the little spring and found her. She had gotten this far, but had been too weak to make the climb up to mam cougar's ledge. Her old mare Sweetie was standing protectively over her crumpled body on the frozen ground. Fortunately Sun had warmed the hillside in the past days melting much of the snow, the rest only a thin frosty crust atop the sage and last year's grasses.

Kneeling beside her, I saw that my sister still lived though she was very weak. Kitahtla smiled at me when I gathered her into my arms and started up the trail to the ledge.

"I almost made it on my own didn't I, big brother?"

"Yes, you did, and I am here to take care of you now and help you finish your journey."

"I knew you would come. Thank you."

When we arrived at the ledge she asked me to sit her with her back propped up against the rocks by the cave mouth so she could look out over the land she loved and watch Sun climb into the sky for the last time. As the day brightened around us I sat beside her and took her hand in mine.

"When you take me down to the rancha, don't let Mathrom make a fuss if his mother wants to bury me in the temple graveyard. I would prefer to rest up here, but I know she and the others will want some place to visit in the years to come, so I guess what is left of me can rest there as well as anywhere."

"I can cut off your braids and burry them within mam cougar's cave," I offered, "so a part of you will remain for a time in this well-loved place."

She let out a wheezing laugh. Her time was near. "Qwadalah isn't going to like it that you scalped me, you wild heathen zaunk, but I think that's a good compromise."

I chuckled and took her into my arms.

As she settled into my warmth a frightened sob escaped her throat. And her brave mask fell away. "Hold me close, big brother. I'm c-cold—and maybe a little frightened," she admitted.

I wrapped my arms around her and kissed her hair. "I know. Be at peace and don't be afraid, my dear one, I will be right here with you and I will see that you pass safely into the waiting embrace of those who love you in the Beyond."

When Sun cleared the horizon and spread his golden light across the gray land below us, Kitahtla's spirit left to join our ancestors. Capturing Sun's light within the circle I made between my two hands I opened the portal and sang my sister's spirit into it.

And for just a moment I saw the ghosts of Amima and Nachoga waiting for her. My song faltered and my heart gave a lurch. Oh how I wanted to go with her... but it wasn't my time, and I had so much to live for in this place and now. I smiled and resumed my song. How could such a thought even enter my mind? My grief was making me a bit crazy.

I stayed on the ledge with her cooling body in my arms and my own tears streaming silently down my face until Sun had climbed high enough to put the ledge in shadow and I got cold in spite of my grief.

Another death to mourn...

I was grateful to the Unseen Ones for the time I had been given with her, but I would regret her passing, my grief a deep ache in my heart.

I cut off her braids and buried them in the cave as she requested, then I lifted her cooling body and started back down the trail to the spring. Sweetie hadn't gone far, still waiting for us. Mounting I drew Kitahtla up into my arms with my Gift and headed back down the trail.

About half way to the rancha house Harley and a couple of the younger hired men met us. They could see right away that I carried only a corpse.

"I knew something was wrong when I saw Sweetie gone from her stall this morning. Did you help her sneak out last night?" Harley asked.

I shook my head. "No, I was in my bed in Seatown last night. I only got here just before dawn when she spoke to me in my dreams and told me to come, because it was her time."

His eyes widened at my answer, but he didn't question me further. "I didn't see no vehicle at the rancha or parked on the road, so I guess you really are an old-time Puhani, like the young ones claim."

I smiled, neither agreeing nor denying what he said. I jerked my head back over my shoulder and changed the subject. "She got to the spring by mam cougar's den on her own. I merely helped her up the rest of the way to the ledge."

He nodded and stared into the hills. "Yeah, she told me before, that she wanted to die up there. She even asked me to take her if she was too weak, but the boss wouldn't have liked it—and it wasn't my place..."

"It's alright, elder. That's why she summoned me. It *wasn't* your place; it was mine, as her oldest relative. That's why she wanted me to carry her out into the hills that last time before we went back to Seatown. She needed to show me the ledge, so I could come there when she called."

When we arrived at the rancha I recognized Rafton's rusty old cart parked near the house, but there were several other vehicles in the yard as well, including a tribal peace defender mecho-cart. A group of people were clustered around a large breed man who seemed to be giving them orders for a search. They all looked up as we rode in.

Harley snorted and muttered in a low voice, "Guess the fendos decided to take the boss's frantic calls this morning seriously after all. But they're too late as usual."

When Qwadalah saw us her face turned ashy. I expected an angry rush and I braced myself for an attack. But she surprised me by just walking slowly over to Sweetie and holding up her arms. I gently lowered her mother down to her and then dismounted myself.

Aware of the eyes watching us, she turned her face away from the group and gave me a murderous glare and then said only loud enough for me and

Harley to hear, "Did you sneak her out of the house last night for some evil heathen purpose?"

"No. I wasn't here last night. I only found her by the little creek by mam cougar's den just before dawn when she called to me in the Dream."

"Did Mathrom and my girl bring you?"

"No, I came by other path ways, but they will be here by tomorrow for the funeral."

Noticing her mother's chopped off hair her scowl deepened. "What did you do to her hair, witch?" she hissed.

"I have only done what she asked of me, niece, and nothing more. She wanted a part of herself to remain in the mountains she loved so well after you take the rest of her body to the temple graveyard. So, at her request, I buried her hair in the hills before returning her to you."

Still scowling Qwadalah took her mother and walked into the house to clean and lay out her body for the gather and the funeral to follow. A weeping Janata and a few other women I had met at the holiday feast, but now couldn't remember their names trailed behind her.

I started to follow the women into the house but the breed man in the tribal peace defender uniform stopped me. Like most goldys he was a bit arrogant and abrasive. "And you are?"

"A relative."

I started to push past him, I was tired and needed a cup of kaf-tea, when he put a hand on my shoulder to stop me. "A relative, eh? I haven't seen you around here before. Care to tell me your name?"

Well I did care, actually, but decided it wasn't worth the hassle to annoy him by withholding it. "My name is Tassele Cougarson. And you haven't seen me around because I left the Preserve to live with my father when I was still a child."

He gave me a noncommittal grunt and glanced back into the barn where Harley was just leading Sweetie to rub her down and feed her. "So how is it that you knew just where to find the old woman when her daughter didn't know where to find her?"

"Because when my family and I came to visit over the winter holidays she showed me where she wanted to go when it was her time to die. And that's where I looked for, and found her."

"Ah, leave him alone, Barnett," a slightly drunk Rafton said as he wove his way over to us. "He is some kind of lost relation that Qwadalah's kids discovered in the city. The old granny stayed with him and his family when she went for tests in Seatown and then they did come for the holidays."

Barnet grunted a reply then gave one last assessing glare before he walked back to his vehicle and climbed inside.

Still watching the vehicle as it turned and drove out of the yard in a cloud of dust, I said to Rafton, who was still standing beside me. "I don't think that man likes me and I wonder why. Was it my long hair, my tattoos or my dusty clothes that got him upset?"

Rafton let out a braying laugh and slapped me on the back. "That was a good one, cousin. Barnet acts like he has a stick up his ass most of the time, but he's not too bad, as fendos go."

Giving me a sly smile he jerked his head towards the barn. "Come have a drink with me. I have a bottle hidden away in the loft. It will help you put up with all the women's noisy yowling and carrying on."

I wanted to smash his face in, and it wouldn't take much provocation for me to do it, but right now there was no point in angering him. With the funeral looming everyone's emotions, including my own, were going to be raw and bleeding before it was over. There was no point starting something now. "No, but thank you. I swore off booze after I got too drunk when I first came to Seatown, and I landed in jail." He shrugged and headed off himself to the barn for more booze.

I sent Aqwissa back to the family for Mathrom or Saskina to wear, once I was safely here and had found my sister. So I wasn't surprised when early the following morning the mud and snow-covered Mecho-cart arrived.

What did surprise me, however, was that the whole family was inside. Gahji laughed when she saw my face. "I called everyone to let them know about the death in the family, before we left. Your sister touched everyone's heart deeply while she lived with us, and we all needed to say our good byes, so we all came."

I hugged her close. Seeing Mathrom coming over to us, I said to both of them, "Everyone must be exhausted. Did you guys stop at all?"

She laughed and snuggled closer. "I could use a cup of kaf-tea, true enough, but I'm alright. We put most of our packs, including the big tent on the rack up top and just put the seats flat and laid all the blankets and pillows on top of the folded seats and then took turns resting on them," Gahji explained.

"For coming so far and so fast I'm surprised that I don't feel that tired," Mathrom said as he joined us. "I guess Aqwissa must have helped us more than I thought. She's probably the one who is exhausted."

I glanced down at the silver bracelet once more adorning my arm. "If she is she will tell me and I will see that she has what she needs for her renewal," I assured him.

Gahji disentangled herself, saying she needed to go and see how Janata was doing and what she could do to help prepare for the funeral. Tuunac and Bijah, not really understanding about death were excited to be back and had raced off to the barn to see the horses almost as soon as the vehicle had rolled to a stop. Saskina and Angika had taken the still sleeping O'siyan and gone to the house.

When we were alone I motioned to a quiet place along the fence near the barn that was out of the wind. Leaning against the top rail, I asked, "How are you doing, really? I'm sorry I haven't been with you to help you come into balance with her death and the Gift of her puwa before now."

"I'm still a bit shaky from her death, the transfer of puwa and the crazy trip, true enough, but I think I will be alright when I have more time to figure everything out."

"Well I'm here if you need me, and I will do the best I can to help you balance your new self to regain your nahawa. And with that thought in mind, before we leave I want you to find the time and take that fine gray stallion, pepper, out for a ride in the hills north and east of here.

"On a high ledge is an old den where a mama cougar raised her kittens for many seasons. That is where I took your grandmother to die. I think she would like it if you go up there to say your good byes and pray. If you can't find it on your own I will take you there, but if you allow the power of Cougar living within you, to guide you, I think you can find it."

In keeping with the old traditions the gathering for a funeral lasted for four days. The family coming from Seatown missed the first day while traveling, but I was so grateful to have my beautiful bear woman with me to help smooth out my tangled feelings and act as a mediator for other family troubles. We remained until the end, but it was a difficult time for everyone, because the immediate family traditionally stayed together for the four days and tempers and old resentments that had been allowed to fester bubbled and burst open under the strain along with the grieving.

Qwadalah was her usual sullen angry self, lashing out at her sister, her children, and especially me. I knew she loved her mother and was hurting; I could see the pain and grief twisting in her spirit fire like a desert wind ready to destroy all around her. She had become a bitter aging woman who feared the lonely years ahead, but was unable to stop herself from driving everyone away who tried to comfort her.

She and Mathrom got into arguments on more than one occasion which either Gahji or I had to break up. I kept encouraging him to go for long rides in the hills to regain his "nahawa", his inner peace, and do a little hunting with Cougar. He did and brought home meat, but often when he returned calm and centered his mother would scold him for not being there to help out and they would start arguing again.

And then there was my other niece and her drunken husband to trouble my mind. After observing Rafton both at the winter holiday and at this funeral I could see why Gahji wanted to defend her. The man was the worst kind of drunk, unpredictable.

I had grown up around people who became addicted to the chamuqwani's fiery drink, so I knew the signs to look for. Matoqwa's father had been such an unpredictable drunk before his early death, which might explain his children's eagerness to use their fists to solve their problems. And Rafton was turning out to be a similar kind of drunk.

Janata was taking her mother's death hard, perhaps because they hadn't seen much of each other since Qwadalah returned to the ranch. She knew Gahji and I loved her mother and we were a sympathetic ear to her troubles, so she spent as much time as she could with one of us, which I found out later irritated her husband very much.

I told her the next morning when she asked me that yes, if she wanted to bring her children and come stay with us for a while until she decided what to do about her marriage that it was alright with me, just as Gahji told her.

Rafton must have seen us talking because later Janata appeared at the evening meal with a bruise on her arm and a blackened eye. Later I overheard

Gahji asking her what had happened, but Janata gave her only a vague answer in reply.

When I went out to help old Harley and Mathrom feed the horses and see to their other needs the reason for her battered condition became clear. Hearing me down below talking to them Rafton came down from the hay loft drunk and wanting to fight. I saw the red spears of rage in his spirit fire as he lurched over to confront me.

"I seen you sniffin' round my woman, and you betta' leave her alone. She already got a better man than you ever be. Me!" He thumped his chest and nearly toppled backwards. Righting himself he belched an alcoholic breath into my face and growled, "And that goes for your ugly fat wife, too. She betta' stop tryin' ta fill my woman's mind with crazy city-folks ideas.

"Control your woman and her mouth—or I'll do it for ya. Janata ain't goin' nowhere. She'z stay'yin here wit me and the kids. Where she belongs."

Though I knew Gahji could lay him flat if he tried to touch her and didn't need my help, I had had enough. Grabbing him by the throat and the crotch with my puwa I slammed him up against an empty stall door. I called him a very insulting name in Kukiyatan and tightened my grip. "I despise a man who beats on women and children. Don't you ever threaten my wife—or lay your filthy hands on her—ever. If you do—"

I stepped forward and yanked out a clump of his greasy hair and held it up to show him. I stepped back and put it in my pants pocket. "Believe me, I *will* know—without them needing to tell me. If you hit Janata, your children—any of my relatives again, dog humper, you are a dead man."

Giving his sack and his throat an extra hard squeeze I let him go. Rafton dropped to the ground whimpering and choking. Harley had retreated to the far shadows of the barn in fear, but Mathrom had come up to stand beside me. I could see out of the corner of my eye that he had called Cougar to him the big cat's faint blue glow curled about his head and shoulders.

He looked down at the blubbering man, folded his arms across his chest and smirked. "Granny always knew Auntie Janata made a bad mistake when she married you. That's why she wrote it into her will that as long as auntie stayed married to you she could never have any part of the rancha. So if you've been hanging around all these years hoping you would inherit your wife's share you can forget about it."

The booze making him brave, in spite of the pain, he said, "Qwadalah ain't gonna live forever what about then, eh?"

Mathrom chuckled and shook his head. "Nah, ain't gonna happen even then. "Her will's set up that next to inherit are me, Saskina and Neko." He grinned. "And you know how much we all love you, eh?"

As we walked back to the house later I asked Mathrom, "Did your granny really put that in her will?"

He shrugged. "I have no idea, but it sounded good at the time and did have a positive result—at least for now."

While we'd been finishing up with the horses we'd heard Rafton's rattily old mecho-cart start up and drive away. I wished him ill and hoped my niece would be better off if he stayed gone for good. Of course, she might decide to stay with him, beaten down women often did, or Rafton might want his revenge and hire another witch to attack me...

Well, I would have to deal with that consequence if it happened. Another enemy wanting my blood would have to take a number and stand in line, as these modern people say.

Grandfather wouldn't have been proud of me for threatening the man with a witch's conjure. For reasons such as this, was why he had hated the power that had been passed on to me through my father's lineage. I recognized the constant temptation to use my Gift unwisely, and how I had paid for my mistakes in the past. I hoped that at least for once it would be worth it and give my niece a bit of time for her to decide what she wanted to do with her life from now on.

The funeral took place in a small wood and stone temple just inside the Preserve's boarder. I couldn't help bracing myself when I saw Djoven's lightning bolt symbol on the roof over the entrance and the blue-robed priest waiting for us. As we filed into the front row set aside for the family Gahji took my hand and squeezed gently to let me know she was here with me. Fortunately, the young priest who hadn't known my sister gave a simple sermon that didn't last long, and then we filed once more outside to walk to the nearby graveyard.

The place chosen for her was beautiful I had to admit, with somber trees and a nice view of the mountains beyond. "Qwadalah must have donated a fair-bit to this temple, to lay her mom in such a nice spot," Gahji murmured close to my ear.

"Yes, my sister would have liked it," I agreed as I watched the work men filling up the hole.

Rafton did stay gone and didn't show up for the funeral. I heard later he was in jail for driving drunk and starting another fight. Mathrom offered to drive her home before we left, but Janata was able to get a ride home with another relative with her four youngest and the old woman. She promised to keep in touch.

To my surprise Qwadalah hired Neko to stay on at the rancha to help out with the spring work. The youth was seventeen and good with horses just like his grandfather, Janata's father, and as Mathrom said, he was more than happy to get away from his home situation. Mathrom told him he could come live in Seatown with him when he finished school if he wanted to go to the Lectorium for more education.

We were ready to head back to Seatown the next day, but then got word that a late-season snow storm had temporarily closed the roads between the Preserve and the coast.

Qwadalah wanted us gone, but wasn't rude enough to kick us out. The extra couple days gave everyone time to help with needed chores and spend a lot of time out on the land as we came to terms with my sister's passing.

I even managed to get Gahji and baby O'siyan to ride out into the mountains for a picnic one afternoon with Saskina and the other children. Not having been on a horse for a very long time I saddled up Sweetie for her. She made me take O'siyan with me, however, claiming she didn't feel confident managing him and the mare.

We had a lovely afternoon. I took them to the creek by mam cougar's den, so I could show Saskina where her granny came at the end. We ate our picnic by the creek, but didn't go up to the ledge.

That evening when we got back to the rancha Qwadalah was waiting for us with the news that the high passes were now open once more.

Though she didn't come right out and say it, I knew she wanted us gone. So, we left next morning after a good night's sleep.

I doubted we would be invited back.

The End

RUSHTON ARCHIVES: CONCLUSION of fifth interview with Zacatik subject 297

Tasimu's story is concluded in Book Six: Memory Reclaimed

Additional Information for the books telling Tasimu's Story
Words in the Qwani'Ya Language:

Qwani'Ya Tsa'adi, or Fish People, what Tas's human family and the other Indigenous people living by Big Ice Lake call themselves

Qwa'osi the Otter Warrior, a guardian spirit protector of the Qwani'Ya

Co'yeh the Lake Seal, the Otter's rival, a spirit with both light and dark aspects related to Tas's father

Siyatli, a child born to a human woman and a being from another dimension, like Tas's Seal father

Qwakaiva, a difficult word to translate in its full meaning, similar to what we might refer to as magic, chi, life force or shamanic medicine

Qwakaihi, someone gifted with great power that uses their gift for the good of others

Malicer, a translated word from the invader's language, referring to a person who uses Qwakaiva to harm others, (a witch)

Aseutl, a snake-like dragon figure some say lives at the bottom of Big Ice Lake, or in the earth

Kunai, a shape-shifting magical being of great power, and benefactor of Tasimu

Qwa'Nayhi a shape-shifting being able to travel between many realms of existence, like the Qwa'Nayhi Seal man who is Tasimu's father

Amima, mother in the Qwani'ya language

Appi, father

Ami grandmother

Ati, grandfather

Chamuqwani, a term the Indigenous people use to refer to the Imperial invaders of their land

Asiya, a greeting like hello

Crokno, the name given the enemy from another dimension that Tas and his father battle, because they wish to destroy Tas's world

Unfamiliar Terms in the Chamuqwani Language

Zacatik, what the imperials called all the indigenous tribal peoples they encountered on their conquests

Zaunk, a degrading term used by soldiers and settlers from the empire to express their contempt for all Indigenous peoples they discovered

Zaunk-Brotha, a term used by tribal people amongst themselves

Bucki, a derogatory term for an Indigenous man or boy

Buckiyo, a more affectionate usage of the term, used by tribal people themselves

Cloocha or Cloocha-whore a demeaning term for an Indigenous woman or girl

Unfamiliar Words in the Kukiya Language

Kukiya, what the Indigenous people living in the desert and mountain country out of which the Empire created their Tribal Preserve call themselves

Puhani, a person with magical powers, the same as a Qwakaihi in Tas's people's language

Puwa, the magical power, like Qwakaiva, that a Puhani can use

UNFAMILIAR WORDS IN the West Coast People's Language

Smotahlik, the name the Indigenous people living on the west coast call themselves

Siiqwah, a spirit guide that a person has throughout life to protect and teach them, often the spirit is connected to a family lineage and can be inherited by an individual.

Bugatzi, masked enforcers, who invoke sacred spirit power to take care of tribal ceremonial affairs when needed

A Drubbing, when the Bugatzi are called to deal with an uncooperative family member, usually family sponsored and comes with family obligations, both to the Bugatzi and the one entrusted into their care.

Don't miss out!

Visit the website below and you can sign up to receive emails whenever Celu Amberstone publishes a new book. There's no charge and no obligation.

https://books2read.com/r/B-A-YGQM-MVMCG

BOOKS 2 READ

Connecting independent readers to independent writers.

Also by Celu Amberstone

Rituals

Blessings of the Blood: A Book of Menstrual Lore and Rituals for Women

Deepening the Power: Community Ritual and Sacred Theatre

Tales of Tasimu

Taste of Memory

When Memory Dies

Abandoning Memory

Bitter Echo of Memory

Reawakening Memory

Memory Reclaimed

Tales of the Kashallans

The Dream-Chosen

The Hunted Kashallan

The Outlawed Bond

Uncertain Refuge

Prey of the Umwira

Blood Magic's Snare

Kashallan Alliance

Treacherous Campaign

Standalone
Refugees and Other Stories

About the Author

Celu is of mixed Cherokee and Scots-Irish ancestry. Celu Amberstone was one of the few young people in her family to take an interest in learning Traditional Native crafts and medicine ways. This interest made several of the older members of her family very happy while annoying others.

Legally blind since birth, she has defied her limitations and spent much of her life avoiding cities. Moving to Canada after falling in love with a Métis-Cree man from Manitoba, she has lived in the rain forests of the west coast, a tepee in the desert and a small village in Canada's arctic. Along the way she also managed to acquire a BA in cultural anthropology and an MA in health education. Celu loves telling stories and reading. She lives in Victoria British Columbia near her grown children and grandchildren.

About the Publisher

Kashallan Press is an independent publisher releasing books by author Celu Amberstone. Among her books are critically-acclaimed works now re-released by Kashallan Press, and new works showcasing her talents in writing both fiction and non-fiction.

www.ingramcontent.com/pod-product-compliance
Lightning Source LLC
Chambersburg PA
CBHW020818260626
47169CB00003B/728